A SELECTED EDITION OF W. D. HOWELLS

Volume 14

The Minister's Charge

W. D. HOWELLS

The Minister's Charge

or

The Apprenticeship of Lemuel Barker

Introduction and Notes to the Text
by Howard M. Munford

Text Established by
David J. Nordloh and David Kleinman

INDIANA UNIVERSITY PRESS

Bloomington and London

1978

CENTER FOR EDITIONS OF
AMERICAN AUTHORS
AN APPROVED TEXT
MODERN LANGUAGE
ASSOCIATION OF AMERICA
®

Editorial expenses for this volume have been met in part by grants from the National Endowment for the Humanities administered through the Center for Editions of American Authors of the Modern Language Association.

Manufactured in the United States of America

160567

Library of Congress Cataloging in Publication Data

Howells, William Dean, 1837–1920.
   The minister's charge.

   (His A selected edition of W. D. Howells ; v. 14)
   Includes bibliographical references.
   I. Title.
PS2020.F68 vol. 14 [PS2025] 818'.4'09s [813'.4] 77–22213
ISBN 0-253-33855-7

Acknowledgments

The editors of this volume and of the Howells Edition Center are grateful for the support given their research by the administrative officers of Indiana University, particularly Herman B Wells, University Chancellor, and Harrison Shull, former Dean of the Office of Research and Development. We are especially happy to thank the Ball Brothers Foundation of Muncie, Indiana, for direct financial assistance which made possible the completion and publication of this book. And we continue to appreciate the kind cooperation of William White Howells and the other heirs of W. D. Howells.

The editors are indebted to the energy and enthusiasm of the staff of the Howells Edition Center: research assistants Dan Rubey and Jerry Herron, secretaries Velma Carmichael and Lia Sayers Barnes, and collators and proofreaders Robert D. Schildgen, Sydelle Grant, and David Lamoureux. They also wish to acknowledge the assistance of Anthony Shipps, Mrs. Gail Mathews, and their associates in the Indiana University Library, Bloomington.

The primary editor wishes to thank Middlebury College for a research grant for the summer of 1970 which helped support his work, and Mary Margaret Fagan, his student assistant, for her interested and able participation in the project.

Contents

Introduction

In the spring of 1885 when he began work on *The Minister's Charge; Or, The Apprenticeship of Lemuel Barker,* Howells was in the fullness of his power and assurance as a professional man of letters. The essays, reviews, travel sketches, and parlor drama issuing steadily from his pen were not allowed to distract him from his main business. His chief energies had been devoted to writing seven novels in as many years. He was currently reading and revising proof for *The Rise of Silas Lapham,* concluding its serial appearance in the *Century,* and was at the same time beginning his next book. He had contracted for a novel described merely as "the story of a country boy in Boston," also to be serialized in the *Century.* The initial chapters were to be submitted in August for appearance in the November issue. He had become accustomed to writing with the printer at his heels and the process did not trouble him, for, he confessed, his books unfolded quite easily and practically wrote themselves once he got underway.

The "country boy" turned out to be uncharacteristically stubborn. In November Howells wrote to Robert Grant that he was limiting himself in all his pleasures in order to drive through a piece of work which threatened in turn to drive him.[1] The task of trying to keep on top of the story, he con-

---

1. WDH to Robert Grant, 22 November 1885. The manuscripts of this and all other letters cited are at Harvard unless otherwise noted. Permission to quote unpublished passages from the letters written by Howells has been granted by William White Howells for the heirs of the Howells Estate. Permission to quote from the notebooks and unpublished letters owned by Harvard has been granted by William H. Bond, Librarian, for the Howells Committee of the Houghton Library. Republication of this material also requires these permissions.

fessed to Clemens, wearied him to the point of his becoming tired of his work "almost for the first time in [his] life."[2] As he approached the conclusion he told his father that the story had bothered him more than usual and had run to greater length than he had expected.[3]

Lemuel Barker had been a long time in gestation. In 1883 James R. Osgood, who was acting as Howells' literary agent as well as his publisher, reported that J. W. Harper would be interested in "a Boston story" for his monthly magazine.[4] Osgood apparently transmitted to the Harper firm a general description of a project Howells had in mind, and in turn relayed to Howells the request of Henry Mills Alden, editor of *Harper's Monthly*, that he submit his story for approval. Howells knew both the market value of his name in a magazine and the method by which he worked best, and refused to meet Alden's terms. He would follow his procedure of submitting a sketch and concluding negotiations on that basis. "I know what his general wish is," he informed Osgood, "and I can conform to it; for the rest, if he wants a story from me he must leave me to be entirely responsible for it."[5]

Some time later, however, Howells relented, and submitted to Alden both manuscript of the opening chapters and a sketch of the novel. Still Alden was reluctant. Howells wrote to Osgood telling him not to push: "We can lose nothing by delay, and if he applies again it will put us in a better position" (29 April 1884). Alden remained unwilling to accept the story unless Howells would "make more of the hero and heroine" (*Life in Letters*, I, 361). While these negotiations faltered, C. L. Webster, the manager of Clemens' publishing

---

2. WDH to Clemens, 11 December 1885; *Mark Twain-Howells Letters* (Cambridge, Massachusetts, 1960), II, 545. All letters to Clemens cited hereafter come from this volume.

3. WDH to William Cooper Howells, 23 January 1886.

4. J. Henry Harper, *The House of Harper* (New York and London, 1912), p. 320.

5. WDH to James R. Osgood, 28 November 1883; quoted in *Life in Letters of William Dean Howells*, ed. Mildred Howells (Garden City, New York, 1928), I, 356.

company, approached Howells about publishing the book, perhaps under the subscription system which had been paying Clemens handsome returns. Howells referred him to Osgood: "You would have to treat with him for the Country Boy in Boston. Perhaps he might consider the notion." [6] At this point Howells dropped the whole matter to pursue other more immediate projects. In the fall of 1884 *Harper's* settled for the previously written *Indian Summer*, although J. W. Harper "was at no pains to hide his humorous disgust" at getting a Florentine story in place of the Boston one he had requested. [7] Howells had also contracted with the *Century* to do a series of five "Italian Papers" and a novel to be serialized beginning in November of 1884. To fulfill these commitments, he quickly hammered out his Italian series and then went steadily to work on the untitled story which was to emerge as *The Rise of Silas Lapham*.

During the year in which he was driving *Silas Lapham* through on schedule, he was looking ahead to what he would take up next. To vary the pace, perhaps, he was entertaining the possibility of doing a series of short stories to be published in one volume after they had appeared separately. The *Century* people were receptive to the project. On the basis of a list of titles and meagerly sketched outlines, the editor, Richard Watson Gilder, selected six which he thought "particularly interesting in theme." [8] Although Howells was not pleased because "too many of the serious subjects" had been chosen, he instructed Osgood to "write at once and close the matter" if the financial arrangements were sufficiently advantageous (12 June 1884).

Lemuel Barker then was allowed to languish from May 1884 until April 1885 when, for an author's reading in New York, Howells dusted off the opening chapters he had earlier submitted to Alden and announced that he would read from

6. WDH to C. L. Webster, 21 June 1884. MS in the Webster Collection.
7. *The House of Harper*, p. 320.
8. Richard Watson Gilder to WDH, 4 June 1884.

an "unwritten" novel which involved "a kindhearted clergyman's mistaken advice to a country youth." [9] This occasion
apparently got him started again and on 6 June 1885, with
Silas Lapham now behind him, he informed Clemens that he
was "sailing on with the country boy I read a little about in
N.Y., that day."

The relationship of his original idea for *The Minister's
Charge* to the projected volume of short stories is not clear.
One of the titles rejected by the *Century* was "A Mistaken
Kindness," which could well have been that of the "kind-
hearted clergyman." Whether "The Country Boy in Boston"
was another of the rejected titles is not indicated. Certainly
Howells had not negotiated earlier with Alden or considered
subscription publication of a short story, yet he had been
emphatic during the negotiations in reserving the right to
change the subject of a story after beginning it, "working it
out on different lines if it seems best." [10] The original idea
may therefore have undergone a metamorphosis. In any event,
when he was working out a schedule with Gilder for the appearance of the first installments, a definite uncertainty existed whether the country boy story would be "long or
short." [11] In August he was writing Osgood that Roswell
Smith, the publisher of the *Century*, "has consented to the
lengthening of Lemuel Barker, so as to cover the ground of
all *six* stories" (20 August 1885). Quite uncharacteristically
he found himself in the situation which constantly plagued
Henry James and his editors of having a story grow under his
hands until it far exceeded the initial conception.

A shift of emphasis as the story progressed probably accounts for the difficulty. In his 1883 sketch of the story, Lemuel was definitely the compositional center and no mention
was made of Sewell, the minister. In 1883 and 1884 and well
into 1885 the story was referred to variously as that of "my

---

9. *Mark Twain-Howells Letters*, II, 528, n. 1.
10. WDH to Osgood, 12 June 1884.
11. Gilder to WDH, 5 August 1885.

pathetic country boy," "The Country Boy in Boston," or simply "Lemuel Barker." By October of 1885, however, Sewell
was moving stage center and the story was being referred to as
"Minister's Charge or the Difficulty with Lemuel Barker."[12]
As in the final version of the title, Lemuel was now getting
second billing.

The stolid Lemuel apparently turned out to be insufficient-
ly illustrative of Howells' general intent. In explaining his
own methods Howells once stated that he commenced a novel
by "choosing the phase of life or the subject that I wish to
illustrate, sketch out in mind the principal characters, and
then plunge into the work."[13] That he had in mind a "subject" as well as a "phase of life" is indicated by an 1884 or
early 1885 jotting in his "Savings Bank" Notebook: "Barker
from thinking how S. depresses & J. elevates him, dimly con-
ceives of the notion of elevating others. (Complicity)."[14] Here
Howells uses as the focal term the topic of Sewell's concluding
sermon: the term and the sermon express an idea adumbrated
in Howells' earlier stories, brought to full consciousness in
The Minister's Charge, and restated as the animating principle in much of his later work. Furthermore, his discovery
of Tolstoy in the fall of 1885 probably led Howells to give
the "notion" greater prominence than he had originally
planned.[15] But his struggles with the book earlier during the
summer and the use of the word with the illustrative details
in his notebook jotting suggest another fundamental source

---

12. Unpublished agreement with Harper and Brothers, 6 October 1885, in
possession of Harper and Row, Publishers, New York.

13. Edwin H. Cady, *The Road to Realism* (Syracuse, New York, 1956), p. 203.

14. MS at Harvard.

15. For a full discussion of how the impact of Tolstoy at this moment in
Howells' career led to a shifting of focus in *The Minister's Charge*, see George
N. Bennett, *William Dean Howells: The Development of a Novelist* (Norman,
Oklahoma, 1959), pp. 164–171. The question of "complicity" in Howells' de-
velopment is treated at length in Clara and Rudolph Kirk's introduction to
William Dean Howells: Representative Selections (New York, 1950); William
McMurray, *The Literary Realism of William Dean Howells* (Carbondale, Illi-
nois, 1967); Arnold Fox, "Howells' Doctrine of Complicity," *Modern Language
Quarterly*, XIII (March 1952), 56–60.

of difficulty: Lemuel Barker, given his character and background, could only "dimly" conceive of the idea of "complicity." Howells had to get beyond that "dimly." He had encountered head-on the problem which Henry James was in the process of solving through selecting always a "fine consciousness" for his compositional center. Howells had to have a consciousness "finer" than that of Lemuel to give adequate expression to what had become for him at this point as well as for Sewell "a complete philosophy of life" (present edition, page 340). Howells tried to resolve his dilemma, it would seem, by moving Sewell to the center of the stage and having him spell out the idea of complicity in his concluding sermon.[16] Howells might well, in James' phrase, "have hung his artistic head in shame" at this violation of one of the cardinal principles of realism. In all probability, committed to an inexorable schedule, he resorted to this expedient as a means of rushing the story to a conclusion. George Parsons Lathrop reported that he found Howells "busy with composition at almost all hours of the day and also in the evening."[17] On 23 January 1886 Howells told his father that "200 more pages . . . ought to finish" *The Minister's Charge*. On 7 February he reported, "I concluded my story yesterday,"[18] and on 7 August he acknowledged receipt of proof for the last installment.[19]

II

Howells knew that he was embarking on troubled waters as he moved into the lower orders of Boston society with Lem-

---

16. The reviewer of the Boston *Evening Transcript*, 11 December 1886, saw what had happened. "Mr. Howells is becoming self-indulgent. He is falling . . . . into the habit of providing himself with mouthpieces through which, with very thinly disguised voice, he can talk to his readers."

17. "W. D. Howells, His Career and His Home," New York *Daily Tribune*, 9 November 1885, p. 3.

18. At this time in his career a manuscript page was the size of a normal piece of typing paper cut in half, containing from twenty-two to twenty-four lines of text with about ten words to a line. This would mean that he had produced about 4,800 words in a week's time.

19. MS at New York Public Library.

uel. During the time he was writing *The Minister's Charge*, the reviews of *Silas Lapham* were appearing. His "vivifying faith," in James' phrase, had been concealed "so little as to afford every facility to those people who [were] anxious to prove that it is the wrong one."[20] The anti-realists did proceed to castigate him for the commonplaceness of his characters and the sordidness of his tentative move toward Boston low life in the Zerilla Dewey scenes. Since he was clearly going to be even more assertively realistic in the story of Lemuel Barker and would provide the anti-realists "a Boston story with a vengeance," as he was later to say,[21] he must have anticipated a rough reception. As with the response to the first numbers of "The Editor's Study" appearing at about the same time, the resulting "spectacle" was, as he said, not "seemly; the passions of the followers of fraud and humbug were aroused; they returned blow for blow, and much mud from afar."[22]

Some of the "mud" came all the way across the Atlantic. The British critics, infuriated by Howells' downgrading of the classic English novelists in his 1882 article on James and by his subsequent strictures in "The Editor's Study," saw *The Minister's Charge* as an opportunely provided club with which to bludgeon him. The reviewer for the *Academy* (25 December 1886) did not conceal his animus: "Mr. W. D. Howells recently wrote some random words anent English fiction as compared with that of Europe and America—words, to be candid, which were as presumptuous as they were uncalled for. He did not know that the following footsteps of Nemesis were so close upon him." The reviewer conceded that "There is the familiar delicacy of touch, the wonted charm of style," but saw in the "mania for the commonplace" which afflicted "this choice product of American culture" a "consummate dulness" which "almost amounts to genius."

20. *Harper's Weekly*, 19 June 1886, p. 394.
21. *The House of Harper*, p. 320.
22. *Harper's Monthly*, LXXXIV (March 1892), 641–642.

"The hearts of his enemies," he concluded, "must be filled with rejoicing." The *Saturday Review* (5 February 1887) was equally scurrilous, remarking with heavy irony that the book was "in every way worthy of the exterminator of George Eliot." Only the *Westminster Review* (May 1887) came to the book's defense in a perfunctory one-paragraph notice. " 'The Minister's Charge; or, The Apprenticeship of Samuel [sic] Barker,' is . . . a wonderfully fine piece of moral and mental analysis. It is the investigation and dissection of human impulse and motive carried, as it were, to the furthest limit . . . . In this class of novel Mr. Howells reigns supreme." Unfortunately, though, the reviewer saw it as another of "Mr. Howells' romances."

At home, the book provided the anti-realists "every facility," as James foresaw. The New York *Daily Tribune* (12 December 1886) saw "the question of realism in literary art . . . raised again in its baldest form." The author had drawn his "scenes of common and sordid life" in a way which "would have made the fortune of a newspaper reporter" with "no particle of imagination." The *Literary World* (8 January 1887), the *Critic* (5 February 1887), and the *Independent* (3 March 1887) were equally severe in their condemnation of dealing with such dull and disagreeable material. The *Nation* (10 February 1887) raised the chief question plaguing the anti-realists. "With the mote 'realism' in our eye, we have cried in despair, Are the qualities in men that we know to be fine not real? Are trivial baseness, petty viciousness, the only truths?"

One of the most savage attacks on *Silas Lapham* had come from the *Catholic World* (November 1885). The reviewer had been horrified by the "degradation" of the material in which Howells "out-Zolas Zola." Howells must therefore have found a not very amusing irony in the opinion of this journal (February 1887) that he did not have the honesty to be sufficiently realistic in *The Minister's Charge*. Turgenev, Tolstoy, and Zola would not have been so gingerly. "The truth is that Mr.

Howells, though he professes to be a realist and describe life as it is, is not a realist .... Lemuel's lovemaking in the boarding-house room is innocent enough; but we feel that it is not Lemuel's tender New England conscience or Statira's principles which make it innocent, but the fact that Mr. Howells ... is a most careful chaperon." "He fits his human beings for presentation in the pages of a family magazine and in novels which may be read by every young girl in the country." Only the Chicago *Tribune* (18 December 1886) responded sympathetically to Howells' governing intent. It quoted at length from Lemuel's visit home to his mother to illustrate how "in common things lurk what is best and greatest in life .... Our generation is learning that every thread of human experience has its unique value." Howells' "sympathy" and "intimate acquaintance with American life and character ... are unapproachable by any living writer."

Howells responded "manfully" to the extravagant hostility of most of the reviews. "I find myself not really caring a great deal for the printed animosity," he reported to James.[23] "As to the things you see about me in the papers," he reassured his father (27 February 1887), "I hope you'll not let them worry you. ... They are inevitable, because I'm now something of a 'shining mark,' and because in fiction I've identified myself with truth and humanity, which you know people always hate. It will pass, and pretty soon I shall be accepted. My ideas are right." He was not pleased, of course. He complained to James that the book's "reception here by most of the reviewers is extremely discouraging. Of all grounds in the world they take the genteel ground, and every 'Half-bred rogue that groomed his mother's cow,' reproaches me for introducing him to low company. ... in the newspapers it hardly stops short of personal defamation."[24] He wrote a note of thanks to George William Curtis, who had come to the book's defense in the March 1887 number of "The Editor's Easy

---

23. 25 December 1886; *Life in Letters*, I, 387.
24. *Ibid.*

Chair" in *Harper's Monthly,* and exclaimed wrathfully, "What really depresses and disheartens me in the outburst against having 'commonplace people' in fiction is that the very, very little culture and elegance . . . with which our refined people have overlaid themselves seems to have hardened their hearts against the common people: they seem to despise and hate them."[25]

Howells' literary friends and acquaintance came to his support. As the story neared its serial conclusion, Lowell gave his erstwhile pupil a pat on the back. "I am happy in your well-earned fame, my dear boy, and have just been reading your last chapters with the feeling Gray had about Crébillon *fils.*"[26] Whittier, John Hay, Cassius Clay, Barrett Wendell, and William James also had kind but unilluminating things to say. Howells could not accept a friendly note from Thomas Wentworth Higginson, however, without admonishing him. In an 1879 critical piece, Higginson had taken exception to his "undersized" characters and "miniature . . . heroes and heroines."[27] If Higginson liked the novel, he would have to accept the principles with the practice. "After your liking my story . . . I ought to be willing you should dislike my literary creed, or my preaching it. But I can't. . . . no reader of mine shall suppose that the true and natural way of writing fiction which is now universal, wherever the fiction is worth reading, is any longer to be taken on sufferance."[28]

III

Howells' response to the animadversions of the reviewers and his taking exception to Higginson's superficial praise in-

25. WDH to Curtis, 27 February 1887.

26. 11 November 1886, *Letters of James Russell Lowell,* ed. Charles Eliot Norton (New York, 1894), II, 320. Thomas Gray had written to Richard West that "as the paradisiacal pleasures of the Mahometans consist in playing upon the flute and lying with Houris be mine to read eternal new romances of Marivaux and Crébillon."

27. "Howells," *Literary World,* 2 August 1879, pp. 249–250; reprinted in *Short Studies of American Authors* (Boston, 1879), pp. 32–39.

28. WDH to Higginson, 31 August 1885. MS at New York Public Library.

dicate that he was sure of his ground. The various motives back of his impulse toward realism which had been steadily emerging over the years culminated in this story of a lowly country boy. He once stated that *April Hopes* (1887) was the first novel he had written "with the distinct consciousness that he was writing as a realist";[29] the story of Lemuel Barker was instrumental in bringing him to this critical awareness.

In his initial correspondence with Alden in 1883 and 1884 one of these motives was clearly stated. Alden had been "disinclined" toward the story because he wanted "a more considerable hero" than Lemuel promised to be. Howells was not to be swayed. "I don't believe in heroes and heroines," he explained to Osgood, "and willingly avoid the heroic . . . . [Alden] appeared to think that I had some poet *manqué* like gifted Hopkins in mind; but I had nothing of the sort. I believe in this story, and am not afraid of its effect before the public."[30]

Another issue was explicitly drawn in the body of the novel. Already in *Silas Lapham* and *Indian Summer* Howells had used a device which was to become characteristic. He could make his point about the sanative nature of realism by measuring the reality of his characters' personal involvements against the distorted expectations and idealism disseminated by popular fiction. Statira, 'Manda, Sibyl Vane, the women in the St. Albans Hotel, and Lemuel himself all have their heads turned to some degree by their novel reading. Even Sewell, who continues the practice observed in *Silas Lapham* of inveighing against the corrupting moral influence of fiction, ironically fails to appreciate the depth of Jessie Carver's trouble by cavalierly dismissing her from his mind as someone whose conduct has been derived from novels. One suspects that the abrupt ending of Lemuel's adventures is to be taken as ironic comment. Statira conveniently drifts away and Lemuel, we are told, will achieve a "union" which will be "hap-

29. Marrion Wilcox, "Works of William Dean Howells," *Harper's Weekly*, 4 July 1896, p. 655.
30. WDH to Osgood, 12 May 1884; *Life in Letters*, I, 361–362.

piness," but how it came about and with whom "must be left for some future inquiry" (present edition, page 344). The reader avid for happy endings can revive Miss Carver and supply the details.

The other issues of realism implicit in Lemuel's story were to be developed while the novel was in the process of composition. In January 1886 Howells began his occupancy of "The Editor's Study" in *Harper's Monthly*. Since each column was written from three to four months in advance of publication, the first was begun no later than October 1885 with the completion of *The Minister's Charge* still four months in the future. Lemuel and his adventures were therefore very much in Howells' mind when he undertook in these critical articles the task of codifying, formulating, and exploring the implications of his basic artistic principles. In the first number, Howells was already writing from a clearly stated platform. In praising some current novels for their intense localism and accurate rendering of the American tongue, he observed: "From the beginning Realism, before she got a name or put on a capital letter had divined this near-at-hand truth." In the second number he found in the fictional *Autobiography of Mark Rutherford* a book which "got rid of that barbaric survival, the 'hero,' " and which had "no excuses to make for asking us to be interested in the psychological experience of a waiter, a salesman, a porter, who are never at all romanced, but are considered simply in their quality of human beings, affected in due degree by their callings." In the succeeding numbers he continued through such critical comment to bring to "distinct consciousness" the issues of realism which he was in the process of exemplifying in the story of Lemuel.

In the May issue appears the eloquent statement of his deepest conviction, a statement which was to become the central passage of *Criticism and Fiction* (1891):

> In life [the realist] finds nothing insignificant; all tells for destiny and character; nothing that God has made is contemptible. He cannot look upon human life and declare this

thing or that thing unworthy of notice, any more than the scientist can declare a fact of the material world beneath the dignity of his inquiry. He feels in every nerve the equality of things and the unity of men; his soul is exalted, not by vain shows and shadows and ideals, but by realities, in which alone the truth lives.

Written just as Howells was putting the finishing touches on *The Minister's Charge*, this passage was in effect an epitome of the book's governing idea.

The crucial issue was raised by the nature of the material Howells found himself treating in turning his "pathetic country boy" loose to find his way through the streets of Boston. J. W. De Forest, who had himself pioneered in the treatment of low-life characters, was almost beside himself with excitement to see his acknowledged master moving so far in the same direction. On 6 December 1886 he wrote, "It is a wonder that the females of America, at least the common born & bred of them, do not stone you in the streets. . . . 'Manda Grier & Stira Dudley are masterpieces of born, unfathomable 'lowness,' incurably commonplace, egotistic, envious, unappreciative of worth, & unconsciously ungrateful." Howells was indeed venturing into areas seldom trod by an American writer; he had, he replied, "struck a new streak" in rendering the "vulgarity of those poor, silly, common girls—especially 'Manda."[31]

The logic of Howells' development was forcing him in the direction of the vulgar and the sordid almost in spite of himself. In 1884, on the eve of *The Minister's Charge*, and with reference to Zola, Henry James observed that he considered his trans-Atlantic friend to be "the great American naturalist," but, he prompted, "I don't think you go far enough."[32] Howells was forced to agree, forced at least to recognize that at this point he must go further. *The Minister's Charge* was,

---

31. WDH to De Forest, 9 December 1886. MS at Yale University.
32. 21 February 1884; quoted in *The Letters of Henry James*, ed. Percy Lubbock (New York, 1920), I, 105.

he said, "the performance of a man who won't and can't keep on doing what's been done already."[33] In his previous novels he had already "done" the middle and upper reaches of Boston society. There was no direction to go other than down if he were to continue to "do" what was for him still "the most interesting town in the world."[34]

In 1886 Howells told an interviewer who had raised the question of Zola, "I would not touch his material with a pair of tongs, a 10-foot pole."[35] Yet, in preparation for the story of Lemuel Barker, he had gone around Boston with notebook in hand collecting material out of what must have seemed to him the sordid depths. Earlier he had sufficiently overcome his youthful shrinking from "the abhorrent contacts" of the Cincinnati Police Court to observe at first hand the "life whose reality asserts itself every day in the newspapers with indisputable force." On two separate occasions he had paid extended visits to the Boston Police Court, and he described for the January 1882 *Atlantic* the procession of tramps, thieves, drunkards, and prostitutes brought before the judge ("Police Report"). In 1883 he visited the Elliott Street Police Station and in 1885 the Joy Street Police Station, noting in detail the booking and interrogation of those who had been arrested, the facilities and housekeeping arrangements. He made equally detailed observations of the city Lodge for Wayfarers, noting the economy, the food, sanitary and sleeping arrangements, the specimens of human wreckage, bits of conversation.

Given a dynamic emotional center by the experience of Lemuel, the book renders these details precisely. Howells hedged a bit by failing to mention that the women in the Chardon Street Home who baked the bread were "unfortunate" girls, usually in "a family way," and by avoiding references to a "very mammalian type" observed sitting op-

---

33. WDH to James, 25 December 1886; *Life in Letters*, I, 387.
34. "A Chat with Howells," Boston *Daily Advertiser*, 3 August 1886, p. 4.
35. *Ibid.*

posite the lodging, but the rest is given almost to the last detail. He even playfully included himself as the visitor to the police station observed by Lemuel while he is being escorted to his cell. His thrifty use of this material perhaps helps to explain why the story expanded under his hand beyond his original plans.

James was pleased to see Howells following his advice to go further into American life. In his article for *Harper's Weekly*, 19 June 1886, he took note of "the history of *Lemuel Barker*, which is unfolding itself from month to month at the moment I write," and saw it as Howells' highest point to date for "imparting a palpitating interest to common things and unheroic lives." In light of James' attitude toward the thinness of American material, one detects a note of irony in his finding "a poem, an idyl, a trait of genius, and a compendium of American good-nature" in the "four (or is it eight?) repeated 'good-mornings' between the liberated Lemuel and the shop-girl." There was no irony, though, in his seeing in Howells a writer of "definite and downright convictions on the subject of the work that calls out to be done," and it was these realistic convictions which were leading Howells down the path toward naturalism, as James had foreseen and promoted. "Lemuel Barker . . . is wholly perfect," he wrote to Howells on 25 February 1887, "better than anything yet—even than Bartley and Silas I think . . . . You are so absolutely in the right track and the right sense."

The Minister's Charge did well. "It sells, and sells bravely," he informed James (*Life in Letters*, I, 387). Over 11,000 copies, through five re-impressions, were printed by 1893. There were eight other smaller re-impressions through 1919 for a total of some 13,000. The story of Lemuel has not, however, taken its place in the canon of Howells' best fiction.[36] Howells himself occasionally referred to his previous work after the initial excitement, but he rarely mentioned *The*

---

36. See Edwin H. Cady, *The Realist at War* (Syracuse, New York, 1958), p. 269.

Minister's Charge. Only James had a lingering affection for Lemuel, including him in a list of Howells' outstanding books on the occasion of his friend's seventy-fifth birthday.

The Minister's Charge was Howells' last excursion into the lower orders of society. Never again was he to treat such "sordid" material in any extended way. He once confessed to a "tenderness for Lemuel" and entertained briefly the idea of writing a sequel by bringing Lemuel back to Boston to "set up a critical book store, in which he sold only books which he respected, ethically and aesthetically."[37] This scheme would have safely removed Lemuel from his low-life associates, but when the "critical book store" did finally find its way into print, Lemuel was not part of it.[38] After one more partially Boston novel, *April Hopes*, Howells avoided having to "keep on doing what's been done already" by moving into other geographical areas where he could remain in the more comfortable middle reaches of American life.

H. M. M.

---

37. WDH to Mrs. Hamer, 5 August 1905. MS in George Arms' collection.
38. "The Critical Bookstore," *Harper's Monthly*, CXXVII (August 1913), 431–442; reprinted in *The Daughter of the Storage and Other Things in Prose and Verse* (New York and London, 1916).

The Minister's Charge

I

————————

ON THEIR WAY back to the farm-house where they were board-ing, Sewell's wife reproached him for what she called his reck-lessness. "You had no right," she said, "to give the poor boy false hopes. You ought to have discouraged him—that would have been the most merciful way—if you knew the poetry was bad. Now, he will go on building all sorts of castles in the air on your praise, and sooner or later they will come tumbling about his ears—just to gratify your passion for saying pleasant things to people."

"I wish you had a passion for saying pleasant things to me, my dear," suggested her husband evasively.

"Oh, a nice time I should have!"

"I don't know about *your* nice time, but I feel pretty cer-tain of my own. How do you know— Oh, *do* get up, you im-placable cripple!" he broke off to the lame mare he was driving, and pulled at the reins.

"Don't saw her mouth!" cried Mrs. Sewell.

"Well, let her get up, then, and I won't. I don't like to saw her mouth; but I have to do something when you come down on me with your interminable consequences. I dare say the boy will never think of my praise again. And besides, as I was saying when this animal interrupted me with her ill-timed at-tempts at grazing, how do you know that I knew the poetry was bad?"

"How? By the sound of your voice. I could tell you were dishonest in the dark, David."

"Perhaps the boy knew that I was dishonest too," suggested Sewell.

"Oh, no, he didn't. I could see that he pinned his faith to every syllable."

"He used a quantity of pins, then; for I was particularly profuse of syllables. I find that it requires no end of them to make the worse appear the better reason to a poet who reads his own verses to you. But come, now, Lucy, let me off a syllable or two. I—I have a conscience, you know well enough, and if I thought— But pshaw! I've merely cheered a lonely hour for the boy, and he'll go back to hoeing potatoes to-morrow, and that will be the end of it."

"I *hope* that will be the end of it," said Mrs. Sewell, with the darkling reserve of ladies intimate with the designs of Providence.

"Well," argued her husband, who was trying to keep the matter from being serious, "perhaps he may turn out a poet yet. You never can tell where the lightning is going to strike. He has some idea of rhyme, and some perception of reason, and—yes, some of the lines *were* musical. His general attitude reminded me of Piers Plowman. Didn't he recall Piers Plowman to you?"

"I'm glad you can console yourself in that way, David," said his wife relentlessly.

The mare stopped again, and Sewell looked over his shoulder at the house, now black in the twilight, on the crest of the low hill across the hollow behind them. "I declare," he said, "the loneliness of that place almost broke my heart. There!" he added, as the faint sickle gleamed in the sky above the roof, "I've got the new moon right over my left shoulder for my pains. That's what comes of having a sympathetic nature."

The boy was looking at the new moon, across the broken gate which stopped the largest gap in the tumbled stone wall. He still gripped in his hand the manuscript which he had been reading to the minister.

"There, Lem," called his mother's voice from the house, "I guess you've seen the last of 'em for one while. I'm 'fraid you'll take cold out there'n the dew. Come in, child."

The boy obeyed. "I was looking at the new moon, mother. I saw it over my right shoulder. Did you hear—hear him," he asked in a broken and husky voice,—"hear how he praised my poetry, mother?"

"Oh, *do* make her get up, David!" cried Mrs. Sewell. "These mosquitoes are eating me alive!"

"I will saw her mouth all to the finest sort of kindling-wood, if she doesn't get up this very instant," said Sewell, jerking the reins so wildly that the mare leaped into a galvanic canter, and continued without further urging for twenty paces. "Of course, Lucy," he resumed, profiting by the opportunity for conversation which the mare's temporary activity afforded, "I should feel myself greatly to blame if I thought I had gone beyond mere kindness in my treatment of the poor fellow. But at first I couldn't realize that the stuff was so bad. Their saying that he read all the books he could get, and was writing every spare moment, gave me the idea that he *must* be some sort of literary genius in the germ, and I listened on and on, expecting every moment that he was coming to some passage with a little lift or life in it; and when he got to the end, and hadn't come to it, I couldn't quite pull myself together to say so. I had gone there so full of the wish to recognize and encourage, that I couldn't turn about for the other thing. Well! I shall know another time how to value a rural neighborhood report of the existence of a local poet. Usually there is some hardheaded cynic in the community with native perception enough to enlighten the rest as to the true value of the phenomenon; but there seems to have been none here. I ought to have come sooner to see him, and then I could have had a chance to go again and talk soberly and kindly with him, and show him gently how much he had mistaken himself. Oh, *get* up!" By this time the mare had lapsed again into her habitual absent-mindedness, and was limping along the dark road with a tendency to come to a full stop, from step to step. The remorse in the minister's soul was so keen that he could not use her with the cruelty necessary to rouse her flagging energies; as he held the reins he flapped his elbows up toward his face, as if they were wings, and contrived to beat away a few of the mosquitoes with them; Mrs. Sewell, in silent exasperation, fought them from her with the bough which she had torn from an overhanging birch-tree.

In the morning they returned to Boston, and Sewell's parish duties began again; he was rather faithfuller and busier in these than he might have been if he had not laid so much stress upon duties of all sorts, and so little upon beliefs. He declared that he envied the ministers of the good old times who had only to teach their people that they would be lost if they did not do right; it was much simpler than to make them understand that they were often to be good for reasons not immediately connected with their present or future comfort, and that they could not confidently expect to be lost for any given transgression, or even to be lost at all. He found it necessary to do his work largely in a personal way, by meeting and talking with people, and this took up a great deal of his time, especially after the summer vacation, when he had to get into relations with them anew, and to help them recover themselves from the moral lassitude into which people fall during that season of physical recuperation.

He was occupied with these matters one morning late in October when a letter came addressed in a handwriting of copybook carefulness, but showing in every painstaking stroke the writer's want of training, which, when he read it, filled Sewell with dismay. It was a letter from Lemuel Barker, whom Sewell remembered, with a pang of self-upbraiding, as the poor fellow he had visited with his wife the evening before they left Willoughby Pastures; and it inclosed passages of a long poem which Barker said he had written since he got the fall work done. The passages were not submitted for Sewell's criticism, but were offered as examples of the character of the whole poem, for which the author wished to find a publisher. They were not without ideas of a didactic and satirical sort, but they seemed so wanting in literary art beyond a mechanical facility of versification, that Sewell wondered how the writer should have mastered the notion of anything so literary as publication, till he came to that part of the letter in which Barker spoke of their having had so much sickness in the family that he thought he would try to do something to help along. The avowal of this meritorious ambition inflicted another wound upon Sewell's guilty consciousness; but what made his blood run cold was Barker's proposal to come down to Boston, if Sewell advised, and find a publisher with Sewell's assistance.

This would never do, and the minister went to his desk with the intention of dispatching a note of prompt and total discouragement. But in crossing the room from the chair into which he had sunk, with a cheerful curiosity, to read the letter, he could not help some natural rebellion against the punishment visited upon him. He could not deny that he deserved punishment, but he thought that this, to say the least, was very ill-timed. He had often warned other sinners who came to him in like resentment that it was this very quality of inopportuneness that was perhaps the most sanative and divine property of retribution; the eternal justice fell upon us, he said, at the very moment when we were least able to bear it, or thought ourselves so; but now in his own case the clear-sighted prophet cried out and revolted in his heart. It was Saturday morning, when every minute was precious to him for his sermon, and it would take him fully an hour to write that letter; it must be done with the greatest sympathy; he had seen that this poor foolish boy was very sensitive, and yet it must be done with such thoroughness as to cut off all hope of anything like literary achievement for him.

At the moment Sewell reached his desk, with a spirit disciplined to the sacrifice required of it, he heard his wife's step outside his study door, and he had just time to pull open a drawer, throw the letter into it, and shut it again before she entered. He did not mean finally to conceal it from her, but he was willing to give himself breath before he faced her with the fact that he had received such a letter. Nothing in its way was more terrible to this good man than the righteousness of that good woman. In their case, as in that of most other couples who cherish an ideal of dutiful living, she was the custodian of their potential virtue, and he was the instrument, often faltering and imperfect, of its application to circumstances; and without wishing to spare himself too much, he was sometimes aware that she did not spare him enough. She worked his moral forces as mercilessly as a woman uses the physical strength of a man when it is placed at her direction.

"What is the matter, David?" she asked, with a keen glance at the face he turned upon her over his shoulder.

"Nothing that I wish to talk of at present, my dear," answered Sewell, with a boldness that he knew would not avail him if she persisted in knowing.

"Well, there would be no time if you did," said his wife. "I'm dreadfully sorry for you, David, but it's really a case you can't refuse. Their own minister is taken sick, and it's appointed for this afternoon at two o'clock, and the poor thing has set her heart upon having you, and you must go. In fact, I promised you would. I'll see that you're not disturbed this morning, so that you'll have the whole forenoon to yourself. But I thought I'd better tell you at once. It's only a child—a little boy. You won't have to say much."

"Oh, of course I must go," answered Sewell, with impatient resignation; and when his wife left the room, which she did after praising him and pitying him in a way that was always very sweet to him, he saw that he must begin his sermon at once, if he meant to get through with it in time, and must put off all hope of replying to Lemuel Barker till Monday at least. But he chose quite a different theme from that on which he had intended to preach. By an immediate inspiration he wrote a sermon on the text, "The tender mercies of the wicked are cruel," in which he taught how great harm could be done by the habit of saying what are called kind things. He showed that this habit arose not from goodness of heart, or from the desire to make others happy, but from the wish to spare one's self the troublesome duty of formulating the truth so that it would perform its heavenly office without wounding those whom it was intended to heal. He warned his hearers that the kind things spoken from this motive were so many sins committed against the soul of the flatterer and the soul of him they were intended to flatter; they were deceits, lies; and he besought all within the sound of his voice to try to practice with one another an affectionate sincerity, which was compatible not only with the brotherliness of Christianity, but the politeness of the world. He enforced his points with many apt illustrations, and he treated the whole subject with so much fullness and fervor, that he fell into the error of the literary temperament, and almost felt that he had atoned for his wrong-doing by the force with which he had portrayed it.

Mrs. Sewell, who did not always go to her husband's sermons, was at church that day, and joined him when some ladies who had lingered to thank him for the excellent lesson he had given them at last left him to her.

"Really, David," she said, "I wondered your congregation could keep their countenances while you were going on. Did you think of that poor boy up at Willoughby Pastures when you were writing that sermon?"

"Yes, my dear," replied Sewell gravely; "he was in my mind the whole time."

"Well, you were rather hard upon yourself; and I think I was rather too hard upon you, that time, though I *was* so vexed with you. But nothing has come of it, and I suppose there are cases where people are so lost to common sense that you can't do anything for them by telling them the truth."

"But you'd better tell it, all the same," said Sewell, still in a glow of righteous warmth from his atonement; and now a sudden temptation to play with fire seized him. "You wouldn't have excused me if any trouble had come of it."

"No, I certainly shouldn't," said his wife. "But I don't regret it altogether if it's made you see what danger you run from that tendency of yours. What in the world made you think of it?"

"Oh, it came into my mind," said Sewell.

He did not find time to write to Barker the next day, and on recurring to his letter he saw that there was no danger of his taking another step without his advice, and he began to postpone it: when he had time he was not in the mood; he waited for the time and the mood to come together, and he also waited for the most favorable moment to tell his wife that he had got that letter from Barker and to ask her advice about answering it. If it had been really a serious matter, he would have told her at once; but being the thing it was, he did not know just how to approach it, after his first concealment. He knew that, to begin with, he would have to account for his mistake in attempting to keep it from her, and would have to bear some just upbraiding for this unmanly course, and would then be miserably led to the distasteful contemplation of the folly by which he had brought this trouble upon himself. Sewell smiled to think how much easier it was to make one's peace with one's God than with one's wife; and before he had brought himself to the point of answering Barker's letter, there came a busy season in which he forgot him altogether.

———————

ONE DAY in the midst of this Sewell was called from his study
to see some one who was waiting for him in the reception-
room, but who sent in no name by the housemaid.

"I don't know as you remember me," the visitor said, rising
awkwardly, as Sewell came forward with a smile of inquiry.
"My name's Barker."

"Barker?" said the minister, with a cold thrill of instant
recognition, but playing with a factitious uncertainty till he
could catch his breath in the presence of the calamity. "Oh,
yes! How do you do?" he said; and then planting himself adventurously upon the commandment to love one's neighbor
as one's self, he added: "I'm very glad to see you!"

In token of his content, he gave Barker his hand and asked
him to be seated.

The young man complied, and while Sewell waited for him
to present himself in some shape that he could grapple with
morally, he made an involuntary study of his personal appearance. That morning, before starting from home by the
milk-train that left Willoughby Pastures at 4:05, Barker had
given his Sunday boots a coat of blacking, which he had eked
out with stove-polish, and he had put on his best pantaloons,
which he had outgrown, and which, having been made very
tight a season after tight pantaloons had gone out of fashion
in Boston, caught on the tops of his boots and stuck there in
spite of his efforts to kick them loose as he stood up, and his
secret attempts to smooth them down when he had reseated

himself. He wore a single-breasted coat of cheap broadcloth, fastened across his chest with a carnelian clasp-button of his father's, such as country youth wore thirty years ago, and a belated summer scarf of gingham, tied in a breadth of knot long since abandoned by polite society.

Sewell had never thought his wife's reception-room very splendidly appointed, but Barker must have been oppressed by it, for he sat in absolute silence after resuming his chair, and made no sign of intending to open the matter upon which he came. In the kindness of his heart Sewell could not refrain from helping him on.

"When did you come to Boston?" he asked with a cheeriness which he was far from feeling.

"This morning," said Barker, briefly, but without the tremor in his voice which Sewell expected.

"You've never been here before, I suppose," suggested Sewell, with the vague intention of generalizing or particularizing the conversation, as the case might be.

Barker abruptly rejected the overture, whatever it was. "I don't know as you got a letter from me a spell back," he said.

"Yes, I did," confessed Sewell. "I did receive that letter," he repeated, "and I ought to have answered it long ago. But the fact is——" He corrected himself when it came to his saying this, and said, "I mean that I put it by, intending to answer it when I could do so in the proper way, until, I'm very sorry to say, I forgot it altogether. Yes, I forgot it, and I certainly ask your pardon for my neglect. But I can't say that as it's turned out I altogether regret it. I can talk with you a great deal better than I could write to you in regard to your" — Sewell hesitated between the words poems and verses, and finally said—"work. I have blamed myself a great deal," he continued, wincing under the hurt which he felt that he must be inflicting on the young man as well as himself, "for not being more frank with you when I saw you at home in September. I hope your mother is well?"

"She's middling," said Barker, "but my married sister that

came to live with us since you was there has had a good deal of
sickness in her family. Her husband's laid up with the rheumatism most of the time."

"Oh!" murmured Sewell sympathetically. "Well! I ought
to have told you at that time that I could not see much hope
of your doing acceptable work in a literary way; and if I had
supposed that you ever expected to exercise your faculty of
versifying to any serious purpose,—for anything but your own
pleasure and entertainment,—I should certainly have done so.
And I tell you now that the specimens of the long poem you
have sent me give me even less reason to encourage you than
the things you read me at home."

Sewell expected the audible crash of Barker's air-castles to
break the silence which the young man suffered to follow upon
these words; but nothing of the kind happened, and for all
that he could see, Barker remained wholly unaffected by what
he had said. It nettled Sewell a little to see him apparently so
besotted in his own conceit, and he added: "But I think I had
better not ask you to rely altogether upon my opinion in the
matter, and I will go with you to a publisher, and you can get
a professional judgment. Excuse me a moment."

He left the room and went slowly upstairs to his wife. It
appeared to him a very short journey to the third story, where
he knew she was decking the guest-chamber for the visit of a
friend whom they expected that evening. He imagined himself saying to her when his trial was well over that he did not
see why she complained of those stairs; that he thought they
were nothing at all. But this sense of the absurdity of the situation which played upon the surface of his distress flickered and
fled at sight of his wife bustling cheerfully about, and he was
tempted to go down and get Barker out of the house, and
out of Boston if possible, without letting her know anything
of his presence.

"Well?" said Mrs. Sewell, meeting his face of perplexity
with a penetrating glance. "What is it, David?"

"Nothing. That is—everything! Lemuel Barker is here!"

"Lemuel Barker? Who is Lemuel Barker?" She stood with the pillow-sham in her hand which she was just about to fasten on the pillow, and Sewell involuntarily took note of the fashion in which it was ironed.

"Why, surely you remember! That simpleton at Willoughby Pastures." If his wife had dropped the pillow-sham, and sunk into a chair beside the bed, fixing him with eyes of speechless reproach; if she had done anything dramatic, or said anything tragic, no matter how unjust or exaggerated, Sewell could have borne it; but she only went on tying the sham on the pillow, without a word. "The fact is, he wrote to me some weeks ago, and sent me some specimens of a long poem."

"Just before you preached that sermon on the tender mercies of the wicked?"

"Yes," faltered Sewell. "I had been waiting to show you the letter."

"You waited a good while, David."

"I know—I know," said Sewell miserably. "I was waiting—waiting—" He stopped, and then added with a burst, "I was waiting till I could put it to you in some favorable light."

"I'm glad you're honest about it at last, my dear!"

"Yes. And while I was waiting I forgot Barker's letter altogether. I put it away somewhere—I can't recollect just where, at the moment. But that makes no difference; he's here with the whole poem in his pocket, now." Sewell gained a little courage from his wife's forbearance; she knew that she could trust him in all great matters, and perhaps she thought that for this little sin she would not add to his punishment. "And what I propose to do is to make a complete thing of it, this time. Of course," he went on convicting himself, "I see that I shall inflict twice the pain that I should have done if I had spoken frankly to him at first; and of course there will be the added disappointment, and the expense of his coming to Boston. But," he added brightly, "we can save him any expense while he's here, and perhaps I can contrive to get him to go home this afternoon."

"He wouldn't let you pay for his dinner out of the house anywhere," said Mrs. Sewell. "You must ask him to dinner here."

"Well," said Sewell, with resignation; and suspecting that his wife was too much piqued or hurt by his former concealment to ask what he now meant to do about Barker, he added: "I'm going to take him round to a publisher and let him convince himself that there's no hope for him in a literary way."

"David!" cried his wife; and now she left off adjusting the shams, and erecting herself looked at him across the bed. "You don't intend to do anything so cruel."

"Cruel?"

"Yes! Why should you go and waste any publisher's time by getting him to look at such rubbish? Why should you expose the poor fellow to the mortification of a perfectly needless refusal? Do you want to shirk the responsibility—to put it on some one else?"

"No; you know I don't."

"Well, then, tell him yourself that it won't do."

"I have told him."

"What does he say?"

"He doesn't say anything. I can't make out whether he believes me or not."

"Very well, then; you've done your duty, at any rate." Mrs. Sewell could not forbear saying also: "If you'd done it at first, David, there wouldn't have been any of this trouble."

"That's true," owned her husband, so very humbly that her heart smote her.

"Well, go down and tell him he must stay to dinner, and then try to get rid of him the best way you can. Your time is really too precious, David, to be wasted in this way. You *must* get rid of him, somehow."

Sewell went back to his guest in the reception-room, who seemed to have remained as immovably in his chair as if he had been a sitting statue of himself. He did not move when Sewell entered.

"On second thoughts," said the minister, "I believe I will

not ask you to go to a publisher with me, as I had intended; it would expose you to unnecessary mortification, and it would be, from my point of view, an unjustifiable intrusion upon very busy people. I must ask you to take my word for it that no publisher would bring out your poem, and it never would pay you a cent if he did." The boy remained silent as before, and Sewell had no means of knowing whether it was from silent conviction or from mulish obstinacy. "Mrs. Sewell will be down presently. She wished me to ask you to stay to dinner. We have an early dinner, and there will be time enough after that for you to look about the city."

"I shouldn't like to put you out," said Barker.

"Oh, not at all," returned Sewell, grateful for this sign of animation, and not exigent of a more formal acceptance of his invitation. "You know," he said, "that literature is a trade, like every other vocation, and that you must serve an apprenticeship if you expect to excel. But first of all you must have some natural aptitude for the business you undertake. You understand?" asked Sewell; for he had begun to doubt whether Barker understood anything. He seemed so much more stupid than he had at home; his faculties were apparently sealed up, and he had lost all the personal picturesqueness which he had when he came in out of the barn, at his mother's call, to receive Sewell.

"Yes," said the boy.

"I don't mean," continued Sewell, "that I wouldn't have you continue to make verses whenever you have the leisure for it. I think, on the contrary, that it will give a grace to your life which it might otherwise lack. We are all in daily danger of being barbarized by the sordid details of life; the constantly recurring little duties which must be done, but which we must not allow to become the whole of life." Sewell was so much pleased with this thought, when it had taken form in words, that he made a mental note of it for future use. "We must put a border of pinks around the potato-patch, as Emerson would say, or else the potato-patch is no better than a field of thistles." Perhaps because the logic of this figure rang a little false, Sewell hastened to add: "But there are many ways in which we can prevent the encroachment of those little duties without being tempted to neglect them, which would be still worse. I have thought a good deal about the condition of our young men in the country, and I have sympathized with them in what seems their want of opportunity, their lack of room for expansion. I have often wished that I could do something for them—help them in their doubts and misgivings, and perhaps find some way out of the trouble for them. I regret this tendency to the cities of the young men from the country. I am sure that if we could give them some sort of social and intellectual life at home, they would not be so restless and dissatisfied."

Sewell felt as if he had been preaching to a dead wall; but now the wall opened, and a voice came out of it, saying: "You mean something to occupy their minds?"

"Exactly so!" cried Sewell. "Something to occupy their minds. Now," he continued, with a hope of getting into some sort of human relations with his guest which he had not felt before, "why shouldn't a young man on a farm take up some scientific study, like geology, for instance, which makes every inch of earth vocal, every rock historic, and the waste places social?" Barker looked so blankly at him that he asked again, "You understand?"

"Yes," said Barker; but having answered Sewell's personal question, he seemed to feel himself in no wise concerned with the general inquiry which Sewell had made, and he let it lie where Sewell had let it drop. But the minister was so well pleased with the fact that Barker had understood anything of what he had said, that he was content to let the notion he had thrown out take its chance of future effect, and rising, said briskly: "Come upstairs with me into my study, and I will show you a picture of Agassiz. It's a very good photograph."

He led the way out of the reception-room, and tripped lightly in his slippered feet up the steps against which Barker knocked the toes of his clumsy boots. He was not large, nor naturally loutish, but the heaviness of the country was in every touch and movement. He dropped the photograph twice in his endeavor to hold it between his stiff thumb and finger.

Sewell picked it up each time for him, and restored it to his faltering hold. When he had securely lodged it there, he asked sweetly: "Did you ever hear what Agassiz said when a scheme was once proposed to him by which he could make a great deal of money?"

"I don't know as I did," replied Barker.

" 'But, gentlemen, *I've no time to make money.*' "

Barker received the anecdote in absolute silence, standing helplessly with the photograph in his hand; and Sewell with a hasty sigh forbore to make the application to the ordinary American ambition to be rich that he had intended. "That's a photograph of the singer Nilsson," he said, cataloguing the other objects on the chimney-piece. "She was a peasant, you know, a country girl in Norway. That's Grévy, the President of the French Republic; his father was a peasant. Lincoln, of course. Sforza, throwing his hoe into the oak," he said, explaining the picture that had caught Barker's eye on the wall above the mantel. "He was working in the field, when a band of adventurers came by, and he tossed his hoe at the tree. If it fell to the ground, he would keep on hoeing; if it caught in the branches and hung there he would follow the adventurers. It caught, and he went with the soldiers and became Duke of Milan. I like to keep the pictures of these great Originals about me," said Sewell, "because in our time, when we refer so constantly to law, we are apt to forget that God is creative as well as operative." He used these phrases involuntarily; they slipped from his tongue because he was in the habit of saying this about these pictures, and he made no effort to adapt them to Barker's comprehension, because he could not see that the idea would be of any use to him. He went on pointing out the different objects in the quiet room, and he took down several books from the shelves that covered the whole wall, and showed them to Barker, who, however, made no effort to look at them for himself, and did not say anything about them. He did what Sewell bade him do in admiring this thing or that; but if he had been an Indian he could not have regarded them with a greater reticence. Sewell made him sit down from time to time, but in a sitting posture Barker's silence became so deathlike that Sewell hastened to get him on his legs again, and to walk him about from one point to another, as if to keep life in him. At the end of one of these otherwise aimless excursions Mrs. Sewell appeared, and infused a gleam of hope into her husband's breast. Apparently she brought none to Barker; or perhaps he did not conceive it polite to show any sort of liveliness before a lady. He did what he could with the hand she gave him to shake, and answered the brief questions she put to him about his family to precisely the same effect as he had already reported its condition to Sewell.

"Dinner's ready now," said Mrs. Sewell, for all comment. She left the expansiveness of sympathy and gratulation to her husband on most occasions, and on this she felt that she had less than the usual obligation to make polite conversation. Her two children came down-stairs after her, and as she unfolded her napkin across her lap after grace she said, "This is my son, Alfred, Mr. Barker; and this is Edith." Barker took the acquaintance offered in silence, the young Sewells smiled with the wise kindliness of children taught to be good to all manner of strange guests, and the girl cumbered the helpless country boy with offers of different dishes.

Mr. Sewell as he cut at the roast beef lengthwise, being denied by his wife a pantomimic prayer to be allowed to cut it crosswise, tried to make talk with Barker about the weather at Willoughby Pastures. It had been a very dry summer, and he asked if the fall rains had filled up the springs. He said he really forgot whether it was an apple year. He also said that he supposed they had dug all their turnips by this time. He had meant to say potatoes when he began, but he remembered that he had seen the farmers digging their potatoes before he came back to town, and so he substituted turnips; afterwards it seemed to him that dig was not just the word to use in regard to the harvesting of turnips. He wished he had said, "got your turnips in," but it appeared to make no difference to Barker, who answered, "Yes, sir," and "No, sir," and "Yes, sir," and let each subject drop with that.

III

The silence grew so deep that the young Sewells talked together in murmurs, and the clicking of the knives on the plates became painful. Sewell kept himself from looking at Barker, whom he nevertheless knew to be changing his knife and fork from one hand to the other, as doubt after doubt took him as to their conventional use, and to be getting very little good of his dinner in the process of settling these questions. The door-bell rang, and the sound of a whispered conference between the visitor and the servant at the threshold penetrated to the dining-room. Some one softly entered, and then Mrs. Sewell called out, "Yes, yes! Come in! Come in, Miss Vane!" She jumped from her chair and ran out into the hall, where she was heard to kiss her visitor; she reappeared, still holding her by the hand, and then Miss Vane shook hands with Sewell, saying in a tone of cordial liking, "*How* d'ye do?" and to each of the young people, as she shook hands in turn with them, "How d'ye *do*, dear?" She was no longer so pretty as she must have once been; but an air of distinction and a delicate charm of manner remained to her from her fascinating youth.

Young Sewell pushed her a chair to the table, and she dropped softly into it, after acknowledging Barker's presentation by Mrs. Sewell with a kindly glance that probably divined him.

"You must dine with us," said Mrs. Sewell. "You can call it lunch."

"No, I can't, Mrs. Sewell," said Miss Vane. "I could once, and should have said with great pleasure, when I went away, that I had been lunching at the Sewells; but I can't now. I've reformed. What have you got for dinner?"

"Roast beef," said Sewell.

"Nothing I dislike more," replied Miss Vane. "What else?" She put on her glasses, and peered critically about the table.

"Stewed tomatoes, baked sweet potatoes, macaroni."

"How unimaginative! What are you going to have afterwards?"

"Cottage pudding."

"The very climax of the commonplace! Well!" Miss Vane began to pull off her gloves, and threw her veil back over her shoulder. "I will dine with you, but when I say dine, and people ask me to explain, I shall have to say 'Why, the Sewells still dine at one o'clock, you know,' and laugh over your old-fashioned habits with them. I should like to do differently, and to respect the sacredness of broken bread and that sort of thing; but I'm trying to practice with every one an affectionate sincerity, which is perfectly compatible not only with the brotherliness of Christianity, but the politeness of the world." Miss Vane looked demurely at Mrs. Sewell. "I can't make any exceptions."

The ladies both broke into a mocking laugh, in which Sewell joined with sheepish reluctance; after all, one does not like to be derided, even by one's dearest friends.

"As soon as I hear my other little sins denounced from the pulpit, I'm going to stop using profane language and carrying away people's spoons in my pocket."

The ladies seemed to think this also a very good joke, and his children laughed in sympathy, but Sewell hung his head; Barker sat bolt upright behind his plate, and stared at Miss Vane. "I never have been all but named in church before," she concluded, "and I've heard others say the same."

"Why didn't you come to complain sooner?" asked Sewell.

"Well, I have been away ever since that occasion. I went

down the next day to Newport, and I've been there ever since, admiring the ribbon-planting."

"On the lawns or on the ladies?" asked Sewell.

"Both. And sowing broadcast the seeds of plain speaking. I don't know what Newport will be in another year if they all take root."

"I dare say it will be different," said Sewell. "I'm not sure it will be worse." He plucked up a little spirit, and added: "Now you see of how little importance you really are in the community; you have been gone these three weeks, and your own pastor didn't know you were out of town."

"Yes, you did, David," interposed his wife. "I told you Miss Vane was away two weeks ago."

"Did you? Well, I forgot it immediately; the fact was of no consequence, one way or the other. How do you like that as a bit of affectionate sincerity?"

"I like it immensely," said Miss Vane. "It's delicious. I only wish I could believe you were honest." She leaned back and laughed into her handkerchief, while Sewell regarded her with a face in which his mortification at being laughed at was giving way to a natural pleasure at seeing Miss Vane enjoy herself. "What do you think," she asked, "since you're in this mood of exasperated veracity,—or pretend to be,—of the flower charity?"

"Do you mean by the barrel, or the single sack? The Graham, or the best Haxall, or the health-food cold-blast?" asked Sewell.

Miss Vane lost her power of answering in another peal of laughter, sobering off, and breaking down again before she could say, "I mean cut flowers for patients and prisoners."

"Oh, that kind! I don't think a single pansy would have an appreciable effect upon a burglar; perhaps a bunch of forget-me-nots might, or a few lilies of the valley carelessly arranged. As to the influence of a graceful little *boutonnière*, in cases of rheumatism or cholera morbus, it might be efficacious; but I can't really say."

"How perfectly cynical!" cried Miss Vane. "Don't you know how much good the flower mission has accomplished among the deserving poor? Hundreds of bouquets are distributed every day. They prevent crime."

"That shows how susceptible the deserving poor are. I don't find that a bowl of the most expensive and delicate roses in the center of a dinner-table tempers the asperity of the conversation when it turns upon the absent. But perhaps it oughtn't to do so."

"I don't know about that," said Miss Vane; "but if you had an impulsive niece to supply with food for the imagination, you would be very glad of anything that seemed to combine practical piety and picturesque effect."

"Oh, if you mean that," began Sewell more soberly, and his wife leaned forward with an interest in the question which she had not felt while the mere joking went on.

"Yes. When Sibyl came in this morning with an imperative demand to be allowed to go off and do good with flowers in the homes of virtuous poverty, as well as the hospitals and prisons, I certainly felt as if there had been an interposition, if you will allow me to say so."

Miss Vane still had her joking air, but a note of anxiety had crept into her voice.

"I don't think it will do the sick and poor any harm," said Sewell, "and it may do Sibyl some good." He smiled a little in adding: "It may afford her varied energies a little scope."

Miss Vane shook her head, and some lines of age came into her face which had not shown themselves there before. "And you would advise letting her go into it?" she asked.

"By all means," replied Sewell. "But if she's going to engage actively in the missionary work, I think you'd better go with her on her errands of mercy."

"Oh, of course, she's going to do good in person. What she wants is the sensation of doing good—of seeing and hearing the results of her beneficence. She'd care very little about it if she didn't."

"Oh, I don't know that you can say that," replied Sewell

in deprecation of this extreme view. "I don't believe," he continued, "that she would object to doing good for its own sake."

"Of course she wouldn't, David! Who in the world supposed she would?" demanded his wife, bringing him up roundly at this sign of wandering, and Miss Vane laughed wildly. "And is this what your doctrine of sincerity comes to? This fulsomeness! You're very little better than one of the wicked, it seems to me! Well, I *hoped* that you would approve of my letting Sibyl take this thing up, but such *unbounded* encouragement!"

"Oh, I don't wish to flatter," said Sewell, in the spirit of her raillery. "It will be very well for her to go round with flowers; but don't let her," he continued seriously—"don't let her imagine it's more than an innocent amusement. It would be a sort of hideous mockery of the good we ought to do one another if there were supposed to be anything more than a kindly thoughtfulness expressed in such a thing."

"Oh, if Sibyl doesn't feel that it's real, for the time being she won't care anything about it. She likes to lose herself in the illusion, she says."

"Well!" said Sewell with a slight shrug, "then we must let her get what good she can out of it as an exercise of the sensibilities."

"Oh, my dear!" exclaimed his wife. "You *don't* mean anything so abominable as that! I've heard you say that the worst thing about fiction and the theater was that they brought emotions into play that ought to be sacred to real occasions."

"Did I say that? Well, I must have been right. I——"

Barker made a scuffling sound with his boots under the table, and rose to his feet. "I guess," he said, "I shall have to be going."

They had all forgotten him, and Sewell felt as if he had neglected this helpless guest. "Why, no, you mustn't go! I was in hopes we might do something to make the day pleasant to you. I intended proposing——"

"Yes," his wife interrupted, believing that he meant to give

up one of his precious afternoons to Barker, and hastening
to prevent the sacrifice, "my son will show you the Public
Garden and the Common, and go about the town with you."
She rose too, and young Sewell, accustomed to suffer, silently
acquiesced. "If your train isn't to start very soon——"

"I guess I better be going," said Barker, and Mrs. Sewell
now gave her husband a look conveying her belief that Barker
would be happier if they let him go. At the same time she
frowned upon the monstrous thought of asking him to stay
the night with them, which she detected in Sewell's face.

She allowed him to say nothing but, "I'm sorry; but if you
really must——"

"I guess I better," persisted Barker. He got himself somehow to the door, where he paused a moment, and contrived
to pant "Well, good-day," and without effort at more cordial
leave-taking, passed out.

Sewell followed him, and helped him find his hat, and made
him shake hands. He went with him to the door, and, beginning to suffer afresh at the wrong he had done Barker, he
detained him at the threshold. "If you still wish to see a publisher, Mr. Barker, I will gladly go with you."

"Oh, not at all, not at all. I guess I don't want to see any
publisher this afternoon. Well, good-afternoon!" He turned
away from Sewell's remorseful pursuit, and clumsily hurrying
down the steps, he walked up the street and round the next
corner. Sewell stood watching him in rueful perplexity, shad-
ing his eyes from the mild October sun with his hand; and
some moments after Barker had disappeared, he remained
looking after him.

When he rejoined the ladies in the dining-room they fell
into a conscious silence.

"Have you been telling, Lucy?" he asked.

"Yes, I've been telling, David. It was the only way. Did you
offer to go with him to a publisher again?"

"Yes, I did. It was the only way," said Sewell.

Miss Vane and his wife both broke into a cry of laughter.
The former got her breath first. "So *that* was the origin of the

famous sermon that turned all our heads gray with good resolutions." Sewell assented with a sickly grin. "What in the world *made* you encourage him?"

"My goodness of heart, which I didn't take the precaution of mixing with goodness of head before I used it."

Everything was food for Miss Vane's laugh, even this confession. "But what is the natural history of the boy? How came he to write poetry? What do you suppose he means by it?"

"That isn't so easy to say. As to his natural history, he lives with his mother in a tumble-down, unpainted wooden house in the deepest fastness of Willoughby Pastures. Lucy and I used to drive by it and wonder what kind of people inhabited that solitude. There were milk-cans scattered round the dooryard, and the Monday we were there a poverty-stricken wash flapped across it. The thought of the place preyed upon me till one day I asked about it at the post-office, and the postmistress told me that the boy was quite a literary character, and read everything he could lay his hands on, and 'sat up nights' writing poetry. It seemed to me a very clear case of genius, and the postmistress's facts rankled in my mind till I couldn't stand it any longer. Then I went to see him. I suppose Lucy has told you the rest?"

"Yes, Mrs. Sewell has told me the rest. But still I don't see how he came to write poetry. I believe it doesn't pay, even in extreme cases of genius."

"Ah, but that's just what this poor fellow didn't know. He must have read somewhere, in some deleterious newspaper, about the sale of some large edition of a poem, and have had his own wild hopes about it. I don't say his work didn't show sense; it even showed some rude strength, of a didactic, satirical sort, but it certainly didn't show poetry. He might have taken up painting by a little different chance. And when it was once known about the neighborhood that he wrote poetry, his vanity was flattered——"

"Yes, I see. But wasn't there any kind soul to tell him that he was throwing his time away?"

"It appears not."

"And even the kind soul from Boston, who visited him," suggested Mrs. Sewell. "Go on, David."

"Visited him in spite of his wife's omniscience,—even the kind soul from Boston paltered with this plain duty. Even he, to spare himself the pain of hurting the boy's feelings, tried to find some of the lines better than others, and left him with the impression that he had praised them."

"Well, that was pretty bad," said Miss Vane. "You had to tell him to-day, I suppose, that there was no hope for him?"

"Yes, I had to tell him at last, after letting him waste his time and money in writing more stuff and coming to Boston with it. I've put him to needless shame, and I've inflicted suffering upon him that I can't lighten in the least by sharing."

"No, that's the most discouraging thing about pitying people. It does them no manner of good," said Miss Vane, "and just hurts you. Don't you think that in an advanced civilization we shall cease to feel compassion? Why don't you preach against common pity, as you did against common politeness?"

"Well, it isn't quite such a crying sin yet. But really, really," exclaimed Sewell, "the world seems so put together that I believe we ought to think twice before doing a good action."

"David!" said his wife warningly.

"Oh, let him go on!" cried Miss Vane, with a laugh. "I'm proof against his monstrous doctrines. Go on, Mr. Sewell."

"What I mean is this." Sewell pushed himself back in his chair, and then stopped.

"Is what?" prompted both the ladies.

"Why, suppose this boy really had some literary faculty, should I have had any right to encourage it? He was very well where he was. He fed the cows and milked them, and carried the milk to the cross-roads, where the dealer collected it and took it to the train. That was his life, with the incidental facts of cutting the hay and fodder, and bedding the cattle; and his experience never went beyond it. I doubt if his fancy ever did, except in some wild, mistaken excursion. Why shouldn't

he have been left to this condition? He ate, he slept, he ful-
filled his use. Which of us does more?"

"How would you like to have been in his place?" asked his
wife.

"I couldn't *put* myself in his place; and therefore I oughtn't
to have done anything to take him out of it," answered Sewell.

"It seems to me that's very un-American," said Miss Vane.
"I thought we had prospered up to the present point by taking
people out of their places."

"Yes, we have," replied the minister, "and sometimes, it
seems to me, the result is hideous. I don't mind people taking
themselves out of their places; but if the particles of this
mighty cosmos have been adjusted by the divine wisdom, what
are we to say of the temerity that disturbs the least of them?"

"I'm sure I don't know," said Miss Vane, rising. "I'm almost
afraid to stir, in view of the possible consequences. But I
can't sit here all day, and if Mrs. Sewell will excuse me, I'll
go at once. Yes, 'I guess I better be going,' as your particle
Barker says. Let us hope he'll get safely back to his infinitesi-
mal little crevice in the cosmos. He's a very pretty particle,
don't you think? That thick, coarse, wavy black hair growing
in a natural bang over his forehead would make his fortune if
he were a certain kind of young lady."

They followed her to the door, chatting, and Sewell looked
quickly out when he opened it for her.

As she shook his hand she broke into another laugh. "Really,
you looked as if you were afraid of finding him on the steps!"

"If I could only have got near the poor boy," said Sewell to
his wife, as they returned within doors. "If I could only have
reached him where he lives, as our slang says! But do what I
would, I couldn't find any common ground where we could
stand together. We were as unlike as if we were of two different species. I saw that everything I said bewildered him more
and more; he couldn't understand me! Our education is un-
christian, our civilization is pagan. They both ought to bring

us in closer relations with our fellow-creatures, and they both only put us more widely apart! Every one of us dwells in an impenetrable solitude! We understand each other a little if our circumstances are similar, but if they are different all our words leave us dumb and unintelligible."

IV

Barker walked away from the minister's door without knowing where he was going, and with a heart full of hot pain. He burned with a confused sense of shame and disappointment and anger. It had turned out just as his mother had said: Mr. Sewell would be mighty different in Boston from what he was that day at Willoughby Pastures. There he made Barker think everything of his poetry, and now he pretended to tell him that it was not worth anything; and he kept hinting round that Barker had better go back home and stay there. Did he think he would have left home if there had been anything for him to do there? Had not he as much as told him that he was obliged to find something to make a living by, and help the rest? What was he afraid of? Was he afraid that Barker wanted to come and live off *him?* He could show him that there was no great danger. If he had known how, he would have refused even to stay to dinner.

What made him keep the pictures of these people who had got along, if he thought no one else ought to try? Barker guessed to himself that if that Mr. Agassiz had had to get a living off the farm at Willoughby Pastures, he would have *found* time to make money. What did Mr. Sewell mean by speaking of that Nilsson lady by her surname, without any Miss or Mrs.? Was that the way people talked in Boston?

Mr. Sewell had talked to him as if he were a baby, and did not know anything; and Barker was mad at himself for having staid half a minute after the minister had owned up that he had got the letter he wrote him. He wished he had said, "Well, that's all I want of *you*, sir," and walked right out; but he had not known how to do it. Did they think it was very polite to go on talking with that woman who laughed so much, and forget all about him? Pretty poor sort of manners to eat with her bonnet on, and tell them she hated their victuals.

Barker tried to rage against them in these thoughts, but at the bottom of all was a simple grief that he should have lost the friend whom he thought he had in the minister; the friend he had talked of and dreamed of ever since he had seen and heard him speak those cordial words; the friend he had trusted through all, and had come down to Boston counting upon so much. The tears came into his eyes as he stumbled and scuffled along the brick pavements with his uncouth country walk.

He was walking up a straight, long street, with houses just alike on both sides, and bits of grass before them, that sometimes were gay with late autumn flowers. A horse-car track ran up the middle, and the cars seemed to be tinkling by all the time, and people getting on and off. They were mostly ladies and children, and they were very well dressed. Sometimes they stared at Barker, as they crossed his way in entering or issuing from the houses, but generally no one appeared to notice him. In some of the windows there were flowers in painted pots, and in others little marble images on stands.

There were more images in the garden that Barker came to presently: an image of Washington on horseback, and some orator speaking, with his hand up, and on top of a monument a kind of Turk holding up a man that looked sick. The man was almost naked, but he was not so bad as the image of a woman in a granite basin; it seemed to Barker that it ought not to be allowed there. A great many people of all kinds were passing through the garden, and after some hesitation he went in too, and walked over the bridge that crossed the pond in the middle of the garden, where there were rowboats and boats with images of swans on them. Barker made a sarcastic reflection that Boston seemed to be a great place for images, and passed rather hurriedly through the garden on the other side of the bridge. There were beds of all kinds of flowers scattered about, and they were hardly touched by the cold yet. If he had been in better heart, he would have liked to look round a little; but he felt strange, being there all alone, and he felt very low-spirited.

He wondered if this were the Public Garden that Mrs. Sewell had spoken of, and if that kind of grove across the street were the Common. He felt much more at home in it, as he wandered up and down the walks, and finally sat down on one of the iron benches beside the path. At first he obscurely doubted whether he had any right to do so, unless he had a lady with him; most of the seats were occupied by couples who seemed to be courting, but he ventured finally to take one; nobody disturbed him, and so he remained.

It was a beautiful October afternoon; the wind, warm and dry, caught the yellow leaves from the trees overhead in little whiffs, and blew them about the grass, which the fall rains had made as green as May; and a pensive golden light streamed through the long loose boughs, and struck across the slopes of the Common. Slight buggies flashed by on the street near which he sat, and glistening carriages, with drivers dressed out in uniform like soldiers, rumbled down its slope.

While he sat looking, now at the street and now at the people sauntering and hurrying to and fro in the Common, he tried to decide a question that had mixed itself up with the formless resentment he had felt ever since Mr. Sewell played him false. It had got out in the neighborhood that he was going to Boston before he left home; his mother must have told it; and people would think he was to be gone a long time. He had warned his mother that he did not know when he should be back, before he started in the morning; and he knew that she would repeat his words to everybody who stopped to ask about him during the day, with what she had said to him in reply: "You better come home to-night, Lem; and I'll have ye a good hot supper waitin' for ye."

The question was whether he should go back on the five

o'clock train, which would reach Willoughby Centre after dark, and house himself from public ignominy for one night at least, or whether self-respect did not demand that he should stay in Boston for twenty-four hours at any rate, and see if something would not happen. He had now no distinct hope of anything; but his pride and shame were holding him fast, while the homesickness tugged at his heart, and made him almost forget the poverty that had spurred him to the adventure of coming to Boston. He could see the cows coming home through the swampy meadow as plain as if they were coming across the Common; his mother was calling them; she and his sister were going to milk in his absence, and he could see her now, how she looked going out to call the cows, in her bare, gray head, gaunt of neck and cheek, in the ugly Bloomer dress in which she was not grotesque to his eyes, though it usually affected strangers with stupefaction or alarm. But it all seemed far away, as far as if it were in another planet that he had dropped out of; he was divided from it by his failure and disgrace. He thought he must stay and try for something, he did not know what; but he could not make up his mind to throw away his money for nothing; at the hotel, down by the depot, where he had left his bag, they were going to make him pay fifty cents for just a room alone.

"Any them beats 'round here been trying to come their games on *you?*"

At first Barker could not believe himself accosted, though the young man who spoke stood directly in front of him, and seemed to be speaking to him. He looked up, and the young man added, "Heigh?"

"Beats? I don't know what you mean," said Barker.

"Confidence sharps, young feller. They're 'round everywheres, and don't you forget it. Move up a little!"

Barker was sitting in the middle of the bench, and at this he pushed away from the young man, who had dropped himself sociably beside him. He wore a pair of black pantaloons, very tight in the legs, and widening at the foot so as almost to cover his boots. His coat was deeply braided, and his waistcoat was cut low, so that his plastron-scarf hung out from the shirt-bosom, which it would have done well to cover.

"I tell you, Boston's full of 'em," he said, excitedly. "One of 'em come up to me just now, and says he, 'Seems to me I've seen you before, but I can't place you.' 'Oh yes,' says I, 'I'll tell you where it was. I happened to be in the police court one morning when they was sendin' you up for three months.' I tell you he got round the corner! Might 'a' played checkers on his coat-tail. Why, what do you suppose would been the next thing if I hadn't have let him know I saw through him?" demanded the young man of Barker, who listened to this adventure with imperfect intelligence. "He'd 'a' said, 'Hain't I seen you down Kennebunk way som'eres?' And when I said, 'No, I'm from Leominster!' or wherever I was from if I was green, he'd say, 'Oh yes, so it *was* Leominster. How's the folks?' and he'd try to get me to think that *he* was from Leominster too; and then he'd want me to go off and see the sights with him; and pretty soon he'd meet a feller that 'ud dun him for that money he owed him; and he'd say he hadn't got anything with him but a check for forty dollars; and the other feller'd say he'd got to have his money, and he'd kind of insinuate it was all a put-up job about the check for forty dollars, any way; and that 'ud make the first feller mad, and he'd take out the check, and ask him what he thought o' that; and the other feller'd say, well, it was a good check, but it wa'n't money, and he wanted money; and then the first feller'd say, 'Well, come along to the bank, and get your money,' and the other'd say the bank was shut. 'Well, then,' the first feller'd say, 'well, sir, I ain't a-goin' to ask any favor of *you*. How much *is* your bill?' and the other feller'd say ten dollars, or fifteen, or may be twenty-five, if they thought I had that much, and the first feller'd say, 'Well, here's a gentleman from up my way, and I guess he'll advance me that much on my check if I make it worth his while. He knows me.' And the first thing you know —he's been treatin' you, and so polite, showin' you round, and ast you to go to the theayter—you advance the money, and you keep on with the first feller, and pretty soon he asks you to hold up a minute, he wants to go back and get a cigar; and he goes round the corner, and you hold up, and *hold* up, and in about a half an hour, or may be less time, you begin to smell a rat, and you go for a policeman, and the next morning you find your name in the papers, 'One more unfortunate!' You look out fer 'em, young feller! Wish I *had* let that one go on till he done something so I could handed him over to the cops. It's a shame they're allowed to go 'round, when the cops knows 'em. Hello! There *comes* my mate, *now*." The young man spoke as if they had been talking of his mate and expecting him, and another young man, his counterpart in dress, but of a sullen and heavy demeanor very unlike his own brisk excitement, approached, flapping a bank-note in his hand. "I just been tellin' this young feller about that beat, you know."

"Oh, he's all right," said the mate. "Just seen him down on Tremont street, between two cops. Must ha' caught him in the act."

"You don't say so! Well, that's good, any way. Why! Didn't you get it changed?" demanded the young man with painful surprise as his mate handed him the bank-note.

"No, I didn't. I been to more'n twenty places, and there ain't no small bills nowhere. The last place, I offered 'em twenty-five cents if they'd change it."

"Why didn't you offer 'em fifty? I'd 'a' give fifty, and glad to do it. Why, I've *got* to have this bill changed."

"Well, I'm sorry for you," said the mate, with ironical sympathy, "because I don't see how you're goin' to git it done. Won't you move up a little bit, young feller?" He sat down on the other side of Barker. "I'm about tired out." He took his head between his hands in sign of extreme fatigue, and drooped forward, with his eyes fixed on the ground.

Lemuel's heart beat. Fifty cents would pay for his lodging, and he could stay till the next day and prolong the chance of something turning up without too sinful a waste of money.

"How much is the bill?" he asked.

"Ten dollars," said the young man despondently.

"And will you give me fifty cents if I change it?"

"Well, I *said* I'd give fifty cents," replied the young man gloomily, "and I *will*."

"It's a bargain," said Lemuel promptly, and he took from his pocket the two five-dollar notes that formed his store, and gave them to the young man.

He looked at them critically. "How do I know they're good?" he asked. "You're a stranger to me, young feller, and how do I know you ain't tryin' to beat me?" He looked sternly at Lemuel, but here the mate interposed.

"How does *he* know that you ain't tryin' to beat *him?*" he asked contemptuously. "I never saw such a feller as you are! Here you make me run half over town to change that bill, and now when a gentleman offers to break it for you, you have to go and accuse him of tryin' to put off counterfeit money on you. If I was him I'd see you furder."

"Oh, well, I don't want any words about it. Here, take your money," said the young man. "As long as I said I'd do it, I'll do it. Here's your half a dollar." He put it, with the bank-note, into Lemuel's hand, and rose briskly. "You stay here, Jimmy, till I come back. I won't be gone a minute."

He walked down the mall, and went out of the gate on Tremont street. Then the mate came to himself. "Why, I've *let* him go off with both them bills now, and he owes me one of 'em." With that he rose from Lemuel's side and hurried after his vanishing comrade; before he was out of sight he had broken into a run.

Lemuel sat looking after them, his satisfaction in the affair alloyed by dislike of the haste with which it had been transacted. His rustic mind worked slowly; it was not wholly content even with a result in its own favor, where the process had been so rapid; he was scarcely able to fix the point at which the talk ceased to be a warning against beats and became his opportunity for speculation. He did not feel quite right at having taken the fellow's half-dollar; and yet a bargain was a bargain. Nevertheless, if the fellow wanted to rue it, Lemuel would give him fifteen minutes to come back and get his money; and he sat for that space of time where the others had left him. He was not going to be mean; and he might have waited a little longer if it had not been for the behavior of two girls who came up and sat down on the same bench with him. They could not have been above fifteen or sixteen years old, and Lemuel thought they were very pretty, but they talked so, and laughed so loud, and scuffled with each other for the paper of chocolate which one of them took out of her pocket, that Lemuel, after first being abashed by the fact that they were city girls, became disgusted with them. He was a stickler for propriety of behavior among girls; his mother had taught him to despise anything like carrying-on among them, and at twenty he was as severely virginal in his morality as if he had been twelve.

People looked back at these tomboys when they had got by; and some shabby young fellows exchanged saucy speeches with them. When Lemuel got up and walked away in reproving dignity, one of the hoydens bounced into his place, and they both sent a cry of derision after him. But Lemuel would not give them the satisfaction of letting them know that he heard them, and at the same time he was not going to let them suppose that they had driven him away. He went very slowly down to the street where a great many horse-cars were passing to and fro, and waited for one marked "Fitchburg, Lowell, and Eastern Depots." He was not going to take it; but he meant to follow it on its way to those stations, in the neighborhood of which was the hotel where he had left his traveling-bag. He had told them that he might take a room there, or he might not; now since he had this half-dollar extra he thought that he would stay for the night; it probably would not be any cheaper at the other hotels.

He ran against a good many people in trying to keep the car in sight, but by leaving the sidewalk from time to time where it was most crowded, he managed not to fall very much behind; the worst was that the track went crooking and turning about so much in different streets, that he began to lose faith in its direction, and to be afraid, in spite of the sign on its side, that the car was not going to the depots after all. But it came in sight of them at last, and then Lemuel, blown with the chase but secure of his ground, stopped and rested himself against the side of a wall to get his breath. The pursuit had been very exhausting, and at times it had been mortifying; for here and there people who saw him running after the car had supposed he wished to board it, and in their good-nature had hailed and stopped it. After this had happened twice or thrice, Lemuel perceived that he was an object of contempt to the passengers in the car; but he did not know what to do about it; he was not going to pay six cents to ride when he could just as well walk, and on the other hand he dared not lose sight of the car, for he had no other means of finding his way back to his hotel.

But he was all right now, as he leaned against the house-wall, panting, and mopping his forehead with his handkerchief; he saw his hotel a little way down the street, and he did not feel anxious about it.

"Gave you the slip after all," said a passer, who had apparently been interested in Lemuel's adventure.

"Oh, I didn't want to catch it," said Lemuel.

"Ah, merely fond of exercise," said the stranger. "Well, it's a very good thing, if you don't overdo it." He walked by, and then after a glance at Lemuel over his shoulder, he returned to him. "May I ask why you wanted to chase the car, if you didn't want to catch it?"

Lemuel hesitated; he did not like to confide in a total stranger; this gentleman looked kind and friendly, but he was all the more likely on that account to be a beat; the expression was probably such as a beat would put on in approaching his intended prey. "Oh, nothing," said Lemuel evasively.

"I beg your pardon," said the stranger, and he walked

away with what Lemuel could only conjecture was the air of a baffled beat.

He waited till he was safely out of sight, and then followed on down the street towards his hotel. When he reached it he walked boldly up to the clerk's desk, and said that he guessed he would take a room for the night, and gave him the check for his bag that he had received in leaving it there.

The clerk wrote the number of a room against Lemuel's name in the register, and then glanced at the bag. It was a large bag of oil-cloth, a kind of bag which is by nature lank and hollow, and must be made almost insupportably heavy before it shows any signs of repletion. The shirt and pair of every-day pantaloons which Lemuel had dropped that morning into its voracious maw made no apparent effect there, as the clerk held it up and twirled it on the crook of his thumb.

"I guess I shall have to get the money for that room in advance," he said, regarding the bag very critically. However he might have been wounded by the doubt of his honesty or his solvency implied in this speech, Lemuel said nothing, but took out his ten-dollar note and handed it to the clerk. The latter said apologetically, "It's one of our rules, where there isn't baggage," and then glancing at the note he flung it quickly across the counter to Lemuel. "That won't do!"

"Won't do?" repeated Lemuel, taking up the bill.

"Counterfeit," said the clerk.

V

LEMUEL stretched the note between his hands, and pored so long upon it that the clerk began to tap impatiently with his finger-tips on the register. "It won't go?" faltered the boy, looking up at the clerk's sharp face.

"It won't go here," replied the clerk. "Got anything else?"

Lemuel's head whirled; the air seemed to darken around him, as he pored again upon the note, and turned it over and over. Two tears scalded their way down his cheeks, and his lips twitched, when the clerk added, "Some beats been workin' you?" but he made no answer. His heart was hot with shame and rage, and heavy with despair. He put the note in his pocket, and took his bag and walked out of the hotel. He had not money enough to get home with now, and besides he could not bear to go back in the disgrace of such calamity. It would be all over the neighborhood, as soon as his mother could tell it; she might wish to keep it to herself for his sake, but she could not help telling it to the first person and every person she saw; she would have to go over to the neighbors to tell it. In a dreary, homesick longing he saw her crossing the familiar meadows that lay between the houses, bareheaded, in her apron, her face set and rigid with wonder at what had happened to her Lem. He could not bear the thought. He would rather die; he would rather go to sea. This idea flashed into his mind as he lifted his eyes aimlessly and caught sight of the tall masts of the coal-ships lying at the railroad wharfs, and he walked quickly in the direction of them, so as not to give himself time to think about it, so as to do it now, quick, right off. But he found his way impeded by all sorts of obstacles; a gate closed across the street to let some trains draw in and out of a station; then a lot of string teams and slow heavy-laden trucks got before him, with a turmoil of express wagons, herdics, and hacks, in which he was near being run over, and was yelled at, sworn at, and laughed at as he stood bewildered, with his lank bag in his hand. He turned and walked back past the hotel again. He felt it an escape, after all, not to have gone to sea; and now a hopeful thought struck him. He would go back to the Common and watch for those fellows who fooled him, and set the police on them, and get his money from them; they might come prowling round again to fool somebody else. He looked out for a car marked like the one he had followed down from the Common, and began to follow it on its return. He got ahead of the car whenever it stopped, so as to be spared the shame of being seen to chase it; and he managed to keep it in sight till he reached the Common. There he walked about looking for those scamps, and getting pushed and hustled by the people who now thronged the paths. At last he was tired out, and on the Beacon street mall, where he had first seen those fellows, he found the very seat where they had all sat together, and sank into it. The seats were mostly vacant now; a few persons sat there reading their evening papers. As the light began to wane, they folded up their papers and walked away, and their places were filled by young men, who at once put their arms round the young women with them, and seemed to be courting. They did not say much, if anything; they just sat there. It made Lemuel ashamed to look at them; he thought they ought to have more sense. He looked away, but he could not look away from them all, there were so many of them. He was all the time very hungry, but he thought he ought not to break into his half-dollar as long as he could help it, or till there was no chance left of catching those fellows. The night came on, the gas-lamps were lighted, and some lights higher up, like moonlight off on the other paths, projected long glares into the night and made the gas look sickly and yellow. Sitting still there while it grew later, he did not feel quite so hungry, but he felt more tired than ever. There were not so many people around now, and he did not see why he should not lie down on that seat and rest himself a little. He made feints of reclining on his arm at first, to see if he were noticed; then he stretched himself out, with his bag under his head, and his hands in his pockets clutching the money which he meant to to make those fellows take back. He got a gas-lamp in range, to keep him awake, and lay squinting his eyes to meet the path of rays running down from it to him. Then he shivered, and rose up with a sudden start. The dull, rich dawn was hanging under the trees around him, while the electric lamps, like paler moons now, still burned among their tops. The sparrows bickered on the grass and the gravel of the path around him.

He could not tell where he was at first; but presently he remembered, and looked for his bag. It was gone; and the money was gone out of both his pockets. He dropped back upon the seat, and leaning his head against the back, he began to cry for utter despair. He had hardly ever cried since he was a baby; and he would not have done it now, but there was no one there to see him.

When he had his cry out he felt a little better, and he got up and went to the pond in the hollow, and washed his hands and face, and wiped them on the handkerchief his mother had ironed for him to use at the minister's; it was still in the folds she had given it. As he shook it out, rising up, he saw that people were asleep on all the benches round the pond; he looked hopelessly at them to see if any of them were those fellows, but he could not find them. He seemed to be the only person awake on the Common, and wandered out of it and down through the empty streets, filled at times with the moony light of the waning electrics, and at times merely with the gray dawn. A man came along putting out the gas, and some milk-carts rattled over the pavement. By and by a market-wagon, with the leaves and roots of cabbages sticking out from the edges of the canvas that covered it, came by, and Lemuel followed it; he did not know what else to do, and it went so slow that he could keep up, though the famine that gnawed within him was so sharp sometimes that he felt as if he must fall down. He was going to drop into a doorway and rest, but when he came to it he found on an upper step a man folded forward like a limp bundle, snoring in a fetid, sodden sleep, and, shocked into new strength, he hurried on. At last the wagon came to a place that he saw was a market. There were no buyers yet, but men were flitting round under the long arcades of the market-houses, with lanterns under their arms, among boxes and barrels of melons, apples, potatoes, onions, beans, carrots, and other vegetables, which the country carts as they arrived continually unloaded. The smell of peaches and cantaloupes filled the air, and made Lemuel giddy as he stood and looked at the abundance. The men were not saying much; now and then one of them priced something, the owner pretended to figure on it, and then they fell into a playful scuffle, but all silently. A black cat lay luxuriously asleep on the canvas top of a barrel of melons, and the man who priced the melons asked if the owner would throw the cat in. There was a butcher's cart laden with carcasses of sheep, and one of the men asked the butcher if he called that stuff mutton. "No; imitation," said the butcher. They all seemed to be very good-natured. Lemuel thought he would ask for an apple; but he could not.

The neighboring restaurants began to send forth the smell of breakfast, and he dragged up and down till he could bear it no longer, and then went into one of them, meaning to ask for some job by which he could pay for a meal. But his shame again would not let him. He looked at the fat, white-aproned boy drawing coffee hot from a huge urn, and serving a countryman with a beefsteak. It was close and sultry in there; the open sugar-bowl was black with flies, and a scent of decaying meat came from the next cellar. "Like some nice fresh doughnuts?" said the boy to Lemuel. He did not answer; he looked around as if he had come in search of some one.

Then he went out, and straying away from the market, he found himself after a while in a street that opened upon the Common.

He was glad to sit down, and he said to himself that now he would stay there, and keep a good lookout for the chaps that had robbed him. But again he fell asleep, and he did not wake now till the sun was high, and the paths of the Common were filled with hurrying people. He sat where he had slept, for he did not know what else to do or where to go. Sometimes he thought he would go to Mr. Sewell, and ask him for money enough to get home; but he could not do it; he could more easily starve.

After an hour or two he went to get a drink at a fountain he saw a little way off, and when he came back some people had got his seat. He started to look for another, and on his way he found a cent in the path, and he bought an apple with it—a small one that the dealer especially picked out for cheapness. It seemed pretty queer to Lemuel that a person should want anything for one apple. The apple when he ate it made him sick. His head began to ache, and it ached all day. Late in the afternoon he caught sight of one of those fellows at a distance; but there was no policeman near. Lemuel called out, "Stop there, you!" but the fellow began to run when he recognized Lemuel, and the boy was too weak and faint to run after him.

The day wore away and the evening came again, and he had been twenty-four hours houseless and without food. He must do something; he could not stand it any longer; there was no sense in it. He had read in the newspapers how they gave soup at the police-stations in Boston in the winter; perhaps they gave something in summer. He mustered up courage to ask a gentleman who passed where the nearest station was, and then started in search of it. If the city gave it, then there was no disgrace in it, and Lemuel had as much right to anything that was going as other people; that was the way he silenced his pride.

But he missed the place; he must have gone down the

wrong street from Tremont to Washington; the gentleman had said the street that ran along the Common was Tremont, and the next was Washington. The cross-street that Lemuel got into was filled with people, going and coming, and lounging about. There were girls going along two or three together with books under their arms, and other girls talking with young fellows who hung about the doors of brightly lighted shops, and flirting with them. One of the girls, whom he had seen the day before in the Common, turned upon Lemuel as he passed, and said, "There goes my young man *now!* Good-evening, Johnny!" It made Lemuel's cheek burn; he would have liked to box her ears for her. The fellows all set up a laugh.

Towards the end of the street the crowd thickened, and there the mixture of gas and the white moony lights that glared higher up, and winked and hissed, shone upon the faces of a throng that had gathered about the doors and windows of a store a little way down the other street. Lemuel joined them, and for pure listlessness waited round to see what they were looking at. By and by he was worked inward by the shifting and changing of the crowd, and found himself looking in at the door of a room, splendidly fitted up with mirrors and marble everywhere, and colored glass and carved mahogany. There was a long counter with three men behind it, and over their heads was a large painting of a woman, worse than that image in the garden. The men were serving out liquor to the people that stood around drinking and smoking, and battening on this picture. Lemuel could not help looking, either. "What place is this?" he asked of the boy next him.

"Why, don't you know?" said the boy. "It's Jimmy Baker's. Just opened."

"Oh," said Lemuel. He was not going to let the boy see that he did not know who Jimmy Baker was. Just then something caught his eye that had a more powerful charm for him than that painting. It was a large bowl at the end of the counter which had broken crackers in it, and near it were two plates, one with cheese, and one with bits of dried fish and smoked meat. The sight made the water come into his mouth; he watched like a hungry dog, with a sympathetic working of the jaws, the men who took a bit of fish, or meat, or cheese, and a cracker, or all four of them, before or after they drank. Presently one of the crowd near him walked in and took some fish and cracker without drinking at all; he merely winked at one of the bartenders, who winked at him in return.

A tremendous tide of daring rose in Lemuel's breast. He was just going to go in and risk the same thing himself, when a voice in the crowd behind him said, "Hain't you had 'most enough, young fellow? Some the rest of us would like a chance to see now."

Lemuel knew the voice, and turning quickly, he knew the impudent face it belonged to. He did not mind the laugh raised at his expense, but launched himself across the intervening spectators, and tried to seize the scamp who had got his money from him. The scamp had recognized Lemuel too, and he fell back beyond his grasp, and then lunged through the crowd, and tore round the corner and up the street. Lemuel followed as fast as he could. In spite of the weakness he had felt before, wrath and the sense of wrong lent him speed, and he was gaining in the chase when he heard a girl's voice, "There goes one of them now!" and then a man seemed to be calling after him, "Stop, there!" He turned round, and a policeman, looking gigantic in his belted blue flannel blouse and his straw helmet, bore down upon the country boy with his club drawn, and seized him by the collar.

"You come along," he said.

"I haven't done anything," said Lemuel, submitting as he must, and in his surprise and terror losing the strength his wrath had given him. He could scarcely drag his feet over the pavement, and the policeman had almost to carry him at arm's length.

A crowd had gathered about them, and was following Lemuel and his captor, but they fell back when they reached the steps of the police station, and Lemuel was pulled up alone, and pushed in at the door. He was pushed through another door, and found himself in a kind of office. A stout man in his shirt-sleeves was sitting behind a desk within a railing, and a large book lay open on the desk. This man, whose blue waistcoat with brass buttons marked him for some sort of officer, looked impersonally at Lemuel and then at the officer, while he chewed a quill toothpick, rolling it in his lips. "What have you got there?" he asked.

"Assaulting a girl down here, and grabbing her satchel," said the officer who had arrested Lemuel, releasing his collar and going to the door, whence he called, "You come in here, lady," and a young girl, her face red with weeping and her hair disordered, came back with him. She held a crumpled straw hat with the brim torn loose, and in spite of her disordered looks she was very pretty, with blue eyes flung very wide open, and rough brown hair, wavy and cut short, almost like a boy's. This Lemuel saw in the frightened glance they exchanged.

"This the fellow that assaulted you?" asked the man at the desk, nodding his head toward Lemuel, who tried to speak; but it was like a nightmare; he could not make any sound.

"There were three of them," said the girl with hysterical volubility. "One of them pulled my hat down over my eyes and tore it, and one of them held me by the elbows behind, and they grabbed my satchel away that had a book in it that I had just got out of the library. I hadn't got it more than——"

"What name?" asked the man at the desk.

" 'A Young Man's Darling,' " said the girl, after a bashful hesitation. Lemuel had read that book just before he left home; he had not thought it was much of a book.

"The captain wants to know your name," said the officer in charge of Lemuel.

"Oh," said the girl with mortification. "Statira Dudley."

"What age?" asked the captain.

"Nineteen last June," replied the girl with eager promptness, that must have come from shame from the blunder she had made. Lemuel was twenty, the 4th of July.

"Weight?" pursued the captain.

"Well, I hain't been weighed very *lately*," answered the girl, with increasing interest. "I don't know as I been weighed since I left home."

The captain looked at her judicially.

"That so? Well, you look pretty solid. Guess I'll put you down at a hundred and twenty."

"Well, I guess it's full as *much* as that," said the girl, with a flattered laugh.

"Dunno how high you are?" suggested the captain, glancing at her again.

"Well, yes, I *do*. I am just five feet two inches and a half."

"You don't look it," said the captain critically.

"Well, I *am*," insisted the girl, with a returning gayety.

The captain apparently checked himself and put on a professional severity.

"What business—occupation?"

"Saleslady," said the girl.

"Residence?"

"No. 2334 Pleasant Avenue."

The captain leaned back in his arm-chair, and turned his toothpick between his lips, as he stared hard at the girl.

"Well, now," he said, after a moment, "you know you've got to come into court and testify to-morrow morning."

"Yes," said the girl, rather falteringly, with a sidelong glance at Lemuel.

"You've got to promise to do it, or else it will be my duty to have you locked up overnight."

"Have me locked up?" gasped the girl, her wide blue eyes filling with astonishment.

"Detain you as a witness," the captain explained. "Of course, we shouldn't put you in a cell; we should give you a good room, and if you ain't sure you'll appear in the morning——"

The girl was not of the sort whose tongues are paralyzed by terror. "Oh, I'll be *sure* to appear, captain! Indeed I will, captain! You needn't lock me up, captain! Lock me *up!*" she broke off indignantly. "It would be a *pretty* idea if I was first to be robbed of my satchel and then put in prison for it overnight! A great kind of law *that* would be! Why, I never heard of such a thing! I think it's a perfect shame! I want to know if that's the way you do with poor things that you don't know about?"

"That's about the size of it," said the captain, permitting himself a smile, in which the officer joined.

"Well, it's a shame!" cried the girl, now carried far beyond her personal interest in the matter.

The captain laughed outright. "It *is* pretty rough. But what you going to do?"

"Do? Why, I'd——" But here she stopped for want of science, and added from emotion, "I'd do *any*thing before I'd do that."

"Well," said the captain, "then I understand you'll come round to the police court and give your testimony in the morning?"

"Yes," said the girl, with a vague, compassionate glance at Lemuel, who had stood there dumb throughout the colloquy.

"If you don't, I shall have to send for you," said the captain.

"Oh, I'll *come*," replied the girl, in a sort of disgust, and her eyes still dwelt upon Lemuel.

"That's all," returned the captain, and the girl, accepting her dismissal, went out.

Now that it was too late, Lemuel could break from his nightmare. "Oh, don't let her go! I ain't the one! I was running after a fellow that passed off a counterfeit ten-dollar bill on me in the Common yesterday. I never touched her satchel. I never saw her before——"

"What's that?" demanded the captain sharply.

"You've got the wrong one!" cried Lemuel. "I never did anything to the girl."

"Why, you fool!" retorted the captain angrily; "why didn't you say that when she was here, instead of standing there like a dumb animal? Heigh?"

Lemuel's sudden flow of speech was stopped at its source again. His lips were locked; he could not answer a word.

The captain went on angrily. "If you'd spoke up in time, maybe I might 'a' let you go. I don't want to do a man any harm if I can't do him some good. Next time, if you've got a tongue in your head, use it. I can't do anything for you now. I got to commit you."

He paused between his sentences, as if to let Lemuel speak, but the boy said nothing. The captain pulled his book impatiently toward him, and took up his pen.

"What's your name?"

"Lemuel Barker."

"I thought maybe there was a mistake all the while," said the captain to the officer, while he wrote down Lemuel's name. "But if a man hain't got sense enough to speak for himself, I can't put the words in his mouth. Age?" he demanded savagely of Lemuel.

"Twenty."

"Weight?"

"A hundred and thirty."

"I could see with half an eye that the girl wa'n't very sanguine about it. But what's the use? *I* couldn't tell her she was mistaken. Height?"

"Five feet six."

"Occupation?"

"I help mother carry on the farm."

"Just as I expected!" cried the captain. "Slow as a yoke of oxen. Residence?"

"Willoughby Pastures."

The captain could not contain himself. "Well, Willoughby Pastures,—or whatever your name is,—you'll get yourself into the papers *this* time, *sure*. And I must say it serves you right. If you can't speak for yourself, who's going to speak for you,

160567

do you suppose? Might send round to the girl's house—— No, she wouldn't be there, ten to one. You've got to go through now. Next time don't be such an infernal fool."

The captain blotted his book and shut it.

"We'll have to lock him up here to-night," he said to the policeman. "Last batch has gone round. Better go through him." But Lemuel had been gone through before, and the officer's search of his pockets only revealed their emptiness. The captain struck a bell on his desk. "If it ain't all right, you can make it right with the judge in the morning," he added to Lemuel.

Lemuel looked up at the policeman who had arrested him. He was an elderly man, with a kindly face, squarely fringed with a chin-beard. The boy tried to speak, but he could only repeat, "I never saw her before. I never touched her."

The policeman looked at him and then at the captain.

"Too late now," said the latter. "Got to go through the mill this time. But if it ain't right, you can make it right."

Another officer had answered the bell, and the captain indicated with a comprehensive roll of his head that he was to take Lemuel away and lock him up.

"Oh, my!" moaned the boy. As they passed the door of a small room opening on an inner corridor, a smell of coffee gushed out of it; the officer stopped, and Lemuel caught sight of two gentlemen in the room with a policeman, who was saying:

"Get a cup of coffee here when we want it. Try one?" he suggested hospitably.

"No, thank you," said one of the gentlemen, with the bland respectfulness of people being shown about an institution. "How many of you are attached to this station?"

"Eighty-one," said the officer. "Largest station in town. Gang goes on at one in the morning, and another at eight and another at six P.M." He looked inquiringly at the officer in charge of Lemuel.

"Any matches?" asked this officer.

"Everything but money," said the other, taking some matches out of his waistcoat pocket.

Lemuel's officer went ahead, lighting the gas along the corridor, and the boy followed, while the other officer brought up the rear with the visitor whom he was lecturing. They passed some neat rooms, each with two beds in it, and he answered some question: "Tramps? Not much! Give *them* a *board* when they're drunk; send 'em round to the Wayfarers' Lodge when they're sober. These officers' rooms."

Lemuel followed his officer downstairs into a basement, where on either side of a white-walled, brilliantly lighted, specklessly clean corridor, there were numbers of cells, very clean and smelling of fresh whitewash. Each had a broad low shelf in it, and a bench opposite, a little wider than a man's body. Lemuel suddenly felt himself pushed into one of them, and then a railed door of iron was locked upon him. He stood motionless in the breadth of light and lines of shade which the gas-light cast upon him through the door, and knew the gentlemen were looking at him as their guide talked.

"Well, fill up pretty well, Sunday nights. Most the arrests for drunkenness. But all the arrests before seven o'clock sent to the City Prison. Only keep them that come in afterwards."

One of the gentlemen looked into the cell opposite Lemuel's. "There seems to be only one bunk. Do you ever put more into a cell?"

"Well, hardly ever, if they're men. Lot o' women brought in 'most always ask to be locked up together for company."

"I don't see where they sleep," said the visitor. "Do they lie on the floor?"

The officer laughed. "Sleep? *They* don't want to sleep. What *they* want to do is to set up all night, and talk it over."

Both of the visitors laughed.

"Some of the cells," resumed the officer, "have two bunks, but we hardly ever put more than one in a cell."

The visitors noticed that a section of the rail was removed in each door near the floor.

"That's to put a dipper of water through, or anything," explained the officer. "There!" he continued, showing them Lemuel's door; "see how the rails are bent there? You wouldn't think a man could squeeze through there, but we found a fellow half out o' that one night—backwards. Captain came down with a rattan and made it hot for him."

The visitors laughed, and Lemuel, in his cell, shuddered.

"I never saw anything so astonishingly clean," said one of the gentlemen. "And do you keep the gas burning here all night?"

"Yes; calculate to give 'em plenty of light," said the officer, with comfortable satisfaction in the visitor's complimentary tone.

"And the sanitary arrangements seem to be perfect, doctor," said the other visitor.

"Oh, perfect."

"Yes," said the officer, "we do the best we can for 'em."

The visitors made a murmur of approbation. Their steps moved away; Lemuel heard the guide saying, "Dunno *what* that fellow's in for. Find out in the captain's room."

"He didn't look like a very abandoned ruffian," said one of the visitors, with both pity and amusement in his voice.

VI

Lemuel stood and leaned his head against the wall of his cell. The tears that had come to his relief in the morning when he found that he was robbed would not come now. He was trembling with famine and weakness, but he could not lie down; it would be like accepting his fate, and every fiber of his body joined his soul in rebellion against that. The hunger gnawed him incessantly, mixed with an awful sickness.

After a long time a policeman passed his door with another prisoner, a drunken woman, whom he locked into a cell at the end of the corridor. When he came back, Lemuel could endure it no longer. "Say!" he called huskily through his door. "Won't you give me a cup of that coffee upstairs? I haven't had anything but an apple to eat for nearly two days. I don't want you to *give* me the coffee. You can take my clasp button——"

The officer went by a few steps, then he came back, and peered in through the door at Lemuel's face. "Oh! that's you?" he said; he was the officer who had arrested Lemuel.

"Yes. Please get me the coffee. I'm afraid I shall have a fit of sickness if I go much longer."

"Well," said the officer, "I guess I can get you something." He went away, and came back, after Lemuel had given up the hope of his return, with a saucerless cup of coffee, and a slice of buttered bread laid on top of it. He passed it in through the opening at the bottom of the door.

"Oh, my!" gasped the starving boy. He thought he should

drop the cup, his hand shook so when he took it. He gulped
the coffee and swallowed the bread in a frenzy.

"Here—here's the button," he said as he passed the empty
cup out to the officer.

"I don't want your button," answered the policeman. He
hesitated a moment. "I shall be round at the court in the
morning, and I guess if it ain't right we can make it so."

"Thank you, sir," said Lemuel, humbly grateful.

"You lay down now," said the officer. "We sha'n't put anybody in on you to-night."

"I guess I better," said Lemuel. He crept in upon the lower
shelf and stretched himself out in his clothes, with his arm
under his head for a pillow. The drunken woman at the end
of the corridor was clamoring to get out. She wished to get
out just half a minute, she said, and settle with that hussy;
then she would come back willingly. Sometimes she sang,
sometimes she swore; but with the coffee still sensibly hot in
his stomach, and the comfort of it in every vein, her uproar
turned into an agreeable, fantastic medley for Lemuel, and
he thought it was the folks singing in church at Willoughby
Pastures, and they were all asking him who the new girl in the
choir was, and he was saying Statira Dudley; and then it all
slipped off into a smooth, yellow nothingness, and he heard
some one calling him to get up.

When he woke in the morning he started up so suddenly
that he struck his head against the shelf above him, and lay
staring stupidly at the iron-work of his door.

He heard the order to turn out repeated at other cells
along the corridor, and he crept out of his shelf, and then sat
down upon it, waiting for his door to be unlocked. He was
very hungry again, and he trembled with faintness. He wondered how he should get his breakfast, and he dreaded the
trial in court less than the thought of going through another
day with nothing to eat. He heard the stir of the other prisoners in the cells along the corridors, the low groans and sighs
with which people pull themselves together after a bad night;
and he heard the voice of the drunken woman, now sober,

poured out in voluble remorse, and in voluble promise of amendment for the future, to every one who passed, if they would let her off easy. She said aisy, of course, and it was in her native accent that she bewailed the fate of the little ones whom her arrest had left motherless at home. No one seemed to answer her, but presently she broke into a cry of joy and blessing, and from her cell at the other end of the corridor came the clink of crockery. Steps approached with several pauses, and at last they paused at Lemuel's door, and a man outside stooped and pushed in, through the opening at the bottom, a big bowl of baked beans, a quarter of a loaf of bread, and a tin cup full of coffee. "Coffee's extra," he said, jocosely. "Comes from the officers. You're in luck, young feller."

"I ha'n't got anything to pay for it with," faltered Lemuel.

"Guess they'll trust you," said the man. "Anyrate, I got orders to leave it." He passed on, and Lemuel gathered up his breakfast, and arranged it on the shelf where he had slept; then he knelt down before it, and ate.

An hour later an officer came and unbolted his door from the outside. "Hurry up," he said; "Maria's waiting."

"Maria?" repeated Lemuel, innocently.

"Yes," returned the officer. "Other name's Black. She don't like to wait. Come out of here."

Lemuel found himself in the corridor with four or five other prisoners, whom some officers took in charge and conducted upstairs to the door of the station. He saw no woman, but a sort of omnibus without windows was drawn up at the curbstone.

"I thought," he said to an officer, "that there was a lady waiting to see me. Maria Black," he added, seeing that the officer did not understand.

The policeman roared, and could not help putting his head in at the office door to tell the joke.

"Well, you must introduce him," called a voice from within.

"Guess you ha'n't got the name exactly straight, young

man," said the policeman to Lemuel, as he guarded him down the steps. "It's Black Maria you're looking for. There she is," he continued, pointing to the omnibus, "and don't you forget it. She's particular to have folks recognize her. She's blacker'n she's painted."

The omnibus was, in fact, a sort of æsthetic drab, relieved with salmon, as Lemuel had time to notice before he was hustled into it with the other prisoners, and locked in.

There were already several there, and as Lemuel's eyes accustomed themselves to the light that came in through the little panes at the sides of the roof, he could see that they were women; and by and by he saw that two of them were the saucy girls who had driven him from his seat in the Common that day, and laughed so at him. They knew him too, and one of them set up a shrill laugh. "Hello, Johnny! That you? You don't say so? What you up for *this* time? Going down to the Island? Well, give us a call there! Do be sociable! Ward 11's the address." The other one laughed, and then swore at the first for trying to push her off the seat.

Lemuel broke out involuntarily in all the severity that was native to him. "You ought to be ashamed of yourselves."

This convulsed the bold things with laughter. When they could get their breath, one of them said, "Pshaw! I know what he's up for: preaching on the Common. Say, young feller! don't you want to hold a prayer-meetin' here?"

They burst into another shriek of laughter, so wild and shrill that the driver rapped on the roof, and called down, "Dry up in there!"

"Oh, you mind your horses, and we'll look after the passengers. Go and set on his knee, Jen, and cheer him up a little."

Lemuel sat in a quiver of abhorrence. The girl appealed to remained giggling beside her companion.

"I—I pity ye!" said Lemuel.

The Irishwoman had not stopped bewailing herself and imploring right and left an easy doom. She now addressed herself wholly to Lemuel, whose personal dignity seemed to clothe him with authority in her eyes. She told him about her children, left alone with no one to look after them; the two little girls, the boy only three years old. When the van stopped at a station to take in more passengers, she tried to get out—to tell the gentlemen at the office about it, she said.

After several of these halts they stopped at the basement of a large stone building, that had a wide flight of steps in front, and columns, like the church at Willoughby Pastures, only the church steps were wood, and the columns painted pine. Here more officers took charge of them, and put them in a room where there were already twenty-five or thirty other prisoners, the harvest of the night before; and presently another van-load was brought in. There were many women among them, but here there was no laughing or joking as there had been in the van. Scarcely any one spoke, except the Irishwoman, who crept up to an officer at the door from time to time, and begged him to tell the judge to let her have it easy this time. Lemuel could not help seeing that she and most of the others were familiar with the place. Those two saucy jades who had mocked him were silent, and had lost their bold looks.

After waiting what seemed a long time, the door was opened, and they were driven up a flight of stairs into a railed inclosure at the corner of a large room, where they remained huddled together, while a man at a long desk rattled over something that ended with "God bless the commonwealth of Massachusetts." On a platform behind the speaker sat a gray-haired man in spectacles, and Lemuel knew that he was in the court-room, and that this must be the judge. He could not see much of the room over the top of the railing, but there was a buzz of voices and a stir of feet beyond, that made him think the place was full. But full or empty, it was the same to him; his shame could not be greater or less. He waited apathetically while the clerk read off the charges against the vastly greater number of his fellow-prisoners arrested for drunkenness. When these were disposed of, he read from the back of a paper, which he took from a fresh pile, "Bridget Gallagher, complained of for habitual drunkenness. Guilty or not guilty?"

"Not guilty, your hanor," answered the Irishwoman who had come from Lemuel's station. "But make it aisy for me this time, judge, and ye'll never catch me in it again. I've three helpless childer at home, your hanor, starvin' and cryin' for their mother. Holy Mary, make it aisy, judge!"

A laugh went round the room, which a stern voice checked with "Silence, there!" but which renewed itself when the old woman took the stand at the end of the clerk's long desk, while a policeman mounted a similar platform outside the rail, and gave his testimony against her. It was very conclusive, and it was not affected by the denials with which the poor woman gave herself away more and more. She had nothing to say when invited to do so except to beg for mercy; the judge made a few inquiries, apparently casual, of the policeman; then after a moment's silence, in which he sat rubbing his chin, he leaned forward and said quietly to the clerk, "Give her three months."

The woman gave a wild Irish cry, "Oh, my poor childer!" and amidst the amusement of the spectators, which the constables could not check at once, was led wailing below.

Before Lemuel could get his breath those bold girls, one after the other, were put upon the stand. The charge against them was not made the subject of public investigation; the judge and some other elderly gentleman talked it over together; and the girls, who had each wept in pleading guilty, were put on probation, as Lemuel understood it, and, weeping still and bridling a little, were left in charge of this elderly gentleman, and Lemuel saw them no more.

One case followed another, and Lemuel listened with the fascination of terror; the sentences seemed terribly severe, and out of all proportion to the offenses. Suddenly his own name was called. His name had been called in public places before: at the school exhibitions, where he had taken prizes in elocution and composition; in church, once, when the minister had mentioned him for peculiar efficiency and zeal among other Sabbath-school teachers. It was sacred to him for his father's sake, who fell in the war, and who was recorded in it on the ugly, pathetic monument on the village green; and hitherto he had made it respected and even honored, and had tried all the harder to keep it so because his family was poor, and his mother had such queer ways and dressed so. He dragged himself to the stand which he knew he must mount, and stole from under his eyelashes a glance at the court-room, which took it all in. There were some people, whom he did not know for reporters, busy with their pencils next the railing; and there was a semicircular table in the middle of the room at which a large number of policemen sat, and they had their straw helmets piled upon it, with the hats of the lawyers who sat among them. Beyond, the seats which covered the floor were filled with the sodden loafers whom the law offers every morning, the best dramatic amusement in the city. Presently, among the stupid eyes fixed upon him, Lemuel was aware of the eyes of that fellow who had passed the counterfeit money on him; and when this scamp got up and coolly sauntered out of the room, Lemuel was held in such a spell that he did not hear the charge read against him, or the clerk's repeated demand, "Guilty or not guilty?"

He was recalled to himself by the voice of the judge. "Young man, do you understand? Are you guilty of assaulting this lady and taking her satchel, or not?"

"Not guilty," said Lemuel, huskily; and he looked, not at the judge, but at the pretty girl, who confronted him from a stand at the other end of the clerk's desk, blushing to find herself there up to her wide-flung blue eyes. Lemuel blushed too, and dropped his eyes; and it seemed to him in a crazy kind of way that it was impolite to have pleaded not guilty against her accusation. He stood waiting for the testimony which the judge had to prompt her to offer.

"State the facts in regard to the assault," he said gravely.

"I don't know as I can do it, very well," began the girl.

"We shall be satisfied if you do your best," said the judge, with the glimmer of a smile, which spread to a laugh among the spectators, unrebuked by the constables, since the judge had invited it.

In this atmosphere of sympathy the girl found her tongue, and with a confiding twist of her pretty head began again: "Well, now, I'll tell you just how it was. I'd just got my book out of the Public Library, and I was going down Neponset street on my way home, hurrying along, because I see it was beginning to be pretty late, and the first thing I know somebody pulled my hat down over my eyes, and tore the brim half off, so I don't suppose I can ever wear it again, it's such a lookin' thing; anyrate it ain't the one I've got on, though it's some like it; and then the next thing, somebody grabbed away the satchel I'd got on my arm; and as soon as I could get my eyes clear again, I see two fellows chasin' up the street, and I told the officer somebody'd got my book; and I knew it was one of those fellows runnin' away, and I said, 'There they go now,' and the officer caught the hind one, and I guess the other one got away; and the officer told me to follow along to the station-house, and when we got there they took my name, and where I roomed, and my age——"

"Do you recognize this young man as one of the persons who robbed you?" interrupted the judge, nodding his head toward Lemuel, who now lifted his head and looked his accuser fearlessly in her pretty eyes.

"Why, no!" she promptly replied. "The first thing I knew, he'd pulled my hat over my eyes."

"But you recognize him as one of those you saw running away?"

"Oh, yes, he's one of *them*," said the girl.

"What made you think he had robbed you?"

"Why, because my satchel was gone!" returned the girl, with logic that apparently amused the gentlemen of the bar.

"But why did you think *he* had taken it?"

"Because I see him running away."

"You couldn't swear that he was the one who took your satchel?"

"Why, of course not! I didn't *see* him till I saw him running. And I don't know as he was the one, now," added the girl, in a sudden burst of generosity. "And if it was to do over again, I should say as much to the officers at the station. But I got confused when they commenced askin' me who I was, and how much I weighed, and what my height was; and *he* didn't say anything; and I got to thinkin' maybe it *was*; and when they told me that if I didn't promise to appear at court in the morning they'd have to lock me up, I was only too glad to get away alive."

By this time all the blackguard audience were sharing, unchecked, the amusement of the bar. The judge put up his hand to hide a laugh. Then he said to Lemuel, "Do you wish to question the plaintiff?"

The two young things looked at each other, and both blushed. "No," said Lemuel.

The girl looked at the judge for permission, and at a nod from him left the stand and sat down.

The officer who had arrested Lemuel took the stand on the other side of the rail from him, and corroborated the girl's story; but he had not seen the assault or robbery, and could not swear to either. Then Lemuel was invited to speak, and told his story with the sort of nervous courage that came to him in extremity. He told it from the beginning, and his adventure with the two beats in the Common made the audience laugh again. Even then, Lemuel could not see the fun of it; he stopped, and the stout ushers in blue flannel sacks commanded silence. Then Lemuel related how he had twice seen one of the beats since that time, but he was ashamed to say how he had let him escape out of that very room half an hour before. He told how he had found the beat in the crowd before the saloon, and how he was chasing him up the street when he heard the young lady hollo out, "There they go now!" and then the officer arrested him.

The judge sat a moment in thought; then said quietly,

"The charge is dismissed"; and before Lemuel well knew what it meant, a gate was opened at the stand, and he was invited to pass out. He was free. The officer who had arrested him shook his hand in congratulation and excuse, and the lawyers and the other policemen gave him a friendly glance. The loafers and beats of the audience did not seem to notice him. They were already intent upon a case of colored assault and battery which had been called, and which opened with the promise of uncommon richness, both of the parties being women.

Lemuel saw that girl who had accused him passing down the aisle on the other side of the room. She was with another girl, who looked older. Lemuel walked fast, to get out of their way; he did not know why, but he did not want to speak to the girl. They walked fast too, and when he got down the stairs on to the ground floor of the court-house they overtook him.

"Say!" said the older girl, "I want to speak to *you*. I think it's a down shame, the way that you've been treated; and Statira, she feels jus's I do about it; and I tell her she's got to say so. It's the least she can do, I tell her, after what she got you *in* for. My name's 'Manda Grier; I room 'th S'tira; 'n' I come 'th her this mornin' t' help keep her up; b't I *didn't* know 't was goin' to be s'ch a *perfect* flat-out!"

As the young woman rattled on she grew more and more glib; she was what they call whopper-jawed, and spoke a language almost purely consonantal, cutting and clipping her words with a rapid play of her whopper-jaw till there was nothing but the bare bones left of them. Statira was crying, and Lemuel could not bear to see her cry. He tried to say something to comfort her, but all he could think of was, "I hope you'll get your book back," and 'Manda Grier answered for her:

"Oh, I guess 't ain't the book 't she cares for. S' far forth's the book goes, I guess she can afford to buy another book, well enough. B't I tell her she's done 'n awful thing, and a thing 't she'll carry to her grave 'th her, 'n't she'll remember to her dyin' day. That's what *I* tell her."

"She ha'n't got any call to feel bad about it," said Lemuel, clumsily. "It was just a mistake." Then, not knowing what more to say, he said, being come to the outer door by this time, "Well, I wish you good-morning."

"Well, good-morning," said 'Manda Grier, and she thrust her elbow sharply into Statira Dudley's side, so that she also said faintly:

"Well, good-morning!" She was fluent enough on the witness-stand and in the police station, but now she could not find a word to say.

The three stood together on the threshold of the court-house, not knowing how to get away from one another.

'Manda Grier put out her hand to Lemuel. He took it, and, "Well, good-morning," he said again.

"Well, good-morning," repeated 'Manda Grier.

Then Statira put out her hand, and she and Lemuel shook hands, and said together, "Well, good-morning," and on these terms of high civility they parted. He went one way and they another. He did not look back, but the two girls, marching off with locked arms and flying tongues, when they came to the corner, turned to look back. They both turned inward and so bumped their heads together.

"Why, you—coot!" cried 'Manda Grier, and they broke out laughing.

Lemuel heard their laugh, and he knew they were laughing at him; but he did not care. He wandered on, he did not know whither, and presently he came to the only place he could remember.

VII

THE PLACE was the Common, where his trouble had begun. He looked back to the beginning, and could see that it was his own fault. To be sure, you might say that if a fellow came along and offered to pay you fifty cents for changing a ten-dollar bill, you had a right to take it; but there was a voice in Lemuel's heart which warned him that greed to another's hurt was sin, and that if you took too much for a thing from a necessitous person, you oppressed and robbed him. You could make it appear otherwise, but you could not really change the nature of the act. He owned this with a sigh, and he owned himself justly punished. He was still on those terms of personal understanding with the eternal spirit of right which most of us lose later in life, when we have so often seemed to see the effect fail to follow the cause, both in the case of our own misdeeds and the misdeeds of others.

He sat down on a bench, and he sat there all day, except when he went to drink from the tin cup dangling by the chain from the nearest fountain. His good breakfast kept him from being hungry for a while, but he was as aimless and as hopeless as ever, and as destitute. He would have gone home now if he had had the money; he was afraid they would be getting anxious about him there, though he had not made any particular promises about the time of returning. He had dropped a postal card into a box as soon as he reached Boston, to tell of his safe arrival, and they would not expect him to write again.

There were only two ways for him to get home: to turn

66

tramp and walk back, or to go to that Mr. Sewell and borrow
the money to pay his passage. To walk home would add in-
tolerably to the public shame he must suffer, and the thought
of going to Mr. Sewell was, even in the secret which it would
remain between him and the minister, a pang so cruel to his
pride that he recoiled from it instantly. He said to himself
he would stand it one day more; something might happen,
and if nothing happened, he should think of it again. In the
mean time he thought of other things: of that girl, among
the rest, and how she looked at the different times. As nearly
as he could make out, she seemed to be a very fashionable
girl; at any rate, she was dressed fashionably, and she was nice-
looking. He did not know whether she had behaved very
sensibly, but he presumed she was some excited.

Toward dark, when Lemuel was reconciling himself to another night's sleep in the open air, a policeman sauntered
along the mall, and as he drew nearer the boy recognized his
friendly captor. He dropped his head, but it was too late.
The officer knew him, and stopped before him.

"Well," he said, "hard at it, I see."

Lemuel made no answer, but he was aware of a friendly
look in the officer's face, mixed with fatherly severity.

"I was in hopes you had started back to Willoughby Pas-
tur's before this. You don't want to get into the habit of
settin' round on the Common, much. First thing you know
you can't quit it. Where you goin' to put up to-night?"

"I don't know," murmured Lemuel.

"Got no friends in town you can go to?"

"No."

"Well, now, look here! Do you think you could find your
way back to the station?"

"I guess so," said Lemuel, looking up at the officer questioningly.

"Well, when you get tired of this, you come round, and
we'll provide a bed for you. And you get back home to-
morrow, quick as you can."

"Thank you," said Lemuel. He was helpless against the advice and its unjust implication, but he could not say anything.

"Get out o' Boston, anyway, wherever you go or don't go," continued the officer. "It's a bad place."

He walked on, and left Lemuel to himself again. He thought bitterly that no one knew better than himself how luridly wicked Boston was, and that there was probably not a soul in it more helplessly anxious to get out of it. He thought it hard to be talked to as if it were his fault; as if he wished to become a vagrant and a beggar. He sat there an hour or two longer, and then he took the officer's advice, so far as concerned his going to the station for a bed, swallowing his pride as he must. He must do that, or he must go to Mr. Sewell. It was easier to accept humiliation at the hands of strangers. He found his way there with some difficulty, and slinking in at the front door, he waited at the threshold of the captain's room while he and two or three officers disposed of a respectably dressed man, whom a policeman was holding up by the collar of his coat. They were searching his pockets and taking away his money, his keys, and his pencil and pen-knife, which the captain sealed up in a large envelope, and put into his desk.

"There! take him and lock him up. He's pretty well loaded," said the captain.

Then he looked up and saw Lemuel. "Hello! Can't keep away, eh?" he demanded jocosely. "Well, we've heard about you. I told you the judge would make it all right. What's wanted? Bed? Well, here!" The captain filled up a blank which he took from a pigeon-hole, and gave it to Lemuel. "I guess that'll fix you out for the night. And to-morrow you put back to Willoughby Pastures tight as you can get there. You're on the wrong track now. First thing you know you'll be a professional tramp, and then you won't be worth the powder to blow you. I use plain talk with you because you're a beginner. I wouldn't waste my breath on that fellow behind you."

Lemuel looked round, and almost touched with his a face

that shone fiery red through the rusty growth of a week's beard, and recoiled from a figure that was fouler as to shirt and coat and trousers than anything the boy had seen; though the tramps used to swarm through Willoughby Pastures before the Selectmen began to lock them up in the town poorhouse and set them to breaking stone. There was no ferocity in the loathsome face; it was a vagrant swine that looked from it, no worse in its present mood than greedy and sleepy.

"Bed?" demanded the captain, writing another blank. "Never been here before, I suppose?" he continued with good-natured irony. "I don't seem to remember you."

The captain laughed, and the tramp returned a husky "Thank you, sir," and took himself off into the street.

Then the captain came to Lemuel's help. "You follow him," he said, "and you'll come to a bed by and by."

He went out, and, since he could do no better, did as he was bid. He had hardly ever seen a drunken man at Willoughby Pastures, where the prohibition law was strictly enforced; there was no such person as a thief in the whole community, and the tramps were gone long ago. Yet here was he, famed at home for the rectitude of his life and the loftiness of his aims, consorting with drunkards and thieves and tramps, and warned against what he was doing by policemen, as if he was doing it of his own will. It was very strange business. If it was *all* a punishment for taking that fellow's half-dollar, it was pretty heavy punishment. He was not going to say that it was unjust, but he would say it was hard. His spirit was now so bruised and broken that he hardly knew what to think.

He followed the tramp as far off as he could and still keep him in sight, and he sometimes thought he had lost him, in the streets that climbed and crooked beyond the Common towards the quarter whither they were going; but he reappeared, slouching and shambling rapidly on, in the glare of some electric lights that stamped the ground with shadows thick and black as if cut in velvet or burnt into the surface. Here and there some girl brushed against the boy, and gave him a joking or jeering word; her face flashed into light for a moment, and then vanished in the darkness she passed into. It was that hot October, and the night was close and still; on the steps of some of the houses groups of fat, weary women were sitting, and children were playing on the sidewalks, using the lamp-posts for goal or tag. The tramp ahead of Lemuel issued upon a brilliantly lighted little square, with a great many horse-cars coming and going in it; a church with stores on the ground floor, and fronting it on one side a row of handsome old stone houses with iron fences, and on another a great hotel, with a high-pillared portico, where men sat talking and smoking. People were waiting on the sidewalk to take the cars; a druggist's window threw its mellow lights into the street; from open cellar-ways came the sound of banjos and violins. At one of these cellar-doors his guide lingered so long that Lemuel thought he should have to find the way beyond for himself. But the tramp suddenly commanded himself from the music, the light, and the smell of strong drink, which Lemuel caught a whiff of as he followed, and turning a corner led the way to the side of a lofty building in a dark street, where they met other like shapes tending toward it from different directions.

VIII

LEMUEL entered a lighted doorway from a bricked court-
yard, and found himself with twenty or thirty houseless comrades in a large, square room, with benching against the wall
for them to sit on. They were all silent and quelled-looking,
except a young fellow whom Lemuel sat down beside, and
who, ascertaining that he was a new-comer, seemed disposed
to do the honors of the place. He was not daunted by the reserve native to Lemuel, or by that distrust of strangers which
experience had so soon taught him. He addressed him promptly as mate, and told him that the high, narrow, three-sided
tabling in the middle of the room was where they would get
their breakfast, if they lived.

"And I guess I shall live," he said. "I notice I 'most always
live till breakfast-time, whatever else I do, or I don't do; but
sometimes it don't seem as if I *could* saw my way through
that quarter of a cord of wood." At a glance of inquiry which
Lemuel could not forbear, he continued: "What I mean by a
quarter of a cord of wood is that they let you exercise that
much free in the morning, before they give you your breakfast:
it's the doctor's orders. This used to be a school-house, but it's
in better business now. They got a kitchen under here, that
beats the Parker House; you'll smell it pretty soon. No whack-
ing on the knuckles here any more. All serene, I tell you.
You'll see. I don't know how I should got along without this
institution, and I tell the manager so, every time I see him.
That's him, hollering 'Next,' out of that room there. It's a

name he gives all of us; he knows it's a name we'll answer to. Don't you forget it when it comes your turn."

He was younger than Lemuel, apparently, but his swarthy, large-mouthed, droll-eyed face affirmed the experience of a sage. He wore a blue flannel shirt, with loose trousers belted round his waist, and he crushed a soft felt hat between his hands; his hair was clipped close to his skull, and as he rubbed it now and then it gave out a pleasant, rasping sound.

The tramps disappeared in the order of their vicinity to the manager's door, and it came in time to this boy and Lemuel.

"You come along with me," he said, "and do as I do." When they entered the presence of the manager, who sat at a desk, Lemuel's guide nodded to him, and handed over his order for a bed.

"Ever been here before?" asked the manager, as if going through the form for a joke.

"Never." He took a numbered card which the manager gave him, and stood aside to wait for Lemuel, who made the same answer to the same question, and received his numbered card.

"Now," said the young fellow, as they passed out of another door, "we ain't either of us 'Next' any more. I'm Thirty-nine, and you're Forty, and don't you forget it. All right, boss," he called back to the manager; "I'll take care of him! This way," he said to Lemuel. "The reason why I said I'd never been here before," he explained on the way down, "was because you got to say something when he asks you. Most of 'em says last fall or last year, but I say never, because it's just as true, and he seems to like it better. We're going down to the dressing-room now, and then we're going to take a bath. Do you know why?"

"No," said Lemuel.

"Because we can't help it. It's the doctor's orders. He thinks it's the best thing you can do, just before you go to bed."

The basement was brightly lighted with gas everywhere,

and a savory odor of onion-flavored broth diffused itself
through the whole place.

"Smell it? You might think that was supper, but it ain't.
It's breakfast. You got a bath and a night's rest as well as the
quarter of a cord of wood between you and that stew.
Hungry?"

"Not very," said Lemuel faintly.

"Because if you say you are they'll give you all the bread
and water you can hold now. But I ruther wait."

"I guess I don't want anything to-night," said Lemuel,
shrinking from the act of beggary.

"Well, I guess you won't lose anything in the long run,"
said the other. "You'll make it up at breakfast."

They turned into a room where eight or ten tramps were
undressing; some of them were old men, quite sodden and
stupefied with a life of vagrancy and privation; others were
of a dull or cunning middle-age. Two or three were as young
as Lemuel and his partner, and looked as if they might be
poor fellows who had found themselves in a strange city
without money or work; but it was against them that they
had known where to come for a night's shelter, Lemuel felt.

There were large iron hooks hanging from the walls and
ceiling, and his friend found the numbers on two of them
corresponding to those given Lemuel and himself, and brass
checks which they hung around their necks.

"You got to hang your things on that hook, all but your
shoes and stockings, and you got to hang on to *them* yourself.
Forty's your number, and forty's your hook, and they give you
the clothes off'n it in the morning."

He led the way through the corridor into a large room
where a row of bath-tubs flanked the wall, half of them filled
with bathers, who chatted in tones of subdued cheerfulness
under the pleasant excitement of unlimited hot and cold
water. As each new-comer appeared a black boy, perched on
a window-sill, jumped down and dashed his head from a large
bottle which he carried.

"Free shampoo," explained Lemuel's mate. "Doctor's orders. Only you have to do the rubbing yourself. I don't suppose *you* need it, but some the pardners here couldn't sleep without it," he continued, as Lemuel shrank a little from the bottle, and then submitted. "It's a regular night-cap."

The tramps recognized the humor of the explanation by a laugh, intended to be respectful to the establishment in its control, which spread along their line, and the black boy grinned.

"There ain't anything mean about the Wayfarer's Hotel," said the mate; and they all laughed again, a little louder.

Each man, having dried himself from his bath, was given a coarse linen night-gown; sometimes it was not quite whole, but it was always clean; and then he gathered up his shoes and stockings and went out.

"Hold on a minute," said the mate to Lemuel, when they left the bath-room. "You ought to see the kitchen." And in his night-gown, with his shoes in his hand, he led Lemuel to the open door which that delicious smell of broth came from. A vast copper-topped boiler was bubbling within, and trying to get its lid off. The odor made Lemuel sick with hunger.

"Refrigerator in the next room," the mate lectured on. "Best beef-chucks in the market; fish for Fridays—we don't make any man go against his religion in *this* house; pots of butter as big as a cheese,—none of your oleomargarine,—the real thing, every time; potatoes and onions and carrots laying around on the floor; barrels of hard-tack; and bread, like sponge,—bounce you up if you was to jump on it,—baked by the women at the Chardon Street Home. Oh, I tell you we do things in style here."

A man who sat reading a newspaper in the corner looked up sharply. "Hello, there! what's wanted?"

"Just dropped in to wish you good-night, Jimmy," said Lemuel's mate.

"You clear out!" said the man good-humoredly, as if to an

old acquaintance, who must not be allowed to presume upon his familiarity.

"All right, Jimmy," said the boy. He set his left hand horizontally on its wrist at his left shoulder and cut the air with it in playful menace as the man dropped his eyes again to his paper. "They're all just so in this house," he explained to Lemuel. "No nonsense, but good-natured. *They're* all right. They know me."

He mounted two flights of stairs in front of Lemuel to a corridor, where an attendant stood examining the numbers on the brass checks hung around the tramps' necks as they came up with their shoes in their hands. He instructed them that the numbers corresponded to the cots they were to occupy, as well as the hooks where their clothes hung. Some of them seemed hardly able to master the facts. They looked wistfully, like cowed animals, into his face as he made the case clear.

Two vast rooms, exquisitely clean, like the whole house, opened on the right and left of the corridor, and presented long phalanxes of cots, each furnished with two coarse blankets, a quilt, and a thin pillow.

"Used to be school-rooms," said Lemuel's mate, in a low tone.

"Cots thirty-nine and forty," said the attendant, looking at their checks. "Right over there, in the corner."

"Come along," said the mate, leading the way, with the satisfaction of an habitué. "Best berth in the room, and about the last they reach in the morning. You see, they got to take us as we come when they call us, and the last feller in at night's the first feller out in the morning, because his bed's the nearest the door."

He did not pull down the blankets of his cot at once, but stretched himself out on the quilt that covered them. "Cool off a little first," he explained. "Well, this is what I call comfort, mate, heigh?"

Lemuel did not answer. He was watching the attendant

with a group of tramps who could not find their cots.

"Can't read, I suppose," said the mate, a little disdainfully. "Well, look at that old chap, will you!" A poor fellow was fumbling with his blankets, as if he did not know quite how to manage them. The attendant had to come to his help, and tuck him in. "Well, there!" exclaimed the mate, lifting himself on his elbow to admire the scene. "I don't suppose he's ever been in a decent bed before. Hayloft's *his* style, or a board-pile." He sank down again, and went on: "Well, you do see all kinds of folks here, that's a fact. Sorry there ain't more in to-night, so's to give you a specimen. You ought to be here in the winter. Well, it ain't so lonesome now in summer as it used to be. Sometimes I used to have nearly the whole place to myself, summer nights, before they got to passin' these laws against tramps in the country, and lockin' 'em up when they ketched 'em. That drives 'em into the city summers now; because they're always sure of a night's rest and a day's board here if they ask for it. But winter's the time. You'll see all these cots full then. They let on the steam-heat, and it's comfortable; and it's always airy and healthy." The vast room was, in fact, perfectly ventilated, and the poor who housed themselves that night, and many well-to-do sojourners in hotels, had reason to envy the vagrants their free lodging.

The mate now got under his quilt, and turned his face toward Lemuel, with one hand under his cheek. "They don't let *every* body into this room, 's I was tellin' ye. This room is for the big-bugs, you know. Sometimes a drunk will get in, though, in spite of everything. Why, I've seen a drunk at the station-house, when I've been gettin' my order for a bed, stiffen up so 't the captain himself thought he was sober; and then I've followed him round here, wobblin' and corkscrewin' all over the sidewalk; and then I've seen him stiffen up in the office again, and go through his bath like a little man, and get into bed as drunk as a fish; and maybe wake up in the night with the man with the poker after him, and make things hum. Well, sir, one night there was a drunk in here that thought the man with the poker was after him, and he just up and jumped out of this window behind you—three stories from the ground."

Lemuel could not help lifting himself in bed to look at it. "Did it kill him?" he asked.

"Kill him? *No!* You can't kill a *drunk*. One night there was a drunk got loose here, and he run down-stairs into the wood-yard, and he got hold of an axe down there, and it took five men to get that axe away from that drunk. He was goin' for the snakes."

"The snakes!" repeated Lemuel. "Are there snakes in the wood-yard?"

The other gave a laugh so loud that the attendant called out, "Less noise over there!"

"I'll tell you about the snakes in the morning," said the mate; and he turned his face away from Lemuel.

The stories of the drunks had made Lemuel a little anxious; but he thought that attendant would keep a sharp lookout, so that there would not really be much danger. He was very drowsy from his bath, in spite of the hunger that tormented him, but he tried to keep awake and think what he should do after breakfast.

IX

"COME, turn out!" said a voice in his ear, and he started up, to see the great dormitory where he had fallen asleep empty of all but himself and his friend.

"Make out a night's rest?" asked the latter. "Didn't I tell you we'd be the last up? Come along!" He preceded Lemuel, still drowsy, down the stairs into the room where they had undressed, and where the tramps were taking each his clothes from their hook, and hustling them on.

"What time is it, Johnny?" asked Lemuel's mate of the attendant. "I left my watch under my pillow."

"Five o'clock," said the man, helping the poor old fellow who had not known how to get into bed to put on his clothes.

"Well, that's a pretty good start," said the other. He finished his toilet by belting himself around the waist, and "Come along, mate," he said to Lemuel. "I'll show you the way to the tool-room."

He led him through the corridor into a chamber of the basement where there were bright rows of wood-saws, and ranks of saw-horses, with heaps of the latter in different stages of construction. "House self-supporting, as far as it can. We don't want to be beholden to anybody if we can help it. We make our own horses here; but we can't make our saws, or we would. Ever had much practice with the wood-saw?"

"No," said Lemuel, with a throb of homesickness, that brought back the hacked log behind the house, and the axe resting against it; "we always chopped our stove-wood."

"Yes, that's the way in the country. Well, now," said the

78

other, "I'll show you how to choose a saw. Don't you be took
in by no new saw because it's bright and looks pretty. You
want to take a saw that's been filed and filed away till it ain't
more'n an inch and a half deep; and then you want to tune
it up, just so, like a banjo,—not too tight, and not too slack,—
and then it'll slip through a stick o' wood like—lyin'." He
selected a saw, and put it in order for Lemuel. "There!" He
picked out another. "Here's *my* old stand-by!" He took up a
saw-horse at random, to indicate that one need not be critical
in that, and led through the open door into the wood-yard,
where a score or two of saws were already shrilling and wheez-
ing through the wood.

It was a wide and lofty shed, with piles of cord-wood and
slabs at either end, and walled on the farther side with kindling, sawed, split, and piled up with admirable neatness.
The place gave out the sweet smell of the woods from the
bark of the logs and from the fresh section of their grain. A
double rank of saw-horses occupied the middle space, and beside each horse lay a quarter of a cord of wood, at which the
men were toiling in sullen silence for the most part, only ex-
changing a grunt or snarl of dissatisfaction with one another.

"Morning, mates," said Lemuel's friend cheerfully, as he
entered the shed, and put his horse down beside one of the
piles. "Thought we'd look in and see how you was gettin'
along. Just stepped round from the Parker House while our
breakfast was a-cookin'. Hope you all rested well?"

The men paused, with their saws at different slopes in the
wood, and looked round. The night before, in the nakedness
in which Lemuel had first seen them, the worst of them had
the inalienable comeliness of nature, and their faces, softened
by their relation to their bodies, were not so bad; they were
not so bad, looking from their white night-gowns; but now,
clad in their filthy rags, and caricatured out of all native
dignity by their motley and misshapen attire, they were a
hideous gang, and all the more hideous for the grin that
overspread their stubbly muzzles at the boy's persiflage.

"Don't let me interrupt you, fellows," he said, flinging a

log upon his horse, and dashing his saw gayly into it. "Don't mind *me!* I know you hate to lose a minute of this fun; I understand just how you feel about it, and I don't want you to stand upon ceremony with *me*. Treat me just like one of yourselves, gents. This beech-wood is the regular Nova Scotia thing, ain't it? Tough and knotty! I can't bear any of your cheap wood-lot stuff from around here. What I want is Nova Scotia wood every time. Then I feel that I'm gettin' the worth of my money." His log dropped apart on each side of his horse, and he put on another. "Well, mates," he rattled on, "this is lovely, ain't it? I wouldn't give up my little quarter of a cord of green Nova Scotia before breakfast for anything; I've got into the way of it, and I can't live without it."

The tramps chuckled at these ironies, and the attendant who looked into the yard now and then did not interfere with them.

The mate went through his stint as rapidly as he talked, and he had nearly finished before Lemuel had half done. He did not offer to help him, but he delayed the remnant of his work, and waited for him to catch up, talking all the while with gay volubility, joking this one and that, and keeping the whole company as cheerful as it was in their dull, sodden nature to be. He had a floating eye that harmonized with his queer, mobile face, and played round on the different figures, but mostly upon Lemuel's dogged, rustic industry as if it really amused him.

"What's your lay after breakfast?" he asked, as they came to the last log together.

"Lay?" repeated Lemuel.

"What you goin' to do?"

"I don't know; I can't tell yet."

"You know," said the other, "you can come back here and get your dinner, if you want to saw wood for it from ten till twelve, and you get your supper if you'll saw from five to six."

"Are you going to do that?" asked Lemuel cautiously.

"No, sir," said the other; "I can't spare the time. I'm goin' to fill up for all day at breakfast, and then I'm goin' up to lay round on the Common till it's time to go to the police court; and when that's over I'm goin' back to the Common ag'in, and lay round the rest of the day. I hain't got any leisure for no such nonsense as wood-sawin'. I don't mind the work, but I hate to waste the time. It's the way with most o' the pardners, unless it's the green hands. That so, pards?"

Some of them had already gone in to breakfast; the smell of the stew came out to the wood-yard through the open door. Lemuel and his friend finished their last stick at the same time, and went in together, and found places side by side at the table in the waiting-room. The attendant within its oblong was serving the men with heavy quart bowls of the steaming broth. He brought half a loaf of light, elastic bread with each, and there were platters of hard-tack set along the board, which every one helped himself from freely, and broke into his broth.

"Morning, Jimmy," said the mate, as the man brought him and Lemuel their portions. "I hate to have the dining-room chairs off a-paintin' when there's so much style about everything else, and I've got a visitor with me. But I tell him he'll have to take us as he finds us, and stand it this mornin'." He wasted no more words on his joke, but, plunging his large tin spoon into his bowl, kept his breath to cool his broth, blowing upon it with easy grace, and swallowing it at a tremendous rate, though Lemuel, after following his example, still found it so hot that it brought the tears into his eyes. It was delicious, and he was ravenous from his twenty-four hours' fast; but his companion was scraping the bottom of his bowl before Lemuel had got half-way down, and he finished his second as Lemuel finished his first.

"Just oncet more for both of us, Jimmy," he said, pushing his bowl across the board; and when the man brought them back he said, "Now I'm goin' to take it easy and enjoy myself. I can't never seem to get the good of it till about the third or fourth bowl. Too much of a hurry."

"Do they give you four bowls?" gasped Lemuel in astonishment.

"They give your four barrels, if you can hold it," replied the other proudly; "and some the mates *can,* pretty near. They got an awful tank, as a general rule, the pards has. There ain't anything mean about this house. They don't scamp the broth, and they don't shab the measure. I do wish you could see that refrigerator oncet. Never been much at sea, have you, mate?"

Lemuel said he had never been at sea at all.

The other leaned forward with his elbows on each side of his bowl, and lazily broke his hard-tack into it. "Well, I have. I was shipped when I was about eleven years old by a shark that got me drunk. I wanted to ship, but I wanted to ship on an American vessel for New Orleans. First thing I knowed I turned up on a Swedish brig bound for Venice. Ever been to It'ly?"

"No," said Lemuel.

"Well, I hain't but oncet. Oncet is enough for *me.* I run away while I was in Venice, and went ashore—if you can call it ashore; it's all water, and you got to go round in boats, gondolas they call 'em there—and went to see the American counsul, and told him I was an American boy, and tried to get him to get me off. But he couldn't do anything. If you ship under the Swedish flag you're a Swede, and the whole United States couldn't get you off. If I'd 'a' shipped under the American flag I'd 'a' been an American, I don't care if I was born in Hottentot. That's what the counsul said. I never want to see that town ag'in. I used to hear songs about Venice: 'Beautiful Venice, Bride of the Sea'; but I think it's a kind of a hole of a place. Well, what I started to say was that when I turn up in Boston now,—and I most generally do,—I don't go to no sailor boardin'-house; I break for the Wayfarer's Lodge every time. It's a temperance house, and they give you the worth o' your money."

"Come! hurry up!" said the attendant. He wiped the table impatiently with his towel, and stood waiting for Lemuel and the other to finish. All the rest had gone.

"Don't you be too fresh, pard," said the mate, with the effect of standing upon his rights. "Guess if you was on your third bowl, you wouldn't hurry."

The attendant smiled. "Don't you want to lend us a hand with the dishes?" he asked.

"Who's sick?" asked the other in his turn.

"Johnny's got a day off."

The boy shook his head. "No; I couldn't. If it was a case of sickness, of course I'd do it. But I couldn't spare the time; I couldn't really. Why, I ought to be up on the Common now."

Lemuel had listened with a face of interest.

"Don't you want to make half a dollar, young feller?" asked the attendant.

"Yes, I do," said Lemuel eagerly.

"Know how to wash dishes?"

"Yes," answered the boy, not ashamed of his knowledge, as the boy of another civilization might have been. Nothing more distinctly marks the rustic New England civilization than the taming of its men to the performance of certain domestic offices elsewhere held dishonorably womanish. The boy learns not only to milk and to keep the milk-cans clean, but to churn, to wash dishes, and to cook.

"Come around here, then," said the attendant, and Lemuel promptly obeyed.

"Well, now," said his mate, "that's right. I'd do it myself if I had the time." He pulled his soft wool hat out of his hip pocket. "Well, good-morning, pards. I don't know as I shall see you again much before night." Lemuel was lifting a large tray, heavy with empty broth-bowls. "What *time* did you say it was, Jimmy?"

"Seven o'clock."

"Well, I just got time to get there," said the other, putting on his hat, and pushing out of the door.

At the moment Lemuel was lifting his tray of empty broth-bowls, Mr. Sewell was waking for the early quarter-to-eight

breakfast, which he thought it right to make—not perhaps as
an example to his parishioners, most of whom had the leisure
to lie later, but as a sacrifice, not too definite, to the lingering
ideal of suffering. He could not work before breakfast,—his
delicate digestion forbade that,—or he would have risen still
earlier; and he employed the twenty minutes he had between his bath and his breakfast in skimming the morning
paper.

Just at present Mr. Sewell was taking two morning papers:
the "Advertiser," which he had always taken, and a cheap
little one-cent paper, which had just been started, and which
he had subscribed for experimentally, with the vague impression that he ought to encourage the young men who had established it. He did not like it very well. It was made up somewhat upon the Western ideal, and dealt with local matters
in a manner that was at once a little more lively and a little
more intimate than he had been used to. But before he had
quite made up his mind to stop it, his wife had come to like
it on that very account. She said it was interesting. On this
point she used her conscience a little less actively than usual,
and he had to make her observe that to be interesting was
not the whole duty of journalism. It had become a matter of
personal pride with them respectively to attack and defend
the "Sunrise," as I shall call the little sheet, though that was
not the name; and Mr. Sewell had lately made some gain
through the character of the police reports, which the "Sunrise" had been developing into a feature. It was not that offensive matters were introduced; the worst cases were in fact
rather blinked; but Sewell insisted that the tone of flippant
gayety with which many facts, so serious, so tragic for their
perpetrators and victims, were treated was odious. He objected to the court being called a Mill, and prisoners Grists,
and the procedure Grinding; he objected to the familiar name
of Uncle for the worthy gentleman to whose care certain offenders were confided on probation. He now read that department of the "Sunrise" the first thing every morning, in

the hope of finding something with which to put Mrs. Sewell hopelessly in the wrong; but this morning a heading in the foreign news of the "Advertiser" caught his eye, and he laid the "Sunrise" aside to read at the breakfast-table. His wife came down in a cotton dress, as a tribute to the continued warmth of the weather, and said that she had not called the children, because it was Saturday, and they might as well have their sleep out. He liked to see her in that dress; it had a leafy rustling that was pleasant to his ear, and as she looked into the library he gayly put out his hand, which she took, and suffered herself to be drawn toward him. Then she gave him a kiss, somewhat less business-like and preoccupied than usual.

"Well, you've got Lemuel Barker off your mind at last," she divined, in recognition of her husband's cheerfulness.

"Yes, he's off," admitted Sewell.

"I hope he'll stay in Willoughby Pastures after this. Of course it puts an end to our going there next summer."

"Oh, I don't know," Sewell feebly demurred.

"*I* do," said his wife, but not despising his insincerity enough to insist that he did also. The mellow note of an apostle's bell—the gift of an æsthetic parishioner—came from below, and she said, "Well, there's breakfast, David," and went before him down the stairs.

He brought his papers with him. It would have been her idea of heightened coziness at this breakfast, which they had once a week alone together, not to have the newspapers; but she saw that he felt differently, and after a number of years of married life a woman learns to let her husband have his own way in some unimportant matters. It was so much his nature to have some sort of reading always in hand, that he was certainly more himself, and perhaps more companionable, with his papers than without them.

She merely said, "Let me take the 'Sunrise,' " when she had poured out his coffee, and he had helped her to cantaloupe and steak, and spread his "Advertiser" beside his plate. He had the "Sunrise" in his lap.

"No, you may have the 'Advertiser,' " he said, handing it over the table to her. "I was down first, and I got both the papers. I'm not really obliged to make any division, but I've seen the 'Advertiser,' and I'm willing to behave unselfishly. If you're very impatient for the police report in the 'Sunrise,' I'll read it aloud for you. I think that will be a very good test of its quality, don't you?"

He opened the little sheet, and smiled teasingly at his wife, who said, "Yes, read it aloud; I'm not at all ashamed of it."

She put the "Advertiser" in her lap, and leaned defiantly forward, while she stirred her coffee, and Sewell unfolded the little sheet, and glanced up and down its columns. "Go on! If you can't find it, I can."

"Never mind! Here it is," said Sewell, and he began to read:

" 'The mill opened yesterday morning with a smaller number of grists than usual, but they made up in quality what they lacked in quantity.'

"Our friend's metaphor seems to have weakened under him a little," commented Sewell, and then he pursued:

" 'A reasonable supply of drunks were dispatched———'

"Come, now, Lucy! you'll admit that this is horrible?" he broke off.

"No," said his wife, "I will admit nothing of the kind. It's flippant, I'll allow. Go on!"

"I can't," said Sewell; but he obeyed.

" 'A reasonable supply of drunks were dispatched, and an habitual drunk, in the person of a burly dame from Tipperary, who pleaded not guilty and then urged the "poor childer" in extenuation, was sent down the harbor for three months; Uncle Cook had been put in charge of a couple of young frailties whose hind name was woman———'

"How do you like that, my dear?" asked Sewell exultantly.

Mrs. Sewell looked grave, and then burst into a shocked laugh. "You must stop that paper, David! I can't have it about for the children to get hold of. But it is funny, isn't it? That will do———"

"No, I think you'd better have it all now. There can't be anything worse. It's funny, yes, with that truly infernal drollery which the newspaper wits seem to have the art of." He read on:

"—'when a case was called that brought the breath of clover-blossoms and hay-seed into the sultry court-room, and warmed the cockles of the habitués' toughened pericardiums with a touch of real poetry. This was a case of assault with intent to rob, in which a lithe young blonde, answering to the good old Puritanic name of Statira Dudley, was the complainant, and the defendant an innocent-looking, bucolic youth, yclept——' "

Sewell stopped and put his hand to his forehead.

"What is it, David?" demanded his wife. "Why don't you go on? Is it too scandalous?"

"No, no," murmured the minister.

"Well?"

"I *can't* go on. But you must read it, Lucy," he said, in quite a passion of humility. "And you must try to be merciful. That poor boy—that——"

He handed the paper to his wife, and made no attempt to escape from judgment, but sat submissive while she read the report of Lemuel's trial. The story was told throughout in the poetico-jocular spirit of the opening sentences; the reporter had felt the simple charm of the affair, only to be ashamed of it and the more offensive about it.

When she had finished Mrs. Sewell did not say anything. She merely looked at her husband, who looked really sick.

At last he said, making an effort to rise from his chair, "I must go and see him, I suppose."

"Yes, if you can find him," responded his wife with a sigh.

"Find him?" echoed Sewell.

"Yes. Goodness knows what more trouble the wretched creature's got into by this time. You saw that he was acquitted, didn't you?" she demanded in answer to her husband's stare.

"No, I didn't. I supposed he was convicted, of course."

"Well, you see it isn't so bad as it might be," she said, using a pity which she did not perhaps altogether feel. "Eat your breakfast now, David, and then go and try to look him up."

"Oh, I don't want any breakfast," pleaded the minister.

He offered to rise again, but she motioned him down in his chair. "David, you shall! I'm not going to have you going about all day with a headache. Eat! And then when you've finished your breakfast, go and find out which station that officer Baker belongs to, and he can tell you something about the boy, if any one can."

Sewell made what shift he could to grasp these practical ideas, and he obediently ate of whatever his wife bade him. She would not let him hurry his breakfast in the least, and when he had at last finished, she said: "Now you can go, David. And when you've found the boy, don't you let him out of your sight again till you've put him aboard the train for Willoughby Pastures, and seen the train start out of the depot with him. Never mind your sermon. I will be setting down the heads of a sermon, while you're gone, that will do *you* good, if you write it out, whether it helps any one else or not."

Sewell was not so sure of that. He had no doubt that his wife would set down the heads of a powerful sermon, but he questioned whether any discourse, however potent, would have force to benefit such an abandoned criminal as he felt himself, in walking down his brown-stone steps, and up the long brick sidewalk of Bolingbroke street toward the Public Garden. The beds of geraniums and the clumps of scarlet-blossomed salvia in the little grass-plots before the houses, which commonly flattered his eye with their color, had a suggestion of penal fires in them now, that needed no lingering superstition in his nerves to realize something very like perdition for his troubled soul. It was not wickedness he had been guilty of, but he had allowed a good man to be made the agency of suffering, and he was sorely to blame, for he had sinned against himself. This was what his conscience said, and though his reason protested against his state of mind as a phase of the religious insanity which we have all inherited in some measure from Puritan times, it could not help him. He went along involuntarily framing a vow that if Providence would mercifully permit him to repair the wrong he had done, he would not stop at any sacrifice to get that unhappy boy back to his home, but would gladly take any open shame or obloquy upon himself in order to accomplish this.

He met a policeman on the bridge of the Public Garden, and made bold to ask him at once if he knew an officer named Baker, and which station he could be found at. The policeman was over-rich in the acquaintance of two officers of the name of Baker, and he put his hand on Sewell's shoulder, in the paternal manner of policemen when they will be friendly, and advised him to go first to the Neponset street station, to which one of these Bakers was attached, and inquire there first. "Anyway, that's what I should do in your place."

Sewell was fulsomely grateful, as we all are in the like case; and at the station he used an urbanity with the captain which was perhaps not thrown away upon him, but which was certainly disproportioned to the trouble he was asking him to take in saying whether he knew where he could find Officer Baker.

"Yes, I do," said the captain; "you can find him in bed, upstairs. But I'd rather you wouldn't wake a man off duty if you don't have to, especially if you don't know he's the one. What's wanted?"

Sewell stopped to say that the captain was quite right, and then he explained why he wished to see Officer Baker.

The captain listened with nods of his head at the names and facts given. "Guess you won't have to get Baker up for that. I can tell you what there is to tell. I don't know where your young man is now, but I gave him an order for a bed at the Wayfarer's Lodge last night, and I guess he slept there. You a friend of his?"

"Yes," said Sewell, much questioning inwardly whether he could be truly described as such. "I wish to befriend him," he added savingly. "I knew him at home, and I am sure of his innocence."

"Oh, I guess he's *innocent* enough," said the captain. "Well, now, I tell you what you do, if you want to befriend him; you get him home quick as you can."

"Yes," said Sewell, helpless to resent the officer's authoritative and patronizing tone. "That's what I wish to do. Do you suppose he's at the Wayfarer's Lodge now?" asked Sewell.

"Can't say," said the captain, tilting himself back in his chair, and putting his quill toothpick between his lips like a cigarette. "The only way is to go and see."

"Thank you very much," said the minister, accepting his dismissal meekly, as a man vowed to ignominy should, but feeling keenly that he was dismissed, and dismissed in disgrace.

At the Lodge he was received less curtly. The manager was there with a long morning's leisure before him, and disposed to friendliness that Sewell found absurdly soothing. He turned over the orders for beds delivered by the vagrants the night before, and "Yes," he said, coming to Lemuel's name, "he slept here; but nobody knows where he is by this time. Wait a bit, sir!" he added to Sewell's fallen countenance. "There was one of the young fellows staid to help us through with the dishes this morning. I'll have him up; or maybe you'd like to go down and take a look at our kitchen? You'll find him there, if it's the one. Here's our card. We can supply you with all sorts of firewood at less cost than the dealers, and you'll be helping the poor fellows to earn an honest bed and breakfast. This way, sir!"

Sewell promised to buy his wood there, put the card respectfully into his pocket, and followed the manager downstairs, and through the basement to the kitchen. He arrived just as Lemuel was about to lift a trayful of clean soup-bowls, to carry it upstairs. After a glance at the minister, he stood still with dropped eyes.

Sewell did not know in what form to greet the boy on whom

he had unwillingly brought so much evil, and he found the greater difficulty in deciding as he saw Lemuel's face hardening against him.

"Barker," he said at last, "I'm very glad to find you—I have been very anxious to find you."

Lemuel made no sign of sympathy, but stood still in his long check apron, with his sleeves rolled up to his elbow, and the minister was obliged to humble himself still further to this figure of lowly obstinacy.

"I should like to speak with you. Can I speak with you a few moments?"

The manager politely stepped into the storeroom, and affected to employ himself there, leaving Lemuel and the minister alone together.

X

SEWELL lost no time. "I want you to go home, Barker. I feel that I am wholly to blame, and greatly to blame, for your coming to Boston with the expectation that brought you, and that I am indirectly responsible for all the trouble that has befallen you since you came. I want to be the means of your getting home, in any way you can let me."

This was a very different way of talking from the smooth superiority of address which the minister had used with him the other day at his own house. Lemuel was not insensible to the atonement offered him, and it was not from sulky stubbornness that he continued silent, and left the minister to explore the causes of his reticence unaided.

"I will go home *with* you, if you like," pursued the minister, though his mind misgave him that this was an extreme which Mrs. Sewell would not have justified him in. "I will go with you, and explain all the circumstances to your friends, in case there should be any misunderstanding—though in that event I should have to ask you to be my guest till Monday." Here the unhappy man laid hold of the sheep, which could not bring him greater condemnation than the lamb.

"I guess they won't know anything about it," said Lemuel, with whatever intention.

It seemed hardened indifference to the minister, and he felt it his disagreeable duty to say, "I am afraid they will. I read of it in the newspaper this morning, and I'm afraid that an exaggerated report of your misfortunes will reach Willoughby Pastures, and alarm your family."

A faint pallor came over the boy's face, and he stood again in his impenetrable, rustic silence. The voice that finally spoke from it said, "I guess I don't want to go home, then."

"You *must* go home!" said the minister, with more of imploring than imperiousness in his command. "What will they make of your prolonged absence?"

"I sent a postal to mother this morning. They lent me one."

"But what will you do here, without work and without means? I wish you to go home with me—I feel responsible for you—and remain with me till you can hear from your mother. I'm sorry you came to Boston; it's no place for you, as you must know by this time, and I am sure your mother will agree with me in desiring your return."

"I guess I don't want to go home," said Lemuel.

"Are you afraid that an uncharitable construction will be placed upon what has happened to you by your neighbors?" Lemuel did not answer. "I assure you that all that can be arranged. I will write to your pastor, and explain it fully. But in any event," continued Sewell, "it is your duty to yourself and your friends to go home and live it down. It would be your duty to do so even if you had been guilty of wrong, instead of the victim of misfortune."

"I don't know," said Lemuel, "as I want to go home and be the laughing-stock."

Against this point Sewell felt himself helpless. He could not pretend that the boy would not be ridiculous in the eyes of his friends, and all the more ridiculous because so wholly innocent. He could only say, "That is a thing which you must bear." And then it occurred to him to ask, "Do you feel that it is right to let your family meet the ridicule alone?"

"I guess nobody will speak to mother about it more than once," said Lemuel, with a just pride in his mother's powers of retort. A woman who, unaided and alone, had worn the Bloomer costume for twenty years in the heart of a commentative community like Willoughby Pastures, was not likely to be without a cutting tongue for her defense.

"But your sister," urged Sewell; "your brother-in-law," he feebly added.

"I guess they will have to stand it," replied Lemuel.

The minister heaved a sigh of hopeless perplexity. "What do you propose to do, then? You can't remain here without means. Do you expect to sell your poetry?" he asked, goaded to the question by a conscience peculiarly sore on that point.

It made Lemuel blush. "No, I don't expect to sell it now. They took it out of my pocket on the Common."

"I am glad of that," said the minister as simply, "and I feel bound to warn you solemnly that there is absolutely *no* hope for you in that direction."

Lemuel said nothing.

The minister stood baffled again. After a bad moment he asked, "Have you anything particular in view?"

"I don't know as I have."

"How long can you remain here?"

"I don't know exactly."

Sewell turned and followed the manager into the refrigerator room, where he had remained patiently whistling throughout this interview.

When he came back, Lemuel had carried one trayful of bowls upstairs, and returned for another load, which he was piling carefully up for safe transportation.

"The manager tells me," said Sewell, "that practically you can stay here as long as you like, if you work; but he doesn't think it desirable you should remain, nor do I. But I wish to find you here again when I come back. I have something in view for you."

This seemed to be a question, and Lemuel said, "All right," and went on piling up his bowls. He added, "I shouldn't want you to take a great deal of trouble."

"Oh, it's no trouble," groaned the minister. "Then I may depend upon seeing you here any time during the day?"

"I don't know as I'm going away," Lemuel admitted.

"Well, then, good-bye for the present," said Sewell; and

after speaking again to the manager, and gratefully ordering some kindling which he did not presently need, he went out, and took his way homeward. But he stopped half a block short of his own door, and rang at Miss Vane's. To his perturbed and eager spirit it seemed nothing short of a divine mercy that she should be at home. If he had not been a man bent on repairing his wrong at any cost to others, he would hardly have taken the step he now contemplated without first advising with his wife, who, he felt sure, would have advised against it. His face did not brighten at all when Miss Vane came briskly in, with the *"How* d'ye do?" which he commonly found so cheering. She pulled up the blind and saw his knotted brow.

"What is the matter? You look as if you had got Lemuel Barker back on your hands."

"I have," said the minister briefly.

Miss Vane gave a wild laugh of delight. "You *don't* mean it!" she sputtered, sitting down before him, and peering into his face. "What *do* you mean?"

Sewell was obliged to possess Miss Vane's entire ignorance of all the facts in detail. From point to point he paused; he began really to be afraid she would do herself an injury with her laughing.

She put her hand on his arm and bowed her head forward, with her face buried in her handkerchief. "What—what—do you suppose-pose—they did with the po-po-*po*em they stole from him?"

"Well, one thing I'm sure they *didn't* do," said Sewell bitterly. "They didn't *read* it."

Miss Vane hid her face in her handkerchief, and then plucked it away, and shrieked again. She stopped, with the sudden calm that succeeds such a paroxysm, and, "Does Mrs. Sewell know all about this?" she panted.

"She knows everything, except my finding him in the dishwashing department of the Wayfarer's Lodge," said Sewell gloomily, "and my coming to you."

"Why do you come to me?" asked Miss Vane, her face twitching and her eyes brimming.

"Because," answered Sewell, "I'd rather not go to her till I have done something."

Miss Vane gave way again, and Sewell sat regarding her ruefully.

"What do you expect me to do?" She looked at him over her handkerchief, which she kept pressed against her mouth.

"I haven't the least idea what I expected you to do. I expected you to tell me. You have an inventive mind."

Miss Vane shook her head. Her eyes grew serious, and after a moment she said, "I'm afraid I'm not equal to Lemuel Barker. Besides," she added with a tinge of trouble, "I have *my* problem already."

"Yes," said the minister sympathetically. "How has the flower charity turned out?"

"She went yesterday with one of the ladies, and carried flowers to the city hospital. But she wasn't at all satisfied with the result. She said the patients were mostly disgusting old men that hadn't been shaved. I think that now she wants to try her flowers on criminals. She says she wishes to visit the prisons."

Sewell brightened forlornly. "Why not let her reform Barker?"

This sent Miss Vane off again. "Poor boy!" she sighed, when she had come to herself. "No, there's nothing that I can do for him, except to order some firewood from his benefactors."

"I did that," said Sewell. "But I don't see how it's to help Barker exactly."

"I would gladly join in a public subscription to send him home. But you say he won't *go* home?"

"He won't go home," sighed the minister. "He's determined to stay. I suspect he would accept employment, if it were offered him in the right spirit."

Miss Vane shook her head. "There's nothing I can think of

except shoveling snow. And as yet it's rather warm October weather."

"There's certainly no snow to shovel," admitted Sewell. He rose disconsolately. "Well, there's nothing for it, I suppose, but to put him down at the Christian Union, and explain his checkered career to everybody who proposes to employ him."

Miss Vane could not keep the laughter out of her eyes; she nervously tapped her lips with her handkerchief, to keep it from them. Suddenly she halted Sewell in his dejected progress toward the door. "I might give him my furnace."

"Furnace?" echoed Sewell.

"Yes. Jackson has 'struck' for twelve dollars a month, and at present there is a 'lock-out,'—I believe that's what it's called. And I had determined not to yield as long as the fine weather lasted. I knew I should give in at the first frost. I will take Barker now, if you think he can manage the furnace."

"I've no doubt he can. Has Jackson really struck?" Miss Vane nodded. "He hasn't said anything to me about it."

"He probably intends to make special terms to the clergy. But he told me he was putting up the rates on all his 'famblies' this winter."

"If he puts them up on me, I will take Barker too," said the minister boldly. "If he will come," he added with less courage. "Well, I will go round to the Lodge, and see what he thinks of it. Of course, he can't live upon ten dollars a month, and I must look him up something besides."

"That's the only thing I can think of at present," said Miss Vane.

"Oh, you're indefinitely good to think of so much," said Sewell. "You must excuse me if my reception of your kindness has been qualified by the reticence with which Barker received mine this morning."

"Oh, do tell me about it!" cried Miss Vane.

"Some time I will. But I can assure you it was such as to make me shrink from another interview. I don't know but

Barker may fling your proffered furnace in my teeth. But I'm sure we both mean well. And I thank you, all the same. Goodbye."

"Poor Mr. Sewell!" said Miss Vane, following him to the door. "May I run down and tell Mrs. Sewell?"

"Not yet," said the minister sadly. He was too insecure of Barker's reception of him to be able to enjoy the joke.

When he got back to the Wayfarer's Lodge, whither he made himself walk in penance, he found Lemuel with a book in his hand, reading, while the cook stirred about the kitchen, and the broth, which he had well under way for the midday meal, lifted the lid of its boiler from time to time and sent out a joyous whiff of steam. The place had really a coziness of its own, and Sewell began to fear that his victim had been so far corrupted by its comfort as to be unwilling to leave the refuge. He had often seen the subtly disastrous effect of bounty, and it was one of the things he trembled for in considering the question of public aid to the poor. Before he addressed Barker, he saw him entered upon the dire life of idleness and dependence, partial or entire, which he had known so many Americans even willing to lead since the first great hard times began; and he spoke to him with the asperity of anticipative censure.

"Barker!" he said, and Lemuel lifted his head from the book he was reading. "I have found something for you to do. I still prefer you should go home, and I advise you to do so. But," he added, at the look that came into Lemuel's face, "if you are determined to stay, this is the best I can do for you. It isn't a full support, but it's something, and you must look about for yourself, and not rest till you've found full work, and something better fitted for you. Do you think you can take care of a furnace?"

"Hot air?" asked Lemuel.

"Yes."

"I guess so. I took care of the church furnace last winter."

"I didn't know you had one," said the minister, brightening in the ray of hope. "Would you be willing to take care of a domestic furnace—a furnace in a private house?"

Lemuel pondered the proposal in silence. Whatever objections there were to it in its difference from the aims of his ambition in coming to Boston he kept to himself; and his ignorance of city prejudices and sophistications probably suggested nothing against the honest work to his pride. "I guess I should," he said at last.

"Well, then, come with me."

Sewell judged it best not to tell him whose furnace he was to take care of; he had an impression that Miss Vane was included in the resentment which Lemuel seemed to cherish toward him. But when he had him at her door, "It's the lady whom you saw at my house the other day," he explained. It was then too late for Lemuel to rebel, and they went in.

If there was any such unkindness in Lemuel's breast toward her, it yielded promptly to her tact. She treated him at once, not like a servant, but like a young person, and yet she used a sort of respect for his independence which was soothing to his rustic pride. She put it on the money basis at once; she told him that she should give him ten dollars a month for taking care of the furnace, keeping the sidewalk clear of snow, shoveling the paths in the back yard for the women to get at their clothes-lines, carrying up and down coal and ashes for the grates, and doing errands. She said that this was what she had always paid, and asked him if he understood and were satisfied.

Lemuel answered with one yes to both her questions, and then Miss Vane said that of course till the weather changed they should want no fire in the furnace, but that it might change any day, and they should begin at once and count October as a full month. She thought he had better go down and look at the furnace and see if it was in order; she had had the pipes cleaned, but perhaps it needed blacking; the cook would show him how it worked. She went with him to the head of the basement stairs, and calling down, "Jane, here is Lemuel, come to look after the furnace," left him and Jane to complete the acquaintance upon coming in sight of each other, and went back to the minister. He had risen to go, and she gave him her hand, while a smile rippled into laughter on her lips.

"Do you think," she asked, struggling with her mirth to keep unheard of those below, "that it is quite the work for a literary man?"

"If he is a man," said Sewell courageously, "the work won't keep him from being literary."

Miss Vane laughed at his sudden recovery of spirit, as she had laughed at his dejection; but he did not care. He hurried home, with a sermon kindling in his mind so obviously that his wife did not detain him beyond a few vital questions, and let him escape from having foisted his burden upon Miss Vane with the simple comment, "Well, we shall see how that will work."

As once before, Sewell tacitly took a hint from his own experience, and, enlarging to more serious facts from it, preached effort in the erring. He denounced mere remorse. Better not feel that at all, he taught; and he declared that what is ordinarily distinguished from remorse as repentance was equally a mere corrosion of the spirit unless some attempt at reparation went with it. He maintained that though some mischiefs—perhaps most mischiefs—were irreparable so far as restoring the original status was concerned, yet every mischief was reparable in the good will and the good deed of its perpetrator. Do what you could to retrieve yourself from error, and then, not leave the rest to Providence, but keep doing. The good, however small, must grow if tended and nurtured like a useful plant, as the evil would certainly grow like a wild and poisonous weed if left to itself. Sin, he said, was a terrible mystery; one scarcely knew how to deal with it or to attempt to determine its nature; but perhaps— he threw out the thought while warning those who heard him of its danger in some aspects—sin was not wholly an evil. We were so apt in this world of struggle and ambition to become centered solely in ourselves, that possibly the wrong done to another—the wrong that turned our thoughts from ourselves, and kept them bent in agony and despair upon the suffering we had caused another, and knew not how to mitigate—possibly this wrong, nay, certainly this wrong was good in disguise. But, returning to his original point, we were to beware how we rested in this despair. In the very extremity of our anguish, our fear, our shame, we were to gird ourselves up to reparation. Strive to do good, he preached; strive most of all to do good to those you have done harm to. His text was "Cease to do evil."

He finished his sermon during the afternoon, and in the evening his wife said they would run up to Miss Vane's. Sewell shrank from this a little, with the obscure dread that Lemuel might have turned his back upon good fortune, and abandoned the place offered him, in which case Sewell would have to give a wholly different turn to his sermon; but he consented, as indeed he must. He was as curious as his wife to know how the experiment had resulted.

Miss Vane did not wait to let them ask. "My dear," she said, kissing Mrs. Sewell and giving her hand to the minister in one, "he is a pearl! And I've kept him from mixing his native luster with Rising Sun Stove Polish by becoming his creditor in the price of a pair of overalls. I had no idea they were so cheap, and you can see that they will fade, with a few washings, to a perfect Millet blue. They were quite his own idea, when he found the furnace needed blacking, and he wanted to use the fifty cents he earned this morning toward the purchase, but I insisted upon advancing the entire dollar myself. Neatness, self-respect, awe-inspiring deference!—he is each and every one of them in person."

Sewell could not forbear a glance of triumph at his wife.

"You leave us very little to ask," said that injured woman.

"But I've left myself a great deal to tell, my dear," retorted Miss Vane, "and I propose to keep the floor; though I don't really know where to begin."

"I thought you had got past the necessity of beginning,"

said Sewell. "We know that the new pearl sweeps clean,"—
Miss Vane applauded his mixed metaphor,—"and now you
might go on from that point."

"Well, you may think I'm rash," said Miss Vane, "but I've
thoroughly made up my mind to keep him."

"Dear, *dear* Miss Vane!" cried the minister. "Mrs. Sewell
thinks you're rash, but I don't. What do you mean by keeping
him?"

"Keeping him as a fixture—a permanency—a continuosity."

"Oh! A continuosity? I know what that is in the ordinary
acceptation of the term, but I'm not sure that I follow your
meaning exactly."

"Why, it's simply this," said Miss Vane. "I have long secretly wanted the protection of what Jane calls a man-body in
the house, and when I saw how Lemuel had blacked the
furnace, I knew I should feel as safe with him as with a whole
body of troops."

"Well," sighed the minister, "you have not been rash, perhaps, but you'll allow that you've been rapid."

"No," said Miss Vane, "I won't allow that. I have simply
been intuitive—nothing more. His functions are not decided
yet, but it is decided that he is to stay; he's to sleep in the little
room over the L, and in my tranquilized consciousness he's
been there years already."

"And has Sibyl undertaken Barker's reformation?" asked
Sewell.

"Don't interrupt! Don't anticipate! I admit nothing till I
come to it. But after I had arranged with Lemuel I began to
think of Sibyl."

"That was like some ladies I have known of," said Sewell.
"You women commit yourselves to a scheme, in order to show
your skill in reconciling circumstances to the irretrievable.
Well?"

"*Don't* interrupt, David!" cried his wife.

"Oh, let him go on," said Miss Vane. "It's all very well,
taking people into your house on the spur of the moment,

and in obedience to a generous impulse; but when you reflect that the object of your good intentions slept in the Wayfarer's Lodge the night before, and in the police station the night before that, and enjoys a newspaper celebrity in connection with a case of assault and battery with intent to rob,—why, then you *do* reflect!"

"Yes," said Sewell, "that is just the point where I should begin."

"I thought," continued Miss Vane, "I had better tell Sibyl all about it, so if by any chance the neighbors' kitchens should have heard of the case—they read the police reports very carefully in the kitchens——"

"They do in some drawing-rooms," interrupted Sewell.

"It's well for you they do, David," said his wife. "Your protégé would have been in your refuge still, if they didn't."

"I see!" cried the minister. "I shall have to take the 'Sunrise' another week."

Miss Vane looked from one to the other in sympathetic ignorance, but they did not explain, and she went on.

"And if they should hear Lemuel's name, and put two and two together, and the talk should get to Sibyl—well, I thought it all over, until the whole thing became perfectly lurid, and I wished Lemuel Barker was back in the depths of Willoughby Pastures——"

"I understand," said Sewell. "Go on!"

Miss Vane did so, after stopping to laugh. "It seemed to me I couldn't wait for Sibyl to get home—she spent the night in Brookline, and didn't come till five o'clock—to tell her. I began before she had got her hat or gloves off, and she sat down with them on, and listened like a three-years' child to the Ancient Mariner, but she lost no time when she understood the facts. She went out immediately and stripped the nasturtium bed. If you could have seen it when you came in, there's hardly a blossom left. She took the decorations of Lemuel's room into her own hands at once; and if there is any saving power in nasturtiums, he will be a changed person.

She says that now the great object is to keep him from feeling that he has been an outcast, and needs to be reclaimed; she says nothing could be worse for him. I don't know how she knows."

"Barker might feel that he was disgraced," said the minister, "but I don't believe that a whole system of ethics would make him suspect that he needed to be reclaimed."

"He makes me suspect that *I* need to be reclaimed," said Miss Vane, "when he looks at me with those beautiful honest eyes of his."

Mrs. Sewell asked, "Has he seen the decorations yet?"

"Not at all. They are to steal upon him when he comes in to-night. The gas is to be turned very low, and he is to notice everything gradually, so as not to get the impression that things have been done with a design upon him." She laughed in reporting these ideas, which were plainly those of the young girl. "Sh!" she whispered at the end.

A tall girl, with a slim vase in her hand, drifted in upon their group like an apparition. She had heavy black eyebrows with beautiful blue eyes under them, full of an intensity unrelieved by humor.

"Aunty!" she said severely, "have you been telling?"

"Only Mr. and Mrs. Sewell, Sibyl," said Miss Vane. "*Their* knowing won't hurt. He'll never know it."

"If he hears you laughing, he'll know it's about him. He's in the kitchen now. He's come in the back way. Do be quiet." She had given her hand without other greeting in her preoccupation to each of the Sewells in turn, and now she passed out of the room.

XI

"What makes Lemuel such a gift," said Miss Vane, in a talk which she had with Sewell a month later, "is that he is so supplementary."

"Do you mean just in the supplementary sense of the term?"

"Well, not in the fifth-wheel sense. I mean that he supplements us, all and singular—if you will excuse the legal exactness."

"Oh, certainly," said Sewell; "I should like even more exactness."

"Yes; but before I particularize I must express my general satisfaction in him as a man-body. I had no idea that man-bodies in a house were so perfectly admirable."

"I've sometimes feared that we were not fully appreciated," said Sewell. "Well?"

"The house is another thing with a man-body in it. I've often gone without little things I wanted, simply because I hated to make Sarah bring them, and because I hated still worse to go after them, knowing we were both weakly and tired. Now I deny myself nothing. I make Lemuel fetch and carry without remorse, from morning till night. I never knew it before, but the man-body seems never to be tired, or ill, or sleepy."

"Yes," said Sewell, "that is often the idea of the woman-body. I'm not sure that it's correct."

"Oh, *don't* attack it!" implored Miss Vane. "You don't

know what a blessing it is. Then, the man-body never complains, and I can't see that he expects anything more in an order than the clear understanding of it. He doesn't expect it to be accounted for in any way; the fact that you say you want a thing is enough. It is very strange. Then the moral support of the presence of a man-body is enormous. I now know that I have never slept soundly since I have kept house alone—that I have never passed a night without hearing burglars or smelling fire."

"And now?"

"And now I shouldn't mind a legion of burglars in the house; I shouldn't mind being burned in my bed every night. I feel that Lemuel is in charge, and that nothing can happen."

"Is he really so satisfactory?" asked Sewell, exhaling a deep relief.

"He is, indeed," said Miss Vane. "I couldn't exaggerate it."

"Well, well! Don't try. We are finite, after all, you know. Do you think it can last?"

"I have thought of that," answered Miss Vane. "I don't see why it shouldn't last. I have tried to believe that I did a foolish thing in coming to your rescue, but I can't see that I did. I don't see why it shouldn't last as long as Lemuel chooses. And he seems perfectly contented with his lot. He doesn't seem to regard it as domestic service, but as domestication, and he patronizes our inefficiency while he spares it. His common sense is extraordinary—it's exemplary; it almost makes one wish to have common sense one's self." They had now got pretty far from the original proposition, and Sewell returned to it with the question, "Well, and how does he supplement you singularly?"

"Oh! oh, yes!" said Miss Vane. "I could hardly tell you without going into too deep a study of character."

"I'm rather fond of that," suggested the minister.

"Yes, and I've no doubt we should all work very nicely into a sermon as illustrations; but I can't more than indicate the different cases. In the first place, Jane's forgetfulness seems to be growing upon her, and since Lemuel came she's abandoned herself to ecstasies of oblivion."

"Yes?"

"Yes. She's quite given over remembering *any*thing, because she knows that he will remember *every*thing."

"I see. And you?"

"Well, you have sometimes thought I was a little rash."

"A little? Did I think it was a little?"

"Well, a good deal. But it was all nothing to what I've been since Lemuel came. I used to keep some slight check upon myself for Sibyl's sake; but I don't now. I know that Lemuel is there to temper, to delay, to modify the effect of every impulse, and so I am all impulse now. And I've quite ceased to rule my temper. I know that Lemuel has self-control enough for all the tempers in the house, and so I feel perfectly calm in my wildest transports of fury."

"I understand," said Sewell. "And does Sibyl permit herself a similar excess in her fancies and ambitions?"

"Quite," said Miss Vane. "I don't know that she consciously relies upon Lemuel to supplement her, any more than Jane does; but she must be unconsciously aware that no extravagance of hers can be dangerous while Lemuel is in the house."

"Unconsciously aware is good. She hasn't got tired of reforming him yet?"

"I don't know. I sometimes think she wishes he had gone a little farther in crime. Then his reformation would be more obvious."

"Yes; I can appreciate that. Does she still look after his art and literature?"

"That phase has changed a little. She thinks now that he ought to be stimulated, if anything—that he ought to read George Eliot. She's put 'Middlemarch' and 'Romola' on his shelf. She says that he looks like Tito Melema."

Sewell rose. "Well, I don't see but what your supplement is a very demoralizing element. I shall never dare to tell Mrs. Sewell what you've said."

"Oh, she knows it," cried Miss Vane. "We've agreed that you will counteract any temptation that Lemuel may feel to abuse his advantages by the ferociously self-denying sermons you preach at him every Sunday."

"Do I preach at him? Do you notice it?" asked Sewell nervelessly.

"Notice it?" laughed Miss Vane. "I should think your whole congregation would notice it. You seem to look at nobody else."

"I know it! Since he began to come, I can't keep my eyes off him. I do deliver my sermons at him. I believe I write them at him! He has an eye of terrible and exacting truth. I feel myself on trial before him. He holds me up to a standard of sincerity that is killing me. Mrs. Sewell was bad enough; I was reasonably bad myself; but this! Couldn't you keep him away? Do you think it's exactly decorous to let your man-servant occupy a seat in your family pew? How do you suppose it looks to the Supreme Being?"

Miss Vane was convulsed. "I had precisely those misgivings! But Lemuel hadn't. He asked me what the number of our pew was, and I hadn't the heart—or else I hadn't the face—to tell him he mustn't sit in it. How could I? Do you think it's so very scandalous?"

"I don't know," said Sewell. "It may lead to great abuses. If we tacitly confess ourselves equal in the sight of God, how much better are we than the Roman Catholics?"

Miss Vane could not suffer these ironies to go on.

"He approves of your preaching. He has talked your sermons over with me. You oughtn't to complain."

"Oh, I don't! Do you think he's really softening a little toward me?"

"Not personally, that I know," said Miss Vane. "But he seems to regard you as a channel of the truth."

"I ought to be glad of so much," said Sewell. "I confess that I hadn't supposed he was at all of our way of thinking. They preached a very appreciable orthodoxy at Willoughby Pastures."

"I don't know about that," said Miss Vane. "I only know that he approves your theology, or your ethics."

"Ethics, I hope. I'm sure *they're* right." After a thoughtful moment the minister asked, "Have you observed that they have softened him socially at all—broken up that terrible rigidity of attitude, that dismaying retentiveness of speech?"

"I know what you mean!" cried Miss Vane, delightedly. "I believe Lemuel *is* a little more supple, a little *less* like a granite bowlder in one of his meadows. But I can't say that he's glib yet. He isn't apparently going to say more than he thinks."

"I hope he thinks more than he says," sighed the minister. "My interviews with Lemuel have left me not only exhausted but bruised, as if I had been hurling myself against a dead wall. Yes, I manage him better from the pulpit, and I certainly oughtn't to complain. I don't expect him to make any response, and I perceive that I am not *quite* so sore as after meeting him in private life."

That evening Lemuel was helping to throng the platform of an overcrowded horse-car. It was Saturday night, and he was going to the provision man up toward the South End, whom Miss Vane was dealing with for the time being, in an economical recoil from her expensive Back Bay provision man, to order a forgotten essential of the Sunday's supplies. He had already been at the grocer's, and was carrying home three or four packages to save the cart from going a third time that day to Bolingbroke street, and he stepped down into the road, when two girls came squeezing their way out of the car.

"Well, I'm glad," said one of them in a voice Lemuel knew at once, " 't there's one man's got the politeness to make a *little* grain o' room for you. Thank you, sir!" she added, with more scorn for the others than gratitude for Lemuel. "*You're* a gentleman, *any*way."

The hardened offenders on the platform laughed, but Lemuel said simply, "You're quite welcome."

"Why, land's sakes!" shouted the girl. "Well, if 'tain't you. S'tira!" she exclaimed to her companion in utter admiration. Then she added to Lemuel, "Why, I didn't s'pose but what you'd 'a' be'n back home long ago. Well, I *am* glad. Be'n in Boston ever since? Well, I want to know!"

The conductor had halted his car for the girls to get off, but, as he remarked with a vicious jerk at his bell-strap, he could not keep his car standing there while a woman was asking about the folks, and the horses started up and left Lemuel behind. "Well, there!" said 'Manda Grier. " 'F I hain't made you lose your car! I never see folks like some them conductors."

"Oh, I guess I can walk the rest of the way," said Lemuel, his face bright with a pleasure visible in the light of the lamp that brought out Statira Dudley's smiles and the forward thrust of 'Manda Grier's whopper-jaw as they turned toward the pavement together.

"Well, I guess 'f I've spoke about you once, I have a hundred times, in the last six weeks. I always told S'tira you'd be'n sure to turn up b'fore this 'f you'd be'n in Boston all the time; 'n' 't I guessed you'd got a disgust for the place, 'n' 't you wouldn't want to see it again for *one* while."

Statira did not say anything. She walked on the other side of 'Manda Grier, who thrust her in the side from time to time with a lift of her elbow, in demand of sympathy and corroboration; but though she only spoke to answer yes or no, Lemuel could see that she was always smiling or else biting her lip to keep herself from it. He thought she looked about as pretty as anybody could, and that she was again very fashionably dressed. She had on a short dolman, and a pretty hat that shaded her forehead but fitted close round, and she wore long gloves that came up on her sleeves. She had a book from the library; she walked with a little bridling movement that he found very ladylike. 'Manda Grier tilted along between them and her tongue ran and ran, so that Lemuel, when they came to Miss Vane's provision man's, could hardly get in a word to say that he guessed he must stop there.

Statira drifted on a few paces, but 'Manda Grier halted abruptly with him. "Well, 'f you're ever up our way we sh'd be much pleased to have you call, Mr. Barker," she said formally.

"I should be much pleased to do so," said Lemuel with equal state.

" 'Tain't but just a little ways round here on the Avenue," she added.

Lemuel answered, "I guess I know where it is." He did not mean it for anything of a joke, but both the girls laughed, and though she had been so silent before, Statira laughed the most.

He could not help laughing either when 'Manda Grier said, "I guess if you was likely to forget the number you could go round to the station and inquire. They got your address too."

" 'Manda Grier, you be still!" said Statira.

"S'tira said that's the way she knew you was from Willoughby Pastures. Her folks is from up that way, themselves. She says the minute she heard the name she knew it couldn't 'a' be'n you, whoever it was done it."

" 'Manda Grier!" cried Statira again.

"I tell her she don't believe 't any harm can come out the town o' Willoughby, anywheres."

" 'Manda!" cried Statira.

Lemuel was pleased, but he could not say a word. He could not look at Statira.

"Well, good-evening," said Amanda Grier.

"Well, good-evening," said Lemuel.

"Well, good-evening," said Statira.

"Well, good-evening," said Lemuel again.

The next moment they were gone round the corner, and he was left standing before the provision man's, with his packages in his hand. It did not come to him till he had transacted his business within, and was on his way home, that he had been very impolite not to ask if he might not see them home. He did not know but he ought to go back and try to find them, and apologize for his rudeness, and yet he did not see how he could do that, either; he had no excuse for it; he was afraid it would seem queer, and make them laugh. Besides, he had those things for Miss Vane, and the cook wanted some of them at once.

He could hardly get to sleep that night for thinking of his blunder, and at times he cowered under the bedclothes for shame. He decided that the only way for him to do was to keep out of their way after this, and if he ever met them anywhere, to pretend not to see them.

The next morning he went to hear Mr. Sewell preach, as usual, but he found himself wandering far from the sermon, and asking or answering this or that in a talk with those girls that kept going on in his mind. The minister himself seemed to wander, and at times, when Lemuel forced a return to him, he thought he was boggling strangely. For the first time Mr. Sewell's sermon, in his opinion, did not come to much.

While his place in Miss Vane's household was still indefinitely ascertained, he had the whole of Sunday, and he always wrote home in the afternoon, or brought up the arrears of the journal he had begun keeping; but the Sunday afternoon that followed, he was too excited to stay in and write. He thought he would go and take a walk, and get away from the things that pestered him. He did not watch where he was going, and after awhile he turned a corner, and suddenly found himself in a long street, planted with shade-trees, and looking old-fashioned and fallen from a former dignity. He perceived that it could never have been fashionable, like Bolingbroke street or Beacon; the houses were narrow and their doors opened from little, cavernous arches let into the brick fronts, and they stood flush upon the pavement. The sidewalks were full of people, mostly girls walking up and down; at the corners young fellows lounged, and there were groups before the cigar stores and the fruit stalls, which were open. It was not very cold yet, and the children who swarmed upon the low door-steps were bareheaded and often summer-clad. The street was not nearly so well kept as the streets on the Back Bay that Lemuel was more used to, but he could see that it was not a rowdy street either. He looked up at a lamp on the first corner he came to, and read Pleasant Avenue on it; then he said that the witch was in it. He dramatized a scene of meeting those girls, and was very glib in it, and they were rather shy, and Miss Dudley kept behind Amanda Grier, who nudged her with her elbow when Lemuel said he had come round to see if anybody had robbed them of their books on the way home after he left them last night.

But all the time, as he hurried along to the next corner, he looked fearfully to the right and left. Presently he began to steal guilty glances at the numbers of the houses. He said to himself that he would see what kind of a looking house they did live in, any way. It was only No. 900 odd when he began, and he could turn off if he wished long before he reached 1334. As he drew nearer he said he would just give a look at it, and then rush by. But 1334 was a house so much larger and nicer than he had expected that he stopped to collect his slow rustic thoughts, and decide whether she really lived there, or whether she had just given that number for a blind. He did not know why he should think that, though; she was dressed well enough to come out of any house.

While he lingered before the house an old man with a cane in his hand and his mouth hanging open stopped and peered through his spectacles, whose glare he fixed upon Lemuel, till he began to feel himself a suspicious character. The old man did not say anything, but stood faltering upon his stick and now and then gathering up his lower lip as if he were going to speak, but not speaking.

Lemuel cleared his throat. "Hmmn! Is this a boarding-house?"

"I don't know," crowed the old man, in a high senile note. "You want table-board or rooms?"

"I don't want board at all," began Lemuel again.

"What?" crowed the old man; and he put up his hand to his ear.

People were beginning to put their heads out of the neighboring windows, and to walk slowly as they went by, so as to hear what he and the old man were saying. He could not run away now, and he went boldly up to the door of the large house and rang.

A girl came, and he asked her, with a flushed face, if Miss Amanda Grier boarded there; somehow he could not bear to ask for Miss Dudley.

"Well," the girl said, "she *rooms* here," as if that might be a different thing to Lemuel altogether.

"Oh!" he said. "Is she in?"

"Well, you can walk in," said the girl, "and I'll see." She came back to ask, "Who shall I say called?"

"Mr. Barker," said Lemuel, and then glowed with shame because he had called himself Mister. The girl did not come back, but she hardly seemed gone before 'Manda Grier came into the room. He did not know whether she would speak to him, but she was as pleasant as could be, and said he must come right up to her and S'tira's room. It was pretty high up, but he did not notice the stairs, 'Manda Grier kept talking so; and when he got to it, and 'Manda Grier dashed the door open, and told him to walk right in, he would not have known but he was in somebody's sitting-room. A curtained alcove hid the bed, and the room was heated by a cheerful little kerosene stove; there were bright folding carpet-chairs, and the lid of the wash-stand had a cloth on it that came down to the floor, and there were plants in the window. There was a mirror on the wall, framed in black walnut with gilt molding inside, and a family-group photograph in the same kind of frame, and two chromos, and a clock on a bracket.

Statira seemed surprised to see him; the room was pretty warm, and her face was flushed. He said it was quite mild out, and she said, "Was it?" Then she ran and flung up the window, and said, "Why, so it was," and that she had been in the house all day, and had not noticed the weather.

She excused herself and the room for being in such a state; she said she was ashamed to be caught in such a looking dress, but they were not expecting company, and she did suppose 'Manda Grier would have given her time to put the room to rights a little. He could not understand why she said all this, for the whole room was clean, and Statira herself was beautifully dressed in the same dress that she had worn the night before, or one just like it; and after she had put up the window, 'Manda Grier said, "S'tira Dudley, do you want to kill yourself?" and ran and pulled aside the curtain in the corner, and took down the dolman from among other clothes that hung there, and threw it on Statira's shoulders, who looked as pretty as a pink in it. But she pretended to be too hot, and wanted to shrug it off, and 'Manda Grier called out, "Mr. Barker! *will* you make her keep it on?" and Lemuel sat dumb and motionless, but filled through with a sweet pleasure.

He tried several times to ask them if they had been robbed on the way home last night, as he had done in the scene he had dramatized; but he could not get out a word, except that it had been pretty warm all day.

Statira said, "I think it's been a very warm fall," and 'Manda Grier said, "I think the summer's goin' to spend the winter with us," and they all three laughed.

"What speeches you do make, 'Manda Grier!" said Statira.

"Well, anything better than Quaker meetin', *I* say," retorted 'Manda Grier; and then they were all three silent, and Lemuel thought of his clothes, and how fashionably both of the girls were dressed.

"I guess," said Statira, "it'll be a pretty sickly winter, if it keeps along this way. They say a green Christmas makes a fat grave-yard."

"I guess you'll see the snow fly long before Christmas," said 'Manda Grier, "or Thanksgiving either."

"I guess so, too," said Lemuel, though he did not like to seem to take sides against Statira.

She laughed as if it were a good joke, and said, " 'Tain't but about a fortnight now till Thanksgiving, anyway."

"If it comes a good fall of snow before Thanksgivin', won't you come round and give us a sleigh-ride, Mr. Barker?" asked 'Manda Grier.

They all laughed at her audacity, and Lemuel said, Yes, he would; and she said, "We'll give you a piece of real Willoughby Center mince-pie, if you will."

They all laughed again.

" 'Manda Grier!" said Statira, in protest.

"Her folks sent her half a dozen last Thanksgivin'," persisted 'Manda Grier.

" *'Manda!*" pleaded Statira.

'Manda Grier sprang up and got Lemuel a folding-chair. "You ain't a bit comfortable in that stiff old thing, Mr. Barker."

Lemuel declared that he was perfectly comfortable, but she would not be contented till he had changed, and then she said, "Why don't you look after your company, S'tira Dudley? I should think you'd be ashamed."

Lemuel's face burned with happy shame, and Statira, who was as red as he was, stole a look at him, that seemed to say that there was no use trying to stop 'Manda Grier. But when she went on, "I don't know but it's the fashion to Willoughby Center," they both gave way again, and laughed more than ever, and Statira said, "*Well*, 'Manda Grier, what do you s'pose Mr. Barker'll think?"

She tried to be sober, but the wild girl set her and Lemuel off laughing when she retorted, "Guess he'll think what he did when he was brought up in court for highway robbery."

'Manda Grier sat upright in her chair, and acted as if she had merely spoken about the weather. He knew that she was talking that way just to break the ice, and though he would have given anything to be able to second her, he could not.

"How you do carry on, 'Manda Grier," said Statira, as helpless as he was.

"Guess I got a pretty good load to carry!" said 'Manda Grier.

They all now began to find their tongues a little, and Statira told how one season when her mother took boarders she had gone over to the Pastures with a party of summer-folks on a straw-ride and picked blueberries. She said she never saw the berries as thick as they were there.

Lemuel said he guessed he knew where the place was; but the fire had got into it last year, and there had not been a berry there this summer.

Statira said, "What a shame!" She said there were some Barkers over East Willoughby way; and she confessed that when he said his name was Barker, and he was from Willoughby Pastures, that night in the station, she thought she should have gone through the floor.

Then they talked a little about how they had both felt, but not very much, and they each took all the blame, and would not allow that the other was the least to blame. Statira said she had behaved like a perfect coot all the way through, and Lemuel said that he guessed he had been the coot, if there was any.

"I guess there was a pair of you," said 'Manda Grier; and at this association of them in 'Manda Grier's condemnation, he could see that Statira was blushing, though she hid her face in her hands, for her ears were all red.

He now rose and said he guessed he would have to be going; but when 'Manda Grier interposed and asked, "Why, what's your hurry?" he said he guessed he had not had any, and Statira laughed at the wit of this till it seemed to him she would perish.

"Well, then, you set right straight down again," said 'Manda Grier, with mock severity, as if he were an obstinate little boy; and he obeyed, though he wished that Statira had asked him to stay too.

"Why, the land sakes!" exclaimed 'Manda Grier, "have you been lettin' him keep his hat all this while, S'tira Dudley? You take it right away from him!" And Statira rose, all smiling and blushing, and said:

"Will you let me take your hat, Mr. Barker?" as if he had just come in, and made him feel as if she had pressed him to stay. She took it and went and laid it on a stand across the room, and Lemuel thought he had never seen a much more graceful person. She wore a full Breton skirt, which was gathered thickly at the hips, and swung loose and free as she stepped. When she came back and sat down, letting the back of one pretty hand fall into the palm of the other in her lap, it seemed to him impossible that such an elegant young lady should be tolerating a person dressed as he was.

"There!" began 'Manda Grier. "*I* guess Mr. Barker won't object a great deal to our going on, if it *is* Sunday. 'S kind of a Sunday game, anyways. You 'posed to games on Sunday?"

"I don't know as I am," said Lemuel.

"Now, 'Manda Grier, don't you!" pleaded Statira.

"Shall, too!" persisted 'Manda. "I guess if there's any harm in the key, there ain't any harm in the Bible, and so it comes out even. D'you ever try your fate with a key and a Bible?" she asked Lemuel.

"I don't know as I did," he answered.

"Well, it's *real* fun, 'n' it's curious how it comes out, oftentimes. Well, *I* don't s'pose there's anything *in* it, but it *is* curious."

"I guess we hadn't better," said Statira. "I don't believe Mr. Barker'll care for it."

Lemuel said he would like to see how it was done, anyway.

'Manda Grier took the key out of the door, and looked at it. "That key'll cut the leaves all to pieces."

"Can't you find some other?" suggested Statira.

"I don't know but maybe I could," said 'Manda Grier. "You just wait a half a second."

Before Lemuel knew what she was doing, she flew out of the door, and he could hear her flying down the stairs.

"Well, I *must* say!" said Statira, and then neither she nor Lemuel said anything for a little while. At last she asked, "That window trouble you any?"

Lemuel said, "Not at all," and he added, "Perhaps it's too cold for you?"

"Oh, no," said the girl, "I can't seem to get anything too cold for me. I'm the greatest person for cold weather! I'm *real* glad it's comin' winter. We had the greatest *time*, last winter," continued Statira, "with those English sparrows. Used to feed 'em crumbs, there on the window-sill, and it seemed as if they got to know we girls, and they'd hop right inside, if you'd let 'em. Used to make me feel kind of creepy to have 'em. They say it's a sign of death to have a bird come into your room, and I was always for drivin' 'em out, but 'Manda, she said she guessed the Lord didn't take the trouble to send birds round to every one, and if the rule didn't work one way it didn't work the other. You believe in signs?"

"I don't know as I do, much. Mother likes to see the new moon over her right shoulder, pretty well," said Lemuel.

"Well, I declare," said Statira, "that's just the way with *my* aunt. Now you're up here," she said, springing suddenly to her feet, "I want you should see what a nice view we got from our window."

Lemuel had it on his tongue to say that he hoped it was not going to be his last chance; he believed he would have said it if 'Manda Grier had been there; but now he only joined Statira at the window, and looked out. They had to stoop over, and get pretty close together, to see the things she wished to show him, and she kept shrugging her sack on, and once she touched him with her shoulder. He said yes to everything she asked him about the view, but he saw very little of it. He saw that her hair had a shade of gold in its brown, and that it curled in tight little rings where it was cut on her neck, and that her skin was very white under it. When she touched him, that time, it made him feel very strange; and when she glanced at him out of her blue eyes, he did not know what he was doing. He did not laugh as he did when 'Manda Grier was there.

Statira said, "Oh, excuse me!" when she touched him, and

he answered, "Perfectly excusable," but he said hardly anything else. He liked to hear her talk, and he watched the play of her lips as she spoke. Once her breath came across his cheek, when she turned quickly to see if he was looking where she was pointing.

They sat down and talked, and all at once Statira exclaimed, "*Well!* I should think 'Manda Grier was *makin'* that key!"

Now, whatever happened, Lemuel was bound to say, "I don't think she's been gone very long."

"Well, you're pretty patient, I *must* say," said Statira, and he did not know whether she was making fun of him or not. He tried to think of something to say, but could not. "I hope she'll fetch a lamp, too, when she comes," Statira went on, and now he saw that it was beginning to be a little darker. Perhaps that about the lamp was a hint for him to go; but he did not see exactly how he could go till 'Manda Grier came back; he felt that it would not be polite.

"Well, there!" said Statira, as if she divined his feeling. "I shall give 'Manda Grier a *good* talking-to. I'm awfully afraid we're keeping you, Mr. Barker."

"Not at all," said Lemuel; "I'm afraid I'm keeping *you.*"

"Oh, not at all," said Statira. She became rather quieter, till 'Manda Grier came back.

'Manda Grier burst into the room, with a key in one hand and a lamp in the other. "Well, I knew you two'd be holdin' Quaker's meetin'."

"We hain't at all! How d'you know we have? Have we, Mr. Barker?" returned Statira, in simultaneous admission and denial.

"Well, if you want to know, I listened outside the door," said 'Manda Grier, "and you wa'n't sayin' a word, either of you. I guess I got a key now that'll do," she added, setting down her lamp, "and I borrowed an old Bible 't I guess 'tain't go'n' to hurt a great deal."

"I don't know as I want to play it much," said Statira.

"Well, I guess you got to, now," said 'Manda Grier, "after all my trouble. Hain't she, Mr. Barker?"

It flattered Lemuel through and through to be appealed to, but he could not say anything.

"Well," said Statira, "if I got to, I got to. But you got to hold the Bible."

"You got to put the key in!" cried 'Manda Grier. She sat holding the Bible open toward Statira.

She offered to put the key in, and then she stopped. "Well! I'm great! Who are we going to find it for first?"

"Oh, company first," said 'Manda Grier.

"You company, Mr. Barker?" asked Statira, looking at Lemuel over her shoulder.

"I hope not," said Lemuel, gallantly, at last.

"Well, I declare!" said Statira.

"Quite one the family," said 'Manda Grier, and that made Statira say, " 'Manda!" and Lemuel blush to his hair. "Well, anyway," continued 'Manda Grier, "you're company enough to have your fate found first. Put in the key, S'tira."

"No, I sha'n't do it."

"Well, *I* shall, then!" She took the key from Statira, and shut the book upon it at the Song of Solomon, and bound it tightly in with a ribbon. Lemuel watched breathlessly; he was not sure that he knew what kind of fate she meant, but he thought he knew, and it made his heart beat quick. 'Manda Grier had passed the ribbon through the ring of the key, which was left outside of the leaves, and now she took hold of the key with her two forefingers. "You got to be careful not to touch the Bible with your fingers," she explained, "or the charm won't work. Now I'll say over two verses, 't where the key's put in, and Mr. Barker, you got to repeat the alphabet at the same time; and when it comes to the first letter of the right name, the Bible will drop out of my fingers, all I can do. Now, then! *Set me as a seal on thine heart——*"

"A, B, C, D," began Lemuel.

"Pshaw, now, 'Manda Grier, you stop!" pleaded Statira.

"You be still! Go on, Mr. Barker!—*As a seal upon thine arm; for love is as strong as death*—don't say the letters so fast —*jealousy as cruel as the grave*—don't look at S'tira; look at me!—*the coals thereof are coals of fire*—you're sayin' it too slow now—*which hath a most vehement flame*. I declare, S'tira Dudley, if you joggle me!—*Many waters cannot quench love; neither can the floods drown it*—you must put just so much time between every letter; if you stop on every particular one, it ain't fair—*if a man would give all the substance of his house for love*—you stop laughin', you two!—*it would be utterly consumed*. Well, there! Now we got to go it all over again, and my arm's most broke *now*."

"I don't believe Mr. Barker wants to do it again," said Statira, looking demurely at him; but Lemuel protested that he did, and the game began again. This time the Bible began to shake at the letter D, and Statira cried out, "Now, 'Manda Grier, you're making it," and 'Manda Grier laughed so that she could scarcely hold the book. Lemuel laughed too; but he kept on repeating the letters. At S the book fell to the floor, and Statira caught it up, and softly beat 'Manda Grier on the back with it. "Oh, you mean thing!" she cried out. "You did it on purpose."

'Manda Grier was almost choked with laughing.

"Do you know anybody of the name of Sarah, Mr. Barker?" she gasped, and then they all laughed together till Statira said, "Well, I shall surely die! Now, 'Manda Grier, it's your turn. And you see if I don't pay you up."

"I guess I ain't afraid any," retorted 'Manda Grier. "The book'll do what it pleases, in spite of you."

They began again, Statira holding the book this time, and Lemuel repeating as before, and he went quite through the alphabet without anything happening. "Well, I declare!" said Statira, looking grave. "Let's try it over again."

"You may try, and you may try, and you may try," said 'Manda Grier. "It won't do you any good. I hain't got any fate in that line."

"Well, that's what we're goin' to find out," said Statira; but again the verses and alphabet were repeated without effect.

"Now you satisfied?" asked 'Manda Grier.

"No, not yet. Begin again, Mr. Barker!"

He did so, and at the second letter the book dropped. Statira jumped up, and 'Manda Grier began to chase her round the room, to box her ears for her, she said. Lemuel sat looking on. He did not feel at all severe toward them, as he usually did toward girls that cut up; he did not feel that this was cutting up, in fact.

"Stop, stop!" implored Statira, "and I'll let you try it over again."

"No, it's your turn now!"

"No, I ain't going to have any," said Statira, folding her arms.

"You got to," said 'Manda Grier. "The rest of us has, and now you've got to. Hain't she got to, Mr. Barker?"

"Yes," said Lemuel, delightedly; "you've got to, Miss Dudley."

"Miss Dudley!" repeated 'Manda Grier. "How that *does* sound."

"I don't know as it sounds any worse than Mr. Barker," said Lemuel.

"Well," said 'Manda Grier, judicially, "I sh'd think it was 'bout time they was both of 'em dropped. 'T any rate, I don't want you should call me Miss Grier—Lemuel."

"Oh!" cried S'tira. "Well, you *are* getting along, 'Manda Grier!"

"Well, don't you let yourself be outdone, then, S'tira."

"I guess Mr. Barker's good enough for me awhile yet," said Statira, and she hastened to add, "The name, I mean," and at this they all laughed till Statira said, "I shall *certainly* die!" She suddenly recovered herself—those girls seemed to do everything like lightning, Lemuel observed—and said, "No, I ain't goin' to have mine told at all. I don't like it. Seems kind of wicked. I ruther talk. I never *could* make it just right to act so with the Bible."

Lemuel was pleased at that. Statira seemed prettier than ever in this mood of reverence.

"Well, don't talk too much when I'm gone," said 'Manda Grier, and before anybody could stop her, she ran out of the room. But she put her head in again to say, "I'll be back as soon's I can take this key home."

Lemuel did not know what to do. The thought of being alone with Statira again was full of rapture and terror. He was glad when she seized the door, and tried to keep 'Manda Grier.

"I—I—guess I better be going," he said.

"You sha'n't go till I get back, anyway," said 'Manda Grier hospitably. "You keep him, S'tira!"

She gave Statira a little push, and ran down the stairs.

Statira tottered against Lemuel, with that round, soft shoulder which had touched him before. He put out his arms to save her from falling, and they seemed to close round her of themselves. She threw up her face, and in a moment he had kissed her. He released her and fell back from her aghast.

She looked at him.

"I—I didn't mean to," he panted. His heart was thundering in his ears.

She put up her hands to her face, and began to cry.

"Oh, my goodness!" he gasped. He wavered a moment, then he ran out of the room.

On the stairs he met 'Manda Grier coming up. "Now, Mr. Barker, you're real mean to go!" she pouted.

"I guess I better be going," Lemuel called back, in a voice so husky that he hardly knew it for his own.

XII

LEMUEL let himself into Miss Vane's house with his key to the back gate, and sat down, still throbbing, in his room over the L, and tried to get the nature of his deed, or misdeed, before his mind. He had grown up to manhood in an austere reverence for himself as regarded the other sex, and in a secret fear, as exacting for them as it was worshipful, of women. His mother had held all show of love-sickness between young people in scorn; she said they were silly things, when she saw them soft upon one another; and Lemuel had imbibed from her a sense of unlawfulness, of shame, in the love-making he had seen around him all his life. These things are very open in the country. Even in large villages they have kissing-games at the children's parties, in the church vestries and refectories; and as a little boy Lemuel had taken part in such games. But as he grew older, his reverence and his fear would not let him touch a girl. Once a big girl, much older than he, came up behind him in the play-ground and kissed him; he rubbed the kiss off with his hand, and scoured the place with sand and gravel. One winter all the big boys and girls at school began courting whenever the teacher was out of sight a moment; at the noon-spell, some of them sat with their arms round one another. Lemuel wandered off by himself in the snows of the deep woods; the sight of such things, the thought of them, put him to shame for those fools, as he tacitly called them; and now what had he done himself? He could not tell. At times he was even proud and glad of it; and then he did not know what would become of him. But mostly it seemed to him that he had been guilty of an enormity that nothing could ever excuse. He must have been crazy to do such a thing to a young lady like that; her tear-stained face looked her wonder at him still.

By this time she had told 'Manda Grier all about it; and he dared not think what their thoughts of him must be. It seemed to him that he ought to put such a monster as he was out of the world. But all the time there was a sweetness, a joy in his heart, that made him half frantic with fear of himself.

"Lemuel!"

He started up at the sound of Sibyl Vane's voice calling to him from the dining-room which opened into the L.

"Yes, ma'am," he answered tremulously, going to his door. Miss Vane had been obliged to instruct him to say ma'am to her niece, whom he had at first spoken of by her Christian name.

"Was that you came in a little while ago?"

"Yes, ma'am, I came in."

"Oh! And have you had your supper?"

"I—I guess I don't want any supper."

"Don't want any supper? You will be ill. Why don't you?"

"I don't know as I feel just like eating anything."

"Well, it won't do. Will you see, please, if Jane is in the kitchen?"

Lemuel came forward, full of his unfitness for the sight of men, but gathering a little courage when he found the dining-room so dark. He descended to the basement and opened the door of the kitchen, looked in, and shut it again. "Yes, ma'am, she's there."

"Oh!" Sibyl seemed to hesitate. Then she said: "Light the gas down there, hadn't you better?"

"I don't know but I had," Lemuel assented.

But before he could obey, "And Lemuel!" she called down again, "come and light it up here too, please."

"I will, as soon as I've lit it here," said Lemuel.

An imperious order came back. "You will light it here *now*, please."

"All right," assented Lemuel. When he appeared in the upper entry and flashed the gas up, he saw Sibyl standing at the reception-room door, with her finger closed into a book which she had been reading.

"You're not to say that you will do one thing when you're told to do another."

Lemuel whitened a little round the lips. "I'm not to do two things at once, either, I suppose."

Sibyl ignored this reply. "Please go and get your supper, and when you've had it come up here again. I've some things for you to do."

"I'll do them now," said Lemuel fiercely. "I don't want any supper, and I sha'n't eat any."

"Why, Lemuel, what is the matter with you?" asked the girl, in the sudden effect of motherly solicitude. "You look very strange, you seem so excited."

"I'm not hungry, that's all," said the boy doggedly. "What is it you want done?"

"Won't you please go up to the third floor," said Sibyl, in a phase of timorous dependence, "and see if everything is right there? I thought I heard a noise. See if the windows are fast, won't you?"

Lemuel turned, and she followed with her finger in her book, and her book pressed to her heart, talking. "It seemed to me that I heard steps and voices. It's very mysterious. I suppose any one could plant a ladder on the roof of the L part, and get into the windows if they were not fastened."

"Have to be a pretty long ladder," grumbled Lemuel.

"Yes," Sibyl assented, "it would. And it didn't sound exactly like burglars."

She followed him half-way up the second flight of stairs, and stood there while he explored the third story throughout.

"There ain't anything there," he reported without looking at her, and was about to pass her on the stairs in going down.

"Oh, thank you very much, Lemuel," she said, with fervent gratitude in her voice. She fetched a tremulous sigh. "I suppose it was nothing. Yes," she added hoarsely, "it must have been nothing. Oh, let *me* go down first!" she cried, putting out her hand to stop him from passing her. She resumed when they reached the ground floor again. "Aunty has gone out, and Jane was in the kitchen, and it began to grow dark while I sat reading in the drawing-room, and all at once I heard the strangest *noise*." Her voice dropped deeply on the last word. "Yes, it was very strange, indeed! Thank you, Lemuel," she concluded.

"Quite welcome," said Lemuel dryly, pushing on towards the basement stairs.

"Oh! And Lemuel! will you let Jane give you your supper in the dining-room, so that you could be here if I heard anything else?"

"I don't want any supper," said Lemuel.

The girl scrutinized him with an expression of misgiving. Then, with a little sigh, as of one who will not explore a painful mystery, she asked: "Would you mind sitting in the dining-room, then, till aunty gets back?"

"I'd just as lives sit there," said Lemuel, walking into the dark dining-room and sitting down.

"Oh, thank you very much. Aunty will be back very soon, I suppose. She's just gone to the Sewells' to tea."

She followed him to the threshold. "You must—I must— light the gas in here, for you."

"Guess I can light the gas," said Lemuel, getting up to intercept her in this service. She had run into the reception-room for a match, and she would not suffer him to prevent her.

"No, no! I insist! And Lemuel," she said, turning upon him, "I must ask you to excuse my speaking harshly to you. I was— agitated."

"Perfectly excusable," said Lemuel.

"I am afraid," said the girl, fixing him with her eyes, "that you are not well."

"Oh, yes, I'm well. I'm—pretty tired; that's all."

"Have you been walking far?"

"Yes—not very."

"The walking ought to do you good," said Sibyl with serious thoughtfulness. "I think," she continued, "you had better have some bryonia. Don't you think you had?"

"No, no! I don't want anything," protested Lemuel.

She looked at him with a feeling of baffled anxiety painted on her face; and as she turned away, she beamed with a fresh inspiration. "I will get you a book." She flew into the reception-room and back again, but she only had the book that she had herself been reading.

"Perhaps you would like to read this? I've finished it. I was just looking back through it."

"Thank you; I guess I don't want to read any, just now."

She leaned against the side of the dining-table, beyond which Lemuel sat, and searched his fallen countenance with a glance contrived to be at once piercing and reproachful. "I see," she said, "you have not forgiven me."

"Forgiven you?" repeated Lemuel blankly.

"Yes—for giving way to my agitation in speaking to you."

"I don't know," said Lemuel, with a sigh of deep inward trouble, "as I noticed anything."

"I told you to light the gas in the basement," suggested Sibyl, "and then I told you to light it up here, and then—I scolded you."

"Oh, yes," admitted Lemuel: "that." He dropped his head again.

Sibyl sank upon the edge of a chair. "Lemuel! you have something on your mind!"

The boy looked up with a startled face.

"Yes! I can see that you have," pursued Sibyl. "What have you been doing?" she demanded sternly.

Lemuel was so full of the truth that it came first to his lips in all cases. He could scarcely force it aside now with the evasion that availed him nothing. "I don't know as I've been doing anything in particular."

"I see that you don't wish to tell me!" cried the girl. "But you might have trusted me. I would have defended you, no matter what you had done—the worse the better."

Lemuel hung his head without answering.

After a while she continued: "If I had been that girl who had you arrested, and I had been the cause of so much suffering to an innocent person, I should never have forgiven myself. I should have devoted my life to expiation. I should have spent my life in going about the prisons, and finding out persons who were unjustly accused. I should have done it as a penance. Yes! even if he had been guilty!"

Lemuel remained insensible to this extreme of self-sacrifice, and she went on: "This book—it is a story—is all one picture of such a nature. There is a girl who's been brought up as the ward of a young man. He educates her, and she expects to be his wife, and he turns out to be perfectly false and unworthy in every way; but she marries him all the same, although she likes some one else, because she feels that she ought to punish herself for thinking of another, and because she hopes that she will die soon, and when her guardian finds out what she's done for him, it will reform him. It's perfectly sublime. It's—ennobling! If every one could read this book, they would be very different."

"I don't see much sense in it," said Lemuel, goaded to this comment.

"You would if you read it. When she dies—she is killed by a fall from her horse in hunting, and has just time to join the hands of her husband and the man she liked first, and tell them everything—it is wrought up so that you hold your breath. I suppose it was reading that that made me think there were burglars getting in. But perhaps you're right not to read it now, if you're excited already. I'll get you something cheerful." She whirled out of the room and back in a series of those swift, nervous movements peculiar to her. "There! that will amuse you, I know." She put the book down on the table before Lemuel, who silently submitted to have it left there.

"It will distract your thoughts, if anything will. And I shall ask you to let me sit just here in the reception-room, so that I can call you if I feel alarmed."

"All right," said Lemuel, lapsing absently to his own troubled thoughts.

"Thank you very much," said Sibyl. She went away, and came back directly. "Don't you think," she asked, "that it's very strange you should never have seen or heard anything of her?"

"Heard of who?" he asked, dragging himself painfully up from the depths of his thoughts.

"That heartless girl who had you arrested."

"She *wasn't* heartless!" retorted Lemuel indignantly.

"You think so because you are generous, and can't imagine such heartlessness. Perhaps," added Sibyl, with the air of being illumined by a happy thought, "she is dead. That would account for everything. She may have died of remorse. It probably preyed upon her till she couldn't bear it any longer, and then she killed herself."

Lemuel began to grow red at the first apprehension of her meaning. As she went on, he changed color more and more.

"She is alive!" cried Sibyl. "She's alive, and you have seen her! You needn't deny it! You've seen her to-day!"

Lemuel rose in clumsy indignation. "I don't know as anybody's got any right to say what I've done, or haven't done."

"Oh, Lemuel!" cried Sibyl. "Do you think any one in this house would intrude in your affairs? But if you need a friend —a sister——"

"I don't need any sister. I want you should let me alone."

At these words, so little appreciative of her condescension, her romantic beneficence, her unselfish interest, Sibyl suddenly rebounded to her former level, which she was sensible was far above that of this unworthy object of her kindness. She rose from her chair, and pursued:

"If you need a friend—a sister—I'm sure that you can safely confide in—the cook." She looked at him a moment, and broke into a malicious laugh very unlike that of a social reformer, which rang shriller at the bovine fury which mounted to Lemuel's eyes. The rattle of a night-latch made itself heard in the outer door. Sibyl's voice began to break, as it rose: "I never expected to be treated in my own aunt's house with such perfect ingratitude and impudence—yes, impudence!— by one of her servants!"

She swept out of the room, and her aunt, who entered it, after calling to her in vain, stood with Lemuel, and heard her mount the stairs, sobbing, to her own room, and lock herself in.

"What is the matter, Lemuel?" asked Miss Vane, breathing quickly. She looked at him with the air of a judge who would not condemn him unheard, but would certainly do so after hearing him. Whether it was Lemuel's perception of this that kept him silent, or his confusion of spirit from all the late rapidly successive events, or a wish not to inculpate the girl who had insulted him, he remained silent.

"Answer me!" said Miss Vane sharply.

Lemuel cleared his throat. "I don't know as I've got anything to say," he answered finally.

"But I *insist* upon your saying something," said Miss Vane. "What is this *impudence?*"

"There hasn't been any impudence," replied Lemuel, hanging his head.

"Very well, then, you can tell me what Sibyl means," persisted Miss Vane.

Lemuel seemed to reflect upon it. "No, I can't tell you," he said at last, slowly and gently.

"You refuse to make any explanation whatever?"

"Yes."

Miss Vane rose from the chair which she had mechanically sunk into while waiting for him to speak, and ceased to be the kindly, generous soul she was, in asserting herself as a gentlewoman who had a contumacious servant to treat with. "You will wait here a moment, please."

"All right," said Lemuel. She had asked him not to receive instructions from her with that particular answer, but he could not always remember.

She went upstairs, and returned with some bank-notes that rustled in her trembling hand. "It is two months since you came, and I've paid you one month," she said, and she set her lips, and tried to govern her head, which nevertheless shook with the vehemence she was struggling to repress. She laid two ten-dollar notes upon the table, and then added a five, a little apart. "This second month was to be twenty instead of ten. I shall not want you any longer, and should be glad to have you go now—at once—to-night! But I had intended to offer you a little present at Christmas, and I will give it you now."

Lemuel took up the two ten-dollar notes without saying anything, and then after a moment laid one of them down. "It's only half a month," he said. "I don't want to be paid for any more than I've done."

"Lemuel!" cried Miss Vane. "I insist upon your taking it. I employed you by the month."

"It don't make any difference about that; I've only been here a month and a half."

He folded the notes, and turned to go out of the room. Miss Vane caught the five-dollar note from the table and intercepted him with it. "Well, then, you shall take it as a present."

"I don't want any present," said Lemuel, patiently waiting her pleasure to release him, but keeping his hands in his pockets.

"You would have taken it at Christmas," said Miss Vane. "You shall take it now."

"I shouldn't take a present any time," returned Lemuel steadily.

"You are a foolish boy!" cried Miss Vane. "You need it, and I tell you to take it."

He made no reply whatever.

"You are behaving very stubbornly—ungratefully," said Miss Vane.

Lemuel lifted his head; his lip quivered a little. "I don't think you've got any right to say I'm ungrateful."

"I don't mean ungrateful," said Miss Vane. "I mean unkind—very silly, indeed. And I wish you to take this money. You are behaving resentfully—wickedly. I am much older than you, and I tell you that you are not behaving rightly. Why don't you do what I wish?"

"I don't want any money I haven't earned."

"I don't mean the money. Why don't you tell me the meaning of what I heard? My niece said you had been impudent to her. Perhaps she didn't understand."

She looked wistfully into the boy's face.

After a long time he said, "I don't know as I've got anything to say about it."

"Very well, then, you may *go*," said Miss Vane, with all her hauteur.

"Well, good-evening," said Lemuel passively, but the eyes that he looked at her with were moist, and conveyed a pathetic reproach. To her unmeasured astonishment, he offered her his hand; her amaze was even greater—*more* infinite, as she afterwards told Sewell—when she found herself shaking it.

He went out of the room, and she heard him walking about in his room in the L, putting together his few belongings. Then she heard him go down and open the furnace-door, and she knew he was giving a final conscientious look at the fire. He closed it, and she heard him close the basement door behind him, and knew that he was gone.

She explored the L, and then she descended to the basement and mechanically looked it over. Everything that could be counted hers by the most fastidious sense of property had been left behind him in the utmost neatness. On their accustomed nail, just inside the furnace-room, hung the blue overalls. They looked like a suicidal Lemuel hanging there.

Miss Vane went upstairs slowly, with a heavy heart. Under

the hall light stood Sibyl, picturesque in the deep shadow it flung upon her face.

"Aunt Hope," she began in a tragic voice.

"Don't *speak* to me, you wicked girl!" cried her aunt, venting her self-reproach upon this victim. "It is *your* doing."

Sibyl turned with the meekness of an ostentatious scapegoat unjustly bearing the sins of her tribe, and went upstairs into the wilderness of her own thoughts again.

XIII

THE SENSE of outrage with which Lemuel was boiling when
Miss Vane came in upon Sibyl and himself had wholly passed
away, and he now saw his dismissal, unjust as between that
girl and him, unimpeachably righteous as between him and
the moral frame of things. If he had been punished for being
ready to take advantage of that fellow's necessity, and charge
him fifty cents for changing ten dollars, he must now be no
less obviously suffering for having abused that young lady's
trust and defenselessness; only he was not suffering one-tenth
as much. When he recurred to that wrong, in fact, and tried
to feel sorry for it and ashamed, his heart thrilled in a curious
way; he found himself smiling and exulting, and Miss Vane
and her niece went out of his mind, and he could not think
of anything but of being with that girl, of hearing her talk
and laugh, of touching her. He sighed; he did not know what
his mother would say if she knew; he did not know where he
was going; it seemed a hundred years since the beginning of
the afternoon.

A horse-car came by, and Lemuel stopped it. He set his bag
down on the platform, and stood there near the conductor,
without trying to go inside, for the bag was pretty large, and
he did not believe the conductor would let him take it in.

The conductor said politely after a while, "See, 'd I get
your fare?"

"No," said Lemuel. He paid, and the conductor went inside and collected the other fares.

When he came back he took advantage of Lemuel's continued presence to have a little chat. He was a short, plump, stubby-mustached man, and he looked strong and well, but he said, with an introductory sigh, "Well, sir, I get sore all over at this business. There ain't a bone in me that hain't got an ache in it. Sometimes I can't tell but what it's the ache got a bone in it, ache seems the biggest."

"Why, what makes it?" asked Lemuel, absently.

"Oh, it's this standin'; it's the hours, and changin' the hours so much. You hain't got a chance to get used to one set o' hours before they get 'em all shifted round again. Last week I was on from eight to eight; this week it's from twelve to twelve. Lord knows what it's going to be next week. And this is one o' the best lines in town, too."

"I presume they pay you pretty well," said Lemuel, with awakening interest.

"Well, they pay a dollar 'n' half a day," said the conductor.

"Why, it's more than forty dollars a month," said Lemuel.

"Well, it is," said the conductor scornfully, "if you work every day in the week. But I can't stand it more than six days out o' seven; and if you miss a day, or if you miss a trip, they dock you. No, sir. It's about the meanest business *I* ever struck. If I wa'n't a married man, 'n' if I didn't like to be regular about my meals and get 'em at home 'th my wife, I wouldn't stand it a minute. But that's where it is. It's regular."

A lady from within signaled the conductor. He stopped the car, and the lady, who had risen with her escort, remained chatting with a friend before she got out. The conductor snapped his bell for starting, with a look of patient sarcasm. "See that?" he asked Lemuel. "Some these women act as if the cars was their private carriage; and *you* got to act so *too*, or the lady complains of you, and the company bounces you in a minute. Stock's owned along the line, and they think they own *you* too. You can't get 'em to set more than ten on a side; they'll leave the car first. I'd like to catch 'em on some

the South End or Cambridge cars; I'd show 'em how to pack
live stock once, anyway. Yes, sir, these ladies that ride on this
line think they can keep the car standin' while they talk about
the opera. But you'd ought to see how they all look if a *poor*
woman tries their little game. Oh, I tell you, rich people are
hard."

Lemuel reflected upon the generalization. He regarded
Miss Vane as a rich person; but though she had blamed him
unjustly, and had used him impatiently, even cruelly, in this
last affair, he remembered other things, and he said:

"Well, I don't know as I should say all of them were hard."

"Well, maybe not," admitted the conductor. "But I don't
envy 'em. The way I look at it, and the way I tell my wife, I
wouldn't want their money 'f I had to have the rest of it.
Ain't any of 'em happy. I saw that when I lived out. No, sir;
what me and my wife want to do is to find us a nice little place
in the country."

At the words a vision of Willoughby Pastures rose upon
Lemuel, and a lump of homesickness came into his throat.
He saw the old wood-colored house, crouching black within
its walls under the cold November stars. If his mother had
not gone to bed yet, she was sitting beside the cooking-stove
in the kitchen, and perhaps his sister was brewing something
on it, potion or lotion, for her husband's rheumatism. Miss
Vane had talked to him about his mother; she had said he
might have her down to visit him, if everything went on right;
but of course he knew that Miss Vane did not understand
that his mother wore bloomers, and he made up his mind
that her invitation was never to be accepted. At the same
time he had determined to ask Miss Vane to let him go up
and see his mother some Sunday.

" 'S fur's we go," said the conductor. " 'F you're goin' on,
you want to take another car here."

"I guess I'll go back with you a little ways," said Lemuel.
"I want to ask you——"

"Guess we'll have to take a back seat, then," said the conductor, leading the way through the car to the other plat-

form; "or a standee," he added, snapping the bell. "What is it you want to ask?"

"Oh, nothing. How do you fellows learn to be conductors? How long does it take you?"

Till other passengers should come the conductor lounged against the guard of the platform in a conversational posture.

"Well, generally it takes you four or five days. You got to learn all the cross streets, and the principal places on all the lines."

"Yes?"

"It didn't take me more'n two. Boston boy."

"Yes," said Lemuel, with a fine discouragement. "I presume the conductors are mostly from Boston."

"They're from everywhere. And some of 'em are pretty streaked, I can tell you; and then the rest of us has got to suffer; throws suspicion on all of us. One fellow gets to stealin' fares, and then everybody's got to wear a bell-punch. I never hear mine go without thinkin' it says, 'Stop thief!' Makes me sick, I can tell you."

After a while Lemuel asked, "How do you get such a position?"

The conductor seemed to be thinking about something else. "It's a pretty queer kind of a world, anyway, the way everybody's mixed up with everybody else. What's the reason, if a man wants to steal, he can't steal and suffer for it himself, without throwin' the shame and the blame on a lot more people that never thought o' stealin'? I don't notice much when a fellow sets out to do right that folks think everybody else is on the square. No, sir, they don't seem to consider that kind of complaint so catching. Now, you take another thing: A woman goes round with the scarlet fever in her clothes, and a whole carful of people take it home to their children; but let a nice young girl get in, fresh as an apple, and a perfect daisy for wholesomeness every way, and she don't give it to a single soul on board. No, sir; it's a world I can't see through, nor begin to."

"I never thought of it that way," said Lemuel, darkened

by this black pessimism of the conductor. He had not, practically, found the world so unjust as the conductor implied, but he could not controvert his argument. He only said, "Maybe the right thing makes us feel good in some way we don't know of."

"Well, I don't want to feel good in some way I don't know of, myself," said the conductor very scornfully.

"No, that's so," Lemuel admitted. He remained silent, with a vague wonder flitting through his mind whether Mr. Sewell could make anything better of the case, and then settled back to his thoughts of Statira, pierced and confused as they were now with his pain from that trouble with Miss Vane.

"What was that you asked me just now?" said the conductor.

"That I asked you?" Lemuel echoed. "Oh, yes! I asked you how you got your place on the cars."

"Well, sir, you have to have recommendations—they won't touch you without 'em; and then you have to have about seventy-five dollars capital to start with. You got to get your coat, and your cap, and your badge, and you got to have about twenty dollars of your own to make change with, first off; company don't start you with a cent."

Lemuel made no reply. After a while he asked, "Do you know any good hotel, around here, where I could go for the night?"

"Well, there's the Brunswick, and there's the Van-dome," said the conductor. "They're both pretty fair houses." Lemuel looked round at the mention of the aristocratic hostelries to see if the conductor was joking. He owned to something of the kind by adding, "There's a little hotel, if you want something quieter, that ain't a great ways from here." He gave the name of the hotel, and told Lemuel how to find it.

"Thank you," said Lemuel. "I guess I'll get off here, then. Well, good-evening."

"Guess I'll have to get another nickel from you," said the conductor, snapping his bell. "New trip," he explained.

"Oh," said Lemuel, paying. It seemed to him a short ride for five cents.

He got off, and as the conductor started up the car, he called forward through it to the driver, "Wanted to try for conductor, I guess. But I guess the seventy-five dollars capital settled that little point for him."

Lemuel heard the voice but not the words. He felt his bag heavy in his hand as he walked away in the direction the conductor had given him, and he did not set it down when he stood hesitating in front of the hotel; it looked like too expensive a place for him, with its stained-glass door, and its bulk hoisted high into the air. He walked by the hotel, and then he came back to it, and mustered courage to go in. His bag, if not superb, looked a great deal more like baggage than the lank sack which he had come to Boston with; he had bought it only a few days before, in hopes of going home before long; he set it down with some confidence on the tessellated floor of cheap marble, and when a shirt-sleeved, drowsy-eyed, young man came out of a little room or booth near the door, where there was a desk, and a row of bells, and a board with keys, hanging from the wall above it, Lemuel said quite boldly that he would like a room. The man said, well, they did not much expect transients; it was more of a family-hotel, like; but he guessed they had a vacancy, and they could put him up. He brushed his shirt-sleeves down with his hands, and looked apologetically at some ashes on his trousers, and said, well, it was not much use trying to put on style, anyway, when you were taking care of a furnace and had to run the elevator yourself, and look after the whole concern. He said his aunt mostly looked after letting the rooms, but she was at church, and he guessed he should have to see about it himself. He bade Lemuel just get right into the elevator, and he put his bag into a cage that hung in one corner of the hallway, and pulled at the wire rope, and they mounted together. On the way up he had time to explain that the clerk, who usually ran the elevator when they had no elevator-boy, had kicked, and they were just between hay and grass, as you

might say. He showed Lemuel into a grandiose parlor or
drawing-room, enormously draped and upholstered, and furnished in a composite application of yellow jute and red
plush to the ashen easy-chairs and sofa. A folding-bed in the
figure of a chiffonier attempted to occupy the whole side of
the wall and failed.

"I'm afraid it's more than I can pay," said Lemuel. "I guess
I better see some other room." But the man said the room
belonged to a boarder that had just gone, and he guessed they
would not charge him very much for it; he guessed Lemuel
had better stay. He pulled the bed down, and showed him
how it worked, and he lighted two bulbous gas-burners, contrived to burn the gas at such a low pressure that they were
like two unsnuffed candles for brilliancy. He backed round
over the spacious floor and looked about him with an un-
familiar, marauding air, which had a certain boldness, but
failed to impart courage to Lemuel, who trembled for fear
of the unknown expense. But he was ashamed to go away,
and when the man left him he went to bed, after some suspicious investigation of the machine he was to sleep in. He
found its comfort unmistakable. He was tired out with what
had been happening, and the events of the day recurred in
a turmoil that helped rather than hindered slumber; none
evolved itself distinctly enough from the mass to pursue him;
what he was mainly aware of was the daring question whether
he could not get the place of that clerk who had kicked.

In the morning he saw the landlady, who was called Mrs.
Harmon, and who took the pay for his lodging, and said he
might leave his bag awhile there in the office. She was a
large, smooth, tranquil person, who seemed ready for any
sort of consent; she entered into an easy conversation with
Lemuel, and was so sympathetic in regard to the difficulties
of getting along in the city, that he had proposed himself as
clerk and been accepted almost before he believed the thing
had happened. He was getting a little used to the rapidity of
urban transactions, but his mind had still a rustic difficulty
in keeping up with his experiences.

"I suppose," said Mrs. Harmon, "it ain't very usual to take anybody without a reference; I never do it; but so long as you haven't been a great while in the city—You ever had a place in Boston before?"

"Well, not exactly what you may call a place," said Lemuel, with a conscience against describing in that way his position at Miss Vane's. "It was only part work." He added, "I wasn't there but a little while."

"Know anybody in the city?"

"Yes," said Lemuel, reluctantly; "I know Rev. David L. Sewell, some."

"Oh, all right," said Mrs. Harmon, with eager satisfaction. "I have to be pretty particular who I have in the house. The boarders are all high-class, and I have to have all the departments accordingly. I'll see Mr. Sewell about you as soon as I get time, and I guess you can take hold right now, if you want to."

Mrs. Harmon showed him in half a minute how to manage the elevator, and then left him with general instructions to tell everybody who came upon any errand he did not understand, that she would be back in a very short time. He found pen and paper in the office, and she said he might write the letter that he asked leave to send his mother; when he mentioned his mother, she said, yes, indeed, with a burst of maternal sympathy which was imagined in her case, for she had already told Lemuel that if she had ever had any children she would not have gone into the hotel business, which she believed unfriendly to their right nurture; she said she never liked to take ladies with children.

He inclosed some money to his mother which he had intended to send, but which, before the occurrence of the good fortune that now seemed opening upon him, he thought he must withhold. He made as little as he could of his parting with Miss Vane, whom he had celebrated in earlier letters to his mother; he did not wish to afflict her on his own account, or incense her against Miss Vane, who, he felt, could not help her part in it; but his heart burned anew against Miss Sibyl while he wrote. He dwelt upon his good luck in getting this new position at once, and he let his mother see that he considered it a rise in life. He said he was going to try to get Mrs. Harmon to let him go home for Thanksgiving, though he presumed he might have to come back the same night.

His letter was short, but he was several times interrupted by the lady boarders, many of whom stopped to ask Mrs. Harmon something on their way to their rooms from breakfast. They did not really want anything, in most cases; but they were strict with Lemuel in wanting to know just when they could see Mrs. Harmon; and they delayed somewhat to satisfy a natural curiosity in regard to him. They made talk with him as he took them up in the elevator, and did what they could to find out about him. Most of them had their door-keys in their hands, and dangled them by the triangular pieces of brass which the keys were chained to; they affected some sort of *négligée* breakfast costume, and Lemuel thought them very fashionable. They nearly all snuffled and whined as they spoke; some had a soft, lazy nasal; others broke abruptly from silence to silence in voices of nervous sharpness, like the cry or the bleat of an animal; one young girl, who was quite pretty, had a high, hoarse voice, like a gander.

Lemuel did not mind all this; he talked through his nose too; and he accepted Mrs. Harmon's smooth characterization of her guests, as she called them, which she delivered in a slow, unimpassioned voice. "I never have any but the highest class people in my house—the very nicest; and I never have any jangling going on. In the first place, I never allow anybody to have anything to complain of, and then if they do complain, I'm right up and down with them; I tell them their rooms are wanted, and they understand what I mean. And I never allow any trouble among the servants; I tell them, if they are not suited, that I don't want them to stay; and if they get to quarreling among themselves, I send them all away, and get a new lot; I pay the highest wages, and I can always do it. If you want to keep up with the times at all, you have got to set a good table, and I mean to set just as good a table as any in Boston; I don't intend to let any one complain of my house on that score. Well, it's as broad as it's long: if you set a good table, you can ask a good price; and if you don't, you can't, that's all. Pay as you go, is my motto."

Mrs. Harmon sat talking in the little den beside the door which she called the office, when she returned from that absence which she had asked him to say would not be more than fifteen minutes at the outside. It had been something more than two hours, and it had ended almost clandestinely; but knowledge of her return had somehow spread through the house, and several ladies came in while she was talking, to ask when their window-shades were to be put up, or to say that they knew their gas-fixtures must be out of order; or that there were mice in their closets, for they had heard them gnawing; or that they were sure their set-bowls smelt, and that the traps were not working. Mrs. Harmon was prompt in every exigency. She showed the greatest surprise that those shades had not gone up yet; she said she was going to send round for the gas-fitter to look at the fixtures all over the house; and that she would get some potash to pour down the bowls, for she knew the drainage was perfect—it was just the pipes down *to* the traps that smelt; she advised a cat for the mice, and said she would get one. She used the greatest sympathy with the ladies, recognizing a real sufferer in each, and not attempting to deny anything. From the dining-room came at times the sound of voices, which blended in a discord loud above the clatter of crockery, but Mrs. Harmon seemed not to hear them. An excited foreigner of some sort finally rushed from this quarter, and thrust his head into the booth where Lemuel and Mrs. Harmon sat, long enough to explode some formula of renunciation upon her, which left her serenity unruffled. She received with the same patience the sarcasm of a boarder who appeared at the office-door with a bag in his hand, and said he would send an express-man for his trunk. He threw down the money for his receipted bill; and when she said she was sorry he was going, he replied that he could not stand the table any longer, and that he believed that French cook of hers had died on the way over; he was tired of the Nova Scotia temporary, who had become permanent.

A gentleman waited for the parting guest to be gone, and then said to the tranquil Mrs. Harmon: "So Mellen has kicked, has he?"

"Yes, Mr. Evans," said Mrs. Harmon; "Mr. Mellen has kicked."

"And don't you want to abuse him a little? You can to me, you know," suggested the gentleman.

He had a full beard, parted at the chin; it was almost white, and looked older than the rest of his face; his eyes were at once sad and whimsical. Lemuel tried to think where he had seen him before.

"Thank you; I don't know as it would do any good, Mr. Evans. But if he could have waited one week longer, I should have had that cook."

"Yes, that is what I firmly believe. Do you feel too much broken up to accept a ticket to the Wednesday matinée at the Museum?"

"No, I don't," said Mrs. Harmon. "But I shouldn't want to deprive Mrs. Evans of it."

"Oh, she wouldn't go," said Mr. Evans, with a slight sigh. "You had better take it. Jefferson's going to do *Bob Acres*."

"Is that so?" asked Mrs. Harmon placidly, taking the ticket. "Well, I'm ever so much obliged to you, Mr. Evans. Mr. Evans, Mr. Barker—our new clerk," she said, introducing them.

Lemuel rose with rustic awkwardness, and shook hands with Mr. Evans, who looked at him with a friendly smile, but said nothing.

"Now Mr. Barker is here, I guess I can get the time." Mr. Evans said, well, he was glad she could, and went out of the street-door. "He's just one of the nicest gentlemen I've got," continued Mrs. Harmon, following him with her eye as far as she conveniently could without turning her head, "him and his wife both. Ever heard of the 'Saturday Afternoon'?"

"I don't know as I have," said Lemuel.

"Well, he's one of the editors. It's a kind of a Sunday paper, I guess, for all it don't come out that day. I presume he could go every night in the week to every theater in town, if he wanted to. I don't know how many tickets he's give me. Some of the ladies seem to think he's always makin' fun of them; but I can't ever feel that way. He used to board with a great friend of mine, him and his wife. They've been with me now ever since Mrs. Hewitt died; she was the one they boarded with before. They say he used to be dreadful easy-going, 'n' 't his wife was all 't saved him. But I guess he's different now. Well, I must go out and see after the lunch. You watch the office and say just what I told you before."

XIV

SEWELL chanced to open his door to go out just as Miss Vane put her hand on the bell-pull, the morning after she had dismissed Lemuel. The cheer of his Monday face died out at the unsmiling severity of hers; but he contrived to ask her in, and said he would call Mrs. Sewell, if she would sit down in the reception-room a moment.

"I don't know," she said, with a certain look of inquiry, not unmixed with compassion. "It's about Lemuel."

The minister fetched a deep sigh. "Yes, I know it. But she will have to know it sooner or later." He went to the stairway and called her name, and then returned to Miss Vane in the reception-room.

"Has Lemuel been here?" she asked.

"No."

"You said you knew it was about him—"

"It was my bad conscience, I suppose, and your face that told me."

Miss Vane waited for Mrs. Sewell's presence before she unpacked her heart. Then she left nothing in it. She ended by saying, "I have examined and cross-examined Sibyl, but it's like cross-questioning a chameleon; she changed color with every new light she was put into." Here Miss Vane had got sorrowfully back to something more of her wonted humor, and laughed.

"Poor Sibyl!" said Mrs. Sewell.

"Poor?" retorted Miss Vane. "Not at all! I could get nothing out of either of them; but I feel perfectly sure that Lemuel was not to blame."

"It's very possible," suggested Mrs. Sewell, "that he did say something in his awkward way that she misconstrued into impertinence."

Miss Vane did not seem to believe this. "If Lemuel had given me the slightest satisfaction," she began in self-exculpation. "But no," she broke off. "It had to be!" She rose. "I thought I had better come and tell you at once, Mr. Sewell. I suppose you will want to look him up, and do something more for him. I wish if you find him you would make him take this note." She gave the minister a ten-dollar bill. "I tried to do so, but he would not have it. I don't know what I shall do without him! He is the best and most faithful creature in the world. Even in this little time I had got to relying implicitly upon his sense, his judgment, his goodness, his—— Well! good-morning!"

She ran out of the door, and left Sewell confronted with his wife.

He did not know whether she had left him to hope or to despair, and he waited for his wife to interpret his emotion, but Mrs. Sewell tacitly refused to do this. After a dreary interval he plucked a random cheerfulness out of space, and said: "Well, if Miss Vane feels in that way about it, I don't see why the whole affair can't be arranged and Barker reinstated."

"David," returned his wife, not vehemently at all, "when you come out with those mannish ideas I don't know what to do."

"Well, my dear," said the minister, "I should be glad to come out with some womanish ideas if I had them. I dare say they would be better. But I do my poor best, under the circumstances. What is the trouble with my ideas, except that the sex is wrong?"

"You think, you men," replied Mrs. Sewell, "that a thing like that can be mended up and smoothed over, and made

just the same as ever. You think that because Miss Vane is
sorry she sent Barker away and wants him back, she can take
him back."

"I don't see why she can't. I've sometimes supposed that the
very highest purpose of Christianity was mutual forgiveness
—forbearance with one another's errors."

"That's all very well," said Mrs. Sewell. "But you know
that whenever I have taken a cook back, after she had shown
temper, it's been an entire failure; and this is a far worse
case, because there is disappointed good-will mixed up with
it. I don't suppose Barker is at all to blame. Whatever has
happened, you may be perfectly sure that it has been partly
a bit of stage-play in Sibyl and partly a mischievous desire to
use her power over him. I foresaw that she would soon be
tired of reforming him. But whatever it is, it's something
that you can't repair. Suppose Barker went back to them;
could they ignore what's happened?"

"Of course not," Sewell admitted.

"Well, and should he ask her pardon, or she his?"

"The Socratic method is irresistible," said the minister
sadly. "You have proved that nothing can be done for Barker
with the Vanes. And now the question is, what *can* be done
for him?"

"That's something I must leave to you, David," said his
wife dispiritedly. She arose, and as she passed out of the room
she added, "You will have to find him, in the *first* place, and
you had better go round to the police stations and the tramps'
lodging-houses and begin looking."

Sewell sighed heavily under the sarcastic advice, but acted
upon it, and set forth upon the useless quest, because he did
not know in the least what else to do.

All that week Barker lay, a lurking discomfort, in his soul,
though as the days passed the burden grew undeniably lighter; Sewell had a great many things besides Barker to think
of. But when Sunday came, and he rose in his pulpit, he could
not help casting a glance of guilty fear toward Miss Vane's

pew and drawing a long breath of guilty relief not to see Lemuel in it. We are so made, that in the reaction the minister was able to throw himself into the matter of his discourse with uncommon fervor.

It was really very good matter, and he felt the literary joy in it which flatters the author even of a happily worded supplication to the Deity. He let his eyes, freed from their bondage to Lemuel's attentive face, roam at large in liberal ease over his whole congregation; and when, toward the close of his sermon, one visage began to grow out upon him from the two or three hundred others, and to concentrate in itself the facial expression of all the rest, and become the only countenance there, it was a perceptible moment before he identified it as that of his inalienable charge. Then he began to preach at it as usual, but defiantly, and with yet a haste to be through and to get speech with it that he felt was ludicrous, and must appear unaccountable to his hearers. It seemed to him that he could not bring his sermon to a close; he ended it in a cloudy burst of rhetoric which he feared would please the nervous, elderly ladies—who sometimes blamed him for a want of emotionality—and knew must grieve the judicious. While the choir was singing the closing hymn, he contrived to beckon the sexton to the pulpit, and described and located Lemuel to him as well as he could without actually pointing him out; he said that he wished to see that young man after church, and asked the sexton to bring him to his room. The sexton did so to the best of his ability, but the young man whom he brought was not Lemuel, and had to be got rid of with apologies.

On three or four successive Sundays Lemuel's face dawned upon the minister from the congregation, and tasked his powers of impersonal appeal and mental concentration to the utmost. It never appeared twice in the same place, and when at last Sewell had tutored the sexton carefully in Lemuel's dress, he was driven to despair one morning when he saw the boy sidling along between the seats in the gallery, and sitting down with an air of satisfaction in an entirely new suit of clothes.

After this defeat the sexton said with humorous sympathy, "Well, there ain't anything for it now, Mr. Sewell, but a detective. Or else an advertisement in the Personals."

Sewell laughed with him at his joke, and took what comfort he could from the evidence of prosperity which Lemuel's new clothes offered. He argued that if Barker could afford to buy them he could not be in immediate need, and for some final encounter with him he trusted in Providence, and was not too much cast down when his wife made him recognize that he was trusting in luck. It was an ordeal to look forward to finding Lemuel sooner or later among his hearers every Sunday; but having prepared his nerves for the shock, as men adjust their sensibilities to the recurrent pain of a disease, he came to bear it with fortitude, especially as he continually reminded himself that he had his fixed purpose to get at Lemuel at last and befriend him in any and every possible way. He tried hard to keep from getting a grudge against him.

At the hotel, Lemuel remained in much of his original belief in the fashion and social grandeur of the ladies who formed the majority of Mrs. Harmon's guests. Our womankind are prone to a sort of helpless intimacy with those who serve them; the ladies had an instinctive perception of Lemuel's trustiness, and readily gave him their confidence and much of their history. He came to know them without being at all able to classify them with reference to society at large, as of that large tribe among us who have revolted from domestic care, and have skillfully unseated the black rider who remains mounted behind the husband of the average lady-boarder. Some of them had never kept house, being young and newly married, though of this sort there were those who had tried it in flats, and had reverted to their natural condition of boarding. They advised Lemuel not to take a flat, whatever he did, unless he wanted to perish at once. Other lady boarders had broken up housekeeping during the first years of the war, and had been boarding round ever since, going from hotels in the city to hotels in the country, and back again with the change of the seasons; these mostly had husbands who had horses, and they talked with equal tenderness of the husbands and the horses, so that you could not always tell which Jim or Bob was; usually they had no children, but occasionally they had a married daughter, or a son who lived West. There were several single ladies: one who seemed to have nothing in this world to do but to come down to her meals, and another a physician who had not been able, in embracing the medical profession, to deny herself the girlish pleasure of her pet name, and was lettered in the list of guests in the entry as Dr. Cissie Bluff. In the attic, which had a north light favorable to their work, were two girls, who were studying art at the Museum; one of them looked delicate at first sight, and afterwards seemed merely very gentle, with a clear-eyed pallor which was not unhealth. A student in the Law School sat at the table with these girls, and seemed sometimes to go with them to concerts and lectures. From his talk, which was almost the only talk that made itself heard in the dining-room, it appeared that he was from Wyoming Territory; he treated the young ladies as representative of Boston and its prejudices, though apparently they were not Bostonians. There were several serious and retiring couples, of whom one or other was an invalid, and several who were poor, and preferred the plated gentility of Mrs. Harmon's hotel—it was called the St. Albans; Mrs. Harmon liked the name—to the genuine poverty of such housekeeping as they could have set up. About each of these women a home might have clung, with all its loves and cares; they were naturally like other women; but here they were ignoble particles, without attraction for one another, or apparently joy for themselves, impermanent, idle, listless; they had got rid of the trouble of housekeeping, and of its dignity and usefulness. There were a few children in the house, not at all noisy; the boys played on the sidewalk, and the little girls staid in their rooms with their mothers, and rarely took the air oftener than they.

They came down rather later to breakfast, and they seemed not to go to school; some of them had piano lessons in their rooms. Their mothers did not go out much; sometimes they went to church or the theater, and they went shopping. But they had apparently no more social than domestic life. Now and then they had a friend to lunch or dinner; if a lady was absent, it was known to Mrs. Harmon, and through her to the other ladies, that she was spending the day with a friend of hers at a hotel in Newton, or Lexington, or Woburn. In a city full of receptions, of dinner-giving, and party-going, Mrs. Harmon's guests led the lives of cloistered nuns, so far as such pleasures were concerned. Occasionally a transient had rooms for a week or two, and was continually going, and receiving visits. She became the object of a certain unenvious curiosity with the other ladies, who had not much sociability among themselves; they waited a good while before paying visits at one another's rooms, and then were very punctilious not to go again until their calls had been returned. They were all doctoring themselves; they did not talk gossip or scandal much; they talked of their diseases and physicians, and their married daughters, and of Mrs. Harmon, whom they censured for being too easy-going. Certain of them devoured novels, which they carried about clasped to their breasts with their fingers in them at the place where they were reading; they did not often speak of them, and apparently took them as people take opium.

The men were the husbands or fathers of the women, and were wholly without the domestic weight or consequence that belongs to men living in their own houses. There were certain old bachelors, among whom were two or three decayed branches of good Boston families, spendthrifts, or invalided bankrupts. Mr. Evans was practically among the single gentlemen, for his wife never appeared in the parlor or dining-room, and was seen only when she went in or out, heavily veiled, for a walk. Lemuel heard very soon that she had suffered a shock from the death of her son on the cars; the other ladies made much of her inability to get over it, and said nothing would induce them to have a son of theirs go in and out on the cars.

Among these people, such as they were, and far as they might be from a final civilization, Lemuel began to feel an ambition to move more lightly and quickly than he had yet known how to do, to speak promptly, and to appear well. Our schooling does not train us to graceful or even correct speech; even our colleges often leave that uncouth. Many of Mrs. Harmon's boarders spoke bad grammar through their noses; but the ladies dressed stylishly, and the men were good arithmeticians. Lemuel obeyed a native impulse rather than a good example in cultivating a better address; but the incentive to thrift and fashion was all about him. He had not been ignorant that his clothes were queer in cut and out of date, and during his stay at Miss Vane's he had taken much counsel with himself as to whether he ought not to get a new suit with his first money instead of sending it home. Now he had solved the question, after sending the money home, by the discovery of a place on a degenerate street, in a neighborhood of Chinese laundries, with the polite name of Misfit Parlors, where they professed to sell the failures of the leading tailors of Boston, New York, and Chicago. After long study of the window of the Parlors, Lemuel ventured within one day, and was told, when he said he could not afford the suit he fancied, that he might pay for it on the installment plan, which the proprietor explained to him. In the mirror he was almost startled at the stylishness of his own image. The proprietor of the Parlors complimented him. "You see, you've got a good figure for a suit of clothes—what I call a ready-made figure. *You* can go into a clothing-store anywheres and fit you."

He took the first installment of the price, with Lemuel's name and address, and said he would send the clothes round;

but in the evening he brought them himself, and no doubt verified Lemuel's statement by this device. It was a Saturday night, and the next morning Lemuel rose early to put them on. He meant to go to church in them, and in the afternoon he did not know just what he should do. He had hoped that some chance might bring them together again, and then he could see from the way Miss Dudley and 'Manda Grier behaved just what they thought. He had many minds about the matter himself, and had gone from an extreme of self-abhorrence to one of self-vindication, and between these he had halted at every gradation of blame and exculpation. But perhaps what chiefly kept him away was the uncertainty of his future; till he could give some shape to that, he had no courage to face the past. Sometimes he wished never to see either of those girls again; but at other times he had a longing to go and explain, to justify himself, or to give himself up to justice.

The new clothes gave him more heart than he had yet had, but the most he could bring himself to do was to walk towards Pleasant Avenue the next Sunday afternoon, which Mrs. Harmon especially gave him, and to think about walking up and down before the house. It ended in his walking up and down the block, first on one side of the street and then on the other. He knew the girls' window; Miss Dudley had shown him it was the middle window of the top story when they were looking out of it, and he glanced up at it. Then he hurried away, but he could not leave the street without stopping at the corner, to cast a last look back at the house. There was an apothecary's at that corner, and while he stood wistfully staring and going round the corner a little way, and coming back to look at the things in the apothecary's window, he saw 'Manda Grier come swiftly towards him. He wanted to run away now, but he could not; he felt nailed to the spot, and he felt the color go out of his face. She pretended not to see him at first; but with a second glance she abandoned the pretense, and at his saying faintly "Good-afternoon," she said, with freezing surprise, "Oh! good-afternoon, Mr. Barker!" and passed into the apothecary's.

He could not go now, since he had spoken, and leave all so inconclusive again; and yet 'Manda Grier had been so repellent, so cutting, in her tone and manner, that he did not know how to face her another time. When she came out he faltered, "I hope there isn't anybody sick at your house, Miss Grier."

"Oh, nobody that you'll care about, Mr. Barker," she answered airily, and began to tilt rapidly away, with her chin thrust out before her.

He made a few paces after her, and then stopped; she seemed to stop too, and he caught up with her.

"I hope," he gasped, "there ain't anything the matter with Miss Dudley?"

"Oh, nothing 't *you'll* care about," said 'Manda Grier; and she added with terrible irony, "You've b'en round to inquire so much that you hain't allowed time for any *great* change."

"Has she been sick long?" faltered Lemuel. "I didn't dare to come!" he cried out. "I've been wanting to come, but I didn't suppose you would speak to me—any of you." Now his tongue was unlocked, he ran on: "I don't know as it's any excuse—there *ain't* any excuse for such a thing! I know she must perfectly despise me, and that I'm not fit for her to look at; but I'd give anything if I could take it all back and be just where I was before. You tell her, won't you, how I feel?"

'Manda Grier, who had listened with a killingly averted face, turned sharply upon him. "You mean about stayin' away so long? I don't know as she cared a great deal, but it's a pretty queer way of showin' you cared for her."

"I didn't mean that!" retorted Lemuel; and he added by an immense effort, "I meant—the way I behaved when I was there; I meant——"

"Oh!" said 'Manda Grier, turning her face away again; she turned it so far away that the back of her head was all that Lemuel could see. "I guess you better speak to Statira about that."

By this time they had reached the door of the boarding-house, and 'Manda Grier let herself in with her latch-key. "Won't you walk in, Mr. Barker?" she said in formal tones of invitation.

"Is she well enough to see—company?" murmured Lemuel. "I shouldn't want to disturb her."

"I don't believe but what she can see you," said 'Manda Grier, for the first time relentingly.

"All right," said Lemuel, gulping the lump in his throat, and he followed 'Manda Grier up the flights of stairs to the door of the girls' room, which she flung open without knocking.

"S'tira," she said, "here's Mr. Barker." And Lemuel, from the dark landing, where he lurked a moment, could see Statira sitting in the rocking-chair in a pretty blue dressing-gown. After a first flush she looked pale, and now and then put up her hand to hide a hoarse little cough.

XV

"WALK right in, Mr. Barker," cried 'Manda Grier, and Lemuel entered, more awkward and sheepish in his new suit from the Misfit Parlors than he had been before in his Willoughby Pastures best clothes.

Statira merely said, "Why, Mr. Barker!" and stood at her chair where she rose. "You're quite a stranger. Won't you sit down?"

Lemuel sat down, and 'Manda Grier said, politely, "Won't you let me take your hat, Mr. Barker?" and they both treated him with so much ceremony and deference that it seemed impossible he could ever have done such a monstrous thing as kiss a young lady like Miss Dudley; and he felt that he never could approach the subject even to accept a just doom at her hands.

They all talked about the weather for a minute, and then 'Manda Grier said, "Well, I guess I shall have to go down and set this boneset to steep"; and as he rose, and stood to let her pass, she caught his arm and gave it a clutch. He did not know whether she did it on purpose, or why she did it, but somehow it said to him that she was his friend, and he did not feel so much afraid.

When she was gone, however, he returned to the weather for conversation; but when Statira said it was lucky for her that the winter held off so, he made out to inquire about her sickness, and she told him that she had caught a heavy cold; at first it seemed just to be a head-cold, but afterwards it seemed to settle on the lungs, and it seemed as if she never *could* throw it off; they had had the doctor twice; but now she was better, and the cough was nearly *all* gone.

"I guess I took the cold that day, from havin' the window open," she concluded; and she passed her hand across her lap, and looked down demurely, and then up at the ceiling, and her head twitched a little and trembled.

Lemuel knew that his hour had come, if ever it were to come, and he said hoarsely: "I guess if I made you take cold that day, it wasn't all I did. I guess I did worse than that."

She did not look at him and pretend ignorance, as 'Manda Grier would have done; but lifting her moist eyes and then dropping them, she said, "Why, Mr. Barker, what can you mean?"

"You know what I mean," he retorted, with courage astonishing to him. "It was because I liked you so much." He could not say loved; it seemed too bold. "There's nothing else can excuse it, and I don't know as *that* can."

She put up her hands to her eyes and began to cry, and he rose and went to her and said, "Oh, don't cry, don't cry!" and somehow he took hold of her hands, and then her arms went round his neck, and she was crying on his breast.

"You'll think I'm rather of a silly person, crying so much about nothing," she said, when she lifted her head from his shoulder to wipe her eyes. "But I can't seem to help it," and she broke down again. "I presume it's because I've been sick, and I'm kind of weak yet. I know you wouldn't have done that, that day, if you hadn't have cared for me; and I wasn't mad a bit—not half as mad as I ought to have been; but when you staid away so long, and never seemed to come near any more, I didn't know what *to* think. But now I can understand just how you felt, and I don't blame you one bit; I should have done just so myself if I'd been a man, I suppose. And now it's all come right, I don't mind being sick, or anything; only when Thanksgiving came, we felt sure you'd call, and we'd got the pies nicely warmed. Oh dear!" She gave way

again, and then pressed her cheek tight against his to revive
herself. "'Manda said she just knew it was because you was
kind of ashamed, and I was too sick to eat any of the pies, any
way; and so it all turned out for the best; and I don't want you
to believe that I'm one to cry over spilt milk, especially when
it's all gathered up again!"

Her happy tongue ran on, revealing, divining everything,
and he sat down with her in his arms, hardly speaking a word,
till her heart was quite poured out. 'Manda Grier left them
a long time together, and before she came back he had told
Statira all about himself since their last meeting. She was
very angry at the way that girl had behaved at Miss Vane's,
but she was glad he had found such a good place now, without
being beholden to any one for it, and she showed that she felt
a due pride in his being a hotel clerk. He described the hotel,
and told what he had to do there, and about Mrs. Harmon
and the fashionableness of all the guests. But he said he did
not think any of the ladies went ahead of her in dress, if they
came up to her; and Statira pressed her lips gratefully against
his cheek, and then lifting her head held herself a little away
to see him again, and said, "*You're* splendidly dressed, *too*;
I noticed it the first thing when you came in. You look just as
if you had always lived in Boston."

"Is that so?" asked Lemuel; and he felt his heart suffused
with tender pride and joy. He told her of the Misfit Parlors
and the installment plan, and she said, well, it was just splendid; and she asked him if he knew she wasn't in the store any
more; and "No," she added delightedly, upon his confession
of ignorance, "I'm going to work in the box-factory, after this,
where 'Manda Grier works. It's better pay, and you have
more control of your hours, and you can set down while you
work, if you're a mind to. I think it's going to be splendid.
What should you say if 'Manda Grier and me took some rooms
and went to housekeepin'?"

"I don't know," said Lemuel; but in his soul he felt jealous
of her keeping house with 'Manda Grier.

"Well, I don't know as we shall do it," said Statira, as if feeling his tacit reluctance.

'Manda Grier came in just then, and cast a glance of friendly satire at them. "Well, I declare!" she said, for all recognition of the situation.

Lemuel made an offer to rise, but Statira would not let him. "I guess 'Manda Grier won't mind it much."

"I guess I can stand it if you can," said 'Manda Grier; and this seemed such a witty speech that they all laughed, till, as Statira said, she thought she should die. They laughed the more when 'Manda Grier added dryly, "I presume you won't want your boneset now." She set the vessel she had brought it up in on the stove, and covered it with a saucer. "I do' know as I should if I was in your place. It's kind o' curious I should bring both remedies home with me at once." At this they all laughed a third time, till 'Manda Grier said, " 'Sh! 'sh! Do you want to raise the roof?"

She began to bustle about, and to set out a little table, and cover it with a napkin, and as she worked she talked on. "I guess if you don't want any boneset tea, a little of the other kind won't hurt any of us, and I kinder want a cup myself." She set it to steep on the stove, and it went through Lemuel's mind that she might have steeped the boneset there too, if she had thought of it; but he did not say anything, though it seemed a pretty good joke on 'Manda Grier. She ran on in that way of hers so that you never could tell whether she really meant a thing or not. "I guess if I have to manage many more cases like yours, S'tira Dudley, I shall want to lay in a whole chest of it. What do you think, Mr. Barker?"

"Mr. Barker!" repeated Statira.

"Well, I'm afraid to say Lemuel any more, for fear he'll fly off the handle, and never come again. What do you think, Mr. Barker, of havin' to set at that window every Sunday for the last three weeks, and keep watch of both sidewalks till you get such a crick in your neck, and your eyes so set in your head, you couldn't move either of 'em?"

"Now, 'Manda Grier!" said Statira from Lemuel's shoulder.

"Well, I don't say I had to do it, and I don't say who the young man was that I was put to look out for——"

" '*Manda!*"

"But I *do* say it's pretty hard to wait on a sick person one side the room, and keep watch for a young man the other side, both at once."

" 'Manda Grier, you're *too* bad!" pouted Statira. "Don't you believe a word she says, Mr. Barker."

"*Mr. Barker!*" repeated 'Manda Grier.

"Well, I don't care!" said Statira. "I know who I mean."

"*I* don't," said 'Manda Grier. "And I didn't know who you meant this afternoon when you was standin' watch't the window, and says you, 'There! there he is!' and I had to run so quick with the dipper of water I had in my hand to water the plants that I poured it all over the front of my dress."

"*Do* you believe her?" asked Statira.

"And I didn't know who you meant," proceeded 'Manda Grier, busy with the cups and saucers, "when you kept hurryin' me up to change it; 'Oh, quick, quick! How long you are! I know he'll get away! I *know* he will!' and I had to just *sling* on a shawl and rush out after this boneset."

"There! Now that *shows* she's makin' it all up!" cried Statira. "She put on a sack, and I helped her on with it myself. So there!"

"Well, if it *was* a sack! And after all, the young man was gone when I got down int' the street," concluded 'Manda Grier solemnly.

Lemuel had thought she was talking about him; but now a pang of jealousy went through him, and showed at the eyes he fixed on her.

"I don't know what I sh'd 'a' done," she resumed demurely, "if I hadn't have found Mr. Barker at the apothecary's, and got *him* to come home 'th me; but of course 'twan't the same as if it was the young man!"

Lemuel's arm fell from Statira's waist in his torment.

"Why, Lemuel!" she said in tender reproach.

"Why, you coot!" cried 'Manda Grier in utter amazement at his single-mindedness, and burst into a scream of laughter. She took the teapot from the stove, and set it on the table. "There, young man—if you *are* the young man—you better pull up to the table, and have something to start your ideas. S'tira! let him come!" and Lemuel, blushing for shame at his stupidity, did as he was bid.

"I've got the greatest mind in the world to set next to S'tira myself," said 'Manda Grier, "for fear she should miss that young man!" and now they both laughed together at Lemuel; but the girls let him sit between them, and Statira let him keep one of her hands under the table, as much as she could. "I never saw such a jealous piece! Why, I shall begin to be afraid for myself. What should you think of S'tira's going to housekeeping with me?"

"I don't believe he likes the idea one bit," Statira answered for him.

"Oh, yes, I do!" Lemuel protested.

" 'D you tell him?" 'Manda Grier demanded of her. She nodded with saucy defiance. "Well, you *have* got along! And about the box-factory?" Statira nodded again, with a look of joyous intelligence at Lemuel. "Well, what *hain't* you told, I wonder!" 'Manda Grier added seriously to Lemuel, "I think it'll be about the best thing in the world for S'tira. I see for the last six months she's been killin' herself in that store. She can't ever get a chance to set down a minute; and she's on her feet from morning till night; and I think it's more'n half that that's made her sick; I don't *say* what the other four-fifths was!"

"Now, 'Manda Grier, stop!"

"Well, that's over with now, and now we want to keep you out that store. I been lookin' out for this place for S'tira a good while. She can go onto the small boxes, if she wants to, and she can set down all the time; and she'll have a whole hour for her dinner; and she can work by the piece, and do as much or as little as she's a mind to; but if she's a mind to work she can make her five and six dollars a week, easy. Mr. Stevens's *real* nice and kind, and he looks out for the girls that ain't exactly strong—not but what S'tira's as strong as anybody, when she's well—and he don't put 'em on the green paper work, because it's got arsenic in it, and it makes your head ache, and you're liable to blood-poisonin'. One the girls fainted and had spasms, and as soon as he found it out he took her right off; and he's just like clockwork to pay. I think it'll do everything for S'tira to be along 'th me there, where I can look after her."

Lemuel said he thought so too; he did not really think at all, he was so flattered at being advised with about Statira, as if she were in his keeping and it was for him to say what was best for her; and when she seemed uncertain about his real opinion, and said she was not going to do anything he did not approve of, he could scarcely speak for rapture, but he protested that he did approve of the scheme entirely.

"But you shouldn't want we girls to set up housekeeping in rooms?" she suggested; and he said that he should, and that he thought it would be more independent and homelike.

"We're half doin' it now," said 'Manda Grier, "and I know some rooms—two of 'em—where we could get along first-rate, and not cost us much more'n half what it does here."

After she cleared up the tea-things she made another errand down-stairs, and Lemuel and Statira went back to their rocking-chair. It still amazed him that she seemed not even to make it a favor to him; she seemed to think it was favor to her. What was stranger yet was that he could not feel that there was anything wrong or foolish about it; he thought of his mother's severity about young folks' sickishness, as she called it, and he could not understand it. He knew that he had never had such right and noble thoughts about girls before; perhaps Statira was better than other girls; she must be; she was just like a child; and he must be very good himself to be anyways fit for her; if she cared so much for him, it must be a sign that he was not so bad as he had sometimes thought. A great many things went through his mind, the silent comment and suggestion of their talk, and all the time while he was saying something or listening to her, he was aware of the overwhelming wonder of her being so frank with him, and not too proud or ashamed to have him know how anxious she had been, ever since they first met, for fear he did not care for her. She had always appeared so stylish and reserved, and now she was not proud at all. He tried to tell her how it had been with him the last three weeks; all that he could say was that he had been afraid to come. She laughed, and said, the idea of his being afraid of *her!* She said that she was glad of everything she had gone through. At times she lifted herself from his shoulder, and coughed; but that was when she had been laughing or crying a little. They told each other about their families. Statira said she had not really any folks of her own; she was just brought up by her aunt; and Lemuel had to tell her that his mother wore bloomers. Statira said she guessed she should not care much for the bloomers; and in everything she tried to make out that he was much better than she was, and just exactly right. She already spoke of his sister by her first name, and she entered into his whole life, as if she had always known him. He said she must come with him to hear Mr. Sewell preach, some time; but she declared that she did not think much of a minister who could behave the way he had done to Lemuel. He defended Sewell, and maintained that if it had not been for him he might not have come to Boston, and so might never have seen her; but she held out that she could not bear Mr. Sewell, and that she knew he was double-faced, and everything. Lemuel said well, he did not know that he should ever have anything more to do with him; but he liked to hear him preach, and he guessed he tried to do what was about right. Statira made him promise that if ever he met Mr. Sewell again, he would not make up to him, any way; and she would not tolerate the thought of Miss Vane.

"What you two quar'lin' about?" demanded 'Manda Grier,

coming suddenly into the room; and that turned their retrospective griefs into joy again.

"I'm scoldin' him because he don't think enough of himself," cried Statira.

"Well, he seems to take it pretty meekly," said 'Manda Grier. "I guess you didn't scold very hard. Now, young man," she added to Lemuel, "I guess you better be goin'. It's five o'clock, and if you should be out after dark, and the bears should get you, I don't know what S'tira would do."

"'T'ain't five yet!" pleaded Statira. "That old watch of yours is always tryin' to beat the town clock."

"Well, it's the clock that's ahead this time," said 'Manda Grier. "My watch says quarter of. Come, now, S'tira, you let him go, or he sha'n't come back any more."

They had a parting that Lemuel's mother would have called sickish, without question; but it all seemed heavenly sweet and right. Statira said now he had got to kiss 'Manda Grier too; and when he insisted, her chin knocked against his and saved her lips, and she gave him a good box on the ear.

"There, I guess that'll do for one while," she said, arranging her tumbled hair; "but there's more kisses where that came from, for both of you, if you want 'em. Coots!"

Once, when Lemuel was little, he had a fever, and he was always seeming to glide down the school-house stairs without touching the steps with his feet. He remembered this dream now, when he reached the street; he felt as if he had floated down on the air; and presently he was back in his little den at the hotel, he did not know how. He ran the elevator up and down for the ladies who called him from the different floors, and he took note of the Sunday difference in their toilet as they passed in to tea, but in the same dreamy way.

After the boarders had supped, he went in as usual with Mrs. Harmon's nephew, less cindery than on week-days, from the cellar, and Mrs. Harmon, silken smooth for her evening worship at the shrine of a popular preacher from New York. The Sunday evening before, she had heard an agnostic lecture in the Boston Theater, and she said she wished to compare notes. Her tranquillity was unruffled by the fact that the head-waitress had left, just before tea; she presumed they could get along just as well without her as with her; the boarders had spoiled her, anyway. She looked round at Lemuel's face, which beamed with his happiness, and said she guessed she should have to get him to open the dining-room doors and seat the transients the next few days, till she could get another head-waitress. It did not seem to be so much a request as a resolution; but Lemuel willingly assented. Mrs. Harmon's nephew said that so long as they did not want him to do it, he did not care who did it; and if a few of them had his furnace to look after, they would not be so anxious to kick.

XVI

LEMUEL had to be up early in the morning to get the bills of fare, which Mrs. Harmon called the Meanyous, written in time for the seven o'clock breakfasters; and after opening the dining-room doors with fit ceremony, he had to run backward and forward to answer the rings at the elevator, and to pull out the chairs for the ladies at the table, and slip them back under them as they sat down. The ladies at the St. Albans expected to get their money's worth; but their exactions in most things were of use to Lemuel. He grew constantly nimbler of hand and foot under them, and he grew quicker-witted; he ceased to hulk in mind and body. He did not employ this new mental agility in devising excuses and delays; he left that to Mrs. Harmon, whose conscience was easy in it; but from seven o'clock in the morning till eleven at night, when the ladies came in from the theater, he was so promptly, so comfortingly at their service, that they all said they did not see how they had ever got along without him.

His activities took the form of interruptions rather than constant occupation, and he found a good deal of broken-up time on his hands, which he passed in reading and in reveries of Statira. At the hours when the elevator was mostly in use he kept a book in it with him, and at other times he had it in the office, as Mrs. Harmon called his little booth. He remained there reading every night after the house quieted down after dinner, until it was time to lock up for the night; and several times Mr. Evans stopped and looked in at him where he sat in the bad combustion of the gas that was taking the country tan out of his cheeks. One night when he came in late, and Lemuel put his book down to take him up in the elevator, he said, "Don't disturb yourself; I'm going to walk up"; but he lingered at the door, looking in with the queer smile that always roused the ladies' fears of tacit ridicule. "I suppose you don't find it necessary," he said finally, "to chase a horse-car now, when you want to find your way to a given point?"

Lemuel reddened and dropped his head; he had already recognized in Mr. Evans the gentleman from whose kindly curiosity he had turned, that first day, in the suspicion that he might be a beat. "No," he said; "I guess I can go pretty near everywhere in Boston, now."

"Well," said Mr. Evans, "it was an ingenious system. How do you like Boston?"

"I like it first-rate, but I've not seen many other places," answered Lemuel cautiously.

"Well, if you live here long enough you won't care to see any other places; you'll know they're not worth seeing." Lemuel looked up as if he did not understand exactly, and Mr. Evans stepped in and lifted the book he had been reading. It was one he had bought at second hand while he was with Miss Vane: a tough little epitome of the philosophies in all times, the crabbed English version of a dry German original. Mr. Evans turned its leaves over. "Do you find it a very exciting story?" he asked.

"Why, it isn't a story," said Lemuel, in simple surprise.

"No?" asked Mr. Evans. "I thought it must be. Most of the young gentlemen who run the elevators I travel in read stories. Do you like this kind of reading?"

Lemuel reflected, and then he said he thought you ought to find out about such things if you got a chance.

"Yes," said the editor, musingly, "I suppose one oughtn't to throw any sort of chance away. But you're sure you don't prefer the novels? You'll excuse my asking you?"

"Oh, perfectly excusable," said Lemuel. He added that he liked a good novel too, when he could get hold of it.

"You must come to my room some day, and see if you can't

get hold of one there. Or if you prefer metaphysics, I've got shelves full that you're welcome to. I suppose," he added, "you hadn't been in Boston a great while when I met you that day?"

"No," said Lemuel, dropping his head again; "I had just come."

As if he saw that something painful lurked under the remembrance of the time for Lemuel, the editor desisted.

The next morning he stopped on his way to breakfast with some books which he handed to Lemuel. "Don't feel at all obliged to read them," he said, "because I lend them to you. They won't be of the least use to you, if you do so."

"I guess that anything you like will be worth reading," said Lemuel, flattered by the trouble so chief a boarder as Mr. Evans had taken with him.

"Not if they supplied a want you didn't feel. You seem to be fond of books, and after a while you'll be wanting to lend them yourself. I'll give you a little hint that I'm too old to profit by: remember that you can lend a person more books in a day than he can read in a week."

His laugh kept Lemuel shy of him still, in spite of a willingness that the editor showed for their better acquaintance. He seemed to wish to know about Lemuel, particularly since he had recognized the pursuer of the horse-car in him, and this made Lemuel close up the more. He would have liked to talk with him about the books Evans had lent him. But when the editor stopped at the office door, where Lemuel sat reading one of them, and asked him what he thought of it, the boy felt that somehow it was not exactly his opinion that Mr. Evans was getting at; and this sense of being inspected and arranged in another's mind, though he could not formulate the operation in his own, somehow wounded and repelled him. It was not that the editor ever said anything that was not kind and friendly; he was always doing kind and friendly things, and he appeared to take a real interest in Lemuel. At the end of the first week after Lemuel had added the head-waitership to his other duties, Evans stopped in going out of the dining-room and put a dollar in his hand.

"What is it for?" asked Lemuel.

"For? Really, I don't know. It must be tribute money," said the editor in surprise, but with a rising curiosity. "I never know what it's for."

Lemuel turned red, and handed it back. "I don't know as I want any money I haven't earned."

That night, after dinner, when Evans was passing the office door on his way out of the hotel, Lemuel stopped him and said with embarrassment, "Mr. Evans, I don't want you should think I didn't appreciate your kindness this morning."

"Ah, I'm not sure it was kindness," said Evans with immediate interest. "Why didn't you take the money?"

"Well, I told you why," said Lemuel, overcoming the obscure reluctance he felt at Evans's manner as best he could. "I've been thinking it over, and I guess I was right; but I didn't know whether I had expressed it the best way."

"The way couldn't be improved. But why did you think you hadn't earned my dollar?"

"I don't do anything but open the doors, and show people to their places; I don't call that anything."

"But if you were a waiter and served at table?"

"I wouldn't *be* one," said Lemuel, with a touch of indignation; "and I shouldn't take presents, anyway."

Evans leaned against the door-jamb.

"Have you heard of the college students who wait at the mountain hotels in vacation? They all take fees. Do you think yourself better than they are?"

"Yes, I do!" cried Lemuel.

"Well, I don't know but you are," said the editor thoughtfully. "But I think I should distinguish. Perhaps there's no shame in waiting at table, but there is in taking fees."

"Yes; that's what I meant," said Lemuel, a little sorry for his heat. "I shouldn't be ashamed to do any kind of work, and to take my pay for it; but I shouldn't want to have folks giving me money over and above, as if I was a beggar."

The editor stood looking him absently in the face. After a

moment he asked, "What part of New England did you come from, Mr. Barker?"

"I came from the middle part of the State—from Willough-by Pastures."

"Do those ideas—those principles—of yours prevail there?"

"I don't know whether they do or not," said Lemuel.

"If you were sure they did, I should like to engage board there for next summer," said the editor, going out.

It was Monday night, a leisure time with him, and he was going out to see a friend, a minister, with whom Monday night was also leisure time.

After he was gone, some of the other boarders began to drop in from the lectures and concerts which they frequented in the evening. The ladies had all some favor to ask of Lemuel, some real or fancied need of his help; in return for his promise or performance, they each gave him advice. What they expressed collectively was that they should think that he would put his eyes out reading by that gas, and that he had better look out, or he would ruin his health anyway, reading so much. They asked him how much time he got for sleep; and they said that from twelve till six was not enough, and that he was just killing himself. They had all offered to lend him books; the least literary among them had a sort of house pride in his fondness for books; their sympathy with this taste of his amused their husbands, who tolerated it, but in their hearts regarded it as a womanish weakness, indicating a want of fiber in Lemuel. Mrs. Harmon, as a business woman, and therefore occupying a middle ground between the sexes, did not exactly know herself what to make of her clerk's studiousness; all that she could say was that he kept up with his work. She assumed that before Lemuel's coming she had been the sole motive power of the house; but it was really a sort of democracy, and was managed by the majority of its inmates. An element of demagoguery tampered with the Irish vote in the person of Jerry, nominally porter, but actually factotum, who had hitherto, pending the strikes of the different functionaries, filled the offices now united in Lemuel. He had never been clerk, because his literature went no further than the ability to write his name, and to read a passage of the Constitution in qualifying for the suffrage. He did not like the new order of things, but he was without a party, and helpless to do more than neglect the gong-bell when he had reason to think Lemuel had sounded it.

About eleven o'clock the law-student came in with the two girl art-students, fresh from the outside air, and gay from the opera they had been hearing. The young man told Lemuel he ought to go to see it. After the girls had opened their door, one of them came running back to the elevator, and called down to Lemuel that there was no ice-water, and would he please send some up.

Lemuel brought it up himself, and when he knocked at the door, the same girl opened it and made a pretty outcry over the trouble she had given him. "I supposed, of course, Jerry would bring it," she said contritely; and as if for some atonement she added, "Won't you come in, Mr. Barker, and see my picture?"

Lemuel stood in the gush of the gas-light hesitating, and the law-student called out to him, jollily, "Come in, Mr. Barker, and help me play art-critic." He was standing before the picture, with his overcoat on and his hat in his hand. "First appearance on any stage," he added, and as Lemuel entered, "If I were you," he said, "I'd fire that porter out of the hotel. He's outlived his usefulness."

"It's a shame, your having to bring the water," said Miss Swan; she was the girl who had spoken before.

The other one came forward and said, "Won't you sit down?"

She spoke to Lemuel; the law-student answered, "Thank you; I don't care if I do."

Lemuel did not know whether to stay, nor what to say of Miss Swan's picture, and he thanked the young lady and remained standing.

"Oh, Jessie, *Jessie,* Jessie!" cried Miss Swan.

The other went to her, tranquilly, as if used to such vehement appeals.

"Just *see* how my poor cow looks since I painted out that grass! She hasn't got a leg to stand on!"

The law-student did nothing but make jokes about the picture. "I think she looks pretty well for a cow that you must have had to study from a milk-can—nearest you could come to a cow in Boston."

Miss Carver, the other young lady, ignored his joking, and after some criticisms on the picture left him and Miss Swan to talk it over. She talked to Lemuel, and asked him if he had read a book he glanced at on the table, and seemed willing to make him feel at ease. But she did not. He thought she was very proud, and he believed she wanted him to go, but he did not know how to go. Her eyes were so still and pure; but they dwelt very coldly upon him. Her voice was like that look put into sound; it was rather high-pitched, but very sweet and pure and cold. He hardly knew what he said; he felt hot, and he waited for some chance to get away.

At last he heard Miss Swan saying, "*Must* you go, Mr. Berry? So *soon!*" and saw her giving the student her hand, with a bow of burlesque desolation.

Lemuel prepared to go, too. All his rusticity came back upon him, and he said, "Well, I wish you good-evening."

It seemed to him that Miss Carver's still eyes looked a sort of starry scorn after him. He found that he had brought away the book they had been talking about, and he was a long time in question whether he had better take it back at once, or give it to her when she came to breakfast.

He went to bed in the same trouble of mind. Every night he had fallen asleep with Statira in his thoughts, but now it was Miss Carver that he thought of, and more and more uncomfortably. He asked himself what she would say if she saw his mother in the bloomers. She was herself not dressed so fashionably as Statira, but very nicely.

XVII

At SEWELL'S HOUSE the maid told Evans to walk up into the study, without seating him first in the reception-room, as if that were needless with so intimate a friend of the family. He found Sewell at his desk, and he began at once, without the forms of greeting:

"If you don't like that other subject, I've got a new one for you, and you could write a sermon on it that would make talk."

"You look at it from the newspaper point of view," returned Sewell, in the same humor. "I'm not an 'enterprise,' and I don't want to make talk in your sense. I don't know that I want to make talk at all; I should prefer to make thought, to make feeling."

"Well," said the editor, "this would do all three."

"Would you come to hear me, if I wrote the sermon?"

"Ah, that's asking a good deal."

"Why don't you develop your idea in an article? You're always bragging that you preach to a larger congregation than I."

"I propose to let you preach to my congregation too, if you'll write this sermon. I've talked to you before about reporting your sermons in 'Saturday Afternoon.' They would be a feature; and if we could open with this one, and have a good 'incisive' editorial on it, disputing some of your positions, and treating certain others with a little satire, at the same time maintaining a very respectful attitude towards you

176

on the whole, and calling attention to the fact that there was a strong and increasing interest in your 'utterances,' which we were the first to recognize,—it would be a card. We might agree beforehand on the points the editorial was to touch, and so make one hand wash another. See?"

"I see that journalism has eaten into your soul. What *is* your subject?"

"Well, in general terms, and in a single word, *Complicity*. Don't you think that would be rather taking? 'Mr. Sewell, in his striking sermon on Complicity,' and so forth. It would be a great hit, and it would stand a chance of sticking, like Emerson's 'Compensation.' "

"Delightful! The most amusing part is that you've really a grain of business in your bushel of chaff." Sewell wheeled about in his swivel-chair, and sat facing his guest, deeply sunken in the low easy seat he always took. "When did this famous idea occur to you?" he pursued, swinging his glasses by their cord.

"About three weeks ago, at the theater. There was one of those pieces on that make you despair of the stage, and ashamed of writing a play even to be rejected by it—a farrago of indecently amusing innuendoes and laughably vile situations, such as, if they were put into a book, would prevent its being sent through the mail. The theater apparently can still be as filthy in suggestion as it was at the Restoration, and not shock its audiences. There were all sorts of people there that night: young girls who had come with young men for an evening's polite amusement; families; middle-aged husbands and wives; respectable-looking single women; and average bachelors. I don't think the ordinary theatrical audience is of a high grade intellectually; it's third or fourth rate; but morally it seems quite as good as other public assemblages. All the people were nicely dressed, and they sat there before that nasty mess—it was an English comedy where all the jokes turn upon the belief of the characters that their wives and husbands are the parents of illegitimate offspring—and listened with as smooth self-satisfaction as if they were not responsible for it. But all at once it occurred to me that they *were* responsible, every one of them—as responsible as the players, as the author himself."

"Did you come out of the theater at that point?" asked Sewell.

"Oh, I was responsible too; but I seemed to be the only one ashamed of my share in the business."

"If you were the only one conscious of it, your merit wasn't very great," suggested the minister.

"Well, I should like the others to be conscious of it too. That's why I want you to preach my sermon. I want you to tell your people and my people that the one who buys sin or shame, or corruption of any sort, is as guilty as the one who sells it."

"It isn't a new theory," said Sewell, still refusing to give up his ironical tone. "It was discovered some time ago that this was so before God."

"Well, I've just discovered that it ought to be so before man," said Evans.

"Still, you're not the first," said Sewell.

"Yes," said the editor, "I think I am, from my peculiar stand-point. The other day a friend of mine—an upright, just, worthy man, no one more so—was telling me of a shocking instance of our national corruption. He had just got home from Europe, and he had brought a lot of dutiable things, that a customs inspector passed for a trifling sum. That was all very well, but the inspector afterwards came round with a confidential claim for a hundred dollars, and the figures to show that the legal duties would have been eight or ten times as much. My friend was glad to pay the hundred dollars; but he defied me to name any country in Europe where such a piece of official rascality was possible. He said it made him ashamed of America!" Evans leaned his head back against his chair and laughed.

"Yes," said Sewell with a sigh, and no longer feigning lightness. "That's awful."

"Well, now," said Evans, "don't you think it your duty to help people realize that they can't regard such transactions *de haut en bas*, if they happen to have taken part in them? I have heard of the shameful condition of things down in Maine, where I'm told the French Canadians who've come in regularly expect to sell their votes to the highest bidder at every election. Since my new system of ethics occurred to me, I've fancied that there must have always been a shameful state of things there, if Americans could grow up in the willingness to buy votes. I want to have people recognize that there is no superiority for them in such an affair; that there's nothing but inferiority; that the man who has the money and the wit to corrupt is a far baser rascal than the man who has the ignorance and the poverty to be corrupted. I would make this principle seek out every weak spot, every sore spot in the whole social constitution. I'm sick to death of the frauds that we practice upon ourselves in order to be able to injure others. Just consider the infernal ease of mind in which men remain concerning men's share in the social evil——"

"Ah, my dear friend, you can't expect me to consider *that* in my pulpit!" cried the minister.

"No; I couldn't consider it in my paper. I suppose we must leave that where it is, unless we can affect it by analogy, and show that there is infamy for both parties to any sin committed in common. You must select your instances in other directions, but you can find plenty of them—enough and to spare. It would give the series a tremendous send-off," said Evans, relapsing into his habitual tone, "if you would tackle this subject in your first sermon for publication. There would be money in it. The thing would make a success in the paper, and you could get somebody to reprint it in pamphlet form. Come, what do you say?"

"I should say that you had just been doing something you were ashamed of," answered Sewell. "People don't have these tremendous moral awakenings for nothing."

"And you don't think my present state of mind is a gradual

outgrowth of my first consciousness of the common responsibility of actors and audience in the representation of a shameless comedy?"

"No, I shouldn't think it was," said the minister securely.

"Well, you're right." Evans twisted himself about in his chair, and hung his legs over one of the arms. "The real reason why I wish you to preach this sermon is because I have just been offering a fee to the head-waiter at our hotel."

"And you feel degraded with him by his acceptance? For it *is* a degradation."

"No, that's the strangest thing about it. I have a monopoly of the degradation, for he didn't take my dollar."

"Ah, then a sermon won't help *you!* Why wouldn't he take it?"

"He said he didn't know as he wanted any money he hadn't earned," said Evans with a touch of mimicry.

The minister started up from his lounging attitude. "Is his name—Barker?" he asked with unerring prescience.

"Yes," said Evans with a little surprise. "Do you know him?"

"Yes," returned the minister, falling back in his chair helplessly, not luxuriously. "So well that I knew it was he almost as soon as you came into the room to-night."

"What harm have you been doing him?" demanded the editor, in parody of the minister's acuteness in guessing the guilty operation of his own mind.

"The greatest. I'm the cause of his being in Boston."

"This is very interesting," said Evans. "We are companions in crime—pals. It's a great honor. But what strikes me as being so interesting is that we appear to feel remorse for our misdeeds; and I was almost persuaded the other day by an observer of our species, that remorse had gone out, or rather had never existed, except in the fancy of innocent people; that real criminals like ourselves were afraid of being found out, but weren't in the least sorry. Perhaps, if we are sorry, it proves that we needn't be. Let's judge each other. I've told you what my sin against Barker is, and I know yours in gen-

eral terms. It's a fearful thing to be the cause of a human
soul's presence in Boston; but what did you do to bring it
about? Who is Barker? Where did he come from? What was
his previous condition of servitude? He puzzles me a good
deal."

"Oh, I'll tell you," said Sewell; and he gave his personal
chapter in Lemuel's history.

Evans interrupted him at one point. "And what became
of the poem he brought down with him?"

"It was stolen out of his pocket, one night when he slept
in the Common."

"Ah, then he can't offer it to me! And he seems very far
from writing any more. I can still keep his acquaintance. Go
on."

Sewell told, in amusing detail, of the Wayfarer's Lodge,
where he had found Barker after supposing he had gone
home. Evans seemed more interested in the place than in
the minister's meeting with Lemuel there, which Sewell fancied he had painted rather well, describing Lemuel's severity
and his own anxiety.

"There!" said the editor. "There you have it—a practical
illustration! Our civilization has had to come to it!"

"Come to what?"

"Complicity."

Sewell made an impatient gesture.

"Don't sacrifice the consideration of a great principle,"
cried Evans, "to the petty effect of a good story on an appreciative listener. I realize your predicament. But don't you see
that in establishing and regulating a place like that the city
of Boston has instinctively sanctioned my idea? You may say
that it is aiding and abetting the tramp-nuisance by giving
vagrants food and shelter, but other philosophers will con-
tend that it is—blindly perhaps—fulfilling the destiny of the
future State, which will at once employ and support all its
citizens; that it is prophetically recognizing my new principle of Complicity?"

"Your new principle!" cried Sewell. "You have merely

given a new name to one of the oldest principles in the moral world."

"And that is a good deal to do, I can tell you," said Evans. "All the principles are pretty old now. But don't give way to an ignoble resentment of my interruption. Go on about Barker."

After some feints that there was nothing more important to tell, Sewell went on to the end; and when he had come to it, Evans shook his head. "It looks pretty black for you, but it's a beautifully perfect case of Complicity. What do you propose to do, now you've rediscovered him?"

"Oh, I don't know! I hope no more mischief. If I could only get him back on his farm!"

"Yes, I suppose that would be the best thing. But I dare say he wouldn't go back!"

"That's been my experience with him."

They talked this aspect of the case over more fully, and Evans said: "Well, I wouldn't go back to such a place myself after I'd once had a glimpse of Boston, but I suppose it's right to wish that Barker would. I hope his mother will come to visit him while he's in the hotel. I would give a good deal to see her. Fancy her coming down in her bloomers, and the poor fellow being ashamed of her! It would be a very good subject for a play. Does she wear a hat or a bonnet? What sort of head-gear goes with that 'sleek odalisque' style of dress? A turban, I suppose."

"Mrs. Barker," said the minister, unable to deny himself the fleeting comfort of the editor's humorous view of the situation, "is as far from a 'sleek odalisque' as any lady I've ever seen, in spite of her oriental costume. If I remember, her *yashmak* was not gathered at the ankles, but hung loose like occidental trousers; and the day we met, she wore simply her own hair. There was not much of it on top, and she had it cut short in the neck. She was rather a terrible figure. Her having ever been married would have been inconceivable, except for her son."

"I should like to have seen her," said Evans, laughing back in his chair.

"She was worth seeing as a survival of the superficial fermentation of the period of our social history when it was believed that women could be like men if they chose, and ought to be if they ever meant to show their natural superiority. But she was not picturesque."

"The son's very handsome. I can see that the lady boarders think him so."

"Do you find him at all remarkable otherwise? What dismayed me more than his poetry even was that when he gave that up he seemed to have no particular direction."

"Oh, he reads a good deal, and pretty serious books; and he goes to hear all the sermons and lectures in town."

"I thought he came to mine only," sighed the minister, with a retrospective suffering. "Well, what can be done for him now? I feel my complicity with Barker as poignantly as you could wish."

"Ah, you see how the principle applies everywhere!" cried the editor joyously. He added: "But I really think that for the present you can't do better than let Barker alone. He's getting on very well at Mrs. Harmon's, and although the conditions at the St. Albans are more transitory than most sublunary things, Barker appears to be a fixture. Our little system has begun to revolve round him unconsciously; he keeps us going."

"Well," said Sewell, consenting to be a little comforted. He was about to go more particularly into the facts; but Mrs. Sewell came in just then, and he obviously left the subject.

Evans did not sit down again after rising to greet her; and presently he said good-night.

She turned to her husband: "What were you talking about when I came in?"

"When you came in?"

"Yes. You both had that look—I can always tell it—of having suddenly stopped."

"Oh!" said Sewell, pretending to arrange the things on his desk. "Evans had been suggesting the subject for a sermon." He paused a moment, and then he continued hardily, "And he'd been telling me about—Barker. He's turned up again."

"Of course!" said Mrs. Sewell. "What's happened to him now?"

"Nothing, apparently, but some repeated strokes of prosperity. He has become clerk, elevator-boy, and head-waiter at the St. Albans."

"And what are you going to do about him?"

"Evans advises me to do nothing."

"Well, that's sensible, at any rate," said Mrs. Sewell. "I really think you've done quite enough, David, and now he can be left to manage for himself, especially as he seems to be doing well."

"Oh, he's doing as well as I could hope, and better. But I'm not sure that I shouldn't have personally preferred a continued course of calamity for him. I shall never be quite at peace about him till I get him back on his farm at Willoughby Pastures."

"Well, that you will never do; and you may as well rest easy about it."

"I don't know as to never doing it," said Sewell. "All prosperity, especially the prosperity connected with Mrs. Harmon's hotel, is transitory; and I may succeed yet."

"Does everything go on there in the old way, does Mr. Evans say?" Mrs. Sewell did not refer to any former knowledge of the St. Albans, but to a remote acquaintance with the character and methods of Mrs. Harmon, with whom the Sewells had once boarded. She was then freshly widowed by the loss of her first husband, and had launched her earliest boarding-house on that sea of disaster, where she had buoyantly outridden every storm and had floated triumphantly on the top of every ingulfing wave. They recalled the difficult navigation of that primitive craft, in which each of the boarders had taken a hand at the helm, and their reminiscences of her financial embarrassments were mixed with those of the unfailing serenity that seemed not to know defeat, and with fond memories of her goodness of heart, and her ideal devotion in any case of sickness or trouble.

"I should think the prosperity of Mrs. Harmon would convince the most negative of agnostics that there was an overruling Providence, if nothing else did," said Sewell. "It's so defiant of all law, so delightfully independent of causation."

"Well, let Barker alone with her, then," said his wife, rising to leave him to the hours of late reading which she had never been able to break up.

XVIII

After agreeing with his wife that he had better leave Barker alone, Sewell did not feel easy in doing so. He had that ten-dollar note which Miss Vane had given him, and though he did not believe, since Evans had reported Barker's refusal of his fee, that the boy would take it, he was still constrained to do something with it. Before giving it back to her, he decided at least to see Barker and learn about his prospects and expectations. He might find some way of making himself useful to him.

In a state of independence he found Lemuel much more accessible than formerly, and their interview was more nearly amicable. Sewell said that he had been delighted to hear of Lemuel's whereabouts from his old friend Evans, and to know that they were housed together. He said that he used to know Mrs. Harmon long ago, and that she was a good-hearted, well-meaning woman, though without much forecast. He even assented to Lemuel's hasty generalization of her as a perfect lady, though they both felt a certain inaccuracy in this, and Sewell repeated that she was a woman of excellent heart, and turned to a more intimate inquest of Lemuel's life. He tried to find out how he employed his leisure time, saying that he always sympathized with young men away from home, and suggesting the reading-room and the frequent lectures at the Young Men's Christian Union for his odd moments. He learned that Lemuel had not many of these during the week, and that on Sundays he spent all the time he could get in hearing the different noted ministers. For the rest, he learned that Lemuel was very much interested in the city, and ap-

186

peared to be rapidly absorbing both its present civilization and its past history. He was unsmilingly amused at the comments of mixed shrewdness and crudity which Lemuel was betrayed into at times beyond certain limits of diffidence that he had apparently set himself; at his blunders and misconceptions, at the truth divined by the very innocence of his youth and inexperience. He found out that Lemuel had not been at home since he came to Boston; he had expected to go at Thanksgiving, but it came so soon after he had got his place that he hated to ask; the folks were all well, and he would send the kind remembrances which the minister asked him to give his mother. Sewell tried to find out, in saying that Mrs. Sewell and himself would always be glad to see him, whether Lemuel had any social life outside of the St. Albans, but here he was sensible that a door was shut against him; and finally he had not the courage to do more about that money from Miss Vane than to say that from time to time he had sums intrusted him, and that if Lemuel had any pressing need of money he must borrow of him. He fancied he had managed that rather delicately, for Lemuel thanked him without severity and said he should get along now, he guessed, but he was much obliged. Neither of them mentioned Miss Vane, and upon the whole the minister was not sure that he had got much nearer the boy, after all.

Certainly he formed no adequate idea of the avidity and thoroughness with which Lemuel was learning his Boston. It was wholly a public Boston which unfolded itself during the winter to his eager curiosity, and he knew nothing of the social intricacies of which it seems solely to consist for so many of us. To him Boston society was represented by the coteries of homeless sojourners in the St. Albans; Boston life was transacted by the ministers, the lecturers, the public meetings, the concerts, the horse-cars, the policemen, the shop-windows, the newspapers, the theaters, the ships at the docks, the historical landmarks, the charity apparatus.

The effect was a ferment in his mind in which there was nothing clear. It seemed to him that he had to change his opinions every day. He was whirled round and round; he never saw the same object twice the same. He did not know whether he learned or unlearned most. With the pride that comes to youth from the mere novelty of its experiences was mixed a shame for his former ignorance, an exasperation at his inability to grasp their whole meaning.

His activities in acquainting himself with Boston interested Evans, who tried to learn just what his impression was; but this was the last thing that Lemuel could have distinctly imparted.

"Well, upon the whole," he asked, one day, "what do you think? From what you've seen of it, which is the better place, Boston or Willoughby Pastures? If you were friendless and homeless, would you rather be cast away in the city or in the country?"

Lemuel did not hesitate about this. "In the city! They haven't got any idea in the country what's done to help folks along in the city!"

"Is that so?" asked Evans. "It's against tradition," he suggested.

"Yes, I know that," Lemuel assented. "And in the country they think the city is a place where nobody cares for you, and everybody is against you, and wants to impose upon you. Well, when I first came to Boston," he continued, with a consciousness of things that Evans did not betray his own knowledge of, "I thought so too, and I had a pretty hard time for a while. It don't seem as if people *did* care for you, except to make something out of you; but if any one happens to find out that you're in trouble, there's ten times as much done for you in the city as there is in the country."

"Perhaps that's because there are ten times as many to do it," said Evans, in the hope of provoking this impartial spirit further.

"No, it isn't that altogether. It's because they've seen ten times as much trouble, and know how to take hold of it better. I think our folks in the country have been flattered up too much. If some of them could come down here and see how things are carried on, they would be surprised. They wouldn't believe it if you told them."

"I didn't know we were so exemplary," said Evans.

"Oh, city folks have their faults too," said Lemuel, smiling in recognition of the irony.

"No! What?"

Lemuel seemed uncertain whether to say it. "Well, they're too aristocratic."

Evans enjoyed this frank simplicity. He professed not to understand, and begged Lemuel to explain.

"Well, at home, in the country, they mightn't want to do so much for you, or be so polite about it, but they wouldn't feel themselves so much above you. They're more on an equality. If I needed help, I'd rather be in town; but if I could help myself, I'd just as soon be in the country. Only," he added, "there are more chances here."

"Yes, there *are* more chances. And do you think it's better not to be quite so kind, and to be more on an equality?"

"Why, don't you?" demanded Lemuel.

"Well, I don't know," said Evans, with a whimsical affectation of seriousness. "Shouldn't you like an aristocracy if you could be one of the aristocrats? Don't you think you're opposed to aristocracy because you don't want to be under? I have spoken to be a duke when we get an order of nobility, and I find that it's a great relief. I don't feel obliged to go in for equality nearly as much as I used."

Lemuel shyly dropped the subject, not feeling himself able to cope with his elder in these railleries. He always felt his heaviness and clumsiness in talking with the editor, who fascinated him. He did not know but he had said too much about city people being aristocratic. It was not quite what he meant; he had really been thinking of Miss Carver, and how proud she was, when he said it.

Lately he had seemed to see a difference between himself and other people, and he had begun to look for it everywhere, though when he spoke to Evans he was not aware how strongly the poison was working in him. It was as if the girl had made that difference; she made it again, whatever it was, between herself and the black man who once brought her a note and a bunch of flowers from one of her young lady pupils. She was very polite to him, trying to put him at ease, just as she had been with Lemuel that night. If he came into the dining-room to seat a transient when Miss Carver was there, he knew that she was mentally making a difference between him and the boarders. The ladies all had the custom of bidding him good-morning when they came in to breakfast, and they all smiled upon him except Miss Carver; she seemed every morning as if more surprised to see him standing there at the door and showing people to their places; she looked puzzled, and sometimes she blushed, as if she were ashamed for him.

He had discovered, in fine, that there were sorts of honest work in the world which one must not do if he would keep his self-respect through the consideration of others. Once all work had been work, but now he had found that there was work which was service, and that service was dishonor. He had learned that the people who did this work were as a class apart, and were spoken of as servants, with slight that was unconscious or conscious, but never absent.

Some of the ladies at the St. Albans had tried to argue with Lemuel about his not taking the fees he refused, and he knew that they talked him over. One day, when he was showing a room to a transient, he heard one of them say to another in the next apartment, "Well, I did hate to offer it to him, just as if he was a common servant"; and the other said, "Well, I don't see what he can expect if he puts himself in the place of a servant." And then they debated together whether his quality of clerk was sufficient to redeem him from the reproach of servitude; they did not call his running the elevator anything, because a clerk might do that in a casual way without loss of dignity; they alleged other cases of the kind.

His inner life became a turmoil of suspicions, that attached themselves to every word spoken to him by those who must think themselves above him. He could see now how far behind in everything Willoughby Pastures was, and how the summer folks could not help despising the people that took them to board, and waited on them like servants in cities. He esteemed the boarders at the St. Albans in the degree that he thought them enlightened enough to contemn him for his station; and he had his own ideas of how such a person as Mr. Evans really felt toward him. He felt toward him and was interested in his reading as a person might feel toward and be interested in the attainments of some anomalous animal, a learned pig, or something of that kind.

He could look back, now, on his life at Miss Vane's, and see that he was treated as a servant, there,—a petted servant, but still a servant,—and that was what made that girl behave so to him; he always thought of Sibyl as that girl.

He would have thrown up his place at once, though he knew of nothing else he could do; he would have risked starving rather than keep it; but he felt that it was of no use; that the stain of servitude was indelible; that if he were lifted to the highest station, it would not redeem him in Miss Carver's eyes. All this time he had scarcely more than spoken with her, to return her good-mornings at the dining-room door, or to exchange greetings with her on the stairs, or to receive some charge from her in going out, or to answer some question of hers in coming in, as to whether any of the pupils who had lessons of her had been there in her absence. He made these interviews as brief as possible; he was as stiff and cold as she.

The law-student, whose full name was Alonzo W. Berry, had one joking manner for all manner of men and women, and Lemuel's suspicion could not find any offensive distinction in it toward himself; but he disabled Berry's own gentility for that reason, and easily learning much of the law-student's wild past in the West from so eager an autobiographer, he could not comfort himself with his friendship. While the student poured out his autobiography without stint upon Lemuel, his shyness only deepened upon the boy. There were things in his life for which he was in equal fear of discovery: his arrest and trial in the police court, his mother's queerness, and his servile condition at Miss Vane's. The thought that Mr. Sewell knew about them all made him sometimes hate the minister, till he reflected that he had evidently told no one of them. But he was always trembling lest they should somehow become known at the St. Albans; and when Berry was going on about himself, his exploits, his escapes, his loves,—chiefly his loves,—Lemuel's soul was sealed within him; a vision of his disgraces filled him with horror.

But in the delight of talking about himself, Berry was apparently unaware that Lemuel had not reciprocated his confidences. He celebrated his familiarity with Miss Swan and her friend, though no doubt he had the greater share of the acquaintance,—that was apt to be the case with him,—and from time to time he urged Lemuel to come up and call on them with him.

"I guess they don't want *me* to call," said Lemuel with feeble bitterness at last, one evening after an elaborate argument from Berry to prove that Lemuel had the time, and that he just knew they would be glad to see him.

"Why?" demanded Berry, and he tried to get Lemuel's reason; but when Lemuel had stated that belief, he could not have given the reason for it on his death-bed. Berry gave the conundrum up for the time, but he did not give Lemuel up; he had an increasing need of him as he advanced in a passion for Miss Swan, which, as he frankly prophesied, was bound to bring him to the popping-point sooner or later; he debated with himself in Lemuel's presence all the best forms of popping, and he said that it was simply worth a ranch to be able to sing to him,

> "She's a darling,
> She's a daisy,
> She's a dumpling,
> She's a lamb,"

and to feel that he knew who *she* was. He usually sang this refrain to Lemuel when he came in late at night after a little supper with some of the fellows, that had left traces of its cheer on his bated breath. Once he came down-stairs alone in the elevator, in his shirt-sleeves and stocking-feet, for the purpose of singing it after Lemuel had thought him in bed.

Every Sunday afternoon during the winter Lemuel went to see Statira, and sometimes in the evening he took her to church. But she could not understand why he always wanted to go to a different church; she did not see why he should not pick out one church and stick to it: the ministers seemed to be all alike, and she guessed one was pretty near as good as another. 'Manda Grier said she guessed they were all Lemuel to her; and Statira said well, she guessed that was pretty much so. She no longer pretended that he was not the whole world to her, either with him or with 'Manda Grier; she was so happy from morning till night, day in and day out, that 'Manda Grier said if she were in her place she should be afraid something would happen.

Statira worked in the box-factory now; she liked it a great deal better than the store, and declared that she was ever so much stronger. The cough lingered still, but none of them noticed it much; she called it a cold, and said she kept catching more. 'Manda Grier told her that she could throw it off soon enough if she would buy a few clothes for warmth and not so many for looks; but they did not talk this over before Lemuel. Before he came Statira took a soothing mixture that she got of the apothecary, and then they were all as bright and gay as could be, and she looked so pretty that he said he could not get used to it. The housekeeping experiment was a great success; she and 'Manda Grier had two rooms now, and they lived better than ever they had, for less money. Of course, Statira said, it was not up to the St. Albans, which Lemuel had told them of at first a little braggingly. In fact she liked to have him brag of it, and of the splendors of his position and surroundings. She was very curious, but not envious of anything, and it became a joke with her and 'Manda Grier, who pretended to despise the whole affair.

At first it flattered Lemuel to have her admire his rise in life so simply and ardently; but after a while it became embarrassing, in proportion as it no longer seemed so superb to him. She was always wanting him to talk of it; after a few Sundays, with the long hours they had passed in telling each other all they could think of about themselves, they had not much else to talk of. Now that she had him to employ her fancy, Statira no longer fed it on the novels she used to devour. He brought her books, but she did not read them; she said that she had been so busy with her sewing she had no time to read; and every week she showed him some pretty new thing she had been making, and tried it on for him to see how she looked in it. Often she seemed to care more to rest with her head on his shoulder, and not talk at all; and for a while this was enough for him too, though sometimes he was disappointed that she did not even let him read to her out of the books she neglected. She would not talk over the sermons they heard together; but once when Mr. Evans offered him tickets for the theater, and Lemuel had got the night off and taken Statira, it seemed as if she would be willing to sit up till morning and talk the play over.

Nothing else ever interested her so much, except what one of the girls in the box-factory had told her about going down to the beach, summers, and waiting on table. This girl had been at Old Orchard, where they had splendid times, with one veranda all to themselves and the gentlemen-help; and in the afternoon the girls got together on the beach—or the grass right in front of the hotel—and sewed. They got nearly as much as they did in the box-factory; and then the boarders all gave you something extra; some of them gave as much as a dollar a week apiece. The head-waiter was a college student, and a perfect gentleman; he was always dressed up in a dress-suit and a white silk neck-tie. Statira said that next summer she wanted they should go off somewhere, she and 'Manda Grier, and wait on table together; and she knew Lemuel could easily get the head-waiter's place, after the St. Albans. She should not want he should be clerk, because then they could not have such good times, for they would be more separated.

Lemuel heard her restively through, and then broke out fiercely and told her that he had seen enough of waiting on table at the St. Albans for him never to want her to do it; and that the boarders who gave money to the waiters despised them for taking it. He said that he did not consider just helping Mrs. Harmon out the same as being head-waiter, and that he would not be a regular waiter for any money: he would rather starve.

Statira did not understand; she asked him meekly if he were mad at her, he seemed so; and he had to do what he could to cheer her up.

'Manda Grier took Statira's part pretty sharply. She said it was one thing to live out in a private family—that *was* a disgrace, if you could keep the breath of life in you any other way—and it was quite another to wait in a hotel; and she did not want to have any one hint around that she would let Statira demean herself. Lemuel was offended by her manner, and her assumption of owning Statira. She defended him, but he could not tell her how he had changed; the influences were perhaps too obscure for him to have traced them all himself; after the first time he had hardly mentioned the art-student girls to her. There were a great many things that Statira could not understand. She had been much longer in the city than Lemuel, but she did not seem to appreciate the difference between that and the country. She dressed very stylishly; no one went beyond her in that; but in many things he could see that she remained countrified. Once on a very mild April evening, when they were passing through the Public Garden, she wished him to sit on a vacant seat they came to. All the others were occupied by young couples who sat with their arms around each other.

"No, no!" shuddered Lemuel, "I don't want people should take you for one of these servant-girls."

"Why, Lem, how proud you're getting!" she cried with easy acquiescence. "You're awfully stuck up! Well, then, you've got to take a horse-car; I can't walk any further."

XIX

LEMUEL had found out about the art-students from Berry. He said they were no relation to each other, and had not even been acquainted before they met at the art-school; he had first met them at the St. Albans. Miss Swan was from the western part of the State, and Miss Carver from down Plymouth way. The latter took pupils, and sometimes gave lessons at their houses; she was, to Berry's thinking, not half the genius and not half the duck that Miss Swan was, though she was a duck in her way too. Miss Swan, as nearly as he could explain, was studying art for the fun of it, or the excitement, for she was well enough off; her father was a lawyer out there, and Berry believed that a rising son-in-law in his own profession would be just the thing for the old man's declining years. He said he should not be very particular about settling down to practice at once; if his wife wanted to go to Europe awhile, and kind of tenderfoot it round for a year or two in the art-centers over there, he would let the old man run the business a little longer; sometimes it did an old man good. There was no hurry; Berry's own father was not excited about his going to work right away; he had the money to run Berry and a wife too, if it came to that; Miss Swan understood that. He had not told her so in just so many words, but he had let her know that Alonzo W. Berry, Senior, was not borrowing money at two per cent. a month any more. He said he did not care to make much of a blow about that part of it till he was ready to act, and he was not going to act till he had a dead-sure thing of it; he was having a very good time as it went along, and he guessed Miss Swan was too; no use to hurry a girl, when she was on the right track.

Berry invented these axioms apparently to put himself in heart; in the abstract he was already courageous enough. He said that these Eastern girls were not used to having any sort of attention; that there was only about a tenth or fifteenth of a fellow to every girl, and that it tickled one of them to death to have a whole man around. He was not meanly exultant at their destitution. He said he just wished one of these pretty Boston girls—nice, well dressed, cultured, and brought up to be snubbed and neglected by the tenths and fifteenths of men they had at home—could be let loose in the West, and have a regular round-up of fellows. Or no, he would like to have about five thousand fellows from out there, that never expected a woman to look at them, unloaded in Boston, and see them open their eyes. "Wouldn't one of 'em get home alive, if kindness could kill 'em. I never saw such a place! I can't get used to it! It makes me tired. *Any* sort of fellow could get married in Boston!"

Berry made no attempt to reconcile his uncertainty as to his own chances with this general theory, but he urged it to prove that Miss Swan and Miss Carver would like to have Lemuel call; he said they had both said they wished they could paint him. He had himself sustained various characters in costume for them, and one night he pretended that they had sent him down for Lemuel to help out with a certain group. But they received him with a sort of blankness which convinced him that Berry had exceeded his authority; there was a helplessness at first, and then an indignant determination to save him from a false position even at their own cost, which Lemuel felt rather than saw. Miss Carver was foremost in his rescue; she devoted herself to this, and left Miss Swan to punish Berry, who conveyed from time to time his sense that he was "getting it," by a wink to Lemuel.

An observer with more social light might have been more

puzzled to account for Berry's toleration by these girls, who apparently associated with him on equal terms. Since he was not a servant, he *was* their equal in Lemuel's eyes; perhaps his acceptance might otherwise be explained by the fact that he was very amusing, chivalrously harmless, and extremely kind-hearted and useful to them. One must not leave out of the reckoning his open devotion for Miss Swan, which in itself would do much to approve him to her, and commend him to Miss Carver, if she were a generous girl, and very fond of her friend. It is certain that they did tolerate Berry, who made them laugh even that night in spite of themselves, till Miss Swan said, "Well, what's the use?" and stopped trying to discipline him. After that they had a very sociable evening, though Lemuel kept his distance, and would not let them include him, knowing what the two girls really thought of him. He would not take part in Berry's buffooneries, but talked soberly and rather austerely with Miss Carver; and to show that he did not feel himself an inferior, whatever she might think, he was very sarcastic about some of the city ways and customs they spoke of. There were a good many books about—novels mostly, but not the kind Statira used to read, and poems; Miss Carver said she liked to take them up when she was nervous from her work; and if the weather was bad, and she could not get out for a walk, a book seemed to do her almost as much good. Nearly all the pictures about in the room seemed to be Miss Swan's; in fact, when Lemuel asked about them, and tried to praise them in such a way as not to show his ignorance, Miss Carver said she did very little in color; her lessons were all in black and white. He would not let her see that he did not know what this was, but he was ashamed, and he determined to find out; he determined to get a drawing-book, and learn something about it himself. To his thinking, the room was pretty harum-scarum. There were shawls hung upon the walls, and rugs, and pieces of cloth, which sometimes had half-finished paintings fastened to them; there were paintings standing round the room on the floor, sometimes right side out, and sometimes faced to the walls; there were two or three fleeces and fox-pelts scattered about instead of a carpet; and there were two easels, and stands with paints all twisted up in lead tubes on them. He compared the room with Statira's, and did not think much of it at first.

Afterwards it did not seem so bad; he began to feel its picturesqueness, for he went there again, and let the girls sketch him. When Miss Swan asked him that night if he would let them he wished to refuse; but she seemed so modest about it, and made it such a great favor on his part, that he consented; she said she merely wished to make a little sketch in color, and Miss Carver a little study of his head in black and white; and he imagined it a trifling affair that could be dispatched in a single night. They decided to treat his head as a Young Roman head; and at the end of a long sitting, beguiled with talk and with thoughtful voluntaries from Berry on his banjo, he found that Miss Carver had rubbed her study nearly all out with a piece of bread, and Miss Swan said she should want to try a perfectly new sketch with the shoulders draped; the coat had confused her; she would not let any one see what she had done, though Berry tried to make her let him.

Lemuel looked a little blank when she asked him for another sitting; but Berry said, "Oh, you'll have to come, Barker. Penalty of greatness, you know. Have you in Williams & Everett's window; notices in all the papers. 'The exquisite studies, by Miss Swan and Miss Carver, of the head of the gentlemanly and accommodating clerk of the St. Albans, as a Roman Youth.' Chromoed as a Christmas card by Prang, and photograph copies everywhere. You're all right, Barker."

One night Miss Swan said, in rapture with some momentary success, "Oh, I'm perfectly in love with this head!"

Berry looked up from his banjo, which he ceased to strum. "Hello, hello, hel-*lo!*"

Then the two broke into a laugh, in which Lemuel helplessly joined.

"What—what is it?" asked Miss Carver, looking up absently from her work.

"Nothing; just a little outburst of passion from our young friend here," said Berry, nodding his head toward Miss Swan.

"What does it mean, Mad?" asked Miss Carver in the same dreamy way, continuing her work.

"Yes, Madeline," said Berry, "explain yourself."

"Mr. Berry!" cried Miss Swan, warningly.

"That's me; Alonzo W., Jr. Go on!"

"You forget yourself," said the girl with imperfect severity.

"Well, you forgot me first," said Berry with affected injury. "Ain't it hard enough to sit here night after night, strumming on the old banjo, while another fellow is going down to posterity as a Roman Youth with a red shawl round his neck, without having to hear people say they're in love with that head of his?"

Miss Carver now stopped her work, and looked from her friend, with her head bowed in laughter on the back of her hand, to that of Berry bent in burlesque reproach upon her, and then at Lemuel, who was trying to control himself.

"But I can tell you what, Miss Swan; you spoke too late, as the man said when he swallowed the chicken in the fresh egg. Mr. Barker has a previous engagement. That so, Barker?"

Lemuel turned fire-red, and looked round at Miss Carver, who met his glance with her clear gaze. She turned presently to make some comment on Miss Swan's sketch, and then, after working a little while longer, she said she was tired, and was going to make some tea.

The girls both pressed Lemuel to stay for a cup, but he would not; and Berry followed him downstairs to explain and apologize.

"It's all right," said Lemuel. "What difference would it make to them whether I was engaged or not?"

"Well, I suppose as a general rule a girl would rather a fellow wasn't," philosophized Berry. He whistled ruefully, and Lemuel drawing a book toward him in continued silence,

he rose from the seat he had taken on the desk in the little
office, and said, "Well, I guess it'll all come out right. Come
to think of it, *I* don't know anything about your affairs, and
I can tell 'em so."

"Oh, it don't matter."

He had pulled the book toward him as if he were going to
read, but he could not read; his head was in a whirl. After a
first frenzy of resentment against Berry, he was now angry
at himself for having been so embarrassed. He thought of a
retort that would have passed it all off lightly; then he reflected again that it was of no consequence to these young
ladies whether he was engaged or not, and at any rate it was
nobody's business but his own. Of course he was engaged to
Statira, but he had hardly thought of it in that way. 'Manda
Grier had joked about the time when she supposed she should
have to keep old maid's hall alone; when she first did this
Lemuel thought it delightful, but afterwards he did not like
it so much; it began to annoy him that 'Manda Grier should
mix herself up so much with Statira and himself. He believed
that Statira would be different, would be more like other
ladies (he generalized it in this way, but he meant Miss Swan
and Miss Carver), if she had not 'Manda Grier there all the
time to keep her back. He convinced himself that if it were
not for 'Manda Grier, he should have had no trouble in telling Statira that the art-students were sketching him; and that
he had not done so yet because he hated to have 'Manda ask her
so much about them, and call them that Swan girl and that
Carver girl, as she would be sure to do, and clip away the
whole evening with her questions and her guesses. It was now
nearly a fortnight since the sketching began, and he had let
one Sunday night pass without mentioning it. He could not
let another pass, and he knew 'Manda Grier would say they
were a good while about it, and would show her ignorance,
and put Statira up to asking all sorts of things. He could not
bear to think of it, and he let the next Sunday night pass without saying anything to Statira. The sittings continued; but

before the third Sunday came Miss Swan said she did not see how she could do anything more to her sketch, and Miss Carver had already completed her study. They criticised each other's work with freedom and good humor, and agreed that the next thing was to paint it out and rub it out.

"No," said Berry; "what you want is a fresh eye on it. I've worried over it as much as you have,—suffered more, I be-lieve,—and Barker can't tell whether he looks like a Roman Youth or not. Why don't you have up old Evans?"

Miss Swan took no apparent notice of this suggestion; and Miss Carver, who left Berry's snubbing entirely to her, said nothing. After a minute's study of the pictures, Miss Swan suggested, "If Mr. Barker had any friends he would like to show them to?"

"Oh, no, thank you," returned Lemuel hastily, "there isn't anybody," and again he found himself turning very red.

"Well, I don't know how we can thank you enough for your patience, Mr. Barker," said the girl.

"Oh, don't mention it. I've—I've enjoyed it," said Lemuel.

"Game—every time," said Berry; and their evening broke up with a laugh.

The next morning Lemuel stopped Miss Swan at the door of the breakfast-room, and said, "I've been thinking over what you said last night, and I *should* like to bring some one —a lady friend of mine—to see the pictures."

"Why, certainly, Mr. Barker. Any time. Some evening?" she suggested.

"Should you mind it if I came to-morrow night?" he asked; and he thought it right to remind her, "It's Sunday night."

"Oh, not at all! To-morrow night, by all means! We shall both be at home, and very glad to see you." She hurried after Miss Carver, loitering on her way to their table, and Lemuel saw them put their heads together, as if they were whisper-ing. He knew they were whispering about him, but they did not laugh; probably they kept themselves from laughing. In coming out from breakfast, Miss Swan said, "I hope your friend isn't *very* critical, Mr. Barker?" and he answered confusedly, "Oh, not at all, thank you." But he said to himself that he did not care whether she was trying to make fun of him or not, he knew what he had made up his mind to do.

Statira did not seem to care much about going to see the pictures, when he proposed it to her the next evening. She asked why he had been keeping it such a great secret, and he could not pretend, as he had once thought he could, that he was keeping it as a surprise for her. "Should *you* like to see 'em, 'Manda?" she asked with languid indifference.

"I d' know as I care much about Lem's picture, s' long 's we've got *him* around," 'Manda Grier whipped out, "but I *should* like t' see those celebrated girls 't we 've heard s' much about."

"Well," said Statira carelessly, and they went into the next room to put on their wraps. Lemuel, vexed to have 'Manda Grier made one of the party, and helpless to prevent her going, walked up and down, wondering what he should say when he arrived with this unexpected guest.

But Miss Swan received both of the girls very politely, and chatted with 'Manda Grier, whose conversation, in defiance of any sense of superiority that the Swan girl or the Carver girl might feel, was a succession of laconic snaps, sometimes witty, but mostly rude and contradictory.

Miss Carver made tea, and served it in some pretty cups which Lemuel hoped Statira might admire, but she took it without noticing, and in talking with Miss Carver she drawled, and said "N-y-e-e-e-s," and "I don't know as I d-o-o-o," and "Well, I should think as m-u-u-ch," with a prolongation of all the final syllables in her sentences which had not observed in her before, and which she must have borrowed for the occasion for the gentility of the effect. She tried to refer everything to him, and she and 'Manda Grier talked together as much as they could, and when the others spoke of him as Mr. Barker, they called him Lem. They did not look at anything, or do anything to betray that they found the studio, on which Lemuel had once expatiated to them, different from other rooms.

At last Miss Swan abruptly brought out the studies of Lemuel's head, and put them in a good light; 'Manda Grier and Statira got into the wrong place to see them.

'Manda blurted out, "Well, he looks 's if he'd had a fit of sickness in *that* one"; and perhaps, in fact, Miss Carver had refined too much upon a delicate ideal of Lemuel's looks.

"So he d-o-o-es!" drawled Statira. "And how funny he looks with that red thing o-o-o-n!"

Miss Swan explained that she had thrown that in for the color, and that they had been fancying him in the character of a young Roman.

"You think he's got a Roman n-o-o-se?" asked Statira through her own.

"I think Lem's got a kind of a pug, m'self," said 'Manda Grier.

"Well, 'Manda Grier!" said Statira.

Lemuel could not look at Miss Carver, whom he knew to be gazing at the two girls from the little distance to which she had withdrawn; Miss Swan was biting her lip.

"So that's the celebrated St. Albans, is it?" said 'Manda Grier, when they got in the street. "Don't know's I really ever expected to see the inside 'f it. You notice the kind of oilcloth they had on that upper entry, S'tira?"

They did not mention Lemuel's pictures, or the artists; and he scarcely spoke on the way home.

When they parted, Statira broke out crying and would not let him kiss her.

XX

"I'M AFRAID your little friend at the St. Albans isn't altogether happy of late," said Evans toward the end of what he called one of his powwows with Sewell. Their talk had taken a vaster range than usual, and they both felt the need, that people know in dealing with abstractions, of finally getting the ground beneath their feet again.

"Ah?" asked Sewell, with a twinge that allayed his satisfaction in this. "What's the matter with him?"

"Oh, the knowledge of good and evil, I suspect."

"I hope there's nothing wrong," said Sewell, anxiously.

"Oh, no. I used the phrase because it came easily. Just what I mean is that I'm afraid his view of our social inequalities is widening and deepening, and that he experiences the dissatisfaction of people who don't command that prospect from the summit. I told you of his censure of our aristocratic constitution?"

"Yes," said Sewell, with a smile.

"Well, I'm afraid he feels it more and more. If I can judge from the occasional distance and *hauteur* with which he treats me, he is humiliated by it. Nothing makes a man so proud as humiliation, you know."

"That's true!"

"There are a couple of pretty girls at the St. Albans, art-students, who have been painting Barker. So I learn from a reformed cow-boy of the plains who is with us as a law-student, and is about with one of the young ladies a good deal. They're rather nice girls; quite nice, in fact; and there's no harm in the cow-boy, and a good deal of fun. But if Barker had conceived of being painted as a social inferior and had been made to feel that he was merely a model, and if he had become at all aware that one of the girls was rather pretty—they both are——"

"I see!"

"I don't say it's so. But he seems low-spirited. Why don't you come round and cheer him up—get into his confidence——"

"Get into the center of the earth!" cried Sewell. "I never saw such an inapproachable creature!"

Evans laughed. "He *is* rather remote. The genuine American youth is apt to be so, especially if he thinks you mean him a kindness. But there ought to be some way of convincing him that he need not feel any ignominy in his employment. After so many centuries of Christianity and generations of Democracy, it ought to be very simple to convince him that there is nothing disgraceful in showing people to their places at table."

"It isn't," said the minister, soberly.

"No, it isn't," said Evans. "I wonder," he added thoughtfully, "why we despise certain occupations? We don't despise a man who hammers stone or saws boards; why should we despise a barber? Is the care of the human head intrinsically less honorable than the shaping of such rude material? Why do we still contemn the tailor who clothes us, and honor the painter who portrays us in the same clothes? Why do we despise waiters? I tried to make Barker believe that I respected all kinds of honest work. But I lied; I despised him for having waited on table. Why have all manner of domestics fallen under our scorn, and come to be stigmatized in a lump as servants?"

"Ah, I don't know," said the minister. "There *is* something in personal attendance upon us that dishonors; but the reasons of it are very obscure; *I* couldn't give them. Perhaps it's because it's work that in a simpler state of things each of us would do for himself, and in this state is too proud to do."

"That doesn't cover the whole ground," said Evans.

"And you think that poor boy is troubled—is really suffering from a sense of inferiority to the other young people?"

"Oh, I don't say certainly. Perhaps not. But if he were, what should you say was the best thing for him to do? Remain a servant; cast his lot with these outcasts; or try to separate and distinguish himself from them, as we all do? Come; we live in the world, which isn't so bad, though it's pretty stupid. He couldn't change it. Now, what ought he to do?"

Sewell mused awhile without answering anything. Then he said with a smile, "It's very much simpler to fit people for the other world than for this, don't you think?"

"Yes, it is. It was a cold day for the clergy when it was imagined that they ought to do both."

"Well," said Sewell, rising to follow his friend to the door, "I will come to see Barker, and try to talk with him. He's a very complicated problem. I supposed that I had merely his material prosperity to provide for, after getting him down here; but if I have to reconcile him to the constitution of society!"

"Yes," said Evans. "I wish you'd let me know the result of your labors. I think I could make a very incisive article on the subject. The topic is always an attractive one. There is nobody who doesn't feel that somebody else is taking on airs with him, and ought to have his comb cut. Or, if you should happen to prove to Barker that his ignominy is in accordance with the Development Theory, and is a necessary Survival, or something of that sort, don't you see what a card it would be for us with the better classes?"

They went down-stairs together, and at the street door Evans stopped again. "Or, I'll tell you what. Make it a simple study of Barker's mind—a sort of psychological interview; and then with what I've been able to get from him we can present the impression that Boston makes upon a young, fresh, shrewd mind. That would be something rather new, wouldn't it? Come! the 'Afternoon' would make it worth your while. And then you could work it into a sermon afterwards."

"You shameless reprobate!" said Sewell, laying his hand affectionately on his friend's arm.

There was nothing in Lemuel's case that seemed to him urgent, and he did not go to see him at once. In the mean time, Fast Day came, and Lemuel got away at last to pay his first visit home.

"Seems to me ye ain't lookin' over and above well, Lem," was the first thing his mother said to him, even before she noticed how well he was dressed.

His new spring overcoat, another prize from the Misfit Parlors, and his new pointed-toe shoes and Derby hat, with the suit of clothes he had kept so carefully all through the winter, were not the complete disguise he had fancied they might be at Willoughby Pastures. The depot-master had known him as soon as he got out of the cars, and ignored his splendor in recognizing him. He said, "Hello, Lem!" and had not time to reconcile himself to the boy's changed appearance before Lemuel hurried away with the bag he had bought so long before for the visit. He met several people on his way home from the depot: two of them were women, and one of these said she knew as soon as she looked at him who it was, and the other said she should have known it was Lem Barker as far as she could see him. She asked him if he was home for good now.

His mother pushed back his thick hair with her hard old hand as she spoke to him, and then she pressed his head down upon her neck, which was mostly collar-bone. But Lemuel could hear her heart beat, and the tears came into his eyes.

"Oh, I'm all right, mother," he said huskily, though he tried to say it cheerfully. He let her hold his head there the longer because mixed with his tenderness for her was a horror of her bloomers, which he was not at once able to overcome. When he gained courage to look, he saw that she had them on, but now he had the strength to bear it.

"Ye had any breakfast?" she asked; and when he said that he had got a cup of coffee at Fitchburg, she said, well, she must get him something; and she drew him a cup of Japan tea, and made him some milk-toast and picked-fish, talking all the time, and telling him how his sister and her husband had gone to the village to have one of her teeth drawn. They had got along through the winter pretty well; but she guessed that they would have had more to complain of if it had not been for him. This was her way of acknowledging the help Lemuel had given them every week, and it was casually sandwiched between an account of an Indian Spirit treatment, which Reuben had tried for his rheumatism, and a question whether Lemuel had seen anything of that Mind Cure down to Boston.

But when he looked about the room, and saw here and there the simple comforts and necessaries which his money had bought the sick man and the two helpless women, his heart swelled with joy and pride; and he realized the pleasure we all feel in being a good genius. At times it had come pretty hard to send the greater part of his week's wages home, but now he was glad he had done it. The poor, coarse food which his mother had served him as a treat; the low, cracked ceilings; the waving floor, covered with rag carpet; the sagging doors, and the old-fashioned trim of the small-paned windows, were all very different from the luxurious abundance, the tessellated pavement, and the tapestry brussels, the lofty studding, and the black walnut moldings of the St. Albans; and Lemuel felt the difference with a curious mixture of pride and remorse in his own escape from the meanness of his home. He felt the self-reproach to which the man who rises without raising with him all those dear to him is destined in some measure all his life. His interests and associations are separated from theirs, but if he is not an ignoble spirit, the ties of affection remain unweakened; he cares for them with a kind of indignant tenderness, and calls himself to account before them in the midst of pleasures which they cannot share, or even imagine.

Lemuel's mother did not ask him much about his life in

Boston; she had not the materials for curiosity about it; but he told her everything that he thought she could understand. She recurred to his hopes when he left home and their disappointment in Sewell, and she asked if Lemuel ever saw him nowadays. She could not reconcile herself to his reconciliation with Sewell, whom she still held to have behaved treacherously. Then she went back to Lemuel's looks, and asked him if he kept pretty well; and when he answered that he did, she smoothed with her hand the knot between her eyes, and did not question him further.

He had the whole forenoon with his mother, and he helped her to get the dinner, as he used to do, pulling the stove-wood out of the snow-drift that still imbedded part of the wood-pile, though the snow was all gone around Boston. It was thawing under the dull, soft April sky, and he saw the first bluebird perched on the clothes-line when he went out for the wood; his mother said there had been lots of them. He walked about the place, and into the barn, taking in the forlornness and shabbiness; and then he went up into the room over the shed, where he used to study and write. His heart ached with self-pity.

He realized as he had not done at a distance how dependent this wretched home was upon him; and after meaning the whole morning to tell his mother about Statira, he decided that he was keeping it from her, not merely because he was ashamed to tell her that he was engaged, but because it seemed such a crazy thing, for a person in his circumstances, if it was really an engagement. He had not seen Statira since that night when he brought her to look at the pictures the art-students had made of him. He felt that he had not parted with her kindly, and he went to see her the night before he started home, though it was not Sunday; but he had found her door locked, and this made him angry with her, he could not have said just why. If he told his mother about Statira now, what should he tell her? He compromised by telling her about the two girls that had painted his likeness.

His mother seemed not to care a great deal about the picture. She said, "I don't want you should let any girl make a fool of you, Lem."

"Oh, no," he answered; and went and looked out of the window.

"I don't say but what they're nice girls enough, but in your place you no need to throw yourself away."

Lemuel thought of the awe of Miss Carver in which he lived, and the difference between them; and he could have laughed at his mother's ignorant pride. What would she say if she knew that he was engaged to a girl that worked in a box-factory? But probably she would not think that studying art and teaching it was any better. She evidently believed that his position in the St. Albans was superior to that of Miss Carver.

His sister and her husband came home before they had finished dinner. His sister had her face all tied up to keep from taking cold after having her tooth drawn, and Lemuel had to go out and help his rheumatic brother-in-law put up the horse. When they came in, his brother-in-law did not wash his hands before going to the table, and Lemuel could not keep his eyes off his black and broken finger-nails; his mother's and sister's nails were black too. It must have been so when he lived at home.

His sister could not eat; she took some tea, and went to bed. His brother-in-law pulled off his boots after dinner, and put up his stocking-feet on the stove-hearth to warm them.

There was no longer any chance to talk with his mother indoors, and he asked her if she would not like to come out; it was very mild. She put on her bonnet, and they strolled down the road. All the time Lemuel had to keep from looking at her bloomers. When they met any one driving, he had to keep himself from trying to look as if he were not with her, but was just out walking alone.

The day wore heavily away. His brother-in-law's rheumatism came on toward evening, and his sister's face had swollen, so that it would not do for her to go out. Lemuel put on some old clothes he found in his room, and milked the cows himself.

"Like old times, Lem," said his mother, when he came in.

"Yes," he assented quietly.

He and his mother had tea together, but pretty soon afterwards she seemed to get sleepy; and Lemuel said he had been up early and he guessed he would go to bed. His mother said she guessed she would go too.

After he had blown out his light, she came in to see if he were comfortable. "I presume it seems a pretty poor place to you, Lem," she said, holding her lamp up and looking round.

"I guess if it's good enough for you it is for me," he answered evasively.

"No, it ain't," she said. "I always b'en used to it, and I can see from your talk that you've got used to something different already. Well, it's right, Lem. You're a good boy, and I want you should get the good of Boston, all you can. We don't any of us begrutch it to ye; and what I came up to say now was, don't you scrimp yourself down there to send home to us. We got a roof over our heads, and we can keep soul and body together somehow; we always have, and we don't need a great deal. But I want you should keep yourself nicely dressed down to Boston, so't you can go with the best; I don't want you should feel anyways meechin' on account of your clothes. You got a good figure, Lem; you take after your father. Sometimes I wish you was a little bigger; but *he* wa'n't; and he had a big spirit. He wa'n't afraid of anything; and they said if he'd come out o' that battle where he was killed, he'd 'a' b'en a captain. He was a good man."

She had hardly ever spoken so much of his father before; he knew now by the sound of her voice in the dim room that the tears must be in her eyes; but she governed herself and went on.

"What I wanted to say was, don't you keep sendin' so much o' your money home, child. It's yours, and I want you should have it. Most of it goes for patent medicines, anyway, when it gets here; we can't keep Reuben from buying 'em, and he's always changin' doctors. And I want you should hold yourself high, Lem. You're as good as anybody. And don't you go with any girls, especially, that ain't of the best. You're gettin' to that time o' life when you'll begin to think about 'em; but don't you go and fall in love with the first little poppet you see, because she's got pretty eyes and curly hair."

It seemed to Lemuel as if she must know about Statira, but of course she did not. He lay still, and she went on.

"Don't you go and get engaged, or any such foolishness, in a hurry, Lem. Them art-student girls you was tellin' about, I presume they're all right enough; but you wait awhile. Young men think it's a kind of miracle if a girl likes 'em, and they're ready to go crazy over it; but it's the most natural thing she can do. You just wait awhile. When you get along a little further, you can pick and choose for yourself. I don't know as I should want you should marry for money; but don't you go and take up with the first thing comes along, because you're afraid to look higher. What's become o' that nasty thing that talked so to you at that Miss Vane's?"

Lemuel said that he had never seen Sibyl or Miss Vane since; but he did not make any direct response to the anxieties his mother had hinted at. Her pride in him, so ignorant of all the reality of his life in the city, crushed him more than the sight and renewed sense of the mean conditions from which he had sprung. What if he should tell her that Miss Carver, whom she did not want him to marry in a hurry, regarded him as a servant, and treated him as she would treat a black man? What if she knew that he was as good as engaged to marry a girl that could no more meet Miss Carver on the same level than she could fly? He could only tell his mother not to feel troubled about him; that he was not going to get married in any great hurry; and pretend to be sleepy and turn his head away.

She pulled the covering up round his neck and tucked it in with her strong, rough old hand, whose very tenderness hurt.

He had expected to stay the greater part of the next day,

but he took an earlier train. His sister was still laid up; she thought she must have taken cold in her jaw; her husband, rumpled, unshaven, with a shawl over his shoulders, cowered about the cook-stove for the heat. He began to hate this poverty and suffering, to long for escape from it to the life which at that distance seemed so rich and easy and pleasant; he trembled lest something might have happened in his absence to throw him out of his place.

All the way to Boston he was under the misery of the home that he was leaving; his mother's pride added to the burden of it. But when the train drew in sight of the city, and he saw the steeples and chimneys, and the thin masts of the ships printed together against the horizon, his heart rose. He felt equal to it, to anything in it.

He arrived in the middle of the afternoon, and he saw no one at the hotel except the Harmons till toward dinner-time. Then the ladies coming in from shopping had a word of welcome for him; some of them stopped and shook hands at the office, and when they began to come down to dinner they spoke to him, and there again some of them offered their hands; they said it seemed an age since he had gone.

The art-students came down with Berry, who shook hands so cordially with him that perhaps they could not help it. Miss Carver seemed to hesitate, but she gave him her hand too, and she asked, as the others had done, whether he had found his family well.

He did not know what to think. Sometimes he felt as if people were trying to make a fool of him, almost. He remained blushing and smiling to himself after the last of them had gone in to dinner. He did not know what Miss Carver meant, but her eyes seemed to have lost that cold distance, and to have come nearer to him.

Late at night Berry came to him where he sat at his desk. "Well, Barker, I'm glad you're back again, old man. Feels as if you'd been gone a month of Sundays. Didn't know whether we should have you with us this *first* evening."

Lemuel grew hot with consciousness, and did not make it

better for himself by saying, "I don't know what you mean."

"Well, I don't suppose *I* should in your *place*," returned Berry. "It's human nature. It's all right. What did the ladies think of the 'Roman Youth' the other night? The distinguished artists weren't sure exactly, and I thought I could make capital with one of 'em if I could find out. Yes, that's my little game, Barker; that's what I dropped in for; Bismarck style of diplomacy. I'll tell you why they want to know, if you won't give me away: Miss Swan wanted to give her 'bit of color'—that's what she calls it—to one of the young ladies; but she's afraid she didn't like it."

"I guess they liked it well enough," said Lemuel, thinking with shame that Statira had not had the grace to say a word of either of the pictures; he attributed this to 'Manda Grier's influence.

"Well, that's good, so far as it goes," said Berry. "But now, to come down to particulars, what did they *say?* That's what Miss Swan will ask *me*."

"I don't remember just what they said," faltered Lemuel.

"Well, they must have said something," insisted Berry, jocosely. "Give a fellow some little clew, and I can piece it out for myself. What did *she* say? I don't ask which she *was*, but I have my suspicions. All I want to know is what she *said*. Anything like beautiful middle distance, or splendid chiaroscuro, or fine perspective, or exquisite modeling? Come, now! Try to think, Barker." He gave Lemuel time, but to no purpose. "Well," he resumed with affected dejection, "I'll have to try to imagine it; I guess I can; I haven't worked my imagination much since I took up the law. But look here, Barker," he continued more briskly, "now you open up a little. Here I've been giving you my confidence ever since I saw you— forcing it on you; and you know just how far I'm gone on Miss Swan, to the hundredth part of an inch; but I don't know enough of your affections to swear that you've got any. Now, which one is it? Don't be mean about it. I won't give you away. Honest Injun!"

Lemuel was goaded to desperation. His face burned, and

the perspiration began to break out on his forehead. He did not know how to escape from this pursuit.

"Which is it, Barker?" repeated his tormentor. "I know it's human nature to deny it, though I never could understand why; if I was engaged, the Sunday papers should have it about as quick!"

"I'm *not* engaged!" cried Lemuel.

"You ain't?" yelled Berry.

"No!"

"Give me your hand! Neither am I!"

He shook Lemuel's helpless hand with mock-heroic fervor. "We are brothers from this time forth, Barker! You can't imagine how closely this tie binds you to me, Barker. Barker, we are one; with no particular prospect, as far as I am concerned, of ever being more."

He offered to dramatize a burst of tears on Lemuel's shoulder; but Lemuel escaped from him.

"Stop! Quit your fooling! What if somebody should come in?"

"They won't," said Berry, desisting, and stretching himself at ease in the only chair besides Lemuel's with which the office was equipped. "It's too late for 'em. Now o'er the one half world nature seems dead-ah, and wicked dreams abuse the curtained sleep-ah. We are safe here from all intrusion, and I can lay bare my inmost thoughts to you, Barker, if I happen to have any. Barker, I'm awfully glad you're not engaged to either of those girls—or both. And it's not altogether because I enjoy the boon companionship of another unengaged man, but it's partly because I don't think—shall I say it?"

"Say what?" asked Lemuel, not without some prescience.

"Well, you can forgive the brotherly frankness, if you don't like it. I don't think they're quite up to you."

Lemuel gave a sort of start, which Berry interpreted in his own way.

"Now, hold on! I know just how you feel. Been there myself. I have seen the time, too, when I thought any sort of a girl was too good for Alonzo W., Jr. But I don't now. I think A. W., Jr., is good enough for the best. I may be mistaken; I was, the other time. But we all begin that way; and the great object is not to keep on that way. See? Now, I suppose you're in love—puppy love—with that little thing. Probably the first girl you got acquainted with after you came to Boston, or maybe a sweet survival of the Willoughby Pastures period. All right. Perfectly natural, in either case. But don't you let it go any further, my dear boy; old man, don't you let it go any further. Pause! Reflect! Consider! Love wisely, but not too well! Take the unsolicited advice of a sufferer."

Pride, joy, shame, remorse, mixed in Lemuel's heart, which eased itself in an involuntary laugh at Berry's nonsense.

"Now, what I want you to do—dear boy, or old man, as the case may be—is to regard yourself in a new light. Regard yourself, for the sake of the experiment, as too good for any girl in Boston. No? Can't fetch it? Try again!"

Lemuel could only laugh foolishly.

"Well, now, that's singular," pursued Berry. "I supposed you could have done it without the least trouble. Well, let's try something a little less difficult. Look me in the eye, and regard yourself as too good, for example, for Miss Carver. Ha!"

An angry flush spread over Lemuel's embarrassed face. "I wish you'd behave yourself," he stammered.

"In any other cause I would," said Berry, solemnly. "But I must be cruel to be kind. Seriously, old man, if you can't think yourself too good for Miss Carver, I wish you'd think yourself good enough. Now, I'm not saying anything against the Willoughby episode, mind. That has its place in the wise economy of nature, just like anything else. But there ain't any outcome in it for you. You've got a future before you, Barker, and you don't want to go and load up with a love affair that you'll keep trying to unload as long as you live. No, sir! Look at me! I know I'm not an example in some things, but in this little business of correctly placed affections

I could give points to Solomon. Why am I in love with M. Swan? Because I can't help it for one thing, and because for another thing she can do more to develop the hidden worth and unsuspected powers of A. W., Jr., than any other woman in the world. She may never feel that it's her mission, but she can't shake my conviction that way; and I shall stay undeveloped to prove that I was right. Well, now, what you want, my friend, is development, and you can't get it where you've been going. She hain't got it on hand. And what you want to do is not to take something else in its place—tender heart, steadfast affections, loyalty; they've got 'em at every shop in town; they're a drug in the market. You've got to say, 'No development, heigh? Well, I'll just look round awhile, and if I can't find it at some of the other stores I'll come back and take some of that steadfast affection. You say it won't come off? Or run in washing?' See?"

"You ought to be ashamed of yourself," said Lemuel, trying to summon an indignant feeling, and laughing with a strange pleasure at heart. "You've got no right to talk to me that way. I want you should leave me alone!"

"Well, since you're so pressing, I will go," said Berry, easily. "But if I find you at our next interview sitting under the shade of the mustard-tree whose little seed I have just dropped, I shall feel that I have not labored in vain. 'She's a darling, she's a daisy, she's a dumpling, she's a lamb!' I refer to Miss Swan, of course; but on other lips the terms are equally applicable to Miss Carver, and don't you forget it!"

He swung out of the office with a mazurka step. His silk hat, gayly tilted on the side of his head, struck against the doorjamb, and fell rolling across the entry floor. Lemuel laughed wildly. At twenty these things are droll.

XXI

A WEEK passed, and Lemuel had not tried to see Statira again. He said to himself that even when he had tried to do what was right, and to show those young ladies how much he thought of her by bringing her to see their pictures, she had acted very ungratefully, and had as good as tried to quarrel with him. Then, when he went to see her before his visit home, she was out; she had never been out before when he called.

Now, he had told Berry that they were not engaged. At first this shocked him as if it were a lie. Then he said to himself that he had a right to make that answer because Berry had no right to ask the questions that led to it. Then he asked himself if he really were engaged to Statira. He had told her that he liked her better than any one else in the world, and she had said as much to him. But he pretended that he did not know whether it could be called an engagement.

There was no one who could solve the question for him, and it kept asking itself that whole week, and especially when he was with Miss Carver, as happened two or three times through Berry's connivance. Once he had spent the greater part of an evening in the studio, where he talked nearly all the time with Miss Carver, and he found out that she was the daughter of an old ship's captain at Corbitant; her mother was dead, and her aunt had kept house for her father. It was an old, square house that her grandfather built, in the days when Corbitant had direct trade with France. She described it minutely, and told how a French gentleman had died there in exile at the time of the French Revolution, and who was said to haunt the house; but Miss Carver had never seen any ghosts in it. They all began to talk of ghosts and weird experiences; even Berry had had some strange things happen to him in the West. Then the talk broke in two again, and Lemuel sat apart with Miss Carver, who told at length the plot of a story she had been reading; it was a story called "Romola," and she said she would lend it to Lemuel; she said she did not see how any one could bear to be the least selfish or untrue after reading it. That made Lemuel feel cold; but he could not break away from her charm. She sat where the shaded lamp threw its soft light on one side of her face; it looked almost like the face of a spirit, and her eyes were full of a heavenly gentleness.

Lemuel asked himself how he could ever have thought them proud eyes. He asked himself at the same time, and perpetually, whether he was really engaged to Statira or not. He thought how different this evening was from those he spent with her. She could not talk about anything but him and her dress; and 'Manda Grier could not do anything but say saucy things which she thought were smart. Miss Swan was really witty; it was as good as the theater to hear her and Berry going on together. Berry was pretty bright; there was no denying it. He sang to his banjo that night; one of the songs was Spanish; he had learnt it in New Mexico.

Lemuel began to understand better how such nice young ladies could go with Berry. At first, after Berry talked so to him that night in the office against Statira, he determined that he would keep away from him; but Berry was so sociable and good-natured that he could not. The first thing he knew, Lemuel was laughing at something Berry said, and then he could not help himself.

Berry was coming now, every chance he had, to talk about the art-students. He seemed to take it for granted that Lemuel was as much interested in Miss Carver as he was himself in Miss Swan; and Lemuel did begin to speak of her in a shy way. Berry asked him if he had noticed that she looked like that Spanish picture of the Virgin that Miss Swan had pinned up next to the door; and Lemuel admitted that there was some resemblance.

"Notice those eyes of hers, so deep, and sorry for everybody in general? If it was anybody in particular, *that* fellow would be in luck. Oh, she's a dumpling, there's no mistake about it! 'Nymph, in thy orisons be all my sins remembered!' That's Miss Carver's style. She looks as if she just *wanted* to forgive somebody something. I'm afraid you ain't wicked enough, Barker. Look here! What's the reason we can't make up a little party for the Easter service at the Catholic cathedral Sunday night? The girls would like to go, I know."

"No, no, I can't! I mustn't!" said Lemuel; and he remained steadfast in his refusal. It would be the second Sunday night that he had not seen Statira, and he felt that he must not let it pass so. Berry went off to the cathedral with the art-students; and he kept out of the way till they were gone.

He said to himself that he would go a little later than usual to see Statira, to let her know that he was not so very anxious; but when he found her alone, and she cried on his neck, and owned that she had not behaved as she should that night when she went to see the pictures, and that she had been afraid he hated her, and was not coming any more, he had staid away so long, his heart was melted, and he did everything to soothe and comfort her, and they were more loving together than they had been since the first time.

'Manda Grier came in, and said through her nose, like an old countrywoman, "'The falling out of faithful friends renewing is of love!'" and Statira exclaimed in the old way, "'*Manda!*" that he had once thought so cunning, and rested there in his arms with her cheek tight pressed against his.

She did not talk; except when she was greatly excited about something, she rarely had anything to say. She had certain little tricks, poutings, bridlings, starts, outcries, which had seemed the most bewitching things in the world to Lemuel. She tried all these now, unaffectedly enough, in listening to his account of his visit home, and so far as she could she vividly sympathized with him.

He came away heavy and unhappy. Somehow, these things no longer sufficed for him. He compared this evening with the last he had spent with the art-students, which had left his brain in a glow, and kept him awake for hours with luminous thoughts. But he had got over that unkindness to Statira, and he was glad of that. He pitied her now, and he said to himself that if he could get her away from 'Manda Grier, and under the influence of such girls as Miss Swan and Miss Carver, it would be much better for her. He did not relent toward 'Manda Grier; he disliked her more than ever, and in the friendship which he dramatized between Statira and Miss Carver, he saw her cast adrift without remorse.

Sewell had told him that he was always at leisure Monday night, and the next evening Lemuel went to pay his first visit to the minister since his first day in Boston. It was early, and Evans, who usually came that evening, had not arrived yet; but Sewell had him in his thought when he hurried forward to meet his visitor.

"Oh, is it you, Mr. Barker?" he asked, in a note of surprise. "I am glad to see you. I had been intending to come and look you up again. Will you sit down? Mr. Evans was here the other night, and we were talking of you. I hope you are well?"

"Very well, thank you," said Lemuel, taking the hand the minister offered, and then taking the chair he indicated. Sewell did not know exactly whether to like the greater ease which Lemuel showed in his presence; but there was nothing presumptuous in it, and he could not help seeing the increased refinement of the young man's beauty. The knot between his eyes gave him interest, while it inflicted a vague pang upon the minister. "I have been at home since I saw you." Lemuel looked down at his neat shoes to see if they were in fit state for the minister's study-carpet, and Sewell's eye, sympathetically following, wandered to the various details of Lemuel's simple and becoming dress,—the light spring suit which he had indulged himself in at the Misfit Parlors since his mother had bidden him keep his money for himself and not send so much of it home.

"Ah, have you?" cried the minister. "I hope you found your people all well? How is the place looking? I suppose the season isn't quite so advanced as it is with us."

"There's some snow in the woods yet," said Lemuel, laying the stick he carried across the hat-brim on his knees. "Mother was well; but my sister and her husband have had a good deal of sickness."

"Oh, I'm sorry for that," said Sewell, with the general sympathy which Evans accused him of keeping on tap professionally. "Well, how did you like the looks of Willoughby Pastures compared with Boston? Rather quieter, I suppose."

"Yes, it was quieter," answered Lemuel.

"But the first touch of spring must be very lovely there! I find myself very impatient with these sweet, early days in town. I envy you your escape to such a place."

Lemuel opposed a cold silence to the lurking didacticism of these sentences, and Sewell hastened to add, "And I wish I could have had your experience in contrasting the country and the town, after your long sojourn here, on your first return home. Such a chance can come but once in a lifetime, and to very few."

"There are some pleasant things about the country," Lemuel began.

"Oh, I am sure of it!" cried Sewell, with cheerful aimlessness.

"The stillness was a kind of rest, after the noise here. I think any one might be glad to get back to such a place———"

"I was sure you would," interrupted Sewell.

"If he was discouraged or broken down any way," Lemuel calmly added.

"Oh!" said Sewell. "You mean that you found more sympathy among your old friends and neighbors than you do here?"

"No," said Lemuel bluntly. "That's what city people think. But it's all a mistake. There isn't half the sympathy in the country that there is in the city. Folks pry into each other's business more, but they don't really care so much. What I mean is that you could live cheaper, and the fight isn't so hard. You might have to use your hands more, but you wouldn't have to use your head hardly at all. There isn't so much opposition—competition."

"Oh," said Sewell, a second time. "But this competition—this struggle—in which one or the other must go to the wall, isn't that painful?"

"I don't know as it is," answered Lemuel, "as long as you're young and strong. And it don't always follow that one must go to the wall. I've seen some things where both got on better."

Sewell succumbed to this worldly wisdom. He was frequently at the disadvantage men of cloistered lives must be, in having his theories in advance of his facts. He now left this point, and covertly touched another that had come up in his last talk with Evans about Barker. "But you find in the country, don't you, a greater equality of social condition? People are more on a level, and have fewer artificial distinctions."

"Yes, there's that," admitted Lemuel. "I've worried a good deal about that, for I've had to take a servant's place in a good many things, and I've thought folks looked down on me for it, even when they didn't seem to intend to do it. But I guess it isn't so bad as I thought when I first began to notice it. Do you suppose it is?" His voice was suddenly tense with personal interest in the question which had ceased to be abstract.

"Oh, certainly not," said the minister, with an ease which he did not feel.

"I presume I had what you may call a servant's place at Miss Vane's," pursued Lemuel unflinchingly, "and I've been what you may call head waiter at the St. Albans since I've been there. If a person heard afterwards, when I had made out something, if I ever did, that I had been a servant, would they—they—despise me for it?"

"Not unless they were very silly people," said Sewell, cordially, "I can assure you."

"But if they had ever seen me doing a servant's work, wouldn't they always remember it, no matter what I was afterwards?" Sewell hesitated, and Lemuel hurried to add, "I ask because I've made up my mind not to be anything but clerk after this."

Sewell pitied the simple shame, the simple pride. "That isn't the question for you to ask, my dear boy," he answered gently, and with an affection which he had never felt for his charge before. "There's another question, more important, and one which you must ask yourself: '*Should I care if they did?*' After all, the matter's in your own hands. Your soul's always your own till you do something wrong."

"Yes, I understand that." Lemuel sat silently thoughtful, fingering his hat-band. It seemed to Sewell that he wished to ask something else, and was mustering his courage; but if this was so, it exhaled in a sigh, and he remained silent.

"I should be sorry," pursued the minister, "to have you dwell upon such things. There are certain ignoble facts in life which we can best combat by ignoring them. A slight of almost any sort ceases to be when you cease to consider it." This did not strike Sewell as wholly true when he had said it, and he was formulating some modification of it in his mind, when Lemuel said:

"I presume a person can help himself some by being ashamed of caring for such things, and that's what I've tried to do."

"Yes, that's what I meant——"

"I guess I've exaggerated the whole thing, some. But if a thing is so, thinking it ain't won't unmake it."

"No," admitted Sewell, reluctantly. "But I should be sorry, all the same, if you let it annoy—grieve you. What has pleased me in what I've been able to observe in you has been your willingness to take hold of any kind of honest work. I liked finding you with your coat off washing dishes, that morning, at the Wayfarer's Lodge, and I liked your going at once to Miss Vane's in a—as you did——"

"Of course," Lemuel interrupted, "I could do it before I knew how it was looked at here."

"And couldn't you do it now?"

"Not if there was anything else."

"Ah, that's the great curse of it; that's what I deplore," Sewell broke out, "in our young people coming from the country to the city. They must all have some genteel occupation! I don't blame them; but I would gladly have saved you this experience—this knowledge—if I could. I felt that I had done you a kind of wrong in being the means, however indirectly and innocently, of your coming to Boston, and I would willingly have done anything to have you go back to the country. But you seemed to distrust me—to find something hostile in me—and I did not know how to influence you."

"Yes, I understand that," said Lemuel. "I couldn't help it, at first. But I've got to see it all in a different light since then. I know that you meant the best by me. I know now that what I wrote wasn't worth anything, and just how you must have looked at it. I didn't know some things then that I do now; and since I have got to know a little more I have understood better what you meant by all you said."

"I am very glad," said Sewell, with sincere humility, "that you have kept no hard feeling against me."

"Oh, not at all. It's all right now. I couldn't explain very well that I hadn't come to the city just to be in the city, but because I had to do something to help along at home. You didn't seem to understand that there wa'n't anything there for me to take hold of."

"No, I'm afraid I didn't, or wouldn't, quite understand that; I was talking and acting, I'm afraid, from a preconceived notion." Lemuel made no reply, not having learned yet to utter the pleasant generalities with which city people left a subject; and after a while Sewell added, "I am glad to have seen your face so often at church. You have been a great deal in my mind, and I have wished to do something to make your life happy and useful to you in the best way here, but I haven't quite known how." At this point Sewell realized that it was nearly eight months since Lemuel had come to Boston, and he said contritely, "I have not made the proper effort, I'm afraid; but I did not know exactly how to approach you. You were rather a difficult subject," he continued, with a smile in which Lemuel consented to join, "but now that we've come to a clearer understanding"— He broke off and asked, "Have you many acquaintances in Boston?"

Lemuel hesitated, and cleared his throat. "Not many."

Something in his manner prompted the minister to say, "That is such a very important thing for young men in a strange place. I wish you would come oftener to see us hereafter. Young men, in the want of companionship, often form disadvantageous acquaintances, which they can't shake off afterwards, when they might wish to do so. I don't mean evil acquaintance; I certainly couldn't mean that in your case; but frivolous ones, from which nothing high or noble can come—nothing of improvement or development."

Lemuel started at the word and blushed. It was Berry's word. Sewell put his own construction on the start and the blush.

"Especially," he went on, "I should wish any young man whom I was interested in to know refined and noble women." He felt that this was perhaps, in Lemuel's case, too much like prescribing port wine and carriage exercise to an indigent patient, and he added, "If you cannot know such women, it is better to know none at all. It is not what women say or do, so much as the art they have of inspiring a man to make the best of himself. The accidental acquaintances that young people are so apt to form are in most cases very detrimental. There is no harm in them of themselves, perhaps, but all irregularity in the life of the young is to be deplored."

"Do you mean," asked Lemuel, with that concreteness which had alarmed Sewell before, "that they ought to be regularly introduced?"

"I mean that a young girl who allowed a young man to make her acquaintance outside of the—the—social sanctions would be apt to be a silly or romantic person, at the best. Of course, there are exceptions. But I should be very sorry if any young man I knew—no; why shouldn't I say *you* at once?—should involve himself in any such way. One thing leads to another, especially with the young; and the very fact of irregularity, of romance, of strangeness in an acquaintance, throws a false glamour over the relation, and appeals to the sentiments in an unwarranted degree."

"Yes, that is so," said Lemuel.

The admission stimulated Sewell in the belief that he had a clew in his hand which it was his duty to follow up. "The whole affair loses proportion and balance. The fancy becomes excited, and some of the most important interests—the very most important interests of life—are committed to impulse." Lemuel remained silent, and it seemed the silence of conviction. "A young man is better for knowing women older than himself, more cultivated, devoted to higher things. Of course, young people must see each other, must fall in love, and get married; but there need be no haste about such things. If there is haste—if there is rashness, thoughtlessness—there is sure to be unhappiness. Men are apt to outgrow their wives intellectually, if their wives' minds are set on home and children, as they should be; and allowance for this ought to be made, if possible. I would rather that in the beginning the wife should be the mental superior. I hope it will be several years yet before you think seriously of such things, but when the time comes, I hope you will have seen some young girl—there are such for every one of us—whom it is civilization and enlightenment, refinement, and elevation, simply to know. On the other hand, a silly girl's influence is degrading and ruinous. She either drags those attached to her down to her own level, or she remains a weight and a clog upon the life of a man who loves her."

"Yes," said Lemuel, with a sigh which Sewell interpreted as that of relief from danger recognized in time.

He pursued eagerly: "I could not warn any one too earnestly against such an entanglement."

Lemuel rose and looked about with a troubled glance.

Sewell continued: "Any such marriage—a marriage upon any such conditions—is sure to be calamitous; and if the conditions are recognized beforehand, it is sure to be iniquitous. So far from urging the fulfillment of even a promise, in such a case, I would have every such engagement broken, in the interest of humanity—of morality——"

Mrs. Sewell came into the room, and gave a little start of surprise, apparently not mixed with pleasure, at seeing Lemuel. She had never been able to share her husband's interest in him, while insisting upon his responsibility; she disliked him not logically, but naturally, for the wrong and folly which he had been the means of her husband's involving himself in; Miss Vane's kindliness toward Lemuel, which still survived, and which expressed itself in questions about him whenever she met the minister, was something that Mrs. Sewell could not understand. She now said, "Oh! Mr. Barker!" and coldly gave him her hand. "Have you been well? Must you go?"

"Yes, thank you. I have got to be getting back. Well, good-evening." He bowed to the Sewells.

"You must come again to see me," said the minister, and looked at his wife.

"Yes, it has been a very long time since you were here," Mrs. Sewell added.

"I haven't had a great deal of time to myself," said Lemuel, and he contrived to get himself out of the room.

Sewell followed him down to the door, in the endeavor to say something more on the subject his wife had interrupted, but he only contrived to utter some feeble repetitions. He came back in vexation, which he visited upon Lemuel. "Silly fellow!" he exclaimed.

"What has he been doing now?" asked Mrs. Sewell, with reproachful discouragement.

"Oh, *I* don't know! I suspect that he's been involving himself in some ridiculous love affair!" Mrs. Sewell looked a silent inculpation. "It's largely conjecture on my part, of course,—he's about as confiding as an oyster!—but I fancy I have said some things in a conditional way that will give him pause. I suspect from his manner that he has entangled himself with some other young simpleton, and that he's ashamed of it, or tired of it, already. If that's the case, I have hit the nail on the head. I told him that a foolish, rash engagement was better broken than kept. The foolish marriages that people rush into are the greatest bane of life!"

"And would you really have advised him, David," asked his wife, "to break off an engagement if he had made one?"

"Of course I should! I——"

"Then I am glad I came in in time to prevent your doing anything so wicked."

"Wicked?" Sewell turned from his desk, where he was about to sit down, in astonishment.

"Yes! Do you think that nobody else is to be considered in such a thing? What about the poor, silly girl if he breaks off with her? Oh, you men are all alike! Even the best! You think it is a dreadful thing for a young man to be burdened with a foolish love affair at the beginning of his career; but you never think of the girl whose whole career is spoiled, perhaps, if the affair is broken off! Hasn't she any right to be considered?"

"I should think," said Sewell, distinctly daunted, "that they were equally fortunate if it were broken off."

"Oh, my dear, you know you don't think anything of the kind! If he has more mind than she has, and is capable of doing something in the world, he goes on and forgets her; but she remembers him. Perhaps it's her one chance in life to get married—to have a home. You know very well that in a case of that kind—a rash engagement, as you call it—both are to blame; and shall one do all the suffering? Very probably his fancy was taken first, and he followed her up, and flattered her into liking him; and now shall he leave her because he's tired of her?"

"Yes," said Sewell, recovering from the first confusion which his wife's unexpected difference of opinion had thrown him into, "I should think that was the very best reason in the world why he should leave her. Would his marrying make matters worse or better if he were tired of her? As for wickedness, I should feel myself guilty if I did not do my utmost to prevent marriages between people when one or other wished to break their engagement, and had not the moral courage to do so. There is no more pernicious delusion than that one's word ought to be kept in such an affair, after the heart has gone out of it, simply because it's been given."

"David!"

But Sewell was not to be restrained. "I am right about this, Lucy, and you know it. Half the miserable marriages in the world could be prevented, if there were only some frank and fearless adviser at hand to say to the foolish things that if they no longer fully and freely love each other they can commit no treason so deadly as being true to their word. I wish," he now added, "that I could be the means of breaking off every marriage that the slightest element of doubt enters into beforehand. I should leave much less work for the divorce courts. The trouble comes from that crazy and mischievous principle of false self-sacrifice that I'm always crying out against. If a man has ceased to love the woman he has promised to marry— or *vice versa*—the best possible thing they can do, the only righteous thing, is not to marry."

Mrs. Sewell could not deny this. She directed an oblique attack from another quarter, as women do, while affecting not to have changed her ground at all. "Very well, then, David, I wish you would have nothing to do with that crazy and mischievous principle yourself. I wish you would let this ridiculous Barker of yours alone from this time forth. He has found a good place, where he is of use, and where he is doing very well. Now I think your responsibility is fairly ended. I hope you won't meddle with his love affairs, if he has any; for if you do, you will probably have your hands full. He is very good-looking, and all sorts of silly little geese will be falling in love with him."

"Well, so far his love troubles are purely conjectural," said

Sewell, with a laugh. "I'm bound to say that Barker himself didn't say a word to justify the conjecture that he was either in love or wished to be out of it. However, I've given him some wholesome advice, which he'll be all the better for taking, merely as a prophylactic, if nothing else."

"I am tired of him," sighed Mrs. Sewell. "Is he going to keep perpetually turning up, in this way? I hope you were not very pressing with him in your invitations to him to call again?"

Sewell smiled. "You were not, my dear."

"You let him take too much of your time. I was so provoked, when I heard you going on with him, that I came down to put an end to it."

"Well, you succeeded," said Sewell easily. "Don't you think he's greatly improved in the short time he's been in the city?"

"He's very well dressed. I hope he isn't extravagant."

"He's not only well dressed, but he's beginning to be well spoken. I believe he's beginning to observe that there is such a thing as not talking through the nose. He still says, 'I don't know as,' but most of the men they turn out of Harvard say that; I've heard some of the professors say it."

Mrs. Sewell was not apparently interested in this.

XXII

THAT NIGHT Lemuel told Mrs. Harmon that she must not expect him to do anything thenceforward but look after the accounts and the general management; she must get a head-waiter, and a boy to run the elevator. She consented to this, as she would have consented to almost anything else that he proposed.

He had become necessary to the management of the St. Albans in every department; and if the lady boarders felt that they could not now get on without him, Mrs. Harmon was even more dependent. With her still nominally at the head of affairs, and controlling the expenses as a whole, no radical reform could be effected. But there were details of the outlay in which Lemuel was of use, and he had brought greater comfort into the house for less money. He rejected her old and simple device of postponing the payment of debt as an economical measure, and substituted cash dealings with new purveyors. He gradually but inevitably took charge of the store-room, and stopped the waste there; early in his administration he had observed the gross and foolish prodigality with which the portions were sent from the carving-room, and after replacing Mrs. Harmon's nephew there, he established a standard portion that gave all the needed variety, and still kept the quantity within bounds. It came to his taking charge of this department entirely, and as steward he carved the meats, and saw that nothing was in a way to become cold before he opened the dining-room doors as head-waiter.

His activities promoted the leisure which Mrs. Harmon had always enjoyed, and which her increasing bulk fitted her to adorn. Her nephew willingly relinquished the dignity of steward. He said that his furnaces were as much as he wanted to take care of; especially as in former years, when it had begun to come spring, he had experienced a stress of mind in keeping the heat just right, when the ladies were all calling down the tubes for more of it or less of it, which he should now be very glad not to have complicated with other cares. He said that now he could look forward to the month of May with some pleasure.

The guests, sensibly or insensibly, according to their several temperaments, shared the increased ease that came from Lemuel's management. The service was better in every way; their beds were promptly made, their rooms were periodically swept; every night when they came up from dinner they found their pitchers of ice-water at their doors. This change was not accomplished without much of that rebellion and renunciation which was known at the St. Albans as kicking. Chambermaids and table-girls kicked, but they were replaced by Lemuel, who went himself to the intelligence office, and pledged the new ones to his rule beforehand. There was even some kicking among the guests, who objected to the new portions, and to having a second bill sent them if the first remained unpaid for a week; but the general sense of the hotel was in Lemuel's favor.

He had no great pleasure in the reform he had effected. His heart was not in it, except as waste and disorder and carelessness were painful to him. He suffered to promote a better state of things, as many a woman whose love is for books or pictures or society suffers for the perfection of her housekeeping, and sacrifices her tastes to achieve it. He would have liked better to read, to go to lectures, to hear sermons; with the knowledge of Mr. Evans's life as an editor and the incentive of a writer near him, he would have liked to try again if he could not write something, though the shame of his failure in Mr. Sewell's eyes had burned so deep. Above all, since he had begun to see how city people regarded the kind of work he had been doing, he would have liked to get out of the hotel business altogether, if he could have been sure of any other.

As the spring advanced his cares grew lighter. Most of the regular boarders went away to country hotels and became regular boarders there. Their places were only partially filled by transients from the South and West, who came and went, and left Lemuel large spaces of leisure, in which he read, or deputed Mrs. Harmon's nephew to the care of the office and pursued his studies of Boston, sometimes with Mr. Evans,— whose newspaper kept him in town, and who liked to prowl about with him, and to frequent the odd summer entertainments,—but mostly alone. They became friends after a fashion, and were in each other's confidence as regarded their opinions and ideas, rather than their history; now and then Evans dropped a word about the boy he had lost, or his wife's health, but Lemuel kept his past locked fast in his breast.

The art-students had gone early in the summer, and Berry had left Boston for Wyoming at the end of the spring term of the law school. He had not been able to make up his mind to pop before Miss Swan departed, but he thought he should fetch it by another winter; and he had got leave to write to her, on condition, he said, that he should conduct the whole correspondence himself.

Miss Carver had left Lemuel dreaming of her as an ideal, yet true, with a slow, rustic constancy, to Statira. For all that had been said and done, he had not swerved explicitly from her. There was no talk of marriage between them, and could not be; but they were lovers still, and when Miss Carver was gone, and the finer charm of her society was unfelt, he went back to much of the old pleasure he had felt in Statira's love. The resentment of her narrow-mindedness, the shame for her ignorance passed; the sense of her devotion remained.

'Manda Grier wanted her to go home with her for part of the summer, but she would not have consented if Lemuel had not insisted. She wrote him back ill-spelt, scrawly little letters, in one of which she told him that her cough was all gone, and she was as well as ever. She took a little more cold when she returned to town in the first harsh September weather, and her cough returned, but she said she did not call it anything now.

The hotel began to fill up again for the winter. Berry preceded the art-students by some nervous weeks, in which he speculated upon what he should do if they did not come at all. Then they came, and the winter passed, with repetitions of the last winter's events, and a store of common memories that enriched the present, and insensibly deepened the intimacy in which Lemuel found himself. He could not tell whither the present was carrying him; he only knew that he had drifted so far from the squalor of his past, that it seemed like the shadow of a shameful dream.

He did not go to see Statira so often as he used; and she was patient with his absences, and defended him against 'Manda Grier, who did not scruple to tell her that she believed the fellow was fooling with her, and who could not always keep down a mounting dislike of Lemuel in his presence. One night toward spring, when he returned early from Statira's, he found Berry in the office at the St. Albans. "That you, old man?" he asked. "Well, I'm glad you've come. Just going to leave a little Billy Ducks for you here, but now I needn't. The young ladies sent me down to ask if you had a copy of Whittier's poems; they want to find something in it. I told 'em Longfellow would do just as well, but I couldn't seem to convince 'em. They say he didn't write the particular poem they want."

"Yes, I've got Whittier's poems here," said Lemuel, unlocking his desk. "It belongs to Mr. Evans; I guess he won't care if I lend it."

"Well, now, I tell you what," said Berry; "don't you let a borrowed book like that go out of your hands. Heigh? You just bring it up yourself. See?" He winked the eye next Lem-

uel with exaggerated insinuation. "They'll respect you all
the more for being so scrupulous, and I guess they won't be
very much disappointed on general principles if you come
along. There's lots of human nature in girls—the best of 'em.
I'll tell 'em I left you lookin' for it. I don't mind a lie or two
in a good cause. But you hurry along up, now."

He was gone before Lemuel could stop him; he could not
do anything but follow.

It appeared that it was Miss Swan who wished to see the
poem; she could not remember the name of it, but she was
sure she should know it if she saw it in the index. She mingled
these statements with her greetings to Lemuel, and Miss Carver seemed as glad to see him. She had a little more color than
usual, and they were all smiling, so that he knew Berry had
been getting off some of his jokes. But he did not care.

Miss Swan found the poem as she had predicted, and, "Now
all keep still," she said, "and I'll read it." But she suddenly
added, "Or no; you read it, Mr. Barker, won't you?"

"If Barker ain't just in voice to-night, *I'll* read it," suggested
Berry.

But she would not let him make this diversion. She ignored his offer, and insisted upon Lemuel's reading. "Jessie
says you read beautifully. That passage in 'Romola,' " she reminded him; but Lemuel said it was only a few lines, and
tried to excuse himself. At heart he was proud of his reading,
and he ended by taking the book.

When he had finished the two girls sighed.

"Isn't it beautiful, Jessie?" said Miss Swan.

"Beautiful!" answered her friend.

Berry yawned.

"Well, I don't see much difference between that and a poem
of Longfellow's. Why wouldn't Longfellow have done just
as well? Honestly, now! Why isn't one poem just as good as
another, for all practical purposes?"

"It is, for some people," said Miss Swan.

Berry figured an extreme anguish by writhing in his chair.

Miss Swan laughed in spite of herself, and they began to talk in their usual banter, which Miss Carver never took part in, and which Lemuel was quite incapable of sharing. If it had come to savage sarcasm or a logical encounter, he could have held his own, but he had a natural weight and slowness that disabled him from keeping up with Berry's light talk; he envied it, because it seemed to make everybody like him, and Lemuel would willingly have been liked.

Miss Carver began to talk to him about the book, and then about Mr. Evans. She asked him if he went much to his rooms, and Lemuel said no, not at all, since the first time Mr. Evans had asked him up. He said, after a pause, that he did not know whether he wanted him to come.

"I should think he would," said Miss Carver. "It must be very gloomy for him, with his wife such an invalid. He seems naturally such a gay person."

"Yes, that's what I think," said Lemuel.

"I wonder," said the girl, "if it seems to you harder for a naturally cheerful person to bear things, than for one who has always been rather melancholy?"

"Yes, it does!" he answered with the pleasure and surprise young people have in discovering any community of feeling; they have thought themselves so utterly unlike each other. "I wonder why it should?"

"I don't know; perhaps it isn't so. But I always pity the cheerful person the most."

They recognized an amusing unreason in this, and laughed. Miss Swan across the room had caught the name.

"Are you talking of Mrs. Evans?"

Berry got his banjo down from the wall, where Miss Swan allowed him to keep it as bric-à-brac, and began to tune it.

"I don't believe it agrees with this banjoseph being an object of virtue," he said. "What shall it be, ladies? Something light and gay, adapted to disperse gloomy reflections?" He played a fandango. "How do you like that? It has a tinge of melancholy in it, and yet it's lively too, as a friend of mine used to say about the Dead March."

"Was his name Berry?" asked Miss Swan.

"Not Alonzo W., Jr.," returned Berry tranquilly, and he and Miss Swan began to joke together.

"I know a friend of Mr. Evans's," said Lemuel to Miss Carver. "Mr. Sewell. Have you ever heard him preach?"

"Oh, yes, indeed. We go nearly every Sunday morning."

"I nearly always go in the evening now," said Lemuel. "Don't you like him?"

"Yes," said the girl. "There's something about him—I don't know what—that doesn't leave you feeling how bad you are, but makes you want to be better. He helps you so; and he's so clear. And he shows that he's had all the mean and silly thoughts that you have. I don't know—it's as if he were talking for each person alone."

"Yes, that is exactly the way I feel!" Lemuel was proud of the coincidence. He said, to commend himself further to Miss Carver, "I have just been round to see him."

"I should think you would value his acquaintance beyond anything," said the girl. "Is he just as earnest and simple as he is in the pulpit?"

"He's just the same, every way." Lemuel went a little further: "I knew him before I came to Boston. He boarded one summer where we live." As he spoke he thought of the gray, old, unpainted house, and of his brother-in-law with his stocking-feet on the stove-hearth, and his mother's bloomers; he thought of his arrest, and his night in the police-station, his trial, and the Wayfarer's Lodge; and he wondered that he could think of such things and still look such a girl in the face. But he was not without the strange joy in their being unknown to her which reserved and latent natures feel in mere reticence, and which we all experience in some degree when we talk with people and think of our undiscovered lives.

They went on a long time, matching their opinions and feelings about many things, as young people do, and fancying that much of what they said was new with them. When he came away after ten o'clock, he thought of one of the things that Sewell had said about the society of refined and noble women: it was not so much what they said or did that helped; it was something in them that made men say and do their best, and help themselves to be refined and noble men, to make the most of themselves in their presence. He believed that this was what Miss Carver had done, and he thought how different it was with him when he came away from an evening with Statira. Again he experienced that compassion for her, in the midst of his pride and exultation; he asked himself what he could do to help her; he did not see how she could be changed.

Berry followed him downstairs, and wanted to talk the evening over.

"I don't see how I'm going to stand it much longer, Barker," he said. "I shall have to pop pretty soon or die, one of the two; and I'm afraid either one'll kill me. Wasn't she lovely to-night? Honey in the comb, sugar in the gourd, *I* say! I wonder what it is about popping, anyway, that makes it so hard, Barker? It's simply a matter of business, if you come to boil it down. You offer a fellow so many cattle, and let him take 'em or leave 'em. But if the fellow happens to have on a long, slim, olive-green dress of some color, and holds her head like a whole floral tribute on a stem, and *you* happen to be the cattle you're offering, you can't feel so independent about it, somehow. Well, what's the use? She's a daisy, if ever there was one. Ever notice what a peculiar blue her eyes are?"

"Blue?" said Lemuel. "They're brown."

"Look here, old man," said Berry compassionately, "do you think I've come down here to fool away my time talking about Miss Carver? We'll take some Saturday afternoon for that, when we haven't got anything else to do; but it's Miss Swan that has the floor at present. What were you two talking about over there, so long? I can't get along with Miss Carver worth a cent."

"I hardly know what we did talk about," said Lemuel dreamily.

"Well, I've got the same complaint. I couldn't tell you ten words that Madeline said—in thine absence let me call thee Madeline, sweet!—but I knew it was making an immortal spirit of me, right straight along, every time. The worst thing about an evening like this is, it don't seem to last any time at all. Why, when those girls began to put up their hands to hide their yawns, I felt like I was just starting in for a short call. I wish I could have had a good phonograph around. I'd put it on my sleepless pillow, and unwind its precious record all through the watches of the night." He imitated the thin phantasmal squeak of the instrument in repeating a number of Miss Swan's characteristic phrases. "Yes, sir, a pocket phonograph is the thing I'm after."

"I don't see how you can talk the way you do," said Lemuel, shuddering inwardly at Berry's audacious freedom, and yet finding a certain comfort in it.

"That's just the way I felt myself at first. But you'll get over it as you go along. The nicest thing about their style of angel is that they're perfectly human, after all. You don't believe it now, of course, but you will."

It only heightened Lemuel's conception of Miss Carver's character to have Berry talk so lightly and daringly of her, in her relation to him. He lay long awake after he went to bed, and in the turmoil of his thoughts one thing was clear: so pure and high a being must never know anything of his shameful past, which seemed to dishonor her through his mere vicinity. He must go far from her, and she must not know why; but long afterwards Mr. Sewell would tell her, and then she would understand. He owed her this all the more because he could see now that she was not one of the silly persons, as Mr. Sewell called them, who would think meanly of him for having, in his ignorance and inexperience, done a servant's work. His mind had changed about that, and he wondered that he could ever have suspected her of such a thing.

About noon the next day the street-door was opened hesitatingly, as if by some one not used to the place; and when

Lemuel looked up from the *menus* he was writing, he saw the figure of one of those tramps who from time to time presented themselves and pretended to want work. He scanned the vagabond sharply, as he stood molding a soft hat on his hands, and trying to superinduce an air of piteous appeal upon the natural gayety of his swarthy face. "Well! what's wanted?"

A dawning conjecture that had flickered up in the tramp's eyes flashed into full recognition.

"Why, mate!"

Lemuel's heart stood still. "What—what do you want here?"

"Why, don't you know me, mate?"

All his calamity confronted Lemuel.

"No," he said, but nothing in him supported the lie he had uttered.

"Wayfarer's Lodge?" suggested the other cheerfully. "Don't you remember?"

"No——"

"I guess you do," said the mate easily. "Anyway, I remember you."

Lemuel's feeble defense gave way. "Come in here," he said, and he shut the door upon the intruder and himself, and submitted to his fate. "What is it?" he asked huskily.

"Why, mate! what's the matter? Nobody's goin' to hurt you," said the other encouragingly. "What's your lay here?"

"Lay?"

"Yes. Got a job here?"

"I'm the clerk," said Lemuel, with the ghost of his former pride of office.

"Clerk?" said the tramp with good-humored incredulity. "Where's your diamond pin? Where's your rings?" He seemed willing to prolong the playful inquiry. "Where's your patent-leather boots?"

"It's not a common hotel. It's a sort of a family hotel, and I'm the clerk. What do you want?"

The young fellow lounged back easily in his chair. "Why, I *did* drop in to beat the house out of a quarter if I could, or may be ten cents. Thank you, sir. God bless you, sir." He interrupted himself to burlesque a professional gratitude. "That style of thing, you know. But I don't know about it now. Look here, mate! what's the reason you couldn't get me a job here too? I been off on a six months' cruise since I saw you, and I'd like a job on shore first-rate. Couldn't you kind of ring me in for something? I ain't afraid of work, although I never did pretend to love it. But I should like to reform now, and get into something steady. Heigh?"

"There isn't anything to do—there's no place for you," Lemuel began.

"Oh, pshaw, now, mate, you think!" pleaded the other. "I'll take any sort of a job; I don't care what it is. I ain't got any o' that false modesty about me. Been round too much. And I don't want to go back to the Wayfarer's Lodge. It's a good place, and I know my welcome's warm and waitin' for me, between two hot plates; but the thing of it is, it's demoralizin'. That's what the chaplain said just afore I left the—ship, 'n' I promised him I'd give work a try, anyway. Now you just think up something! I ain't in any hurry." In proof he threw his soft hat on the desk, and took up one of the *menus*. "This your bill of fare? Well, it ain't bad! Vurmiselly soup, boiled holibut, roast beef, roast turkey with cranberry sauce, roast pork with apple sauce, chicken croquettes, ditto patties, three kinds of pie; bread puddin', both kinds of sauce; ice cream, nuts, and coffee. Why, mate!"

Lemuel sat dumb and motionless. He could see no way out of the net that had entangled him. He began feebly to repeat, "There isn't anything," when some one tried the door.

"Mr. Barker!" called Mrs. Harmon. "You in there?"

He made it worse by waiting a moment before he rose and opened the door. "I didn't know I'd locked it." The lie came unbidden; he groaned inwardly to think how he was telling nothing but lies. Mrs. Harmon did not come in. She glanced with a little question at the young fellow who had gathered his hat from the table, and risen with gay politeness.

It was a crisis of the old sort; the elevator-boy had kicked, and Mrs. Harmon said, "I just stopped to say that I was going out and I could stop at the intelligence office myself to get an elevator-boy——"

The mate took the word with a joyous laugh at the coincidence. "It's just what me and Mr. Barker was talkin' about! I'm from up his way, and I've just come down to Boston to see if I couldn't look up a job; and he was tellin' me, in here, about your wantin' a telegraph—I mean a elevator-boy, but he didn't think it would suit me. But I should like to give it a try, anyway. It's pretty dull up our way, and I got to do something. Mr. Barker'll tell you who I am."

He winked at Lemuel with the eye not exposed to Mrs. Harmon, and gave her a broad, frank, prepossessing smile.

"Well, of course," said Mrs. Harmon smoothly, "any friend of Mr. Barker's——"

"We just been talkin' over old times in here," interrupted the mate. "I guess it was me shoved that bolt in. I didn't want to have anybody see me talkin' with him till I'd got some clothes that would be a little more of a credit to him."

"Well, that's right," said Mrs. Harmon appreciatively. "I always like to have everybody around my house looking neat and respectable. I keep a first-class house, and I don't have any but first-class help, and I expect them to dress accordingly, from the highest to the lowest."

"Yes, ma'am," said the mate, "that's the way I felt about it myself, me and Mr. Barker both; and he was just tellin' me that if I was a mind to give the elevator a try, he'd lend me a suit of *his* clothes."

"Very well, then," said Mrs. Harmon; "if Mr. Barker and you are a mind to fix it up between you——"

"Oh, we are!" said the mate. "There won't be any trouble about that."

"I don't suppose I need to stop at the intelligence office. I presume Mr. Barker will show you how to work the elevator. He helped us out with it himself at first."

"Yes, that's what he said," the other chimed in. "But I guess I better go and change my clothes first. Well, mate," he added to Lemuel, "I'm ready when you're ready."

Lemuel rose trembling from the chair where he had been chained, as it seemed to him, while the mate and Mrs. Harmon arranged their affair with his tacit connivance. He had not spoken a word; he feared so much to open his lips lest another lie should come out of them, that his sense of that danger was hardly less than his terror at the captivity in which he found himself.

"Yes," said Mrs. Harmon, "I'll look after the office till you get back. Mr. Barker'll show you where you can sleep."

"Thank you, ma'am," said the mate, with gratitude that won upon her.

"And I'm glad," she added, "that it's a friend of Mr. Barker's that's going to have the place. We think everything of Mr. Barker here."

"Well, you can't think more of him than what we do up home," rejoined the other with generous enthusiasm.

In Lemuel's room he was not less appreciative. "Why, mate, it does me good to see how you've got along. I got to write a letter home at once, and tell the folks what friends you've got in Boston. I don't believe they half understand it." He smiled joyously upon Lemuel, who stood stock still, with such despair in his face that probably the wretch pitied him.

"Look here, mate, don't you be afraid now! I'm on the reform lay with all my might, and I mean business. I ain't a-goin' to do you any harm, you bet your life. These your things?" he asked, taking Lemuel's winter suit from the hooks where they hung, and beginning to pull off his coat. He talked on while he changed his dress. "I was led away, and I got my come-uppings, or the other fellow's come-uppings, for *I* wa'n't to blame any, and I always said so, and I guess the judge would say so too, if it was to do over again."

A frightful thought stung Lemuel to life. "The judge? Was it a passenger-ship?"

The other stopped buttoning Lemuel's trousers round him to slap himself on the thigh. "Why, mate! don't you know enough to know what a *sea voyage* is? Why, I've been down to the *Island* for the last six months! Hain't you never heard it called a sea voyage? Why, we *always* come off from a cruise when we git back! You don't mean to say you never *been* one?"

"Oh, my goodness!" groaned Lemuel. "Have—have you been in prison?"

"Why, of course."

"Oh, what am I going to do?" whispered the miserable creature to himself.

The other heard him. "Why, you hain't got to do anything! I'm on the reform, and you might leave everything layin' around loose, and I shouldn't touch it. Fact! You ask the ship's chaplain."

He laughed in the midst of his assertions of good resolutions, but sobered to the full extent, probably, of his face and nature, and tying Lemuel's cravat on at the glass, he said, solemnly, "Mate, it's all right. I'm on the reform."

XXIII

LEMUEL'S friend entered upon his duties with what may almost be called artistic zeal. He showed a masterly touch in managing the elevator from the first trip. He was ready, cheerful, and obliging; he lacked nothing but a little more reluctance and a Seaside Library novel to be a perfect elevator-boy.

The ladies liked him at once; he was so pleasant and talkative, and so full of pride in Lemuel that they could not help liking him; and several of them promptly reached that stage of confidence where they told him, as an old friend of Lemuel's, they thought Lemuel read too much, and was going to kill himself if he kept on a great deal longer. The mate said he thought so too, and had noticed how bad Lemuel looked the minute he set eyes on him. But, he asked, what was the use? He had said everything he could to him about it. He was always just so, up at home. As he found opportunity he did what he could to console Lemuel with furtive winks and nods.

Lemuel dragged absently and haggardly through the day. In the evening he told Mrs. Harmon that he had to go round and see Mr. Sewell a moment. It was then nine o'clock, and she readily assented; she guessed Mr. Williams—he had told her his name was Williams—could look after the office while he was gone. Mr. Williams was generously glad to do so. Behind Mrs. Harmon's smooth, large form, he playfully threatened her with his hand leveled at his shoulder; but even this failed to gladden Lemuel.

247

It was half-past nine when he reached the minister's house, and the maid had a visible reluctance at the door in owning that Mr. Sewell was at home. Mrs. Sewell had instructed her not to be too eagerly candid with people who came so late; but he was admitted, and Sewell came down from his study to see him in the reception-room.

"What is the matter?" he asked at once, when he caught sight of Lemuel's face; "has anything gone wrong with you, Mr. Barker?" He could not help being moved by the boy's looks; he had a fleeting wish that Mrs. Sewell were there to see him, and be moved too; and he prepared himself as he might to treat the trouble which he now expected to be poured out.

"Yes," said Lemuel, "I want to tell you; I want you to tell me what to do."

When he had put the case fully before the minister, his listener was aware of wishing that it had been a love-trouble, such as he foreboded at first.

He drew a long and deep breath, and before he began to speak he searched himself for some comfort or encouragement, while Lemuel anxiously scanned his face.

"Yes—yes! I see your—difficulty," he began, making the futile attempt to disown any share in it. "But perhaps—perhaps it isn't so bad as it seems. Perhaps no harm will come. Perhaps he really means to do well; and if you are vigilant in—in keeping him out of temptation——" Sewell stopped, sensible that he was not coming to anything, and rubbed his forehead.

"Do you think," asked Lemuel, dry-mouthed with misery, "that I ought to have told Mrs. Harmon at once?"

"Why, it is always best to be truthful and above-board—as a principle," said the minister, feeling himself somehow dragged from his moorings.

"Then I had better do it yet!"

"Yes," said Sewell, and he paused. "Yes. That is to say— As the mischief is done— Perhaps—perhaps there is no haste.

If you exercise vigilance— But if he has been in prison— Do you know what he was in for?"

"No. I didn't know he had been in at all till we got to my room. And then I couldn't ask him—I was afraid to."

"Yes," said Sewell, kindly if helplessly.

"I was afraid, if I sent him off—or tried to—that he would tell about my being in the Wayfarer's Lodge that night, and they would think I had been a tramp. I could have done it, but I thought he might tell some lie about me; and they might get to know about the trial——"

"I see," said Sewell.

"I hated to lie," said Lemuel piteously, "but I seemed to have to."

There was another yes on the minister's tongue; he kept it back; but he was aware of an instant's relief in the speculation—the question presented itself abstractly—as to whether it was ever justifiable or excusable to lie. Were the Jesuitical casuists possibly right in some slight, shadowy sort? He came back to Lemuel groaning in spirit. "No—no—no!" he sighed; "we mustn't admit that you *had* to lie. We must never admit that." A truth flashed so vividly upon him that it seemed almost escape. "What worse thing could have come from telling the truth than has come from withholding it? And that would have been some sort of end, and this—this is only the miserable beginning."

"Yes," said Lemuel, with all desirable humility. "But I couldn't see it at once."

"Oh, I don't blame you; I don't blame *you*," said Sewell. "It was a sore temptation. I blame *myself!*" he exclaimed, with more comprehensiveness than Lemuel knew; but he limited his self-accusal by adding, "I ought to have told Mrs. Harmon myself what I knew of your history; but I refrained because I knew you had never done any harm, and I thought it cruel that you should be dishonored by your misfortunes in a relation where you were usefully and prosperously placed; and so—and so I didn't. But perhaps I was wrong. Yes, I was wrong. I have only allowed the burden to fall more heavily upon you at last."

It was respite for Lemuel to have some one else accusing himself, and he did not refuse to enjoy it. He left the minister to wring all the bitterness he could for himself out of his final responsibility. The drowning man strangles his rescuer.

Sewell looked up, and loosened his collar as if really stifling. "Well, well. We must find some way out of it. I will see —see what can be done for you to-morrow."

Lemuel recognized his dismissal. "If you say so, Mr. Sewell, I will go straight back and tell Mrs. Harmon all about it."

Sewell rose too. "No—no. There is no such haste. You had better leave it to me now. I will see to it—in the morning."

"Thank you," said Lemuel. "I hate to give you so much trouble."

"Oh," said Sewell, letting him out at the street-door, and putting probably less thought and meaning into the polite words than they had ever contained before, "it's no trouble."

He went upstairs to his study, and found Mrs. Sewell waiting there. "Well, *now*—what, David?"

"Now what?" he feebly echoed.

"Yes. What has that wretched creature come for now?"

"You may well call him a wretched creature," sighed Sewell.

"Is he really engaged? Has he come to get you to marry him?"

"I think he'd rather have me bury him at present." Sewell sat down, and, bracing his elbow on his desk, rested his head heavily on his hand.

"Well," said his wife, with a touch of compassion tempering her curiosity.

He began to tell her what had happened, and he did not spare himself in the statement of the case. "There you have the whole affair now. And a very pretty affair it is. But, I declare," he concluded, "I can't see that any one is to blame for it."

"No one, David?"

"Well, Adam, finally, of course. Or Eve. Or the Serpent," replied the desperate man.

Seeing him at this reckless pass, his wife forbore reproach, and asked, "What are you going to do?"

"I am going around there in the morning to tell Mrs. Harmon all about Barker."

"She will send him away instantly."

"I dare say."

"And what will the poor thing do?"

"Goodness knows."

"I'm afraid Badness knows. It will drive him to despair."

"Well, perhaps not—perhaps not," sighed the minister. "At any rate, we must not *let* him be driven to despair. You must help me, Lucy."

"Of course."

Mrs. Sewell was a good woman, and she liked to make her husband feel it keenly.

"I knew that it must come to that," she said. "Of course, we must not let him be ruined. If Mrs. Harmon insists upon his going at once—as I've no doubt she will—you must bring him here, and we must keep him till he can find some other home." She waited, and added, for a final stroke of merciless beneficence, "He can have Alfred's room, and Alf can take the front attic."

Sewell only sighed again. He knew she did not mean this.

Barker went back to the St. Albans, and shrunk into as small space in the office as he could. He pulled a book before him and pretended to read, hiding the side of his face toward the door with the hand that supported his head. His hand was cold as ice, and it seemed to him as if his head were in a flame. Williams came and looked in at him once, and then went back to the stool which he occupied just outside the elevator-shaft, when not running it. He whistled softly between his teeth, with intervals of respectful silence, and then went on whistling in absence of any whom it might offend.

Suddenly a muffled clamor made itself heard from the depths of the dining-room, like that noise of voices which is heard behind the scenes at the theater when an armed mob is about to burst upon the stage. Irish tones, high, windy, and angry, yells, and oaths defined themselves, and Mrs. Harmon came obesely hurrying from the dining-room toward the office, closely followed by Jerry, the porter. When upon duty, or, as some of the boarders contended, when in the right humor, he blacked the boots, and made the hard-coal fires, and carried the trunks up and down stairs. When in the wrong humor, he had sometimes been heard to swear at Mrs. Harmon, but she had excused him in this eccentricity because, she said, he had been with her so long. Those who excused it with her on these grounds conjectured arrears of wages as another reason for her patience. His outbreaks of bad temper had the Celtic uncertainty; the most innocent touch excited them, as sometimes the broadest snub failed to do so; and no one could foretell what direction his zigzag fury would take. He had disliked Lemuel from the first, and had chafed at the subordination into which he had necessarily fallen. He was now yelling after Mrs. Harmon, to know if she was not satisfied with *wan* gutther-snoipe, that she must nades go and pick up another, and whether the new wan was going to be too good too to take prisints of money for his worruk from the boarthers, and put all the rest of the help under the caumpliment of refusin' ut, or else demanin' themselves by takin' ut? If this was the case, he'd have her to know that she couldn't kape anny other help; and the quicker she found it out the betther. Mrs. Harmon was trying to appease him by promising to see Lemuel at once, and ask him about it.

The porter raised his voice an octave. "D'ye think I'm a loyar, domn ye? Don't ye think I'm tellin' the thruth?"

He followed her to the little office, whither she had retreated on a purely mechanical fulfillment of her promise to speak to Lemuel, and crowded in upon them there.

"Here he is now!" he roared in his frenzy. "He's too good

to take the money that's offered to 'um! He's too good to be waither! He wannts to play the gintleman! He thinks 'umself too good to do what the other servants do, that's been tin times as lahng in the house!"

At the noise some of the ladies came hurrying out of the public parlor to see what the trouble was. The street-door opened, and Berry entered with the two art-students. They involuntarily joined the group of terrified ladies.

"What's the row?" demanded Berry. "Is Jerry on the kick?"

No one answered. Lemuel stood pale and silent, fronting the porter, who was shaking his fist in his face. He had not heard anything definite in the outrage that assailed him. He only conjectured that it was exposure of Williams's character, and the story of his own career in Boston.

"Why don't you fire him out of there, Barker?" called the law-student. "Don't be afraid of him!"

Lemuel remained motionless; but his glance sought the pitying eyes of the assembled women, and then dropped before the amaze that looked at him from those of Miss Carver. The porter kept roaring out his infamies.

Berry spoke again.

"Mrs. Harmon, do you want that fellow in there?"

"No, goodness knows I don't, Mr. Berry."

"All right." Berry swung the street-door open with his left hand, and seemed with the same gesture to lay his clutch upon the porter's collar. "Fire him out myself!" he exclaimed, and with a few swiftly successive jerks and bumps, the burly shape of the porter was shot into the night. "I want you to get me an officer, Jerry," he said, putting his head out after him. "There's been a blackguard makin' a row here. Never mind your hat! Go!"

"Oh, my good gracious, Mr. Berry!" gasped Mrs. Harmon, "what have you done?"

"If it's back pay, Mrs. Harmon, we'll pass round the hat. Don't you be troubled. That fellow wasn't fit to be in a decent house."

Berry stopped a moment and looked at Lemuel. The art-students did not look at him at all; they passed on upstairs with Berry.

The other ladies remained to question and to comment. Mrs. Harmon's nephew, to whom the uproar seemed to have penetrated in his basement, came up and heard the story from them. He was quite decided. He said that Mr. Berry had done right. He said that he was tired of having folks damn his aunt up hill and down dale; and that if Jerry had kept on a great deal longer, he would have said something to him himself about it.

The ladies justified him in the stand he took; they returned to the parlor to talk it all over, and he went back to his basement. Mrs. Harmon, in tears, retired to her room, and Lemuel was left standing alone in his office. The mate stole softly to him from the background of the elevator, where he had kept himself in safety during the outbreak.

"Look here, mate. This thing been about your ringin' me in here?"

"Oh, go away, go away!" Lemuel huskily entreated.

"Well, that's what I intend to do. I don't want to stay here and git you into no more trouble, and I know that's what's been done. You never done me no harm, and I don't want to do you none. I'm goin' right up to your room to git my clo'es, and then I'll skip."

"It won't do any good now. It'll only make it worse. You'd better stay now. You must."

"Well, if you say so, mate."

He went back to his elevator, and Lemuel sat down at his desk, and dropped his face upon his arms there. Toward eleven o'clock Evans came in and looked at him, but without speaking; he must have concluded that he was asleep; he went upstairs, but after a while he came down again and stopped again at the office door, and looked in on the haggard boy, hesitating as if for the best words. "Barker, Mr. Berry has been telling me about your difficulty here. I know all about you—from Mr. Sewell." Lemuel stared at him. "And I will stand your friend, whatever people think. And I don't blame you for not wanting to be beaten by that ruffian; you could have stood no chance against him; and if you had thrashed him it wouldn't have been a great triumph."

"I wish he had killed me," said Lemuel from his dust-dry throat.

"Oh, no; that's foolish," said the elder, with patient, sad kindness. "Who knows whether death is the end of trouble? We must live things down, not die them down." He put his arm caressingly across the boy's shoulder.

"I can never live this down," said Lemuel. He added passionately, "I wish I could die!"

"No," said Evans. "You must cheer up. Think of next Saturday. It will soon be here, and then you'll be astonished that you felt so bad on Tuesday."

He gave Lemuel a parting pressure with his arm, and turned to go upstairs.

At the same moment the figure of Mrs. Harmon's nephew, distracted, violent, burst up through the door leading to the basement.

"Good heavens!" exclaimed the editor, "is Mr. Harmon going to kick?"

"The house is on fire!" yelled the apparition.

A thick cloud of smoke gushed out of the elevator-shaft, and poured into the hall, which it seemed to fill instantly. It grew denser, and in another instant a wild hubbub began. The people appeared from every quarter, and ran into the street, where some of the ladies began calling up at the windows to those who were still in their rooms. A stout little old lady came to an open window, and paid out hand over hand a small cable, on which she meant to descend to the pavement; she had carried this rope about with her many years against the exigency to which she was now applying it. Within, the halls and the stairway became the scene of frantic encounter between wives and husbands rushing down to save themselves, and then rushing back to save their forgotten friends. Many appeared in the simple white in which they had left their beds, with the addition of such shawls or rugs as chance suggested. A house was opened to the fugitives on the other side of the street, and the crowd that had collected could not repress its applause when one of them escaped from the hotel-door and shot across. It applauded impartially men, women, and children, and, absorbed in the spectacle, no one sounded the fire-alarm; the department began to be severely condemned among the bystanders before the engines appeared.

Most of the ladies, in their escape or their purpose of rescue, tried each to possess herself of Lemuel, and keep him solely in her interest. "Mr. Barker! Mr. Barker! Mr. Barker!" was called for in various sopranos and contraltos, till an outsider took up the cry and shouted "Barker! Barker! Speech! Speech!" This made him very popular with the crowd, who in their enjoyment of the fugitives were unable to regard the fire seriously. A momentary diversion was caused by an elderly gentleman who came to the hotel-door, completely dressed except that he was in his stockings, and demanded Jerry. The humorist who had called for a speech from Lemuel volunteered the statement that Jerry had just gone round the corner to see a man. "I want him," said the old gentleman savagely. "I want my boots; I can't go about in my stockings."

Cries for Jerry followed; but in fact the porter had forgotten all his grudges and enmities; he had reappeared, in perfect temper, and had joined Lemuel and Berry in helping to get the women and children out of the burning house.

The police had set a guard at the door, in whom Lemuel recognized the friendly old officer who had arrested him. "All out?" asked the policeman.

The smoke, which had reddened and reddened, was now a thin veil drawn over the volume of flame that burned strongly and steadily up the well of the elevator, and darted its tongues out to lick the framework without. The heat was intense. Mrs. Harmon came panting and weeping from the dining-room with some unimportant pieces of silver, driven forward by Jerry and her nephew.

They met the firemen, come at last, and pulling in their hose, who began to play upon the flames; the steam filled the place with a dense mist.

Lemuel heard Berry ask him through the fog, "Barker, where's old Evans?"

"Oh, I don't know!" he lamented back. "He must have gone up to get Mrs. Evans."

He made a dash toward the stairs. A fireman caught him and pulled him back. "You can't go up; smoke's thick as hell up there." But Lemuel pulled away, and shot up the stairs. He heard the firemen stop Berry.

"You can't go, I tell you! Who's runnin' this fire anyway, I'd like to know?"

He ran along the corridor which Evans's apartment opened upon. There was not much smoke there; it had drawn up the elevator-well, as if in a chimney.

He burst into the apartment and ran to the inner room, where he had once caught a glimpse of Mrs. Evans sitting by the window.

Evans stood leaning against the wall, with his hand at his breast. He panted, "Help her—help——"

"Where *is* she? Where *is* she?" demanded Lemuel.

She came from an alcove in the room, holding a handkerchief drenched with cologne in her hand, which she passed to her husband's face. "Are you better now? Can you come, dear? Rest on me!"

"I'm—I'm all right! Go—go! I can get along——"

"I'll go when *you* go," said Mrs. Evans. She turned to Lemuel. "Mr. Evans fainted; but he is better now." She took his hand with a tender tranquillity that ignored all danger or even excitement, and gently chafed it.

"But come—come!" cried Lemuel. "Don't you know the house is on fire?"

"Yes, I know it," she replied. "We must get Mr. Evans down. You must help me." Lemuel had seldom seen her before; but he had so long heard and talked of her hopeless invalidism that she was like one risen from the dead, in her sudden strength and courage, and he stared at the miracle of her restoration. It was she who claimed and bore the greater share of the burden in getting her husband away. He was helpless; but in the open air he caught his breath more fully, and at last could tremulously find his way out of the sympathetic crowd. "Get a carriage," she said to Lemuel; and then she added, as it drove up and she gave an address, "I can manage him now."

Evans weakly pressed Lemuel's hand from the seat to which he had helped him, and the hack drove away. Lemuel looked crazily after it a moment, and then returned to the burning house.

Berry called to him from the top of the outside steps, "Barker, have you seen that partner of yours?"

Lemuel ran up to him. "No!"

"Well, come in here. The elevator's dropped, and they're afraid he went down with it."

"I know he didn't! He wouldn't be such a fool!"

"Well, we'll know when they get the fire under."

"I thought I saw something in the elevator, and as long as you don't know where he is——" said a fireman.

"Well," said Berry, "if you've got the upper hands of this thing, I'm going to my room a minute."

Lemuel followed him upstairs, to see if he could find Williams. The steam had ascended and filled the upper halls; little cascades of water poured down the stairs, falling from step to step; the long strips of carpeting in the corridors swam in the deluge which the hose had poured into the building, and a rain of heavy drops burst through the ceilings.

Most of the room-doors stood open, as the people had flung them wide in their rush for life. At the door of Berry's room a figure appeared, which he promptly seized by the throat.

"Don't be in a hurry!" he said, as he pushed it into the room. "I want to see you."

It was Williams.

"I want to see what you've got in your pockets. Hold on to him, Barker."

Lemuel had no choice. He held Williams by the arms while Berry went through him, as he called the search. He found upon him whatever small articles of value there had been in his room.

The thief submitted without a struggle, without a murmur.

Berry turned scornfully to Lemuel. "This a friend of yours, Mr. Barker?"

Still the thief did not speak, but he looked at Lemuel.

"Yes," he dryly gasped.

"Well!" said Berry, staring fiercely at him for a moment. "If it wasn't for something old Evans said to me about you, a little while ago, I'd hand you both over to the police."

Williams seemed to bear the threat with philosophic resignation, but Lemuel shrank back in terror. Berry laughed.

"Why, you *are* his pal. Go along! I'll get Jerry to attend to you."

Lemuel slunk downstairs with Williams. "Look here, mate," said the rogue; "I guess I ha'n't used you just right."

Lemuel expected himself to cast the thief off with bitter rejection. But he heard himself saying hopelessly, "Go away, and try to behave yourself," and then he saw the thief make the most of the favor of heaven and vanish through the crowd.

He would have liked to steal away too; but he remained, and began mechanically helping again wherever he saw help needed. By and by Berry came out; Lemuel thought that he would tell some policeman to arrest him; but he went away without speaking to any one.

In an hour the firemen had finished their share of the havoc, and had saved the building. They had kept the fire to the elevator-shaft and the adjoining wood-work, and but for the water they had poured into the place the ladies might have returned to their rooms, which were quite untouched by the flames. As it was, Lemuel joined with Jerry in fetching such things to them as their needs or fancies suggested; the refugees across the way were finally clothed by their efforts, and were able to quit their covert indistinguishable in dress from any of the other boarders.

The crowd began to go about its business. The engines had disappeared from the little street with exultant shrieks; in the morning the insurance companies would send their workmen to sweep out the extinct volcano, and mop up the shrunken deluge, preparatory to ascertaining the extent of the damage done; in the mean time the police kept the boys and loafers out of the building, and the order that begins to establish itself as soon as chaos is confessed took possession of the ruin.

But it was all the same a ruin and a calamitous conclusion for the time being. The place that had been in its grotesque and insufficient fashion a home for so many homeless people was uninhabitable; even the Harmons could not go back to it. The boarders had all scattered, but Mrs. Harmon lingered, dwelling volubly upon the scene of disaster. She did not do much else; she was not without a just pride in it, but she was not puffed up by all the sympathy and consolation that had been offered her. She thought of others in the midst of her own troubles, and she said to Lemuel, who had remained working with Jerry under her direction in putting together such things as she felt she must take away with her:

"Well, I don't know as I feel much worse about myself than I do about poor Mr. Evans. Why, I've got the ticket in my pocket now that he give me for the Wednesday matinée! I do wonder how he's gettin' along! I guess they've got you to thank, if they're alive to tell the tale. What *did* you do to get that woman out alive?" Lemuel looked blankly at her, and did not answer. "And Mr. Evans too! You must have had your hands full, and that's what I told the reporters; but I told 'em I guessed you'd be equal to it if any one would. Why, I don't suppose Mrs. Evans has been out of her room for a month, or hardly stepped her foot to the floor. Well, I don't want to see many people look as he did when you first got him out the house."

"Well, I don't know as I want to see many more fires where I live," said her nephew, as if with the wish to be a little more accurate.

Jerry asked Lemuel to watch Mrs. Harmon's goods while he went for a carriage, and said sir to him. It seemed to Lemuel that this respect, and Mrs. Harmon's unmerited praises, together with the doom that was secretly upon him, would drive him wild.

XXIV

THE EVENING after the fire Mrs. Sewell sat talking it over with her husband, in the light of the newspaper reports, which made very much more of Lemuel's part in it than she liked. The reporters had flattered the popular love of the heroic in using Mrs. Harmon's version of his exploits, and represented him as having been most efficient and daring throughout, and especially so in regard to the Evanses.

"Well, that doesn't differ materially from what they told us themselves," said Sewell.

"You know very well, David," retorted his wife, "that there couldn't have been the least danger at any time; and when he helped her to get Mr. Evans downstairs, the fire was nearly all out."

"Very well, then; he would have saved their lives if it had been necessary. It was a case of potential heroism, that contained all the elements of self-sacrifice."

Mrs. Sewell could not deny this, but she was not satisfied. She was silent a moment before she asked, "What do you suppose that wretched creature will do now?"

"I think very likely he will come to me," answered Sewell.

"I dare say." The bell rang. "And I suppose that's he now!"

They listened and heard Miss Vane's voice at the door, asking for them.

Mrs. Sewell ran down the stairs and kissed her. "Oh, I'm *so* glad you came. Isn't it wonderful? I've just come from them, and she's taking the whole care of him, as if he had always been the sick one, and she strong and well."

"What do you mean, Lucy? He isn't ill!"

"Who isn't?"

"What are you talking about?"

"About Mr. Evans——"

"Oh!" said Miss Vane, with cold toleration. She arrived at the study door and gave Sewell her hand. "I scarcely knew him, you know; I only met him casually here. I've come to see," she added nervously, "if you know where Lemuel is, Mr. Sewell. Have you seen anything of him since the fire? How nobly he behaved! But I never saw anything he wasn't equal to!"

"Mrs. Sewell objects to his saving human life," said Sewell, not able to deny himself.

"I don't see how you can take the slightest interest in him," began Mrs. Sewell, saying a little more than she meant.

"You would, my dear," returned Miss Vane, "if you had wronged him as I have."

"Or as I," said Sewell.

"I'm thankful I haven't, then," said his wife. "It seems to me that there's nothing else of him. As to his noble behavior, it isn't possible you believe these newspaper accounts? He didn't save any one's life; there was no danger!"

Miss Vane, preoccupied with her own ideal of the facts, stared at her without replying, and then turned to Sewell.

"I want to find him and ask him to stay with me till he can get something else to do." Sewell's eyebrows arched themselves involuntarily. "Sibyl has gone to New York for a fortnight; I shall be quite alone in the house, and I shall be very glad of his company," she explained to the eyebrows, while ignoring them. Her chin quivered a little, as she added, "I shall be *proud* of his company. I wish him to understand that he is my *guest*."

"I suppose I shall see him soon," said Sewell, "and I will give him your message."

"Will you tell him," persisted Miss Vane, a little hysterically, "that if he is in any way embarrassed I insist upon his coming to me immediately—at *once?*"

Sewell smiled, "Yes."

"I know that I'm rather ridiculous," said Miss Vane, smiling in sympathy, "and I don't blame Mrs. Sewell for not entering into my feelings. Nobody could, who hadn't felt the peculiar Lemuel-glamour."

"I don't imagine he's embarrassed in any way," said Sewell. "He seems to have the gift of lighting on his feet. But I'll tell him how peremptory you are, Miss Vane."

"Well, upon my word," cried Mrs. Sewell, when Miss Vane had taken leave of them in an exaltation precluding every recurrent attempt to enlighten her as to the true proportions of Lemuel's part in the fire, "I really believe people like to be made fools of. Why didn't *you* tell her, David, that he had done nothing?"

"What would have been the use? She has her own theory of the affair. Besides, he did do something; he did his duty, and my experience is that it's no small thing to do. It wasn't his fault that he didn't do more."

He waited some days for Lemuel to come to him, and he inquired each time he went to see the Evanses if they knew where he was. But they had not heard of him since the night of the fire.

"It's his shyness," said Evans; "I can understand how if he thought he had put me under an obligation he wouldn't come near me—and couldn't."

Evans was to go out of town for a little while; the proprietors of the "Saturday Afternoon" insisted upon his taking a rest, and they behaved handsomely about his salary. He did not want to go, but his wife got him away finally, after he had failed in two or three attempts at writing.

Lemuel did not appear to Sewell till the evening of the day when the Evanses left town. It seemed as if he had waited till they were gone, so that he could not be urged to visit them. At first the minister scolded him a little for his neglect; but Lemuel said he had heard about them, and knew they were getting along all right. He looked as if he had not been getting along very well himself; his face was thin, and had an air at once dogged and apprehensive. He abruptly left talking of Evans, and said, "I don't know as you heard what happened that night before the fire just after I got back from your house?"

"No, I hadn't."

Lemuel stopped. Then he related briefly and clearly the whole affair, Sewell interrupting him from time to time with murmurs of sympathy, and "Tchk, tchk, tchk!" and "Shocking, shocking!" At the end he said, "I had hoped somehow that the general calamity had swallowed up your particular trouble in it. Though I don't know that general calamities ever do that with particular troubles," he added, more to himself than to Lemuel; and he put the idea away for some future sermon.

"Mr. Evans stopped and said something to me that night. He said we had to live things down, and not die them down; he wanted I should wait till Saturday before I was sure that I couldn't get through Tuesday. He said, How did we know that death was the end of trouble?"

"Yes," said the minister with a smile of fondness for his friend; "that was like Evans all over."

"I sha'n't forget those things," said Lemuel. "They've been in my head ever since. If it hadn't been for them, I don't know what I should have done."

He stopped, and after a moment's inattention Sewell perceived that he wished to be asked something more. "I hope," he said, "that nothing more has been going wrong with you?" and as he asked this he laid his hand affectionately on the young man's shoulder, just as Evans had done. Lemuel's eyes dimmed and his breath thickened. "What has become of the person—the discharged convict?"

"I guess I had better tell you," he said; and he told him of the adventure with Berry and Williams.

Sewell listened in silence, and then seemed quite at a loss what to say; but Lemuel saw that he was deeply afflicted. At last he asked, lifting his eyes anxiously to Sewell's, "Do you think I did wrong to say the thief was a friend of mine, and get him off that way?"

"That's a very difficult question," sighed Sewell. "You had a duty to society."

"Yes, I've thought of that since!"

"If I had been in your place, I'm afraid I should be glad not to have thought of it in time; and I'm afraid I'm glad that, as it is, it's too late. But doesn't it involve you with him in the eyes of the other young man?"

"Yes, I presume it does," said Lemuel. "I shall have to go away."

"Back to Willoughby Pastures?" asked Sewell, with not so much faith in that panacea for Lemuel's troubles as he had once had.

"No, to some other town. Do you know of anything I could get to do in New York?"

"Oh, no, no!" said the minister. "You needn't let this banish you. We must seek this young Mr.—"

"Berry."

"—Mr. Berry out and explain the matter to him."

"Then you'll have to tell him all about me?"

"Yes. Why not?"

Lemuel was silent, and looked down.

"In the mean time," pursued the minister, "I have a message for you from Miss Vane. She has heard, as we all have, of your behavior during the fire——"

"It wasn't anything," Lemuel interrupted. "There wasn't the least danger; and Mrs. Evans did it all herself, anyway. It made me sick to see how the papers had it. It's a shame!"

Sewell smiled. "I'm afraid you couldn't make Miss Vane think so; but I can understand what you mean. She has never felt quite easy about the way—the terms—on which she parted with you. She has spoken to me several times of it, and—ah—expressed her regret; and now, knowing that you have been—interrupted in your life, she is anxious to have you come to her——"

An angry flash lighted up Lemuel's face. "I couldn't go back there! I wouldn't do any such work again."

"I don't mean that," Sewell hastened to say. "Miss Vane wished me to ask you to come as her guest until you could find something—Miss Sibyl Vane has gone to New York——"

"I'm very much obliged to her," said Lemuel, "but I shouldn't want to give her so much trouble, or any one. I—I liked her very much, and I shouldn't want she should think I didn't appreciate her invitation."

"I will tell her," said the minister. "I had no great hope you would see your way to accepting it. But she will be glad to know that you received it." He added, rather interrogatively than affirmatively, "In the right spirit."

"Oh, yes," said Lemuel. "Please to tell her I did."

"Thank you," said Sewell with bland vagueness. "I don't know that I've asked yet where you are staying at present?"

"I'm at Mrs. Nash's, 13 Canary Place. Mrs. Harmon went there first."

"Oh! And are you looking forward to rejoining her in a new place?"

"I don't know as I am. I don't know as I should want to go into a hotel again."

Sewell manifested a little embarrassment. "Well, you won't forget your promise to let me be of use to you—pecuniarily, if you should be in need of a small advance at any time."

"Oh, no! But I've got enough money for a while yet—till I can get something to do." He rose, and after a moment's hesitation he said, "I don't know as I want you should say anything to that fellow about me. To Mr. Berry, I mean."

"Oh! certainly not," said Sewell, "if you don't wish it."

Whatever it was in that reticent and elusive soul which prompted this request, the minister now felt that he could not know; but perhaps the pang that Lemuel inflicted on himself had as much transport as anguish in it. He believed that he had forever cut himself off from the companionship that seemed highest and holiest on earth to him; he should never see that girl again; Berry must have told Miss Swan, and long before this Miss Carver had shuddered at the thought of him as the accomplice of a thief. But he proudly said to himself that he must let it all go; for if he had not been a thief, he had been a beggar and a menial, he had come out of a hovel at home, and his mother went about like a scarecrow, and it mattered little what kind of shame she remembered him in.

He thought of her perpetually now, and, in those dialogues which we hold in revery with the people we think much about, he talked with her all day long. At first, when he began to do this, it seemed a wrong to Statira; but now, since the other was lost to him beyond other approach, he gave himself freely up to the mystical colloquies he held with her, as the devotee abandons himself to imagined converse with a saint. Besides, if he was in love with Statira, he was not in love with Jessie; that he had made clear to himself; for his feeling toward her was wholly different.

Most of the time, in these communings, he was with her in her own home, down at Corbitant, where he fancied she had gone, after the catastrophe at the St. Albans, and he sat there with her on a porch at the front door, which she had once described to him, and looked out under the silver poplars at the vessels in the bay. He formed himself some image of it all from pictures of the seaside which he had seen; and there were times when he tried to go back with her into the life she had led there as a child. Perhaps his ardent guesses at this were as near reality as anything that could be made to appear, for, after her mother and brothers and sisters had died out of the wide old house, her existence there was as lonely as if she had been a little ghost haunting it. She had inherited her mother's temperament with her father's constitution; she was the child born to his last long absence at sea and her mother's last solitude at home. When he returned, he found his wife dead and his maiden sister caring for the child in the desolate house.

This sister of Captain Carver's had been disappointed, as

the phrase is, when a young girl; another girl had won her lover from her. Her disappointment had hardened her to the perception of the neighbors; and, by a strange perversion of the sympathies and faculties, she had turned from gossip and censure, from religion, and from all the sources of comfort that the bruised heart of Corbitant naturally turned to, and found such consolation as came to her in books, that is to say romances, and especially the romances that celebrated and deified such sorrow as her own. She had been a pretty little thing when young, and Jessie remembered her as pretty in her early old age. At heart she must still have been young when her hair was gray, for she made a friend and companion of the child, and they fed upon her romances together. When the aunt died, the child, who had known no mother but her, was stricken with a grief so deep and wild that at first her life and then her mind was feared for. To get her away from the associations and influences of the place, her father sent her to school in the western part of the State, where she met Madeline Swan, and formed one of those friendships which are like passions between young girls. During her long absence, her father married again; and she was called home to his death-bed. He was dead when she arrived; he had left a will that made her dependent on her stepmother. When Madeline Swan wrote to announce that she was coming to Boston to study art, Jessie Carver had no trouble in arranging with her stepmother, by the sacrifice of her final claim on her father's estate, to join her friend there, with a little sum of money on which she was to live till she should begin to earn something.

Her life had been a series of romantic episodes; Madeline said that if it could be written out it would be fascinating; but she went to work very practically, and worked hard. She had not much feeling for color; but she drew better than her friend, and what she hoped to do was to learn to illustrate books.

One evening, after a day of bitter-sweet reveries of Jessie,

Lemuel went to see Statira. She and 'Manda Grier were both very gay, and made him very welcome. They had tea for him; Statira tried all her little arts, and 'Manda Grier told some things that had happened in the box-factory. He could not help laughing at them; they were really very funny; but he felt somehow that it was all a preparation for something else. At last the two girls made a set at him, as 'Manda Grier called it, and tried to talk him into their old scheme of going to wait on table at some of the country hotels, or the seaside. They urged that now, while he was out of a place, it was just the time to look up a chance.

He refused, at first kindly, and at last angrily; and he would have gone away in this mood if Statira had not said that she would never say another word to him about it, and hung upon his neck, while 'Manda Grier looked on in sullen resentment. He came away sick and heavy at heart. He said to himself that they would be willing to drag him into the mire; they had no pride; they had no sense; they did not know anything and they could not learn. He tried to get away from them to Miss Carver in his thoughts; but the place where he had left her was vacant and he could not conjure her back. Out of the void, he was haunted by a look of grieving reproach and wonder from her eyes.

XXV

THAT evening Sewell went to see an old parishioner of his
who lived on the Hill, and who among his eccentricities had
the habit of occupying his city house all summer long, while
his family flitted with other people of fashion to the seashore.
That year they talked of taking a cottage for the first time
since they had sold their own cottage at Nahant, in a day of
narrow things now past. The ladies urged that he ought to
come with them, and not think of staying in Boston now that
he had a trouble of the eyes which had befallen him, and Boston would be so dull if he could not get about freely and read
as usual.

He answered that he would rather be blind in Boston than
telescopic at Beverly, or any other summer resort; and that
as for the want of proper care, which they urged, he did not
think he should lack in his own house, if they left him where
he could reach a bell. His youngest daughter, a lively little
blonde, laughed with a cousin of his wife's who was present,
and his wife decorously despaired. The discussion of the
topic was rather premature, for they were not thinking of
going to Beverly before the middle of May, if they took the
cottage; but an accident had precipitated it, and they were
having it out, as people do, each party in the hope that the
other would yield if kept at long enough before the time of
final decision came.

"Do you think," said the husband and father, who looked
a whimsical tyrant at the worst, but was probably no easier

to manage for his whimsicality, "that I am going to fly in the face of prosperity, and begin to do as other people wish because I'm pecuniarily able to do as I please?"

The little blonde rose decisively from the low chair where she had been sitting. "If papa has begun to *reason* about it, we may as well yield the point for the present, mamma. Come, Lily! Let us leave him to Cousin Charles."

"Oh, but I say!" cried Cousin Charles, "if I'm to stay and fight it out with him, I've got to know which side I'm on."

"You're on the right side," said the young lady over her shoulder; "you always are, Cousin Charles."

Cousin Charles, in the attempt to kiss his hand toward his flatterer, pulled his glasses off his nose by their cord. "Bromfield," he said, "I don't see but this commits me against you." And then, the ladies having withdrawn, the two men put on that business air with which our sex tries to atone to itself for having unbent to the lighter minds of the other; heaven knows what women do when the men with whom they have been talking go away.

"If you should happen to stay in town," continued the cousin treacherously, "I shall be very glad, for I don't know but I shall be here the greater part of the summer myself."

"I shall stay," said the other, "but there won't be anything casual about it."

"What do you hear from Tom?" asked the cousin, feeling about on the mantel for a match. He was a full-bodied, handsome, amiable-looking old fellow, whose breath came in quick sighs with this light exertion. He had a blond complexion, and what was left of his hair, a sort of ethereal down on the top of his head, and some cherished fringes at the temples, was turning the yellowish gray that blond hair becomes.

The other gentleman, stretched at ease in a deep chair, with one leg propped on a cricket, had the distinction of long forms, which the years had left in their youthful gracility; his snow-white mustache had been allowed to droop over the handsome mouth, whose teeth were beginning to go. "They're on the other side of the clock," he said, referring to the matches. He added, with another glance at his relative, "Charles, you ought to bant. It's beginning to affect your wind."

"*Beginning!* Your memory's going, Bromfield. But they say there's a new system that allows you to eat everything. I'm waiting for that. In the mean time, I've gone back to my baccy."

"They've cut mine off," sighed the other. "Doesn't it affect your heart?"

"Not a bit. But what do you do, now you can't smoke and your eyes have given out?"

"I bore myself. I had a letter from Tom yesterday," said the sufferer, returning to the question that his cousin's obesity had diverted him from. "He's coming on in the summer."

"Tom's a lucky fellow," said the cousin. "I wish you had insisted on my taking some of that stock of his when you bought in."

"Yes, you made a great mistake," said the other with whimsical superiority. "You should have taken my advice. You would now be rolling in riches, as I am, with a much better figure for it."

The cousin smoked a while. "Do you know, I think Tom's about the best fellow I ever knew."

"He's a good boy," said the other, with the accent of a father's pride and tenderness.

"Going to bring his pretty chickens and their dam?" asked the cousin, parting his coat-skirts to the genial influence of the fire.

"No; it's a short visit. They're going into the Virginia mountains for the summer." A man-servant came in and said something in a low voice. "Heigh? What? Why, of course! Certainly! By all means! Show him in! Come in, parson; come in!" called the host to his yet unseen visitor, and he held out his hand for Sewell to take when he appeared at the door. "Glad to see you! I can't get up,—a little gouty to-day,—but Bellingham's on foot. *His* difficulty is sitting down."

Bellingham gave the minister a near-sighted man's glare

through his glasses, and then came eagerly forward and shook hands. "Oh, Mr. Sewell! I hope you've come to put up some job on Corey. Don't spare him! With Kanawha Paint Co. at the present figures he merits any demand that Christian charity can make upon him. The man's prosperity is disgraceful."

"I'm glad to find you here, Mr. Bellingham," said Sewell, sitting down.

"Oh, is it double-barreled?" pleaded Bellingham.

"I don't know that it's a deadly weapon of any kind," returned the minister. "But if one of you can't help me, perhaps the other can."

"Well, let us know what the job is," said Corey. "We refuse to commit ourselves beforehand."

"I shall have to begin at the beginning," said Sewell warningly, "and the beginning is a long way off."

"No matter," said Bellingham, adventurously. "The farther off, the better. I've been dining with Corey—he gives you a very good dinner now, Corey does—and I'm just in the mood for a deserving case."

"The trouble with Sewell is," said Corey, "that he doesn't always take the trouble to have them deserving. I hope this is interesting, at least."

"I suspect you'll find it more interesting than I shall," said the minister, inwardly preparing himself for the amusement which Lemuel's history always created in his hearers. It seemed to him, as he began, that he was always telling this story, and that his part in the affair was always becoming less and less respectable. No point was lost upon his hearers; they laughed till the ladies in the drawing-room above wondered what the joke could be.

"At any rate," said Bellingham, "the fellow behaved magnificently at the fire. I read the accounts of it."

"I think his exploits owe something to the imagination of the reporters," said Sewell. "He tells a different story, himself."

"Oh, of course!" said Bellingham.

"Well; and what else?" asked Corey.

"There isn't any more. Simply he's out of work, and wants something to do—anything to do—anything that isn't menial."

"Ah, that's a queer start of his," said Bellingham, thoughtfully. "I don't know but I like that."

"And do you come to such effete posterity as we are for help in a case like that?" demanded Corey. "Why, the boy's an Ancestor!"

"So he is! Why, so he is—so he is!" said Bellingham, with delight in the discovery. "Of course he is!"

"All you have to do," pursued Corey, "is to give him time, and he'll found a fortune and a family, and his children's children will be cutting ours in society. Half of our great people have come up in that way. Look at the Blue-book, where our nobility is enrolled; it's the apotheosis of farm-boys, mechanics, inside-men, and I don't know what!"

"But in the mean time this ancestor is now so remote that he has nothing to do," suggested Sewell. "If you give him time you kill him."

"Well, what do you want me to do? Mrs. Corey is thinking of setting up a Buttons. But you say this boy has a soul above buttons. And besides, he's too old."

"Yes."

"Look here, Bromfield," said Bellingham, "why don't you get *him* to read to you?"

Corey glanced from his cousin to the minister, whose face betrayed that this was precisely what he had had in his own mind.

"Is that the job?" asked Corey.

Sewell nodded boldly.

"He would read through his nose, wouldn't he? I couldn't stand that. I've stopped talking through mine, you know."

"Why, look here, Bromfield!" said Bellingham for the second time. "Why don't you let me manage this affair for you? I'm not of much use in the world, but from time to time I like to do my poor best; and this is just one of the kind of things I think I'm fitted for. I should like to see this young man.

When I read in the newspapers of some fellow who has done a fine thing, I always want to see what manner of man he is; and I'm glad of any chance that throws him in my way."

"Your foible's notorious, Charles. But I don't see why you keep my cigars all to yourself," said Corey.

"My dear fellow," said Bellingham, making a hospitable offer of the cigar-box from the mantel, "you said they'd cut you off."

"Ah, so they have. I forgot. Well, what's your plan?"

"My plan," said Bellingham, "is to have him to breakfast with me, and interview him generally, and get him to read me a few passages, without rousing his suspicions. Heigh?"

"I don't know that I believe much in your plan," said Corey. "I should like to hear what my spiritual adviser has to say."

"I shouldn't know what to advise, exactly," said Sewell. "But I won't reject any plan that gives my client a chance."

"Isn't client rather euphuistic?" asked Corey.

"It is, rather. But I've got into the habit of handling Barker very delicately, even in thought. I'm not sure he'll come," added Sewell, turning to Bellingham.

"Oh, yes, he will," said Bellingham. "Tell him it's business. There won't be anybody there. Will nine be too late for him?"

"I imagine he's more accustomed to half-past five at home, and seven here."

"Well, we'll say nine, anyway. I can't imagine the cause that would get me up earlier. Here!" He turned to the mantel and wrote an invitation upon his card, and handed it to Sewell. "Please give him that from me, and beg him to come. I really want to see him, and if he can't read well enough for this fastidious old gentleman, we'll see what else he can do. Corey tells me he expects Tom on this summer," he concluded, in dismissal of Lemuel as a topic.

"Ah," said Sewell, putting the card in his pocket, "I'm very glad to hear that."

He had something, but not so much, of the difficulty in overcoming Lemuel's reluctance that he had feared, and on the morning named Lemuel presented himself at the address on Bellingham's card exactly at nine. He had the card in his hand, and he gave it to the man who opened the street door of the bachelors' apartment house where Bellingham lived. The man read it carefully over, and then said, "Oh, yes; second floor," and, handing it back, left Lemuel to wander upstairs alone. He was going to offer the card again at Bellingham's door, but he had a dawning misgiving. Bellingham had opened the door himself, and, feigning to regard the card as offered by way of introduction, he gave his hand cordially, and led him into the cozy room where the table was already laid for breakfast.

"Glad to see you—glad to see you, Mr. Barker. Give me your coat. Ah, I see you scorn the effeminacy of half-season things. Put your hat anywhere. The advantage of bachelors' quarters is that you *can* put anything anywhere. We haven't a woman on the premises, and you can fancy how unmolested we are."

Lemuel had caught sight of one over the mantel, who had nothing but her water-colors on, and was called an "Étude"; but he no longer trembled, for evil or for good, in such presences. "That's one of those Romano-Spanish things," said Bellingham, catching the direction of his eye. "I forget the fellow's name; but it isn't bad. We're pretty snug here," he added, throwing open two doors in succession, to show the extent of his apartment. "Here you have the dining-room and drawing-room and library in one; and here's my bedroom, and here's my bath."

He pulled an easy-chair up toward the low fire for Lemuel. "But perhaps you're hot from walking? Sit wherever you like."

Lemuel chose to sit by the window. "It's very mild out," he said, and Bellingham did not exact anything more of him. He talked at him, and left Lemuel to make his mental inventory of the dense Turkey rugs on the slippery hard-wood floor, the pictures on the walls, the deep, leather-lined seats, the bric-à-brac on the mantel, the tall, colored chests of drawers in two corners, the delicate china and quaint silver on the table.

Presently steps were heard outside, and Bellingham threw open the door as he had to Lemuel, and gave a hand to each of the two guests whom he met on his threshold.

"Ah, Meredith! Good-morning, venerable father!" He drew them in. "Let me introduce you to Mr. Barker, Mr. Meredith. Mr. Barker, the Rev. Mr. Seyton. You fellows are pretty prompt."

"We're pretty hungry," said Mr. Meredith. "I don't know that we should have got here if we hadn't leaned up against each other as we came along. Several policemen regarded us suspiciously, but Seyton's cloth protected us."

"It was terrible, coming up Beacon street with an old offender like Meredith, at what he considered the dead hour of the night," said Mr. Seyton. "I don't know what I should have done if any one had been awake to see us."

"You shall have breakfast instantly," said Bellingham, touching an annunciator, and awakening a distant electric titter somewhere.

Mr. Seyton came toward Lemuel, who took the young ritualist for a Catholic priest, but was not proof against the sweet friendliness which charmed every one with him, and was soon talking at more ease than he had felt from all Bellingham's cordial intention. He was put at his host's right hand when they sat down, and Mr. Seyton was given the foot, so that they continued their talk.

"Mr. Bellingham tells me you know my friend Sewell," said the clergyman.

Lemuel's face kindled. "Oh, yes! Do you know him too?"

"Yes, I've known him a long time. He's a capital fellow, Sewell is."

"I think he's a great preacher," ventured Lemuel.

"Ah—well—yes? Is he? I've never heard him lecture," said Mr. Seyton, looking down at his bread.

"I swear, Seyton," said Meredith, across the table, "when

you put on that ecclesiastical superciliousness of yours, I want to cuff you."

"I've no doubt he'd receive it in a proper spirit," said Bellingham, who was eating himself hot and red from the planked shad before him. "But you mustn't do it here."

"Of course," said Mr. Seyton, "Sewell is a very able man, and no end of a good fellow, but you can't expect me to admit he's a priest."

He smiled in sweet enjoyment of his friend's wrath. Lemuel observed that he spoke with an accent different from the others, which he thought very pleasant, but he did not know it for that neat utterance which the Anglican church bestows upon its servants.

"He's no Jesuit," growled Meredith.

"I'm bound to say he's not a pagan, either," laughed the clergyman.

"These gentlemen exchange these little knocks," Bellingham explained to Lemuel's somewhat puzzled look, "because they were boys together at school and college, and can't realize that they've grown up to be lights of the bar and the pulpit." He looked round at the different plates. "Have some more shad?" No one wanted more, it seemed, and Bellingham sent it away by the man, who replaced it with broiled chicken before Bellingham, and lamb chops in front of Mr. Seyton. "This is all there is," the host said.

"It's enough for me," said Meredith, "if no one else takes anything."

But in fact there was also an omelet, and bread and butter delicious beyond anything that Lemuel had tasted; and there was a bouquet of pink radishes with fragments of ice dropped among olives, and other facts of a polite breakfast. At the close came a dish of what Bellingham called premature strawberries.

"Why! they're actually *sweet!*" said Meredith, "and they're as natural as emery-bags."

"Yes, they're all you say," said Bellingham. "You can have strawberries any time nowadays after New Year's, if you send far enough for them; but to get them ripe and sound, or distinguishable from small turnips in taste, is another thing."

Lemuel had never imagined a breakfast like that; he wondered at himself for having respected the cuisine of the St. Albans. It seemed to him that he and the person he had been—the farm boy, the captive of the police, the guest of the Wayfarer's Lodge, the servant of Miss Vane, and the head-waiter at the hotel—could not be the same person. He fell into a strange revery, while the talk, in which he had shared so little, took a range far beyond him. Then he looked up, and found all the others' eyes upon him, and heard Bellingham saying, "I fancy Mr. Barker can tell us something about that," and at Lemuel's mystified stare he added, "About the amount of smoke at a fire that a man could fight through. Mr. Seyton was speaking of the train that was caught in the forest fires, down in Maine, the other day. How was it with you at the St. Albans?"

Lemuel blushed. It was clear that Mr. Bellingham had been reading that ridiculous newspaper version of his exploit. "There was hardly any smoke at all, where I was. It didn't seem to have got into the upper entries much."

"That's just what I was saying!" triumphed Bellingham. "If a man has anything to do, he can get on. That's the way with the firemen. It's the rat-in-a-trap *idea* that paralyzes. Do you remember your sensations at all, when you were coming through the fire? Those things are very curious, sometimes," Bellingham suggested.

"There was no fire where I was," said Lemuel, stoutly, but helpless to make a more comprehensive disclaimer.

"I imagine you wouldn't notice that, any more than the smoke," said Bellingham, with a look of satisfaction in his hero for his other guests. "It's a sort of ecstasy. Do you remember that fellow of Bret Harte's, in 'How Christmas came to Simpson's Bar,' who gets a shot in his leg, or something, when he's riding to get the sick boy a Christmas present, and doesn't know it till he drops off his horse in a faint when he gets back?" He jumped actively up from the table, and found the book on his shelf. "There!" He fumbled for his glasses without finding them. "Will you be kind enough to read the passage, Mr. Barker? I think I've found the page. It's marked." He sat down again, and the others waited.

Lemuel read, as he needs must, and he did his best.

"Ah, that's very nice. Glad you didn't dramatize it; the drama ought to be in the words, not the reader. I like your quiet way."

"Harte seems to have been about the last of the story-tellers to give us the great, simple heroes," said Seyton.

When the others were gone, and Lemuel, who had been afraid to go first, rose to take himself away, Bellingham shook his hand cordially and said, "I hope you weren't bored? The fact is, I rather promised myself a *tête-à-tête* with you, and I told Mr. Sewell so; but I fell in with Seyton and Meredith yesterday—you can't help falling in with one when you fall in with the other; they're inseparable when Seyton's in town— and I couldn't resist the temptation to ask them."

"Oh, no, I wasn't bored at all," said Lemuel.

"I'm very glad. But—sit down a moment. I want to speak to you about a little matter of business. Mr. Sewell was telling us something of you the other night, at my cousin Bromfield Corey's, and it occurred to me that you might be willing to come and read to him. His eyes seem to be on the wane, some way, and he's rather sleepless. He'd give you a bed, and some-times you'd have to read to him in the night; you'd take your meals where you like. How does it strike you, supposing the 'harnsome pittance' can be arranged?"

"Why, if you think I can do it," began Lemuel.

"Of course I do. You don't happen to read French?"

Lemuel shook his head hopelessly. "I studied Latin some at school——"

"Ah! Well! I don't think he'd care for Latin. I think we'd better stick to English for the present."

Bellingham arranged for Lemuel to go with him that after-noon to his cousin's and make, as he phrased it, a stagger at the job.

XXVI

THE STAGGER seemed to be sufficiently satisfactory. Corey could not repress some twinges at certain characteristics of Lemuel's accent, but he seemed, in a critical way, to take a fancy to him, and he was conditionally installed for a week.

Corey was pleased from the beginning with Lemuel's good looks, and justified himself to his wife with an Italian proverb: *"Novanta su cento, chi è bello di fuori è buono di dentro."* She had heard that proverb before, and she had always considered it shocking; but he insisted that most people married upon no better grounds, and that what sufficed in the choice of a husband or wife was enough for the choice of an intellectual nurse. He corrected Lemuel's pronunciation where he found it faulty, and amused himself with Lemuel's struggles to conceal his hurt vanity, and his final good sense in profiting by the correction. But Lemuel's reading was really very good; it was what, even more than his writing, had given him a literary reputation in Willoughby Pastures; and the old man made him exercise it in widely different directions. Chiefly, however, it was novels that he read, which, indeed, are the chief reading of most people in our time; and as they were necessarily the novels of our language, his elder was not obliged to use that care in choosing them which he must have exacted of himself in the fiction of other tongues. He liked to hear Lemuel talk, and he used the art of getting at the boy's life by being frank with his own experience. But this was not always successful, and he was interested to find Lemuel keep-

282

ing doors that Sewell's narrative had opened carefully closed against him. He betrayed no consciousness that they existed, and Lemuel maintained intact the dignity and pride which come from the sense of ignominy well hidden.

The week of probation had passed without interrupting their relation, and Lemuel was regularly installed, and began to lead a life which was so cut off from his past in most things that it seemed to belie it. He found himself dropped in the midst of luxury stranger to him than the things they read of in those innumerable novels. The dull, rich colors in the walls and the heavily rugged floors and dark-wooded leathern seats of the library where he read to the old man; the beautiful forms of the famous bronzes, and the Italian saints and martyrs in their baroque or gothic frames of dim gold; the low shelves with their ranks of luxurious bindings, and all the seriously elegant keeping of the place, flattered him out of his strangeness; and the footing on which he was received in this house, the low-voiced respect with which the man-servant treated him, the master's light, cordial frankness, the distant graciousness of the mistress, and the unembarrassed, unembarrassing kindliness of the young ladies, both so much older than himself, contributed to an effect that afterwards deepened more and more, and became a vital part of the struggle which he was finally to hold with himself.

The first two or three days he saw no one but Mr. Corey, and but for the women's voices in the other parts of the house, he might have supposed himself in another bachelor's apartments, finer and grander than Bellingham's. He was presented to Mrs. Corey when she came into the library, but he did not see the daughters of the house till he was installed in it. After that, his acquaintance with them seemed to go no further. They were all polite and kind when they met him, in the library or on the stairs, but they showed no curiosity about him; and his never meeting them at table helped to keep him a stranger to them under the same roof. He ate at a boarding-house in a neighboring street, but he slept at the Coreys' after he had read their father asleep, and then, going out to his late breakfast, he did not return till Mr. Corey had eaten his own, much later.

He wondered at first that neither of those young ladies read to their father, not knowing the disability for mutual help that riches bring. Later, he saw how much Miss Lily Corey was engrossed with charity and art, and how constantly Miss Nannie Corey was occupied with social cares, and was perpetually going and coming in their performance. Then he saw that they could not have rendered nor their father have received from his family the duty which he was paid to do, as they must have done if they had been poorer. But they were all fond of one another, and the father had a way of joking with his daughters, especially the youngest; and they talked with a freedom of themselves which puzzled Lemuel. It appeared from what they said, at different times, that they had not always been so rich, or that they had once had money, and then less, and now much more. It appeared, also, that their prosperity was due to a piece of luck, and that the young Mr. Corey, whom they expected in the summer, had brought it about. His father was very proud of him, and, getting more and more used to Lemuel's companionship, he talked a great deal about his Tom, as he called him, and about Tom's wife, and his wife's family, who were somehow, Lemuel inferred, not all that his own family could wish them, but very good people. Once when Mr. Corey was talking of them, Mrs. Corey came in upon them, and seemed to be uneasy, as if she thought he was saying too much. But the daughters did not seem to care, especially the youngest.

He found out that Mr. Corey used to be a painter, and had lived a long time in Italy when he was young, and he recalled with a voluptuous thrill of secrecy that Williams had once been in Italy. Mr. Corey seemed to think better of it than Williams; he liked to talk of Rome and Florence, and of Venice, which Williams had said was a kind of hole. The old man said this or that picture was of this or that school, and vague lights of knowledge and senses of difference that flattered Lemuel's intellectual vanity stole in upon him. He began to feel that the things Mr. Corey had lived for were the great and high objects of life.

He now perceived how far from really fine or fashionable anything at the St. Albans had been, and that the simplicity of Miss Vane's little house, which the splendor of the hotel had eclipsed in his crude fancy, was much more in harmony with the richness of Mr. Corey's. He oriented himself anew, and got another view of the world which he had dropped into. Occasionally he had glimpses of people who came to see the Coreys, and it puzzled him that this family, which he knew so kind and good, took with others the tone hard and even cynical which seemed the prevailing tone of society; when their acquaintances went away they dropped back, as if with relief, into their sincere and amiable fashions of speech. Lemuel asked himself if every one in the world was playing a part; it did not seem to him that Miss Carver had been; she was always the same, and always herself. To be one's self appeared to him the best thing in the world, and he longed for it the more as he felt that he too was insensibly beginning to play a part. Being so much in this beautiful and luxurious house, where every one was so well dressed and well mannered, and well kept in body and mind, and passing from his amazement at all its appointments into the habit of its comfortable beauty, he forgot more and more the humility and the humiliations of his past. He did not forget its claims upon him; he sent home every week the greater part of his earnings, and he wrote often to his mother; but now, when he could have got the time to go home and see her, he did not go. In the exquisite taste of his present environment, he could scarcely believe in that figure, grizzled, leathern and gaunt, and costumed in a grotesque unlikeness to either sex. Sometimes he played with the fantastic supposition of some other origin for himself, romantic and involved like that of some of the heroes he was always reading of, which excluded her.

Another effect of this multifarious literature through which his duties led him was the awakening of the ambition to write, stunned by his first disastrous adventures in Boston, and dormant almost ever since, except as it had stirred under the promptings of Evans's kindly interest. But now it did not take the form of verse; he began to write moralistic essays, never finished, but full of severe comment on the folly of the world as he saw it. Sometimes they were examinations of himself, and his ideas and principles, his doctrines and practice, penetrating quests such as the theologians of an earlier day used to address to their consciences.

Meantime, the deeply underlying mass of his rustic crudity and raw youth took on a far higher polish than it had yet worn. Words dropped at random in the talk he now heard supplied him with motives and shaped his actions. Once Mr. Bellingham came in laughing about a sign which he saw in a back street, of Misfit Parlors, and Lemuel spent the next week's salary for a suit at a large clothing store, to replace the dress Sewell had thought him so well in. He began insensibly to ape the manners of those about him.

It drew near the time when the ladies of the Corey family were to leave town, where they had lingered much longer than they meant, in the hope that Mr. Corey might be so much better, or so much worse, that he would consent to go to the shore with them. But his disabilities remained much the same, and his inveterate habits indomitable. By this time that trust in Lemuel which never failed to grow up in those near him, reconciled the ladies to the obstinate resolution of the master of the house to stay in it as usual. They gave up the notion of a cottage, and they were not going far away, nor for long at any one time; in fact, one or other of them was always in the house. Mrs. Corey had grown into the habit of confidence with Lemuel concerning her husband's whims and foibles; and this motherly frankness from a lady so stately and distant at first was a flattery more poisonous to his soul than any other circumstance of his changed life.

It came July, and even Sewell went away then. He went with a mind at rest concerning Lemuel's material prospects, and his unquestionable usefulness and acceptability; but something, at the bottom of his satisfaction, teased him still; a dumb fear that the boy was extravagant, a sense that he was somehow different, and not wholly for the better, from what he had been. He had seen, perhaps, nothing worse in him than that growth of manner which amused Corey.

"He is putting us on," he said to Bellingham, one day, "and making us fit as well as he can. I don't think we're altogether becoming, but that's our fault, probably. I can't help thinking that if we were of better cut and material we should show to better effect upon that granite soul. I wish Tom were here. I've an idea that Tom would fit him like a glove. Charles, why don't *you* pose as a model for Barker?"

"I don't see why I'm not a very good model without posing," said Bellingham. "What do you want me to do for him? Take him to the club? Barker's *not* very conversational."

"You don't take him on the right topics," said Corey, not minding that he had left the point. "I assure you that Barker, on any serious question that comes up in our reading, has a clear head and an apt tongue of his own. It isn't our manners alone that he emulates. I can't find that any of us ever dropped an idea or suggestion of value that Barker didn't pick it up, and turn it to much more account than the owner. He's as true as a Tuscan peasant, as proud as an Indian, and as quick as a Yankee."

"Ah! I *hoped* you wouldn't go abroad for that last," said Bellingham.

"No; and it's delightful, seeing the great variety of human nature there is in every human being here. Our life isn't stratified; perhaps it never will be. At any rate, for the present, we're all in vertical sections. But I always go back to my first notion of Barker: he's ancestral, and he makes me feel like degenerate posterity. I've had the same sensation with Tom; but Barker seems to go a little farther back. I suppose there's such a thing as getting too far back in these Origin of Species days; but he isn't excessive in that or in anything. He's confoundedly temperate, in fact; and he's reticent; he doesn't allow any unseemly intimacy. He's always turning me out-of-doors."

"Of course! But what can we old fellows hope to know of what's going on in any young one? Talk of strangeness! I'd undertake to find more in common with a florid old fellow of fifty from the red planet Mars than with any young Bostonian of twenty."

"Yes; but it's the youth of my sires that I find so strange in Barker. Only, theoretically, there's no Puritanism. He's a thorough believer in Sewell. I suspect he could formulate Sewell's theology a great deal better than Sewell could."

XXVII

Statira and 'Manda Grier had given up their plan of getting places in a summer hotel when Lemuel absolutely refused to take part in it, and were working through the summer in the box-factory. Lemuel came less regularly to see them now, for his Sunday nights had to be at Mr. Corey's disposition; but Statira was always happy in his coming, and made him more excuses than he had thought of, if he had let a longer interval than usual pass. He could not help feeling the loveliness of her patience, the sweetness of her constancy; but he disliked 'Manda Grier more and more, and she grew stiffer and sharper with him. Sometimes the aimlessness of his relation to Statira hung round him like a cloud, which he could not see beyond. When he was with her he contented himself with the pleasure he felt in her devotion, and the tenderness this awakened in his own heart; but when he was away from her there was a strange disgust and bitterness in these.

Sometimes, when Statira and 'Manda Grier took a Saturday afternoon off, he went with them into the country on one of the horse-car lines, or else to some matinée at a garden-theater in the suburbs. Statira liked the theater better than anything else; and she used to meet other girls whom she knew there, and had a gay time. She introduced Lemuel to them, and after a few moments of high civility and distance they treated him familiarly, as Statira's beau. Their talk, after that he was now used to, was flat and foolish, and their pert ease incensed him. He came away bruised and burning, and feeling himself unfit to breathe the refined and gentle air to which he returned in Mr. Corey's presence. Then he would vow in his heart never to expose himself to such things again; but he could not tell Statira that he despised the friends she was happy with; he could only go with a reluctance it was not easy to hide, and atone by greater tenderness for a manner that wounded her. One day toward the end of August, when they were together at a suburban theater, Statira wandered off to a pond there was in the grounds with some other girls who had asked him to go and row them, and had called him a bear for refusing, and told him to look out for Barnum. They left him sitting alone with 'Manda Grier, at a table where they had all been having ice-cream at his expense; and though it was no longer any pleasure to be with her, it was better than to be with them, for she was not a fool, at any rate. Statira turned round at a little distance to mock them with a gesture and a laugh, and the laugh ended in a cough, long and shattering, so that one of her companions had to stop with her, and put her arm round her till she could recover herself and go on.

It sent a cold thrill through Lemuel, and then he turned angry. "What is it Statira does to keep taking more cold?"

"Oh, I guess 'tain't 'ny *more* cold," said 'Manda Grier.

"What do you mean?"

"I guess 'f you cared a great deal you'd noticed that cough 'f hers before now. 'Tain't done it any too much good workin' in that arsenic paper all summer long."

'Manda Grier talked with her face turned away from him.

It provoked him more and more. "I *do* care," he retorted, eager to quarrel, "and you know it. Who got her into the box-factory, I should like to know?"

"*I* did!" said 'Manda Grier, turning sharply on him, "and you *kept* her there; and between us we've killed her."

"How have I kept her there, I should like to know?"

" 'F you'd done's she wanted you should, she might 'a' been at some pleasant place in the country—the mount'ns, or somewhere 't she'd been ov'r her cough by this time. But no! You was too nasty proud for that, Lemuel Barker!"

A heavy load of guilt dropped upon Lemuel's heart, but he flung it off, and he retorted furiously, "You ought to have been ashamed of yourself to ever want her to take a servant's place."

"Oh, a servant's place! If she'd been ashamed of a servant when you came meechin' round her, where'd you been, I sh'd like to know? And now I wish she had; 'n' if she wa'n't such a little fool, 'n' all wrapped in you, the way't she is, I could wish't she'd never set eyes on you again, servant or no servant. But I presume it's too late now, and I presume she's got to go on suff'rin' for you and wonderin' what she's done to offend you when you don't come, and what she's done when you do, with your stuck-up, masterful airs, and your double-faced ways. But don't you try to pretend to me, Lemuel Barker, 't you care the least mite for her any more, 'f you ever did, because it won't go down! 'N' if S'tira wa'n't such a perfect little blind fool, she could see 't you didn't care for her any more than the ground 't you walk on, 'n' 't you'd be glad enough if she was under it, if you couldn't be rid of her any other way!" 'Manda Grier pulled her handkerchief out and began to cry into it.

Lemuel was powerfully shaken by this attack; he did feel responsible for Statira's staying in town all summer; but the spectacle of 'Manda Grier publicly crying at his side in a place like that helped to counteract the effect of her words. " 'Sh! Don't cry!" he began, looking fearfully round him. "Everybody'll see you!"

"I don't care! Let them!" sobbed the girl. "If they knowed what I know, and could see you *not* cryin', I guess they'd think you looked worse than I do!"

"You don't understand—I can explain—"

"No, you can't explain, Mr. Barker!" said 'Manda Grier, whipping down her handkerchief and fiercely confronting him across the table. "You can't explain anything so's to blind *me* any longer! I was a big fool to ever suppose you had any heart *in* you; but when you came round at first, and was so meek you couldn't say your soul was your own, and was so glad if S'tira spoke to you, or looked at you, that you was ready to go crazy, I *did* suppose there was some *little* something to you! And yes, I helped you on, all I could, and helped you to fool that poor thing that you ain't worthy to kiss the ground she walks on, Lord forgive me *for* it! But it's all changed now! You seem to think it's the greatest favor if you come round once a fortnight, and set and let her talk to you, and show you how she dotes upon you, the poor little silly coot! And if you ever speak a word, it's like the Lord unto Moses, it's so grand! But I understand! You've got other friends now! *You after that art-student?* Oh, you can blush and try to turn it off! I've seen you blush before, and I know you! And I know you're in love with that girl, and you're just waitin' to break off with S'tira; but you hain't got the spirit to up and do it like a man! You want to let it lag along, and *lag* along, and see 'f something won't happen to get you out of it! *You waitin' for her to die?* Well, you won't have to wait long! But if I was a man, I'd spoil your beauty for you first!"

The torrent of her words rolled him on, bruising and tearing his soul, which their truth pierced like jagged points. From time to time he opened his lips to protest or deny, but no words came, and in his silence a fury of scorn for the poor, faithful, scolding thing, so just, so wildly unjust, gathered head in him.

"Be still!" he ground between his teeth. "Be still, you——" He stopped for the word, and that saved him from the outrage he had meant to pay her back with. He rose from the table. "You can tell Statira what you've said to me. I'm going home."

He rushed away; the anger was like strong drink in his brain; he was like one drunk all the way back to the city in the car.

He could not go to Mr. Corey's at once; he felt as if physically besmeared with shame; he could not go to his boarding-house; it would have been as if he had shown himself there in a coat of tar and feathers. Those insolent, true, degrading words hissed in his ears, and stung him incessantly. They accused, they condemned with pitiless iteration; and yet there were instants when he knew himself guiltless of all the wrong of which in another sense he knew himself guilty. In his room, he renewed the battle within himself that he had fought so long in his wanderings up and down the street, and he conquered himself at last into the theory that Statira had authorized or permitted 'Manda Grier to talk to him in that way. This simplified the whole affair: it offered him the release which he now knew he had longed for. As he stretched himself in the sheets at daybreak, he told himself that he need never see either of them again. He was free.

XXVIII

LEMUEL went through the next day in that license of revolt which every human soul has experienced in some measure at some time. We look back at it afterwards, and see it a hideous bondage. But for the moment Lemuel rejoiced in it; and he abandoned himself boldly to thoughts that had hitherto been a furtive and trembling rapture.

In the afternoon, when he was most at leisure, he walked down to the Public Garden, and found a seat on a bench near the fountain where the Venus had shocked his inexperience the first time he saw her; he remembered that simple boy with a smile of pity, and then went back into his cloud of revery. There, safely hid from trouble and wrong, he told his ideal how dear she was to him, and how she had shaped and governed his life, and made it better and nobler from the first moment they had met. The fumes of the romances which he had read mixed with the love-born delirium in his brain: he was no longer low, but a hero of lofty line, kept from his rightful place by machinations that had failed at last, and now he was leading her, his bride, into the ancient halls which were to be their home, and the source of beneficence and hope to all the poor and humbly-born around them. His eyes were so full of this fantastic vision, the soul of his youth dwelt so deeply within this dream-built tabernacle, that it was with a shock of anguish he saw coming up the walk towards him the young girl herself. His airy structure fell in ruins around him; he was again common and immeasurably beneath her; she was again in her own world, where, if she thought of him at all, it must be as a squalid vagabond and the accomplice of a thief. If he could have escaped, he would, but he could not move; he sat still and waited, with fallen eyes, for her to pass him.

At sight of him she hesitated and wavered; then she came towards him, and at a second impulse held out her hand, smiling with a radiant pleasure.

"I didn't know it was you, at first," she said. "It seems so strange to see any one that I know!"

"I didn't expect to see you, either," he stammered out, getting somehow upon his feet and taking her hand, while his face burned, and he could not keep his eyes on hers; "I—didn't know you were here."

"I've only been here a few days. I'm drawing at the Museum. I've just got back. Have you been here all summer?"

"Yes—all summer. I hope you've been well—I suppose you've been away——"

"Yes, I've just got back," she repeated.

"Oh, yes! I meant that!"

She smiled at his confusion, as kindly as the ideal of his day-dream. "I've been spending the summer with Madeline, and I've spent most of it out-of-doors, sketching. Have you been well?"

"Yes—not very; oh, yes, I'm well——" She had begun to move forward with the last question, and he found himself walking with her. "Did she—has Miss Swan come back with you?" he asked, looking her in the eyes with more question than he had put into his words.

"No, I don't think she'll come back this winter," said the girl. "You know," she went on, coloring a little, "that she's married now?"

"No," said Lemuel.

"Yes. To Mr. Berry. And I have a letter from him for you."

"Was he there with you, this summer?" asked Lemuel, ignoring alike Berry's marriage and the letter from him.

"Oh, yes; of course! And I liked him better than I used to. He is very good, and if Madeline didn't have to go so far West to live! He will know how to appreciate her, and there are not many who can do that! Her father thinks he has a great deal of ability. Yes, if Madeline *had* to get married!"

She talked as if convincing and consoling herself, and there was an accent of loneliness in it all that pierced Lemuel's preoccupation; he had hardly noted how almost pathetically glad she was to see him. "You'll miss her here," he ventured.

"Oh, I don't dare to think of it!" cried the girl. "I don't know what I shall do! When I first saw you, just now, it brought up Madeline and last winter so that it seemed too much to bear!"

They had walked out of the Garden across Charles street, and were climbing the slope of Beacon street Mall, in the Common. "I suppose," she continued, "the only way will be to work harder, and try to forget it. They wanted me to go out and stay with them; but of course I couldn't. I shall work, and I shall read. I shall not find another Madeline Swan! You must have been reading a great deal this summer, Mr. Barker," she said, in turning upon him from her bereavement. "Have you seen any of the old boarders? Or Mrs. Harmon? I shall never have another winter like that at the poor old St. Albans!"

Lemuel made what answer he could. There was happiness enough in merely being with her to have counterbalanced all the pain he was suffering; and when she made him partner of her interests and associations, and appealed to their common memories in confidence of his sympathy, his heavy heart stirred with strange joy. He had supposed that Berry must have warned her against him; but she was treating him as if he had not. Perhaps he had not, and perhaps he had done so, and this was her way of showing that she did not believe it. He tried to think so; he knew it was a subterfuge, but he lingered in it with a fleeting, fearful pleasure. They had crossed from the Common, and were walking up under the lindens of

Chestnut street, and from time to time they stopped in the earnestness of their parley, and stood talking, and then loitered on again, in the summer security from oversight which they were too rapt to recognize. They reached the top of the hill, and came to a door where she stopped. He fell back a pace. "Good-bye—" It was eternal loss, but it was escape.

She smiled in timorous hesitation. "Won't you come in? And I will get Mr. Berry's letter."

She opened the door with a latch-key, and he followed her within; a servant girl came half-way up the basement stairs to see who it was, and then went down. She left him in the dim parlor a moment, while she went to get the letter. When she returned, "I have a little room for my work at the top of the house," she said, "but it will never be like the St. Albans. There's no one else here yet, and it's pretty lonesome—without Madeline."

She sank into a chair, but he remained standing, and seemed not to heed her when she asked him to sit down. He put Berry's letter into his pocket without looking at it, and she rose again.

She must have thought he was going, and she said, with a smile of gentle trust, "It's been like having last winter back again to see you. We thought you must have gone home right after the fire; we didn't see anything of you again. We went ourselves in about a week."

Then she did not know, and he must tell her himself.

"Did Mr. Berry say anything about me—at the fire—that last day?" he began bluntly.

"No!" she said, looking at him with surprise; there was a new sound in his voice. "He had no need to say anything! I wanted to tell you—to write and tell you—how much I honored you for it—how ashamed I was for misunderstanding you just before, when——"

He knew that she meant when they all pitied him for a coward.

Her voice trembled; he could tell that the tears were in her eyes. He tried to put the sweetness of her praise from him. "Oh, it wasn't that that I meant," he groaned; and he wrenched the words out. "That fellow who said he was a friend of mine, and got into the house that way, was a thief; and Mr. Berry caught him robbing his room the day of the fire, and treated me as if I knew it, and was helping him on——"

"Oh!" cried the girl. "How cruel! How could he do that?"

Lemuel could not suffer himself to take refuge in her generous faith now.

"When I first came to Boston I had my money stolen, and there were two days when I had nothing to eat; and then I was arrested by mistake for stealing a girl's satchel; and when I was acquitted, I slept the next night in the tramps' lodging-house, and that fellow was there, and when he came to the St. Albans I was ashamed to tell where I had known him, and so I let him pass himself off for my friend."

He kept his eyes fixed on hers, but he could not see them change from their pity of him, or light up with a sense of any squalor in his history.

"And I used to think that *my* life had been hard!" she cried. "Oh, how much you have been through!"

"And after that," he pursued, "Mr. Sewell got me a place, a sort of servant's place, and when I lost that I came to be the man-of-all-work at the St. Albans."

In her eyes the pity was changing to admiration; his confession which he had meant to be so abject had kindled her fancy like a boastful tale.

"How little we know about people and what they have suffered! But I thank you for telling me this—oh, yes!—and I shall always think of myself with contempt. How easy and pleasant my life has been! And you——"

She stopped, and he stood helpless against her misconception. He told her about the poverty he had left at home, and the wretched circumstance of his life, but she could not see it as anything but honorable to his present endeavor. She listened with breathless interest to it all, and, "Well," she sighed at last, "it will always be something for you to look back to, and be proud of. And that girl—did she never say or do anything to show that she was sorry for that cruel mistake? Did you ever see her afterwards?"

"Yes," said Lemuel, sick at heart, and feeling how much more triumphantly he could have borne ignominy and rejection than this sweet sympathy. She seemed to think he would say something more, but he turned away from her, and after a little silence of expectance she let him go, with promises to come again which she seemed to win from him for his own sake.

In the street he took out Berry's letter and read it.

"DEAR OLD MAN: I've been trying to get off a letter to you almost any time the last three months, but I've been round so much, and upside down so much since I saw you—out to W. T. and on my head in Western Mass.—that I've not been able to fetch it. I don't know as I could fetch it now, if it wasn't for the prospective Mrs. A. W. B., Jr., standing over me with a revolver, and waiting to see me do it. I've just been telling her about that little interview of ours with Williams, that day, and she thinks I ought to be man enough to write and say that I guess I was all wrong about you; I had a sneaking idea of the kind from the start almost, but if a fellow's proud at all, he's proud of his mistakes, and he hates to give them up. I'm pretty badly balled up, now, and I can't seem to get the right words about remorse, and so forth; but you know how it is yourself. I *am* sorry, there's no two ways about that; but I've kept my suspicions as well as my regrets to myself, and now I do the best thing I can by way of reparation. I send this letter by Miss Carver. She hasn't read it, and she don't know what it's all about; but I guess you'd better tell her. Don't spare yours truly,

"A. W. BERRY, JR."

The letter did not soften Lemuel at all towards Berry, and he was bitterly proud that he had spoken without this bidding, though he had seemed to speak to no end that he had expected. After a while he lost himself in his day-dreams

again, and in the fantastic future which he built up this became a great source of comfort to him and to his ideal. Now
he parted with her in sublime renunciation, and now he
triumphed over all the obstacles between them; but, whatever turn he willed his fortunes to take, she still praised him,
and he prided himself that he had shown himself at his worst
to her of his own free impulse. Sewell praised him for it in
his revery; Mr. Corey and Mr. Bellingham both made him
delicate compliments upon his noble behavior, which he
feigned had somehow become known to them.

XXIX

At the usual hour he was at Mr. Corey's house, where he arrived footsore and empty from supperless wanderings, but not hungry and not weary. The serving-man at the door met him with the message that Mr. Corey had gone to dine at his club and would not be at home till late. He gave Lemuel a letter, which had all the greater effect from being presented to him on the little silver tray employed to bring up the cards and notes of the visitors and correspondents of the family. The envelope was stamped in that ephemeral taste which configured the stationery of a few years ago with the lines of alligator leather, and it exhaled a perfume so characteristic that it seemed to breathe Statira visibly before him. He knew this far better than the poor, scrawly, uncultivated handwriting which he had seen so little. He took the letter, and, turning from the door, read it by the light of the next street lamp.

"Dear Lemuel—Manda Grier has told me what she said to you and Ime about crazy about it dear Lem I want you should come and see mee O Lem you dont Suppose i could of let Manda Grier talk to you that way if I had of none it but of course you dident only do Say so I give her a real good goen over and she says shes sory she done it i dont want any body should care for mee without itse there free will but I shall alwayes care for you if you dont care for me dont come but if you do Care I want you should come as soon as ever you can I can explane everything Manda Grier dident mean anything but for the best but sometimes she dont know what she is sayin O Lem you mussent be mad But if you are and

you dont want to come ennymore dont come But O i hope you
wouldent let such a thing set you againste mee recollect that I
never done or Said anything to set you against me.

"STATIRA."

A cruel disgust mingled with the remorse that this letter
brought him. Its illiteracy made him ashamed, and the helpless fondness it expressed was like a millstone hanged about
his neck. He felt the deadly burden of it drag him down.

A passer-by on the other side of the street coughed slightly
in the night air, and a thought flashed through Lemuel, from
which he cowered as if he had found himself lifting his hand
against another's life.

His impulse was to turn and run, but there was no escape
on any side. It seemed to him that he was like that prisoner
he had read of, who saw the walls of his cell slowly closing
together upon him, and drawing nearer and nearer till they
should crush him between them. The inexperience of youth
denies it perspective; in that season of fleeting and unsub-
stantial joys, of feverish hopes, despair wholly darkens a world
which after years find full of chances and expedients.

If Mr. Sewell had been in town there might have been
some hope through him; or if Mr. Evans were there; or even
if Berry were at hand, it would be some one to advise with,
to open his heart to in his extremity. He walked down into
Bolingbroke street, knowing well that Mr. Sewell was not at
home, but pretending to himself, after the fashion of the
young, that if he should see a light in his house it would be a
sign that all should come out right with him, and if not, it
would come out wrong. He would not let himself lift his eyes
to the house front till he arrived before it. When he looked
his heart stood still; a light streamed bright and strong from
the drawing-room window.

He hurried across the street and rang; and after some delay, in which the person coming to the door took time to
light the gas in the hall, Mr. Sewell himself opened to him.

They stood confronted in mutual amazement, and then Sewell said, with a cordiality which he did not keep free from reluctance, "Oh—Mr. Barker! Come in! Come in!" But after they had shaken hands, and Lemuel had come in, he stood there in the hall with him, and did not offer to take him up to his study. "I'm so glad to have this glimpse of you! How in the world did you happen to come?"

"I was passing and saw the light," said Lemuel.

Sewell laughed. "To be sure! We never have any idea how far our little candle throws its beams! I'm just here for the night, on my way from the mountains to the sea; I'm to be the 'supply' in a friend's pulpit at New Bedford; and I'm here quite alone in the house, scrambling a sermon together. But I'm *so* glad to see you! You're well, I hope? You're looking a little thin, but that's no harm. Do you enjoy your life with Mr. Corey? I was sure you would. When you come to know him, you will find him one of the best of men—kindly, thoughtful, and sympathetic. I've felt very comfortable about your being with him, whenever I've thought of you, and you may be sure that I've thought of you often. What about our friends of the St. Albans? Do you see Mrs. Harmon? You knew the Evanses had gone to Europe."

"Yes; I got a letter from him yesterday."

"He didn't pick up so fast as they hoped, and he concluded to try the voyage. I hear very good accounts of him. He said he was going to write you. Well! And Mr. Corey is well?" He smiled more beamingly upon Lemuel, who felt that he wished him to go, and stood haplessly trying to get away.

In the midst of his own uneasiness Sewell noted Lemuel's. "Is there anything—something—you wished to speak with me about?"

"No. No, not anything in particular. I just saw the light, and——"

Sewell took his hand and wrung it with affection. "It was so good of you to run in and see me. Don't fancy it's been any disturbance. I'd got into rather a dim place in my work, but since I've been standing here with you—ha, ha, ha! those things do happen so curiously!—the whole thing has become perfectly luminous. I'm delighted you're getting on so nicely. Give my love to Mr. Corey. I shall see you soon again. We shall all be back in a little over a fortnight. Glad of this moment with you, if it's *only* a moment! Good-bye!"

He wrung Lemuel's hand again, this time in perfect sincerity, and eagerly shut him out into the night.

The dim place had not become so luminous to him as it had to the minister. A darkness, which the obscurity of the night faintly typified, closed round him, pierced by one ray only, and from this he tried to turn his face. It was the gleam that lights up every labyrinth where our feet wander and stumble, but it is not always easy to know it from those false lights of feeble-hearted pity, of mock-sacrifice, of sick conscience, which dance before us to betray to worse misery yet.

Some sense of this, broken and faltering, reached Lemuel where he stood, and tried to deal faithfully with his problem. In that one steadfast ray he saw that whatever he did he must not do it for himself; but what his duty was he could not make out. He knew now, if he had not known before, that whatever his feeling for Statira was, he had not released himself from her, and it seemed to him that he could not release himself by any concern for his own advantage. That notion with which he had so long played, her insufficiency for his life now and for the needs of his mind hereafter, revealed itself in its real cruelty. The things that Mr. Sewell had said, that his mother had said, that Berry had said, in what seemed a fatal succession, and all to the same effect, against throwing himself away upon some one inadequate to him at his best, fell to the ground like withered leaves, and the fire of that steadfast ray consumed them.

But whom to turn to for counsel now? The one friend in whom he had trusted, to whom he had just gone ready to fling down his whole heart before him, had failed him, failed him unwittingly, unwillingly, as he had failed him once before, but this time in infinitely greater stress. He did not blame him now, fiercely, proudly, as he had once blamed him, but again he wandered up and down the city streets, famished and outcast through his defection.

It was late when he went home, but Mr. Corey had not yet returned, and he had time to sit down and write the letter which he had decided to send to Statira, instead of going to see her. It was not easy to write, but after many attempts he wrote it.

"DEAR STATIRA: You must not be troubled at what Amanda said to me. I assure you that, although I was angry at first, I am entirely willing to overlook it at your request. She probably spoke hastily, and I am now convinced that she spoke without your authority. You must not think that I am provoked at you.

"I received your letter this evening; and I will come to see you very soon.

"LEMUEL BARKER."

The letter was colder than he meant to make it, but he felt that he must above all be honest, and he did not see how he could honestly make it less cold. When it came to Statira's hands she read it silently to herself, over and over again, while her tears dripped upon it.

'Manda Grier was by, and she watched her till she could bear the sight no longer. She snatched the letter from the girl's hands, and ran it through, and then she flung it on the ground. "Nasty, cold-hearted, stuck-up, shameless thing!"

"Oh, don't, 'Manda; don't, 'Manda!" sobbed Statira, and she plunged her face into the pillows of the bed where she sat.

"Shameless, cold-hearted, stuck-up, nasty thing!" said 'Manda Grier, varying her denunciation in the repetition, and apparently getting fresh satisfaction out of it in that way. "Don't? St'ira Dudley, if you was a woman—if you was *half* a woman—you'd never speak to that little corpse-on-ice again."

"Oh, 'Manda, don't call him names! I can't bear to have you!"

"Names? If you was anybody at all, you wouldn't *look* at him! You wouldn't *think* of him!"

"Oh, 'Manda, 'Manda! You know I can't let you talk so," moaned Statira.

"Talk? I could talk my *head* off! 'You must not think I was provoked with you,' " she mimicked Lemuel's dignity of diction in mincing falsetto. " 'I will come to see you very soon.' Miserable, worthless, conceited whipper-snapper!"

"Oh, 'Manda, you'll break my heart if you go on so!"

"Well, then, give him up! He's goin' to give you up."

"Oh, he ain't; you know he ain't! He's just busy, and I know he'll come. I'll bet you he'll be here to-morrow. It'll kill me to give him up."

She had lifted herself from the pillow, and she began to cough.

"He'll kill you anyway," cried 'Manda Grier, in a passion of pity and remorse. She ran across the room to get the medicine which Statira had to take in these paroxysms. "There, there! Take it! I sha'n't say anything more about him."

"And do you take it all back?" gasped Statira, holding the proffered spoon away.

"Yes, yes! But *do* take your med'cine, St'ira, 'f you don't want to die where you set."

"And do you think he'll come?"

"Yes, he'll come."

"Do you say it just to get me to take the medicine?"

"No, I really do believe he'll come."

"Oh, 'Manda, 'Manda!" Statira took her medicine, and then wildly flung her arms round 'Manda Grier's neck, and began to sob and to cry there. "Oh, how hard I *am* with you, 'Manda! I should think if *I* was as hard with everybody else, they'd perfectly hate me."

"*You* hard!"

"Yes, and that's why he hates me. He does hate me. You said he did."

"No, St'ira, I didn't. You never was hard to anybody, and the meanest old iceberg in creation couldn't hate you."

"Then you think he does care for me?"

"Yes."

"And you know he'll come soon?"

"Yes."

"To-morrow?"

"Yes, to-morrow."

"Oh, 'Manda, oh, 'Manda!"

XXX

LEMUEL had promised himself that if he could gain a little time he should be able better to decide what it was right for him to do. His heart lifted as he dropped the letter into the box, and he went through the chapters which Mr. Corey asked him to read, after he came in, with an ease incredible to himself. In the morning he woke with a mind that was almost cheerful. He had been honest in writing that letter, and so far he had done right; he should keep his word about going soon to see Statira, and that would be honest too. He did not look beyond this decision, and he felt as we all do more or less vaguely when we have resolved to do right, that he had the merit of a good action.

Statira showed herself so glad to see him that he could not do less than seem to share her joy in their making-up, as she called it, though he insisted that there had been no quarrel between them; and now there began for him a strange double life, the fact of which each reader must reject or accept according to the witness of his own knowledge.

He renewed as far as he could the old warmth of his feeling for Statira, and in his compunction experienced a tenderness for her that he had not known before, the strange tenderness that some spirits feel for those they injure. He went oftener than ever to see her, he was very good to her, and cheered her with his interest in all her little interests; he petted her and comforted her; but he escaped from her as soon as he could, and when he shut her door behind him he shut her within it.

He made haste to forget her, and to lose himself in thoughts that were never wholly absent even in her presence. Sometimes he went directly from her to Jessie, whose innocent Bohemianism kept later hours, and who was always glad to see him whenever he came. She welcomed him with talk that they thought related wholly to the books they had been reading, and to the things of deep psychological import which they suggested. He seldom came to her without the excuse of a book to be lent or borrowed; and he never quitted her without feeling inspired with the wish to know more and to be more: he seemed to be lifted to purer and clearer regions of thought. She received him in the parlor, but their evenings commonly ended in her little studio, whither some errand took them, or some intrusion of the other boarders banished them. There he read to her poems or long chapters out of the essayists or romancers; or else they sat and talked about the strange things they had noticed in themselves that were like the things they found in their books. Once when they had talked a long while in this strain, he told how when he first saw her he thought she was very proud and cold.

She laughed gayly. "And I used to be afraid of you," she said. "You used to be always reading there in your little office. Do you think I'm very proud now?"

"Are you very much afraid of me now?" he retorted.

They laughed together.

"Isn't it strange," she said, "how little we really know about people in the world?"

"Yes," he answered. "I wonder if it will ever be different. I've been wrong about nearly every one I've met since I came to Boston."

"And I have too!" she cried, with that delight in the coincidence of experience which the young feel so keenly.

He had got the habit with his growing ease in her presence, of walking up and down the room, while she sat, forgetful of everything but the things they were saying, and followed him with her eyes. As he turned about in his walk, he saw how

pretty she was, with her slender form cased in the black silk
she wore. Her eyes were very bright, and her soft lips, small
and fine, were red.

He faltered, and lost the thread of his speech. "I forgot
what I was going to say!"

She clasped her hands over her laughing face a moment.
"And I don't remember what you were saying!" They both
laughed a long time at this; it seemed incomparably droll,
and they became better comrades.

They spent the rest of the evening in laughing and joking.

"I didn't know you were so fond of laughing," he said,
when he went away.

"And I always supposed you were very solemn," she replied.

This again seemed the drollest thing in the world.

"Well, I always was," he said.

"And I don't know when I've laughed so much before!"
She stood at the head of the stairs, and held her lamp up for
him to find his way down.

Again looking back, he saw her in the grace that had bewildered him before.

When he came next they met very seriously, but before the
evening was past they were laughing together; and so it happened now whenever he came. They both said how strange
it was that laughing with any one seemed to make you feel
so much better acquainted. She told of a girl at school that
she had always disliked till one day something made them
laugh, and after that they became the greatest friends.

He tried to think of some experience to match this, but he
could not; he asked her if she did not think that you always
felt a little gloomy after you had been laughing a great deal.
She said, yes; after that first night when they laughed so, she
felt so depressed that she was sure she was going to have bad
news from Madeline. Then she said she had received a letter
from Madeline that morning, and she and Mr. Berry had
both wished her to give him their regards if she ever saw

him. This, when she had said it, seemed a very good joke too; and they laughed at it a little consciously, till he boldly bade her tell them he came so very seldom that she did not know when she could deliver their message.

She answered that she was afraid Madeline would not believe that; and then it came out that he had never replied to Berry's letter.

She said, "Oh! Is that the way you treat your correspondents?" and he was ashamed to confess that he had not forgiven Berry.

"I will write to him to-night, if you say so," he answered hardily.

"Oh, you must do what you think best," she said, lightly refusing the responsibility.

"Whatever you say will be best," he said with a sudden, passionate fervor that surprised himself.

She tried to escape from it. "Am I so infallible as that?"

"You are for me!" he retorted.

A silence followed, which she endeavored to break, but she sat still across the little table from him where the shaded lamp spread its glow, leaving the rest of the room, with its red curtains and its sketches pinned about, in a warm, luxurious shadow. Her eyes fell, and she did not speak.

"It must sound very strange to you, I know," he went on; "and it's strange to me too; but it seems to me that there isn't anything I've done without my thinking whether you would like me to do it."

She rose involuntarily. "You make me ashamed to think that you're so much mistaken about me! I know how we all influence each other—I know I always try to be what I think people expect me to be—I can't be myself—I know what you mean; but you—you must be yourself, and not let——" She stopped in her wandering speech, in strange agitation, and he rose too.

"I hope you're not offended with me!"

"Offended? Why? Why do you—go so soon?"

"I thought you were going," he answered stupidly.

"Why, I'm at *home!*"

They looked at each other, and then they broke into a happy laugh.

"Sit down again! I don't know what I got up for. It must have been to make some tea. Did you know Madeline had bequeathed me her tea-kettle—the one we had at the St. Albans?" She bustled about, and lit the spirit-lamp under the kettle.

"Blow out that match!" he cried. "You'll set your dress on fire!" He caught her hand, which she was holding with the lighted match in it at her side, after the manner of women with lighted matches, and blew it out himself.

"Oh, thank you!" she said indifferently. "Can you take it without milk!"

"Yes, I like it so."

She got out two of the cups he remembered, and he said, "How much like last winter that seems!"

And "Yes, doesn't it?" she sighed.

The lamp purred and fretted under the kettle, and in the silence in which they waited, the elm tree that rose from the pavement outside seemed to look in consciously upon them.

When the kettle began to sing, she poured out the two cups of tea, and in handing him his their fingers touched, and she gave a little outcry. "Oh! Madeline's precious cup! I thought it was going to drop!"

The soft night-wind blew in through the elm leaves, and their rustling seemed the expression of a profound repose, an endless content.

XXXI

THE NEXT NIGHT Lemuel went to see Statira, without promising himself what he should say or do, but if he were to tell her everything, he felt that she would forgive him more easily than 'Manda Grier. He was aware that 'Manda always lay in wait for him, to pierce him at every undefended point of conscience. Since the first break with her, there had never been peace between them, and perhaps not kindness for long before that. Whether or not she felt responsible for having promoted Statira's affair with him, and therefore bound to guard her to the utmost from suffering by it, she seemed always to be on the alert to seize any advantage against him. Sometimes Statira accused her of trying to act so hatefully to him that he would never come any more; she wildly blamed her; but the faithful creature was none the less constant and vigilant on that account. She took patiently the unjust reproaches which Statira heaped upon her like a wayward child, and remitted nothing of her suspicion or enmity towards Lemuel. Once, when she had been very bitter with him, so bitter that it had ended in an open quarrel between them, Statira sided with him against her, and when 'Manda Grier flounced out of the room she offered him, if he wished, to break with her, and never to speak to her again, or have anything more to do with such a person. But at this his anger somehow fell; and he said no, she must not think of such a thing; that 'Manda Grier had been her friend long before he was, and that, whatever she said to him, she was always good and true to her. Then Statira fell upon his neck and cried, and praised him, and said he was a million times more to her than 'Manda Grier, but she would do whatever he said; and he went away sick at heart.

When he came now, with his thoughts clinging to Jessie, 'Manda Grier hardly gave him time for the decencies of greeting. She was in a high nervous exaltation, and Statira looked as if she had been crying.

"What's become o' them art-students you used to have 't the St. Albans?" she began, her whopper-jaw twitching with excitement, and her eyes glaring vindictively upon Lemuel.

He had sat down near Statira on the lounge, but she drew a little away from him in a provisional fashion, as if she would first see what came of 'Manda Grier's inquisition.

"Art-students?" he repeated aimlessly, while he felt his color go.

"Yes!" she snapped. "Them girls 't used to be 't the St. Albans, 't you thought so wonderful!"

"I didn't know I thought they were very wonderful."

"Can't you answer a civil question?" she demanded, raising her voice.

"I haven't heard any," said Lemuel with sullen scorn.

"Oh! Well!" she sneered. "I forgot that you've b'en used to goin' with such fine folks that you can't bear to be spoken to in plain English."

" 'Manda!" began Statira, with an incipient whimper.

"You be still, S'tira Dudley! Mr. Barker," said the poor foolish thing in the mincing falsetto which she thought so cutting, "have you any idea what's become of your young lady artist friends,—them that took your portrait as a Roman youth, you know?"

Lemuel made no answer whatever, for a time. Then, whether he judged it best to do so, or was goaded to the defiance by 'Manda Grier's manner, he replied, "Miss Swan and Miss Carver? Miss Swan is married, and lives in Wyoming Territory now." Before he had reached the close of the sentence he had controlled himself sufficiently to be speaking quite calmly.

"Oh, indeed, Mr. Barker! And may I ask where Miss Carver is? She married and livin' in Wyoming Territory too?"

"No," said Lemuel quietly. "She's not married. She's in Boston."

"Indeed! Then it *was* her I see in the Garden to-day, S'tira! She b'en back long, Mr. Barker?"

"About a month, I think," said Lemuel.

"Quite a spell! *You* seen her, Mr. Barker?"

"Yes, quite often."

"I want to know! She still paintin' Roman Boys, Mr. Barker? Didn't seem to make any great out at it last winter! But practice makes perfect, they say. I s'pose *you* seen her in the Garden too?"

"I usually see her at home," said Lemuel. "*You* probably receive your friends on the benches in the Garden, but young ladies prefer to have them call at their residences." He astonished himself by this brutality, he who was all gentleness with Miss Carver.

"Very well, Mr. Barker! That's all right. That's all I wanted to know. Never mind about where I meet my friends. Wherever it is, they're *gentlemen*; and they ain't generally goin' with three or four other girls 't the same time."

"No, one like you would be enough," retorted Lemuel.

Statira sat cowering away from the quarrel, and making little ineffectual starts as if to stay it. Heretofore their enmity had been covert if not tacit, in her presence.

Lemuel saw her wavering, and the wish to show 'Manda his superior power triumphed over every other interest and impulse in him. He got upon his feet. "There is no use in this sort of thing going on any longer. I came here because I thought I was wanted. If it's a mistake, it's easy enough to mend it, and it's easy not to make it again. I wish you good-evening."

Statira sprang from the lounge, and flung her arms around his neck. "No, no! You sha'n't go! You mustn't go, Lem! I know you're all right, and I won't have you talked to so! I ain't a bit jealous, Lem; indeed I ain't. I know you wouldn't fool with me, any more than I would with you; and that's what I tell 'Manda Grier, I'll leave it to her if I don't. I don't care who you go with, and I hain't, never since that first time. I know you ain't goin' to do anything underhanded. Don't go, Lem; oh, *don't* go!"

He was pulling towards the door; her trust, her fond generosity drove him more than 'Manda Grier's cutting tongue: that hurt his pride, his vanity, but this pierced his soul; he had only a blind, stupid will to escape from it.

Statira was crying; she began to cough; she released his neck from her clasp, and reeled backward to the lounge, where she would have fallen, if 'Manda Grier had not caught her. The paroxysm grew more violent; a bright stream of blood sprang from her lips.

"Run! Run for the doctor! Quick, Lemuel! Oh, quick!" implored 'Manda Grier, forgetting all enmity in her terror.

Statira's arms wavered towards him, as if to keep him, but he turned and ran from the house, cowed and conscience-stricken by the sight of that blood, as if he had shed it.

He did not expect to see Statira alive when he came back with the doctor whom he found at the next apothecary's. She was lying on the lounge, white as death, but breathing quietly, and her eyes sought him with an eagerness that turned to a look of tender gratitude at the look they found in his.

The doctor bent over her for her pulse and her respiration; then when he turned to examine the crimson handkerchief which 'Manda Grier showed him, Lemuel dropped on his knees beside her, and put his face down to hers.

With her lips against his cheek, she made, "Don't go!"

And he whispered, "No, I'll not leave you now!"

The doctor looked round with the handkerchief still in his hand, as if doubting whether to order him away from her. Then he mutely questioned 'Manda Grier with a glance which her glance answered. He shrugged his shoulders, with a puzzled sigh. An expression of pity crossed his face, which he hardened into one of purely professional interest, and he went on questioning 'Manda Grier in a low tone.

Statira had slipped her hand into Lemuel's, and she held it fast, as if in that clasp she were holding on to her chance of life.

XXXII

SEWELL returned to town for the last time in the third week of September, bringing his family with him.

This was before the greater part of his oddly assorted congregation had thought of leaving the country, either the rich cottagers whose family tradition or liberal opinions kept them in his church, or the boarding and camping elements who were uniting a love of cheapness with a love of nature in their prolonged sojourn among the woods and fields. Certain families, perhaps half of his parish in all, were returning because the schools were opening, and they must put their children into them; and it was both to minister to the spiritual needs of these and to get his own children back to their studies that the minister was at home so early.

It was, as I have hinted already, a difficult and laborious season with him; he himself was always a little rusty in his vocation after his summer's outing and felt weakened rather than strengthened by his rest. The domestic machine started reluctantly; there was a new cook to be got in, and Mrs. Sewell had to fight a battle with herself, in which she invited him to share, before she could settle down for the winter to the cares of housekeeping. The wide skies, the dim mountain slopes, the long, delicious drives, the fresh mornings, the sweet, silvery afternoons of their idle country life, haunted their nerves and enfeebled their wills.

One evening in the first days of this moral disability, while Sewell sat at his desk trying to get himself together for a sermon, Barker's name was brought up to him.

318

"Really," said his wife, who had transmitted it from the maid, "I think it's time you protected yourself, David. You can't let this go on forever. He has been in Boston nearly two years now; he has regular employment, where, if there's anything in him at all, he ought to prosper and improve without coming to you every other night. What *can* he want now?"

"I'm sure I don't know," said the minister, leaning back in his chair, and passing his hand wearily over his forehead.

"Then send down and excuse yourself. Tell him you're busy, and ask him to come another time!"

"Ah, you know I can't do that, my dear."

"Very well, then; I will go down and see him. You sha'n't be interrupted."

"Would you, my dear? That would be very kind of you! Do get me off some way; tell him I'm coming to see him very soon." He went stupidly back to his writing without looking to see whether his wife had meant all she said; and after a moment's hesitation she descended in fulfillment of her promise; or, perhaps rather it was a threat.

She met Lemuel not unkindly, for she was a kind-hearted woman; but she placed duty before charity even, and she could not help making him feel that she was there in the discharge of a duty. She explained that Mr. Sewell was very unusually busy that evening, and had sent her in his place, and hoped soon to see him. She bade Lemuel sit down, and he obeyed, answering all the questions as to the summer and his occupations and health, and his mother's health, which she put to him in proof of her interest in him; in further evidence of it, she gave him an account of the Sewell family's doings since they last met. He did not stay long, and she returned slowly and pensively to her husband.

"Well?" he asked, without looking round.

"Well, it's all right," she answered, with rather a deep breath. "He didn't seem to have come for anything in particular; I told him that if he wished specially to speak with you, you would come down."

Sewell went on with his writing, and after a moment his

wife said, "But you must go and see him very soon, David; you must go to-morrow."

"Why?"

"He looks wretchedly, though he says he's very well. It made my heart ache. He looks perfectly wan and haggard. I wish," she burst out, "I wish I had let you go down and see him!"

"Why—why, what was the matter?" asked Sewell, turning about now. "Did you think he had something on his mind?"

"No, but he looked fairly sick. Oh, I wish he had never come into our lives!"

"I'm afraid he hasn't got much good from us," sighed the minister. "But I'll go round and look him up in the morning. His trouble will keep overnight, if it's a real trouble. There's that comfort, at least. And now, do go away, my dear, and leave me to my writing."

Mrs. Sewell looked at him, but turned and left him, apparently reserving whatever sermon she might have in her mind till he should have finished his.

The next morning he went to inquire for Lemuel at Mr. Corey's. The man was sending him away from the door with the fact merely that Lemuel was not then in the house, when the voice of Mr. Corey descending the stairs called from within: "Is that you, Sewell? Don't go away! Come in!"

The old gentleman took him into the library, and confessed in a bit of new slang, which he said was delightful, that he was all balled up by Lemuel's leaving him, and asked Sewell what he supposed it meant.

"Left you? Meant?" echoed Sewell.

When they got at each other it was understood that Lemuel, the day before, had given up his employment with Mr. Corey, expressing a fit sense of all his kindness and a fit regret at leaving him, but alleging no reasons for his course; and that this was the first that Sewell knew of the affair.

"It must have been that which he came to see me about last night," he said with a sort of anticipative remorse. "Mrs. Sewell saw him—I was busy."

"Well! Get him to come back, Sewell," said Mr. Corey, with his whimsical imperiousness; "I can't get on without him. All my moral and intellectual being has stopped like a watch."

Sewell went to the boarding-house where Lemuel took his meals, but found that he no longer came there and had left no other address. He knew nowhere else to ask, and he went home to a day of latent trouble of mind, which whenever it came to the light defined itself as helpless question and self-reproach in regard to Barker.

That evening as he sat at tea, the maid came with the announcement that there was a person in the reception-room who would not send in any name, but wished to see Mr. Sewell, and would wait.

Sewell threw down his napkin, and said, "I'll bring him in to tea."

Mrs. Sewell did not resist; she bade the girl lay another plate.

Sewell was so sure of finding Lemuel in the reception-room, that he recoiled in dismay from the girlish figure that turned timidly from the window to meet him with a face thickly veiled. He was vexed too; here, he knew from the mystery put on, was one of those cases of feminine trouble, real or unreal, which he most disliked to meddle with.

"Will you sit down?" he said as kindly as he could, and the girl obeyed.

"I thought they would let me wait. I didn't mean to interrupt you," she began, in a voice singularly gentle and unaffected.

"Oh, no matter!" cried Sewell. "I'm very glad to see you."

"I thought you could help me. I'm in great trouble—doubt——"

The voice was almost childlike in its appealing innocence.

Sewell sat down opposite the girl and bent sympathetically forward. "Well?"

She waited a moment. Then, "I don't know how to begin," she said hoarsely, and stopped again.

Sewell was touched. He forgot Lemuel; he forgot every-thing but the heartache which he divined before him, and his Christ-derived office, his holy privilege, of helping any in want of comfort or guidance. "Perhaps," he said, in his loveliest way,—the way that had won his wife's heart, and that still provoked her severest criticism for its insincerity, it was so purely impersonal,—"perhaps that isn't necessary, if you mean beginning at the beginning. If you've any trouble that you think I can advise you in, perhaps it's better for both of us that I shouldn't know very much of it."

"Yes?" murmured the girl, questioningly.

"I mean that if you tell me much, you will go away feeling that you have somehow parted with yourself, that you're no longer in your own keeping, but in mine; and you know that in everything our help must really come from within our own free consciences."

"Yes," said the girl again, from behind the veil which com-pletely hid her face. She now hesitated a long time. She put her handkerchief under her veil; and at last she said, "I know what you mean." Her voice quivered pathetically; she tried to control it. "Perhaps," she whispered huskily, after another interval, "I can put it in the form of a question."

"That would be best," said Sewell.

She hesitated; the tears fell down upon her hands behind her veil; she no longer wiped them. "It's because I've often—heard you; because I know you will tell me what's true and right——"

"Your own heart must do that," said the minister, "but I will gladly help you all I can."

She did not heed him now, but continued as if rapt quite away from him.

"If there was some one—something—if there was something that it would be right for you to do—to have, if there was no one else; but if there were some one else that had a right first——" She broke off and asked abruptly, "Don't you think it is always right to prefer another—the interest of another to your own?"

Sewell could not help smiling. "There is only one thing for us to do when we are in any doubt or perplexity," he said cheerily, "and that is the unselfish thing."

"Yes," she gasped; she seemed to be speaking to herself. "I saw it, I knew it! Even if it kills us, we must do it! Nothing ought to weigh against it! Oh, I thank you!"

Sewell was puzzled. He felt dimly that she was thanking him for anguish and despair. "I'm afraid that I don't quite understand you."

"I thought I told you," she answered, with a certain reproach and a fall of courage in view of the fresh effort she must make. It was some moments before she could say "If you knew that some one—some one who was—everything to you—and that you knew—believed—"

At fifty it is hard to be serious about these things, and it was well for the girl that she was no longer conscious of Sewell's mood.

"—Cared for you; and if you knew that before he had cared for you, there had been some else—some else that he was as much to as he was to you, and that couldn't give him up, what—should you——"

Sewell fetched a long sigh of relief; he had been afraid of a much darker problem than this. He almost smiled.

"My dear child,"—she seemed but a child there before the mature man with her poor little love-trouble, so intricate and hopeless to her, so simple and easy to him,—"that depends upon a great many circumstances."

He could feel through her veil the surprise with which she turned to him: "You said, whenever we are in doubt, we must act unselfishly."

"Yes, I said that. But you must first be sure what is really selfish——"

"I *know* what is selfish in this case," said the girl with a sublimity which, if foolish, was still sublimity. "She is sick—it will kill her to lose him— You have said what I expected, and I thank you, thank you, *thank* you! And I will do it! Oh, don't fear now but I shall; I *have* done it! No matter," she went on in her exaltation, "no matter how much we care for each other, now!"

"No," said Sewell, decidedly. "That doesn't follow. I have thought of such things; there was such a case within my experience once,"—he could not help alleging this case, in which he had long triumphed,—"and I have always felt that I did right in advising against a romantic notion of self-sacrifice in such matters. You may commit a greater wrong in that than in an act of apparent self-interest. You have not put the case fully before me, and it isn't necessary that you should, but if you contemplate any rash sacrifice, I warn you against it."

"You said that we ought to act unselfishly."

"Yes, but you must beware of the refined selfishness which shrinks from righteous self-assertion because it is painful. You must make sure of your real motive; you must consider whether your sacrifice is not going to do more harm than good. But why do you come to me with your trouble? Why don't you go to your father—your mother?"

"I have none."

"Ah——"

She had risen and pushed by him to the outer door, though he tried to keep her. "Don't be rash," he urged. "I advise you to take time to think of this——"

She did not answer; she seemed now only to wish to escape, as if in terror of him.

She pulled open the door, and was gone.

Sewell went back to his tea, bewildered, confounded.

"What's the matter? Why didn't he come in to tea with you?" asked his wife.

"Who?"

"Barker."

"What Barker?"

"David, what *is* the matter?"

Sewell started from his daze, and glanced at his children: "I'll tell you by and by, Lucy."

XXXIII

A MONTH passed, and Sewell heard nothing of Lemuel. His charge, always elusive and evanescent, had now completely vanished, and he could find no trace of him. Mr. Corey suggested advertising. Bellingham said, why not put it in the hands of a detective? He said he had never helped work anything up with a detective; he rather thought he should like to do it. Sewell thought of writing to Barker's mother at Willoughby Pastures, but he postponed it; perhaps it would alarm her if Barker were not there. Sewell had many other cares and duties; Lemuel became more and more a good intention of the indefinite future. After all, he had always shown the ability to take care of himself, and except that he had mysteriously disappeared there was no reason for anxiety about him.

One night his name came up at a moment when Sewell was least prepared by interest or expectation to see him. He smiled to himself, in running downstairs, at the reflection that he never seemed quite ready for Barker. But it was a relief to have him turn up again; there was no question of that, and Sewell showed him a face of welcome that dropped at sight of him. He scarcely knew the gaunt, careworn face or the shabby figure before him, in place of the handsome, well-dressed young fellow whom he had come to greet. There seemed a sort of reversion in Barker's whole presence to the time when Sewell first found him in that room; and in whatever trouble he now was, the effect was that of his original rustic constraint.

Trouble there was of some kind, Sewell could see at a glance, and his kind heart prompted him to take Lemuel's hand between both of his. "Why, my dear boy!" he began; but he stopped and made Lemuel sit down, and waited for him to speak, without further question or comment.

"Mr. Sewell," the young man said abruptly, "you told me once you—that you sometimes had money put into your hands that you could lend."

"Yes," replied Sewell, with eager cordiality.

"Could I borrow about seventy-five dollars of you?"

"Why, certainly, Barker!" Sewell had not so much of what he called his flying-charity fund by him, but he instantly resolved to advance the difference out of his own pocket.

"It's to get me an outfit for horse-car conductor," said Lemuel. "I can have the place if I can get the outfit."

"Horse-car conductor!" reverberated Sewell. "What in the world for?"

"It's work I can do," answered Lemuel, briefly, but not resentfully.

"But there are so many other things—better—fitter—more profitable! Why did you leave Mr. Corey? I assure you that you have been a great loss to him—in every way. You don't know how much he valued you, personally. He will be only too glad to have you come back."

"I can't go back," said Lemuel. "I'm going to get married."

"Married!" cried Sewell in consternation.

"My—the lady that I'm going to marry—has been sick ever since the first of October, and I haven't had a chance to look up any kind of work. But she's better now, and I've heard of this place I can get. I don't like to trouble you; but—everything's gone—I've got my mother down here helping take care of her; and I must do something. I don't know just when I can pay you back, but I'll do it sometime."

"Oh, I'm sure of that," said Sewell, from the abyss of hopeless conjecture into which these facts had plunged him; his wandering fancy was dominated by the presence of Lemuel's mother with her bloomers in Boston. "I—I hope there's nothing serious the trouble with your—the lady?" he said, rubbing

away with his hand the smile that came to his lips in spite
of him.

"It's lung trouble," said Lemuel, quietly.

"Oh!" responded Sewell. "Well! Well!" He shook himself
together, and wondered what had become of the impulse he
had felt to scold Barker for the idea of getting married. But
such a course now seemed not only far beyond his province,—
he heard himself saying that to Mrs. Sewell in self-defense
when she should censure him for not doing it,—but utterly
useless in view of the further complications. "Well! This is
great news you tell me—a great surprise. You're—you're going
to take an important step—— You—you—— Of course, of
course! You must have a great many demands upon you, under
the circumstances. Yes, yes! And I'm very glad you came to
me. If your mind is quite made up about——"

"Yes, I've thought it over," said Lemuel. "The lady has had
to work all her life, and she—she isn't used to what I thought—
what I intended—any other kind of people; and it's better for
us both that I should get some kind of work that won't take
me away from her too much——" He dropped his head, and
Sewell with a flash of intelligence felt a thrill of compassionate
admiration for the poor, foolish, generous creature, for so
Lemuel complexly appeared to him.

Again he forbore question or comment.

"Well—well! we must look you up, Mrs. Sewell and I. We
must come to see your—the lady." He found himself falling
helplessly into Lemuel's way of describing her. "Just write
me your address here,"—he put a scrap of paper before Lemuel
on the davenport,—"and I'll go and get you the money."

He brought it back in an envelope which held a very little
more than Lemuel had asked for—Sewell had not dared to
add much—and Lemuel put it in his pocket.

He tried to say something; he could only make a husky
noise in his throat.

"Good-night!" said Sewell, pressing his hand with both of
his again, at the door. "We shall come very soon."

"MARRIED!" said Mrs. Sewell, when he returned to her;

and then she suffered a silence to ensue, in which it seemed to Sewell that his inculpation was visibly accumulating mountains vast and high. "*What did you say?*"

"Nothing," he answered, almost gayly; the case was so far beyond despair. "What should *you* have said?"

XXXIV

Lemuel got a conductor's overcoat and cap at half-price from a man who had been discharged, and put by the money saved to return to Sewell when he should come. He entered upon his duties the next morning, under the instruction of an old conductor, who said "Hain't I seen you som'eres before?" and he worked all day, taking money and tickets, registering fares, helping ladies on and off the car, and monotonously journeying back and forth over his route. He went on duty at six o'clock in the morning, after an early breakfast that 'Manda Grier and his mother got him, for Statira was not strong enough yet to do much, and he was to be relieved at eight. At nightfall, after two half-hour respites for dinner and tea, he was so tired that he could scarcely stand.

"Well, how do you like it, as fur's you've gone?" asked the instructing conductor, in whom Lemuel had recognized an old acquaintance. "Sweet life, ain't it? There! That switch hain't worked again! Jump off, young man, and put your shoulder to the wheel!"

The car had failed to take the right-hand turn where the line divided; it had to be pushed back, and while the driver tugged and swore under his breath at his horses, Lemuel set himself to push the car.

" 'S no use!" said the driver finally. "I got to hitch 'em on at the other end, and pull her back."

He uncoupled the team from the front of the car, and swung round with it. Lemuel felt something strike him on

329

the leg, and he fell down. He scrambled to his feet again, but his left leg doubled under him; it went through his mind that one of the horses must have lashed out and broken it; then everything seemed to stop.

The world began again for him in the apothecary's shop where he had been carried, and from which he was put into an ambulance, by a policeman. It stopped again, as he whirled away; it renewed itself in anguish, and ceased in bliss as he fainted from the pain or came to.

They lifted him up some steps, at last, and carried him into a high, bright room, where there were two or three cots, and a long glass case full of surgical instruments. They laid him on a cot, and some one swiftly and skillfully undressed him. A surgeon had come in, and now he examined Lemuel's leg. He looked once or twice at his face.

"This is a pretty bad job. I can't tell how bad till you've had the ether. Will you leave it to me?"

"Yes. But do the best you can for me."

"You may be sure I will."

Lemuel believed that they meant to cut off his leg. He knew that he had a right to refuse and to take the consequences, but he would not; he had no right to choose death, when he had others to live for.

He woke deathly sick at first, and found himself lying in bed, one of the two rows in a long room, where there were some quiet women in neat caps and seersucker dresses going about, with bowls of food and bottles of medicine.

Lemuel still felt his leg, and the pain in it, but he had heard how mutilated men felt their lost limbs all their lives, and he was afraid to make sure by the touch of his hand.

A nurse who saw his eyes open came to him. He turned them upon her, but he could not speak. She must have understood. "The doctor thinks he can save your leg for you; but it's a bad fracture. You must be careful to keep very still."

He fell asleep; and life began again for him, in the midst of suffering and death. He saw every day broken and mangled men, drunk with ether, brought up as he had been, and laid in beds; he saw the priest of the religion to which most of the poor and lowly still belong, go and come among the cots, and stand by the pillows where the sick feebly followed him in the mystical gestures which he made on his brow and breast; he learned to know the use of the white linen screen which was drawn about a bed to hide the passing of a soul; he became familiar with the helpless sympathy, the despair of the friends who came to visit the sick and dying.

He had not lacked for more attention and interest from his own than the rules of the hospital allowed. His mother and 'Manda Grier came first, and then Statira when they would let her. She thought it hard that she was not suffered to do the least thing for him; she wished to take him away to their own rooms, where she could nurse him twice as well. At first she cried whenever she saw him, and lamented over him, so that the head nurse was obliged to explain to her that she disturbed the patients, and could not come any more unless she controlled herself. She promised, and kept her word; she sat quietly by his pillow and held his hand, when she came, except when she put up her own to hide the cough which she could not always restrain. The nurse told her that of course she was not accountable for the cough, but she had better try to check it. Statira brought troches with her, and held them in her mouth for this purpose.

Lemuel's family was taken care of in this time of disaster. The newspapers had made his accident promptly known, and not only Sewell, but Miss Vane and Mrs. Corey had come to see if they could be of any use.

One day a young girl brought a bouquet of flowers and set it by Lemuel's bed, when he seemed asleep. He suddenly opened his eyes, and saw Sybil Vane for the first time since their quarrel.

She put her finger to her lip, and smiled with the air of a lady benefactress; then, with a few words of official sympathy, she encouraged him to get well, and flitted to the next bed, where she bestowed a jacqueminot rosebud on a Chinaman dying of cancer.

Sewell came often to see him, at first in the teeth of his mother's obvious hostility, but with her greater and greater relenting. Nothing seemed gloomier than the outlook for Lemuel, but Sewell had lived too long not to know that the gloom of an outlook has nothing to do with a man's real future. It was impossible, of course, for Lemuel to go back to Mr. Corey's now with a sick wife, who would need so much of his care. Besides, he did not think it desirable on other accounts. He recurred to what Lemuel had said about getting work that should not take him too far away from the kind of people his betrothed was used to, and he felt a pity and respect for the boy whom life had already taught this wisdom, this resignation. He could see that before his last calamity had come upon him, Barker was trying to adjust his ambition to his next duty, or rather to subordinate it; and the conviction that he was right gave Sewell courage to think that he would yet somehow succeed. It also gave him courage to resist, on Barker's behalf, the generous importunities of some who would have befriended him. Mr. Corey and Charles Bellingham drove up to the hospital one day to see Lemuel; and when Sewell met them the same evening, they were full of enthusiasm. Corey said that the effect of the hospital, with its wards branching from the classistic building in the center, was delightfully Italian; it was like St. Peter's on a small scale, and he had no idea how interesting the South End was; it was quite a bit of foreign travel to go up there. Bellingham had explored the hospital throughout; he said he had found it the thing to do—it was a thing for everybody to do; he was astonished that he had never done it before. They united in praising Barker, and they asked what could be done for him. Corey was strenuous for his coming back to him; at any rate, they must find something for him. Bellingham favored the notion of doing something for his education; a fellow like that could come to almost anything.

Sewell shook his head. "All that's impossible now. With that girl——"

"Oh, confound her!" cried Bellingham.

"I was rather disappointed at not seeing his mother," said Corey. "I had counted a good deal, I find, upon Mrs. Barker's bloomers."

"With a girl like that for his wife," pursued Sewell, "the conditions are all changed. He must cleave to her in mind as well as body, and he must seek the kind of life that will unite them more and more, not less and less. In fact, he was instinctively doing so when this accident happened. That's what marriage means."

"Oh, not always," suggested Corey.

"He must go back to Willoughby Pastures," Sewell concluded, "to his farm."

"Oh, come now!" said Bellingham, with disgust.

"If that sort of thing is to go on," said Corey, "what is to become of the ancestry of the future *élite* of Boston? I counted upon Barker to found one of our first families. Besides, any Irishman could take his farm and do better with it. The farm would be meat to the Irishman, and poison to Barker, now that he's once tasted town."

"Yes, I know all that," said Sewell, sadly. "I once thought the greatest possible good I could do Barker, after getting him to Boston, was to get him back to Willoughby Pastures; but if that was ever true, the time is past. Now, it merely seems the only thing possible. When he gets well, he will still have an invalid wife on his hands; he must provide her a home; she could have helped him once, and would have done so, I've no doubt; but now she must be taken care of."

"Look here!" said Bellingham. "What's the reason these things can't be managed as they are in the novels? In any well-regulated romance that cough of hers would run into quick consumption and carry Barker's fiancée off in six weeks; and then he could resume his career of usefulness and prosperity here, don't you know. He could marry some one else and found that family that Corey wants."

They all laughed, Sewell ruefully.

"As it is," said Corey, "I suppose she'll go on having hemorrhages to a good old age, and outlive him, after being a clog and burden to him all his life. Poor devil! What in the world possesses him to want to marry her? But I suppose the usual thing."

This gave Sewell greater discomfort than the question of Lemuel's material future. He said listlessly, "Oh, I suppose so," but he was far from thinking precisely that. He had seen Lemuel and the young girl together a great deal, and a painful misgiving had grown up in his mind. It seemed to him that while he had seen no want of patience and kindness towards her in Lemuel, he had not seen the return of her fondness, which, silly as it was in some of its manifestations, he thought he should be glad of in him. Yet he was not sure. Barker was always so self-contained that he might very well feel more love for her than he showed; and, after all, Sewell rather weakly asked himself, was the love so absolutely necessary?

When he repeated this question in his wife's presence, she told him she was astonished at him.

"You know that it is *vitally* necessary! It's all the more necessary, if he's so superior to her, as you say. I can't think what's become of your principles, my dear!"

"I do: you've got them," said Sewell.

"I really believe I have," said his wife, with that full conviction of righteousness which her sex alone can feel. "I have always heard you say that marriage without love was not only sinful in itself, but the beginning of sorrow. Why do you think now that it makes no difference?"

"I suppose I was trying to adapt myself to circumstances," answered Sewell, frankly at least. "Let's hope that my facts are as wrong as my conclusions. I'm not sure of either. I suppose if I saw him idolizing so slight and light a person as she seems to be, I should be more disheartened about his future than I am now. If he overvalued her, it would only drag him lower down."

"Oh, his future! Drag him down! Why don't you think of *her*, going up there to that dismal wilderness, to spend her days in toil and poverty, with a half-crazy mother-in-law, and a rheumatic brother-in-law, in such a looking hovel?" Mrs. Sewell did not group these disadvantages conventionally, but they were effective. "You have allowed your feelings about that baffling creature to blind you to everything else, David. Why should you care so much for his future, and nothing for hers? Is that so very bright?"

"I don't think that either is dazzling," sighed the minister. Yet Barker's grew a little lighter as he familiarized himself with it, or rather with Barker. He found that he had a plan for getting a teacher's place in the academy, if they reopened it, at Willoughby Pastures, as they talked of doing, under the impulse of such a course in one of the neighboring towns, and that he was going home, in fancy at least, with purposes of enlightenment and elevation which would go far to console him under such measure of disappointment as they must bring. Sewell hinted to Barker that he must not be too confident of remodeling Willoughby Pastures upon the pattern of Boston.

"Oh, no; I don't expect that," said Lemuel. "What I mean is that I shall always try to remember myself what I've learnt here—from the kind of men I've seen, and the things that I know people are all the time doing for others. I told you once that they haven't got any idea of that in the country. I don't expect to preach it into them; they wouldn't like it if I did; and they'd make fun of it; but if I could try to *live* it?"

"Yes," said Sewell, touched by this young enthusiasm.

"I don't know as I can all the time," said Lemuel. "But it seems to me that that's what I've learnt here, if I've learnt anything. I think the world's a good deal better than I used to."

"Do you, indeed, my dear boy?" asked Sewell, greatly interested. "It's a pretty well meaning world—I hope it is."

"Yes, that's what I mean," said Lemuel. "I presume it ain't

perfect—isn't, I should say," and Sewell smiled. "Mr. Corey was always correcting me on that. But if I were to do nothing but pass along the good that's been done me since I came here, I should be kept busy the rest of my life."

Sewell knew that this emotion was largely the physical optimism of convalescence; but he could not refuse the comfort it gave him to find Barker in such a mood, and he did not conceive it his duty to discourage it. Lofty ideals, if not indulged at the expense of lowly realities, he had never found hurtful to any; and it was certainly better for Barker to think too well than too ill of Boston, if it furnished him incentives to unselfish living. He could think of enough things in the city to warrant a different judgment, but if Barker's lesson from his experience there was this, Sewell was not the person to weaken its force with him. He said, with a smile of reserved comment, "Well, perhaps you'll be coming back to us, some day."

"I don't look forward to that," said Lemuel soberly; and then his face took a sterner cast, as if from the force of his resolution. "The first thing I've got to do after I've made a home for her is to get Statira away from the town where she can have some better air, and see if she can't get her health back. It'll be time enough to talk of Boston again when she's fit to live here."

The minister's sympathetic spirit sank again. But his final parting with Barker was not unhopeful. Lemuel consented to accept from him a small loan, to the compass of which he reduced the eager bounty of Miss Vane and Mr. Corey, representing that more would be a burden and an offense to Barker. Statira and his mother came with him to take leave of the Sewells.

They dismounted from the horse-car at the minister's door; and he saw, with sensibility, the two women helping Lemuel off; he walked with a cane, and they went carefully on either side of him. Sewell hastened to meet them at the door himself, and he was so much interested in the spectacle of this mutual affection that he failed at first to observe that Mrs. Barker wore the skirts of occidental civilization instead of the bloomers which he had identified her with.

"She *says* she's goin' to put 'em on again as soon as she gets back to Willoughby," the younger woman explained to Mrs. Sewell in an aside, while the minister was engaged with Lemuel and his mother. "But I tell her as long as it ain't the fashion in Boston, I guess she hadn't better *he*-e-e-re." Statira had got on her genteel prolongation of her last syllables again. "I guess I shall get along with her. She's kind of queer when you first get acquainted, but she's *real* good-*heart*-e-e-d." She was herself very prettily dressed, and though she looked thin, and at times gave a deep, dismal cough, she was so bright and gay that it was impossible not to feel hopeful about her. She became very confidential with Mrs. Sewell, whom she apparently brevetted Lemuel's best friend, and obliged to a greater show of interest in him than she had ever felt. She told her the whole history of her love affair, and of how much 'Manda Grier had done to help it on at first, and then how she had wanted her to break off with Lemuel. "But," she concluded, "*I* think we're goin' to get along real nice together. I don't know as we shall live all in the same *hou*-ou-se; I guess it'll be the best thing for Lem and I if we can board till we get some little of our health back; I'm more scared for him than what I am for my-*se*-e-lf. I don't presume but what we shall both miss the city some; but he might be out of a job all winter in town; I shouldn't want he should go back on them *ca*-a-rs. Most I hate is leavin' 'Manda Grier; she is the one that I've roomed with ever since I first came to Boston; but Lem and her don't get on very well; they hain't really either of 'em *got* anything against each other, now, but they don't *like* very *we*-e-ll; and, of course, I got to have the friends that he wants me to have, and that's what 'Manda Grier says *to*-o-o; and so it's just as well we're goin' to be where they won't *cla*-a-sh."

She talked to Mrs. Sewell in a low voice; but she kept her

eyes upon Lemuel all the time; and when Sewell took him and his mother the length of the front drawing-room away, she was quite distraught, and answered at random till he came back.

Sewell did not know what to think. Would this dependence warm her betrothed to greater tenderness than he now showed, or would its excess disgust him? He was not afraid that Lemuel would ever be unkind to her; but he knew that in marriage kindness was not enough. He looked at Lemuel, serious, thoughtful, refined in his beauty by suffering; and then his eye wandered to Statira's delicate prettiness, so sweet, so full of amiable cheerfulness, so undeniably light and silly. What chiefly comforted him was the fact of an ally whom the young thing had apparently found in Lemuel's mother. Whether that grim personage's ignorant pride in her son had been satisfied with a girl of Statira's style and fashion, and proved capableness in housekeeping, or whether some fancy for butterfly prettiness lurking in the fastnesses of the old woman's rugged nature had been snared by the gay face and dancing eyes, it was apparent that she at least was in love with Statira. She allowed herself to be poked about, and re-arranged as to her shawl and the narrow-brimmed youthful hat which she wore on the peak of her skull, and she softened to something like a smile at the touch of Statira's quick hands.

They had all come rather early to make their parting visit at the Sewells', for the Barkers were going to take the two o'clock train for Willoughby Pastures, while Statira was to remain in Boston till he could make a home for her. Lemuel promised to write as soon as he should be settled, and tell Sewell about his life and his work; and Sewell, beyond earshot of his wife, told him he might certainly count upon seeing them at Willoughby in the course of the next summer. They all shook hands several times. Lemuel's mother gave her hand from under the fringe of her shawl, standing bolt upright at arm's length off, and Sewell said it felt like a collection of corn-cobs.

XXXV

"WELL?" said Sewell's wife, when they were gone.

"Well," he responded; and after a moment he said, "There's this comfort about it, which we don't always have in such cases: there doesn't seem to be anybody else. It would be indefinitely worse if there were."

"Why, of course. What in the world are you thinking about?"

"About that foolish girl who came to me with her miserable love-trouble. I declare, I can't get rid of it. I feel morally certain that she went away from me and dismissed the poor fellow who was looking to her love to save him."

"At the cost of some other poor creature who'd trusted and believed in him till his silly fancy changed? I hope for the credit of women that she did. But you may be morally certain she did nothing of the kind. Girls don't give up all their hopes in life so easily as that. She might think she would do it, because she had read of such things, and thought it was fine, but when it came to the pinch, she wouldn't."

"I hope not. If she did she would commit a great error, a criminal error."

"Well, you needn't be afraid. Look at Mrs. Tom Corey. And that was her own sister!"

"That was different. Corey had never thought of her sister, much less made love to her, or promised to marry her. Besides, Mrs. Corey had her father and mother to advise her, and support her in behaving sensibly. And this poor creature had nothing but her own novel-fed fancies, and her crazy conscience. She thought that because she inflicted suffering upon herself she was acting unselfishly. Really, the fakirs of India and the Penitentes of New Mexico are more harmless, for they don't hurt any one else. If she has forced some poor fellow into a marriage like this of Barker's, she's committed a deadly sin. She'd better driven him to suicide, than condemned him to live a lie to the end of his days. No doubt she regarded it as a momentary act of expiation. That's the way her romances taught her to look at loveless marriage—as something spectacular, transitory, instead of the enduring, degrading squalor that it is!"

"What in the world are you talking about, David? I should think *you* were a novelist yourself, by the wild way you go on! You have no proof whatever that Barker isn't happily engaged. I'm sure he's got a much better girl than he deserves, and one that's fully his equal. She's only too fond of that dry stick. Such a girl as the one you described,—like that mysterious visitor of yours,—what possible relation could she have with him? She was a lady!"

"Yes, yes! Of course it's absurd. But everybody seems to be tangled up with everybody else. My dear, will you give me a cup of tea? I think I'll go to writing at once."

Before she left her husband to order his tea Mrs. Sewell asked, "And do you think you have got through with him now?"

"I have just begun with him," replied Sewell.

His mind, naturally enough in connection with Lemuel, was running upon his friend Evans, and the subject they had once talked of in that room. It was primarily in thinking of him that he began to write his sermon on Complicity, which made a great impression at the time, and had a more lasting effect as enlarged from the newspaper reports, and reprinted in pamphlet form. His evolution from the text, "Remember them that are in bonds as bound with them," of a complete philosophy of life, was humorously treated by some of his critics as a phase of Darwinism, but upon the whole the sermon met with great favor. It not only strengthened Sewell's hold upon the affections of his own congregation, but carried his name beyond Boston, and made him the topic of editorials in the Sunday editions of leading newspapers as far off as Chicago. It struck one of those popular moods of intelligent sympathy when the failure of a large class of underpaid and worthy workers to assert their right to a living wage against a powerful monopoly had sent a thrill of respectful pity through every generous heart in the country; and it was largely supposed that Sewell's sermon referred indirectly to the telegraphers' strike. Those who were aware of his habit of seeking to produce a personal rather than a general effect, of his belief that you can have a righteous public only by the slow process of having righteous men and women, knew that he meant something much nearer home to each of his hearers, when he preached the old Christ-humanity to them, and enforced again the lesson that no one for good or for evil, for sorrow or joy, for sickness or health, stood apart from his fellows, but each was bound to the highest and the lowest by ties that centered in the hand of God. No man, he said, sinned or suffered to himself alone; his error and his pain darkened and afflicted men who never heard of his name. If a community was corrupt, if an age was immoral, it was not because of the vicious, but the virtuous who fancied themselves indifferent spectators. It was not the tyrant who oppressed, it was the wickedness that had made him possible. The gospel —Christ—God, so far as men had imagined him,—was but a lesson, a type, a witness from everlasting to everlasting of the spiritual unity of man. As we grew in grace, in humanity, in civilization, our recognition of this truth would be transfigured from a duty to a privilege, a joy, a heavenly rapture. Many men might go through life harmlessly without realizing this, perhaps, but sterilely; only those who had had the care of others laid upon them, lived usefully, fruitfully. Let no one shrink from such a burden, or seek to rid himself of it. Rather let him bind it fast upon his neck, and rejoice in it. The wretched, the foolish, the ignorant whom we found at every turn, were something more; they were the messengers of God, sent to tell his secret to any that would hear it. Happy he in whose ears their cry for help was a perpetual voice, for that man, whatever his creed, knew God, and could never forget him. In his responsibility for his weaker brethren he was God-like, for God was but the impersonation of loving responsibility, of infinite and never-ceasing care for us all.

When Sewell came down from his pulpit, many people came up to speak to him of his sermon. Some of the women's faces showed the traces of tears, and each person had made its application to himself. There were two or three who had heard between the words. Old Bromfield Corey, who was coming a good deal more to church since his eyes began to fail him, because it was a change and a sort of relief from being read to, said:

"I didn't know that they had translated it Barker in the revised version. Well, you must let me know how he's getting on, Sewell, and give me a chance at the revelation too, if he ever gets troublesome to you again."

Miss Vane was standing at the door with his wife when Sewell came out. She took his hand and pressed it.

"Do you think I threw away my chance?" she demanded. She had her veil down, and at first Sewell thought it was laughter that shook her voice, but it was not that.

He did not know quite what to say, but he did say, "He was sent to *me*."

As they walked off alone, his wife said:

"Well, David, I hope you haven't preached away all your truth and righteousness."

"I know what you mean, my dear," answered Sewell humbly. He added, "You shall remind me, if I seem likely to forget." But he concluded seriously, "If I thought I could never do anything more for Barker, I should be very unhappy; I should take it as a sign that I had been recreant to my charge."

XXXVI

THE MINISTER heard directly from Barker two or three times
during the winter, and as often through Statira, who came to
see Mrs. Sewell. Barker had not got the place he had hoped
for at once, but he had got a school in the country a little way
off, and he was doing something; and he expected to do better.

The winter proved a very severe one. "I guess it's just as
well I staid in town," said Statira, the last time she came, with
a resignation which Mrs. Sewell, fond of the ideal in others,
as most ladies are, did not like. " 'Manda Grier says 'twould
killed me up there; and I d' know but what it would. I done
so well here, since the cold weather set in, that 'Manda Grier
she thinks I hadn't better get married right away; well, not
till it comes summer, anyway. I tell her I guess she don't want
I should get married at all, after all she done to help it along
first off. Her and Mr. Barker don't seem to get along very
well."

Now that Statira felt a little better acquainted with Mrs.
Sewell, she dropped the genteel elongation of her final syllables, and used such vernacular forms of speech as came first
to her. The name of 'Manda Grier seemed to come in at
every fourth word with her, and she tired Mrs. Sewell with
visits which she appeared unable to bring to a close of herself.

A long relief from them ended in an alarm for her health
with Mrs. Sewell, who went to find her. She found her still
better than before, and Statira frankly accounted for her absence by saying that 'Manda thought she had better not come

any more till Mrs. Sewell returned some of her calls. She laughed, and then she said:

"I don't know as you'd found me here if you'd come much later. 'Manda Grier don't want I should be here in the east winds, now it's comin' spring so soon; and she's heard of a chance at a box factory in Philadelphia. She wants I should go there with her, and I don't know but what it *would* be about the best thing."

Mrs. Sewell could not deny the good sense of the plan, though she was sensible of liking Statira less and less for it.

The girl continued: "Lem—Mr. Barker, I *should* say— wants I should come up *there*, out the east winds. But 'Manda Grier she's opposed to it; she thinks I'd ought to have more of a mild climate, and he better come down *there* and get a school, if he wants me *to*-o." Statira broke into an impartial little titter. "I'm sure I don't know which of 'em 'll win the day!"

Mrs. Sewell's report of this speech brought a radiant smile of relief to Sewell's face. "Ah, well, then! That settles it! I feel perfectly sure that 'Manda Grier will win the day. That poor, sick, flimsy little Statira is completely under 'Manda Grier's thumb, and will do just what she says, now that there's no direct appeal from her will to Barker's; they will never be married. Don't you see that it was 'Manda Grier's romance in the beginning, and that when she came to distrust, to dislike Barker, she came to dislike her romance too—to hate it?"

"Well, don't *you* romance him, David," said Mrs. Sewell, only conditionally accepting his theory.

Yet it may be offered to the reader as founded in probability and human nature. In fact, he may be assured here that the marriage which eventually took place was not that of Lemuel and Statira; though how the union, which was not only happiness for those it joined, but whatever is worthier and better in life than happiness, came about, it is aside from the purpose of this story to tell, and must be left for some future inquiry.

THE END

Notes to the Text

4.6–7   to make the worse appear the better reason: Milton, *Paradise Lost*, Book II, ll. 13–14.

16.34–17.1   "We must . . . thistles.": Sewell's attempt at an Emersonian figure has not been located in Emerson's writings.

18.7ff.   "Did you ever hear what Agassiz said . . . .": when Louis Agassiz (1807–1873) gave the Lowell Lectures at Harvard in 1846, he was paid the highest lecturing fee then known. In refusing an earlier invitation to come to America, he is reported to have said, "I cannot afford to waste my time making money."

18.16   the singer Nilsson: Christine Nilsson (1843–1921), the Swedish diva, appeared in Boston three times between 1871 and 1874.

18.20   Sforza, throwing his hoe into the oak: according to legend Muzio Attendolo (1369–1424), a peasant who took the name Sforza, threw an ax. He was the father of Francesco Sforza (1401–1466), who became Duke of Milan.

23.23–24   the flower charity: the Fruit and Flower Mission was one of the Associated Charities of Boston.

32.26ff.   more images in the garden: Lemuel sees in turn the equestrian statue by Thomas Ball, the Edward Everett statue by William Wetmore Story, and the Ether Monument. See Bartley Hubbard's quite different reaction to the semi-draped Venus in the fountain, in *A Modern Instance*, chapter XVII.

34.15   Bloomer dress: an overskirt reaching somewhat below the knees and a pair of moderately full trousers gathered in at the ankle; named after Mrs. Amelia Bloomer, the crusading feminist, and affected by some women's rights advocates during the 1850's.

36.7   'One more unfortunate!': Thomas Hood, "The Bridge of Sighs," l. 1.

46.31   Jimmy Baker's: the description of the place (46.21–28) was developed from a notebook jotting Howells made after a visit to a popular Boston saloon with his brother-in-law, Edwin Mead, in 1883: "Great crowd before Sullivan's bar-room. Went in: carved mahogany train[?], marble everywhere, large, lewd painting with two fellows battening on it. Large counter with 3 keepers, serving beer to blackguardly crowd" (Notebook: Venice and Boston, 1883; MS at Harvard).

48.31   'A Young Man's Darling': a generic title devised by Howells as a comment on current popular fiction.

58.16–17   the Island: Deer Island, at the foot of Fleet Street, used since 1858 for the confinement of convicts; at the time of *The Minister's Charge*, it was officially called the House of Industry.

74.10ff.   Wayfarer's Hotel: during the time Howells was writing *The Minister's Charge*, the Boston *Evening Transcript* was carrying the following advertisement for the Wayfarers Lodge on Hawkins Street: "The Householders of Boston and Vicinity, who are desirous of helping the worthy poor to help themselves, are respectfully requested to BUY OUR WOOD, as every foot sawed (and sold) gives some poor man a meal and a night's lodging, or his family 20 cents worth of groceries."

74.30   Chardon Street Home: a charitable facility for
         women; see the Introduction to this volume, page
         xxiv.

82.28   'Beautiful Venice, Bride of the Sea': title of a popu-
         lar song (1844); words by J. E. Carpenter, music by
         Joseph P. Knight.

107.33   She says that he looks like Tito Melema.: an exam-
         ple of the expectations aroused in Sibyl by her novel
         reading. That darkly handsome Tito Melema of
         Romola had the "finished fascination . . . of a fleet,
         soft-coated, dark-eyed animal that delights you by
         not bounding away in indifference from you, and
         unexpectedly pillows its chin in your palm, and
         looks up at you desiring to be stroked as if it loved
         you" (Book I, chapter VI).

113.16   1334: for prudential reasons Howells occasionally
         changed a location or a place name while still main-
         taining literal accuracy. "In 'Pleasant Avenue,'
         where 'Stira Dudley and 'Manda Grier had their
         lodgings, it is easy to recognize Harrison Avenue
         [in Boston]; but as the numbers there do not go to
         1334, there is no danger that any one can be an-
         noyed by having his house fixed upon as the place"
         (Sylvester Baxter, "Howells's Boston," *New Eng-
         land Magazine*, IX [October 1893], 151).

118.5   Breton skirt: traditional garment of women of
         Britanny; a full-length, dark-colored skirt of a heavy
         wool, usually worn with a white bib apron.

121.32ff. *Set me as a seal on thine heart* . . .: 'Manda is read-
         ing from Canticles, VIII.

130.13ff. "This book . . . .": for Howells' views on the kind of
         fiction Sibyl is reading, see *Criticism and Fiction*,
         Section XVIII.

137.2ff.   little chat: Lemuel's conversation is a transcription, with minor modifications, of a conversation between Howells and a horse-car conductor recorded in his "Savings Bank" Notebook (MS at Harvard).

146.20–21   the Museum: the Boston Museum on Tremont near Court Street maintained a famous stock company.

146.25   Jefferson's going to do *Bob Acres*: Joseph Jefferson (1829–1909) for many years played alternately the roles of Bob Acres, in his own version of Sheridan's *The Rivals*, and Rip Van Winkle.

168.1   the Boston Theater: Boston's largest, with an entrance on Washington Street and another on Mason.

173.3–4   Willoughby Pastures: the name of Lemuel's town is derived from Lake Willoughby and transposed from the northern to the middle part of the state.

179.3   *de haut en bas*: *French*—from top to bottom.

182.25   that 'sleek odalisque' style of dress: the Bloomer costume was supposedly oriental in design, and the pantaloons were sometimes referred to as "Turkish trousers."

182.31   *yashmak*: a double veil concealing the part of the face below the eyes.

194.23   Old Orchard: a beach resort area in Maine, about ten miles south of Portland.

199.25–26   Williams & Everett's: a fine-art gallery on Washington Street.

199.29   Prang: L. Prang & Company, chromo-lithographers, did a worldwide business in Christmas, Easter, and anniversary cards.

207.26–27   the Development Theory: a theory gaining popularity at the time of *The Minister's Charge* which stressed the continuity of human development and the understanding of human action by the identification of past experiences and situations.

208.5   Fast Day: the law requiring the governor of Massachusetts to proclaim an annual day of fasting and prayer was repealed in 1895; it usually came on the fourth Monday in April.

209.2   picked-fish: fish that has been totally cleaned of all refuse parts.

209.9   an Indian Spirit treatment: a spiritualist belief, supposedly derived from the Indians, that doctors from the spirit world—those who have "passed over" —work through a dedicated medium on earth to aid in the curing of diseases.

209.11   the Mind Cure: a theory in Christian Science and other systems that disease can be cured mainly by mental influence.

216.22–24   Now o'er the one half world . . .: *Macbeth*, II, i, 49.

221.7   'Nymph, in thy orisons be all my sins remembered!': *Hamlet*, III, i, 89.

221.28–29   'The falling out of faithful friends renewing is of love!': Richard Edwards (1523?–1566), "The Paradise of Dainty Devices."

236.25   a little Billy Ducks: *slang—billet doux.*

238.37   the Dead March: from Handel's oratorio "Saul" (1739); part of the traditional pomp and ceremony of a British military funeral.

240.17 Honey in the comb, sugar in the gourd: *slang*—easily obtainable money.

247.5 a Seaside Library novel: the most popular of the several cheap reprint series of standard British writers or American authors whose copyrighted books could not compete with the pirated foreign reprints.

273.2 bant: a treatment for corpulence involving the avoidance of fat, starch, and sugar; the word is a humorous derivation from Banting, an English cabinet-maker who devised the treatment and published a much-discussed book about it in 1864.

274.3 Kanawha Paint Co.: the West Virginia paint company whose competition finally ran Silas Lapham out of business and for which Tom Corey went to work.

277.20 "Étude": perhaps a study of the famous Egyptian nude produced by John Singer Sargent during his Spanish and Moroccan period.

282.7 *Novanta . . . dentro*: *Italian*—ninety out of a hundred, he who is beautiful on the outside is good on the inside.

302.14ff. that prisoner he had read of . . .: an allusion to Poe's "The Pit and the Pendulum."

340.3–4 the fakirs of India and the Penitentes of New Mexico: religious sects which believe in the spiritual discipline of self-flagellation.

340.34–35 "Remember them . . .": Sewell's text comes from Hebrews, XII, 3.

341.10–11 the telegraphers' strike: the national telegraphers' strike of 1883; the public was generally sympathetic, but the strikers gave up after a month.

TEXTUAL APPARATUS

Textual Commentary

Four forms of *The Minister's Charge; Or, The Apprenticeship of Lemuel Barker* are of potential relevance to the establishment of the text of the present edition. The first is the series of eleven installments printed in *The Century Illustrated Monthly Magazine* from February through December 1886 (volumes XXXI–XXXIII). The second is the set of eight parts, constituting like the magazine installments a full text of the novel, registered at Stationers' Hall in London and deposited in appropriate British libraries; these parts, prepared by David Douglas of Edinburgh and registered for the purpose of securing British copyright on the material, bear dates in the British Museum set from 25 January through 22 November 1886.[1] The third form is the first book edition, also prepared by Douglas and issued in a single printing of 1,000 copies which was completed on 28 October 1886 and first advertised as published in the *Athenæum* on 6 November (BAL 9626).[2] The last significant form to be produced during Howells' lifetime was the series of book impressions released under the imprint of Ticknor and Company, Boston, and later by that firm's successor as Howells' Boston publisher, Houghton Mifflin; these impressions were all printed from the same plates as the Douglas single-impression edition. The first impression of 5,668 copies was completed on 18 November 1886 but released with the title-page date 1887 (BAL 9627).[3] No manuscript or other form of the

---

1. A record of the exact dates of deposit for each part and the portions of text represented therein is provided below, p. 357.

2. The information on the date of printing is derived from the records of T. & A. Constable, Limited, London, Douglas' printer, volume XVI, 274. These records are cited with the permission of P. J. W. Kilpatrick.

3. There were at least thirteen more impressions between 1888 and 1919, in both Ticknor and Houghton Mifflin hardbound and paperbound formats. The information about these impressions is derived from the business records of the publishing firm of Ticknor and Fields and that firm's successors, who included Ticknor and Company and Houghton Mifflin. The records are now

text, including galleys or proofs of any of the printed versions, is known to exist.

The general relationships among the extant texts are very simple, and consistent both with the usual process of transmission of Howells' serialized novels and with the patterns of his attention to revision and correction during that process. The *Century* serial installments represent the first typesetting from manuscript. As the individual installments were being prepared, some form of them—as galleys, proofs, or printed sheets—was forwarded to David Douglas. Early in the 1880's Howells and Douglas had devised a method of British copyright registration of Howells' works which satisfied them as fulfilling the basic requirements of the law: by officially registering and effecting the sale of text set and printed in Great Britain before publication took place in the United States, author and publisher could secure protection on that material. Thus Howells generally attempted to get copy to Douglas quickly enough to have type set, proofs pulled, and bound sets of proofs submitted as printed copies and as deposit parts before the release of the American magazine in Great Britain. Then that same Douglas typesetting formed the basis for stereotype plates of the full text. From these Douglas ran off a limited impression under his own imprint, with the sale of the copies enabling him to bear the cost of typesetting and plating of the same text in a different form for release in his customary "shilling editions." (There was, however, no such edition—in smaller format and paper binding—for *The Minister's Charge*.) The original plates were forwarded to Howells' American publisher when Douglas had finished with them, and were used in printing the American impressions. It was to Howells' further advantage to commission the manufacture of these plates at his own expense and to supply them to his American publisher; by reducing the publisher's manufacturing cost in this way, he could typically negotiate a more advantageous royalty position.[4]

---

on deposit at the Houghton Library, Harvard University. For a description of the records and their general contents, see the Textual Commentary to *The Rise of Silas Lapham* (Bloomington and London: Indiana University Press, 1971), pp. 373–374, n. 2.

4. In the case of *The Minister's Charge*, the last original Howells work to be published in Boston before Howells' affiliation with Harper and Brothers in New York, the royalty was 10% on the first ten thousand copies and 16⅔% thereafter.

The references in Howells' correspondence and in publishing records and the collation of extant copies of the different forms of the text indicate that the procedures outlined here were generally followed in the preparation of *The Minister's Charge*.[5] Letters of 13 December 1885 and 26 July 1886 from Howells to a Mr. Carey of the *Century* office, for example, cover the transmittal of installments of the novel in manuscript and request proofs of them.[6] And a letter to Carey of 7 August 1886 acknowledges receipt of sheets and proofs of earlier sections of the text and requests plate proofs of the October installment for Howells' forwarding to Edinburgh.[7] A reference in the Ticknor records dated 1 October 1886 provides information concerning the cost in pounds of the plates made for Howells as well as import duties on those plates and the additional expense of making "titles, &c." (i.e., plates of the Ticknor title and copyright pages) for the American edition.[8] Collation of magazine, deposit parts, and English and American impressions of the book edition demonstrates that the majority of textual variants involve differences between the magazine on the one hand and the forms of the Douglas typesetting on the other.

The coherence of the available evidence about *The Minister's Charge* with the pattern of Howells' other serialized texts of this period makes it possible to set the basic editorial policy for the present edition. The *Century* installments have been chosen as copy-text—the primary authority for both substantives and accidentals—for this edition. Since the typesetting of the *Century* text

---

5. The following printed texts, including first and latest available impressions, were collated in the preparation of the present edition: copies of the *Century* magazine in the Indiana University and Middlebury College libraries; copies of the Douglas copyright deposit installments in the British Museum (12706.de.40) and in the Bodleian Library (2712.f.52); copies of the Douglas 1886 printing of the first edition, BAL 9626, in the British Museum (12707.ff.22), the Islington Public Library (I 1575) and the Barrett Collection at the University of Virginia; copies of the Ticknor impressions, BAL 9627, in the Howells Edition Center (HE9627.1.1, HE9627.2.1), in the Indiana University (PS2025.M58), Duke University (813.43 H859MD), McGill University (YF.H833mc), Northwestern University (813.4 H8mi), Ohio State University (EL 140.H859Mi, PS2025.M66), Yale University (Ix H847.887m), University of Chicago (PS2025.M57 1887, PS2025.M57 1914) and University of California at Santa Barbara (PS2025.M45) libraries, and in the collections of John Reeves and Howard Munford.

6. MSS at Harvard.

7. MS at New York Public Library.

8. Ticknor Cost Books, XIII, 23.

was based on the now-missing manuscript, it is not only the earliest of the extant materials in point of time but also, more importantly, closest to Howells' hand and likely to reflect with greater consistency than texts derived from it both the major and minor details of his manuscript.

Identification of Howells' revisions of his text in the various extant forms constitutes potentially a difficult problem. Given the sequence of preparation of the printed documents, Howells could have had the opportunity to revise the magazine proofs set from his manuscript before the publication of the *Century* installments which constitute the copy-text—in fact, to revise in more than one stage of galleys or proofs; to revise separately whatever version of the magazine material he sent to Douglas for copyright parts; to revise the Douglas typesetting before the manufacture of plates for the printing of the Douglas first edition; and even to request revision in the book plates after the Douglas printing and both before and between the numerous Ticknor impressions.

The kind or extent of Howells' revision between manuscript and the printing of the *Century* installments cannot be determined, since neither manuscript nor proofs exist to allow comparison or verification. Further, there is little evidence in the substantive variants among the different forms of the Douglas typesetting (copyright parts, Douglas edition, Ticknor and Houghton Mifflin impressions) that authorial revision took place after the initial Douglas typesetting. The only problematic variants identified by collation, in fact, occur between the magazine installments and the Douglas parts. And even here possible authorial revision is slight, since there are only six differences between the texts which cannot be explained as either compositorial error or unnecessary editorial sophistication—and those six readings are concentrated in the April and November magazine installments and corresponding copyright parts.

Determination of the final authorial reading in each of the six sets of problematic variants requires first the establishment of the chronological order of the variants, since by definition the "final" reading is that created the latest by the author in the sequence of his revisions. Once chronology is known, the latest reading can be accepted as authorial if it is consistent with—not necessarily an improvement of—the context. That the specific variants in question occur between the *Century* installments and the Douglas deposit parts thus involves an examination of the calendar of the publishing sequence for these texts. Depending on the date on which Howells forwarded material to Douglas, he could possibly have had sufficient time to revise another copy of his proofs or galleys for the magazine even after sending one copy of them to Douglas. On the other hand, if he forwarded the material to Douglas very close to the time of the final press run of the *Century* issue in which it was also to appear, he could have made revisions in the Douglas copy after his opportunity to revise for the magazine had passed. The relative dates of preparation and publication of the April and November magazine installments and corresponding deposit parts are crucial, therefore, to determining the sequence of Howells' revision of the points in question. For convenience in dealing with the chronological relationships of the two forms of the text, the list below records the official month of publication of the *Century* issues and the date of deposit in the British Museum of Douglas parts which contain the portions of the novel corresponding with the magazine's contents.[9]

Date Printed on Magazine	Chapters	British Museum Deposit Date
February 1886	1–4	25 January 1886
March 1886	5–7	[not dated]
April 1886	8–10	19 March 1886
May 1886	11–13	16 April 1886
June 1886	14–16	17 May 1886
July 1886	17–19	16 July 1886
August 1886	20–21	16 July 1886
September 1886	22–23	16 September 1886
October 1886	24–27	16 September 1886
November 1886	28–31	16 September 1886
December 1886	32–36	22 November 1886

9. There are eleven magazine installments but only eight deposit parts because the July and August magazine installments were deposited together as one part on 16 July 1886 and the September–November installments as one part on 16 September.

The Bodleian Library set of deposit parts, though complete, is not so fully dated as the British Museum set: the second and third deposit parts are dated 29 July 1886, and the fourth is dated 4 December 1886; the rest of the sections are undated.

Two of the six sets of significant variants occur in chapter X in the April installment (99.5 and 99.15 in the present text; see Rejected Substantives); the other four occur in chapter XXX in the November installment (309.34, 310.2, 310.6, and 310.20). The chronology of preparation of the magazine and deposit forms of both of these installments would have allowed Howells to make revisions in magazine material after another form of that same material had gone to Douglas. Mailing time from Howells to Douglas was approximately ten days, and Douglas needed another two weeks to set type, proof, and then register the equivalent of a serial installment of the text. Thus text deposited by Douglas on a certain date had to leave Howells' hands at the least three and a half weeks before that date. For the portions of *The Minister's Charge* in question here, then, the April installment, deposited on 19 March, had to be mailed by Howells by 23 February at the latest, and the November installment, deposited on 16 September, by 24 August at the latest. Printing and binding of the magazine itself, on the other hand, generally took place three weeks before the formal publication date of the first of the month stated on the cover of an issue.[10] Thus the April *Century* would be in press beginning about 10 March, and the November *Century* about 10 September. In both instances, therefore, Howells had time to make further revisions and corrections in the magazine version of his text after sending copy to Douglas. If both readings involved in each of the six sets of variants were initiated by Howells—they seem to be so, since neither reading can be easily dismissed as compositorial error or editorial intervention—then in each case the magazine reading which appeared in the *Century* represents the later revision and thus Howells' final intention.

Critical evaluation of these sets of readings coincides with the chronological evidence. The magazine readings in the April installment represent an effective compression of unnecessary descriptive material: the Douglas reading "the city of Boston" at 99.5 (see Rejected Substantives) is not only an overly elaborate qualification, but also an awkward echo of the more crucial use

---

10. For example, when on 16 June 1886 Howells asked Mr. Carey of the *Century* office for sheets—i.e., final printed text—of the July installment (MS at Harvard), he presumably was requesting this material as soon as it was conveniently available in that form.

of the word "city" in the next line—"his ignorance of city prejudices and sophistications"; the condition expressed in the Douglas reading at 99.15 ("rebel if he had wished") is ineffective because it anticipates and is included in the condition which begins the next paragraph—"If there was any such unkindness in Lemuel's breast toward her, it yielded promptly to her tact." The superiority of the four magazine readings in the November installment is even clearer: the readings, concentrated like those of April in one brief section, all involve a description of Miss Carver. The variants in the Douglas material elaborate a sense of either naive or designing sexuality in the girl that is completely inappropriate to Lemuel's sense of her as it is developed elsewhere: physical attraction was a major element in his feelings for Statira Dudley; intellectual and spiritual kinship, latent though they may be, are rather the bond between him and Miss Carver. In all six cases, therefore, both chronology and critical judgment point to the magazine readings as Howells' final coherent intentions for his text.

The *Century* publication is thus both copy-text and final authority for points of substantive difference among the texts. Since Howells' latest revisions of his text were made in what was also the form of the extant material which was closest to his hand, no authorial revisions from other documents need be introduced. The only emendations made to the copy-text are necessary corrections of errors (for example, the misspelling at 107.33 of the name of a character in George Eliot's *Romola*) made on editorial authority. Some of these corrections were first made in one of the texts originally set from the magazine, but those early occurrences are cited not for potential authority but simply as historical fact.

The arrangement of the apparatus to this edition could not be logically consistent with the chronological relationships of the texts, particularly in matters of substantive difference between the *Century* and the copyright parts. Since the Emendations list records only changes introduced into the magazine copy-text from other sources, it does not list those instances where specific readings in the copyright parts may actually have preceded those of the magazine. Instead, the copyright readings appear on the Rejected Substantives list, where no distinction is made between them and readings rejected because they are typographical mistakes or compositorial lapses or editorial sophistications.

The text of the present edition is in all but sixteen readings a republication of the original *Century* text. Since the *Century* preserves forms of spelling and punctuation that are generally characteristic of Howells' known manuscript style, adherence to it in all possible details has seemed the best policy. In addition to the changes recorded on the Emendations list, the only exceptions to this policy involve the styling in the present edition of strictly visual appurtenances: type style, styling of chapter openings, spacing of indentations, and normalization of italic punctuation.[11]

D.J.N.

---

11. We have normalized the use of italic punctuation after italic letters. As in the other volumes in this series, only question marks and exclamation points are set in italics after italicized letters in our text, and all others in roman; this policy differs from that of the *Century* only in the use of semicolons, which the serial consistently set in italics after italics. This difference in styling affects only five semicolons after italicized words, at 63.9, 121.36, 122.3, 161.21, and 315.21.

Emendations

The following list records all substantive and accidental changes introduced into the copy-text, with the exception of the typographical normalizations specified in the Textual Commentary. The reading of the present edition appears to the left of the bracket; the authority for that reading, followed by a semicolon, the copy-text reading and the copy-text symbol appear to the right the bracket. The readings of texts which fall between the copy-text and the authority cited for the reading of the present edition may be assumed to agree substantively with the copy-text reading if not listed.

Within an entry, the curved dash ∼ represents the same word that appears before the bracket and is used in recording punctuation variants. The abbreviation HE indicates emendation made for the first time in the present edition and not found in any of the editions examined in the preparation of this text. If the form adopted here has appeared in an earlier printing, that printing is cited for historical interest, even though it has no textual authority.

The following texts are referred to:

S   *Century,* XXXI–XXXIII (February-December 1886)
A   David Douglas, 1886: Copyright Deposit Parts
B   Douglas, 1886: First Edition
C   Ticknor, 1887: First American Impression

33.33	everybody]A; everbody S
49.20	occupation?"]A; ∼ ? S
51.20	Lemuel.] A; ∼ S
107.33	Melema]HE; Malema S; Malemma A–C
116.3	'Manda]A; Manda S
141.29	He]A; His S
147.7	always]A; alway's S
189.21	Shouldn't]A; Should/n't S

203.4	not,]A; ~ S
204.22	Albans]A; Alban's S
272.12	Charles,] A; ~ S
281.14	*tête-à-tête*]B; *tête-à-tete* S
315.3	"She's]A; ~ S
340.11–12	degrading]A; ~, S
343.18	Sewell,]A; ~. S

Rejected Substantives

The following list records all substantive variants in texts other than the copy-text which were rejected in the present edition. The reading of the present edition appears to the left of the bracket; the authority for that reading, followed by a semicolon, the variant reading and its source or sources appear to the right of the bracket. The curved dash ∼ represents the same word that appears before the bracket and is used in recording punctuation and paragraphing variants. *Om.* means that the reading to the left of the bracket does not appear in the text cited to the right of the semicolon. The reading of any available text other than copy-text, if not listed here, may be presumed to agree with the reading to the left of the bracket, unless recorded in Emendations.

The following texts are referred to:

S *Century,* XXXI–XXXIII (February-December 1886)
A David Douglas, 1886: Copyright Deposit Parts
B Douglas, 1886: First Edition
C Ticknor, 1887: First American Impression

11.19	4:05] S; 4.5 A–C
26.5	acquiesced] S; acniesced A
28.29	this] S; the A–C
34.1	Centre] S; Cenre A
36.8	fer] S; for B–C
55.13	had] S; bad A
55.24	on] S; on the A–C
60.5	hanor] S; honour A–C
60.8	hanor] S; honour A–C
61.13	railing] S; railings A–C
61.18	morning,] S; ∼ A–C
74.13	coarse] S; course A
75.11	around the] S; around A–C
75.33	on] S; in A–C

93.28	which] S; *om.* A–C
98.7	of him] S; *om.* A–C
99.5	Boston] S; the city of Boston A–C
99.15	rebel] S; rebel if he had wished A–C
108.6	nervelessly] S; nervously A–C
112.18	still] S; *om.* A–C
123.24	S'tira] S; Statira A–C
125.6	worshipful,] S; ~ A–C
134.24–25	about in] S; about A–C
143.16	hold right] S; right hold A–C
151.36	sidling] S; sliding A–C
155.19	counsel] S; council A–C
159.4–5	clothes. ¶ Statira] S; ~. ~ A–C
161.2	just knew it was] S; knew it was just A–C
161.32	you're] S; you've B–C
164.28	morning] S; mornin' A–C
171.16	fond] S; found A
180.6	arms. "The] S; ~. ¶ "~ A–C
199.14	trifling] S; triffling A
200.8	warningly] S; warmingly A
211.1–2	picture] S; pictures A–C
212.11–12	round. ¶ "I] S; ~," ~ A
214.8	throw] S; have thrown A–C
215.33	to the] S; to a A–C
217.1	a] S; *om.* A–C
221.26–27	time. ¶ 'Manda] S; time. 'Manda A–C
222.24	are] S; are all A–C
227.22	women] S; woman A–C
229.1–2	glance. ¶ Sewell] S; ~. ~ A–C
234.32	tastes] S; taste A–C
239.23	live] S; lived A–C
239.29	without the] S; without that A–C
244.8	talkin'] S; talking A–C
247.1–2	almost] S; also A–C
252.24	good too] S; good A–C
257.9	back. "He] S; ~. ¶ "~ A–C
258.7	getting] S; gettin' A
260.29	give] S; gave A–C
261.3	out] S; out of A–C

263.21	these] S; those A–C
267.1	face. "I] S; ~. ¶ " "~ A–C
267.32	this] S; his A–C
277.11	room] S; ~, A–C
298.13	tramps'] S; tramp's A–C
309.34	sat,] S; sat, with her arms lifted and clasped above her head, A–C
310.2	wore.] S; wore, and thrown into full relief by the lifted arms; he saw the little hands knit above her head, and white as flowers on her dark hair. A–C
310.6	clasped her hands] S; took down her hands to clasp them A–C
310.20	grace] S; undefended grace A–C
315.2	livin'] S; living A–C
315.22	other] S; *om.* A–C
315.36	you're] S; your A–C
322.34	some one] S; some A–C
325.20	knew] S; new A–C
325.20	shabby] S; shappy A
326.3	and waited] S; waited A–C
329.5	som'eres] S; som'ere's A–C
330.16	you've] S; you have A–C
330.17	to] S; with A–C
335.14	it,] S; ~ A–C
338.22	narrow-brimmed] S; narrow-brimed A
338.26	Sewells'] S; Sewells A–C
339.3	it,] S; ~ A–C
341.17	lesson] S; lessons A–C
344.5	comin'] S; coming A–C
344.15	*to*-o."] S; too," A–C
344.31–32	Lemuel and] S; Lemuel with A–C

Word-Division

List A records compounds or possible compounds hyphenated at the end of the line in the copy-text and resolved as hyphenated or one word as listed below. If the words occur elsewhere in the copy-text or if Howells' manuscripts of this period fairly consistently followed one practice respecting the particular compound or possible compound, the resolution was made on that basis. Otherwise his *Century*, *Harper's*, and other periodical texts of this period were used as guides. List B is a guide to transcription of compounds or possible compounds hyphenated at the end of the line in the present text: compounds recorded here should be transcribed as given; words divided at the end of the line and not listed should be transcribed as one word.

	LIST A		
		50.31	ten-dollar
		53.11	white-walled
13.22	upstairs	58.25	prayer-meetin'
17.33	upstairs	59.29	gray-haired
19.29	lengthwise	67.12–13	nice-looking
26.15	good-day	68.19–20	pen-knife
26.16	leave-taking	69.5	Selectmen
26.30	dining-room	69.5–6	poorhouse
27.10	tumble-down	72.31	dressing-room
34.7	homesickness	73.1	onion-flavored
35.1	waistcoat	74.26	oleomargarine
36.6	policeman	74.36	good-humoredly
38.14	carrying-on	78.19	saw-horses
41.20	bareheaded	78.24	homesickness
44.25	good-natured	79.18	saw-horses
45.30	police-stations	79.34	misshapen
46.3	cross-street	81.8	wood-yard
49.31	overnight	85.4	Sunrise

87.11	innocent-looking	211.22	finger-nails
88.26	sidewalk	211.35	brother-in-
95.26	suppose-	213.10	art-student
97.14	lock-out	216.11	mock-heroic
105.16	man-body	231.35	good-looking
110.16	whopper-jaw	233.18	store-room
111.24	anywheres	233.26	head-waiter
112.27	old-fashioned	238.32	banjoseph
115.32	Thanksgiving	242.31	good-humored
121.26	forefingers	244.3	elevator-boy
127.5	reception-room	248.29	dry-mouthed
129.16	dining-table	252.15	outbreaks
133.9	ten-dollar	254.16	background
134.26	furnace-door	255.35	stairway
138.19	homesickness	257.11	fireman
139.32	carful	257.19	elevator-well
140.20	seventy-five	259.35	elevator-shaft
141.11	stained-glass	268.5	scarecrow
141.23–24	family-hotel	268.24	seaside
145.35	express-man	275.15	inside-men
146.34	street-door	276.23	half-past
148.2	bell-pull	278.1	-à-brac
154.12	party-going	279.32–33	strawberries
156.10	self-vindication	280.24	firemen
156.36	Good-afternoon	281.14	-à-tête
158.15	dressing-gown	283.18	man-servant
165.9	clockwork	289.19	garden-theater
168.7	dining-room	292.7	fortnight
170.6	horse-car	292.33–34	boarding-house
171.35	head-waitership	293.10	daybreak
177.29	respectable-looking	297.3	oversight
179.28	send-off	298.24	-of-all-
186.15	good-hearted	316.32	handkerchief
193.1	down-stairs	324.9	self-interest
204.24–25	oil-cloth	324.14	self-assertion
205.25	cow-boy	331.36	rosebud
206.7	low-spirited	337.11	good-*heart*-
208.11	pointed-toe	337.25	my-*se*-
211.19	brother-in-		

LIST B

		126.27	dining-room
		128.29	reception-room
5.10	kindling-wood	130.12	self-sacrifice
6.8	birch-tree	135.6	scape-goat
11.2	reception-room	141.18	drowsy-eyed
22.16	old-fashioned	141.23	family-hotel
23.32	forget-me-	147.11	easy-going
27.13	door-yard	152.30	lady-boarder
35.2	shirt-bosom	156.9	self-abhorrence
38.29	traveling-bag	158.1	boarding-house
39.18	house-wall	166.29	double-faced
42.33	half-dollar	186.2	ten-dollar
42.35	gas-lamps	186.15	well-meaning
44.31	white-aproned	195.21	art-student
46.10	Good-evening	204.24	oil-cloth
65.13	court-house	205.23	art-students
66.4	ten-dollar	218.29	door-jamb
67.12	nice-looking	229.19	good-evening
67.35	to-morrow	233.3	head-waiter
68.19	pen-knife	242.33	patent-leather
72.23	Thirty-nine	247.5	elevator-boy
76.19	steam-heat	254.1	art-students
77.8	wood-yard	275.14	farm-boys
83.34	broth-bowls	283.35	boarding-house
87.5	clover-blossoms	288.4	-of-doors
88.27	scarlet-blossomed	290.29	box-factory
95.34	dish-washing	292.33	boarding-house
98.2	Good-bye	298.13	lodging-house
105.12	man-bodies	315.32	good-evening
105.24	woman-body	316.19	conscience-stricken
108.16	man-servant	321.8	self-reproach
112.36	summer-clad	333.30	well-regulated
113.30	boarding-house		

THIS EDITION OF

THE MINISTER'S CHARGE

has been set in Linotype Baskerville,

printed on Warren's Olde Style by Heritage Printers, Inc.

and bound by The Delmar Company.

The format is after a design by Bert Clarke.